BUCKINGHAM PALACE GARDENS

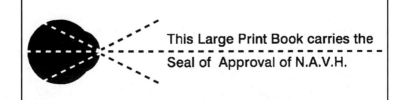

BUCKINGHAM PALACE GARDENS

A NOVEL

ANNE PERRY

THORNDIKE PRESS

A part of Gale, Cengage Learning

Detroit • New York • San Francisco • New Haven, Conn • Waterville, Maine • London

GALE
CENGAGE Learning·

LIBRARY OF CONGRESS CATALOGING-IN-PUBLICATION DATA

Perry, Anne.
    Buckingham Palace gardens / by Anne Perry.
        p. cm. — (Thorndike Press large print basic)
    ISBN-13: 978-1-4104-0368-1 (hardcover : alk. paper)
    ISBN-10: 1-4104-0368-8 (hardcover : alk. paper)
    1. Pitt, Thomas (Fictitious character) — Fiction. 2. Prostitutes
    — Crimes against — Fiction. 3. Murder — Investigation —
    Fiction. 4. London (England) — Fiction. 5. Great Britain — His-
    tory — Victoria, 1837-1901 — Fiction. 6. Large type books.
    I. Title.
    PR6066.E693B83 2008b
    823'.914—dc22
                                                        2008000675

Published in 2008 in arrangement with The Ballantine Publishing Group, a division of Random House, Inc.

Printed in the United States of America
2 3 4 5 6 7 12 11 10 09 08

To my friends Meg MacDonald and Meg Davis for their unfailing help and encouragement. All best wishes.

CHAPTER ONE

"She was apparently found in the linen cupboard, poor creature," Narraway replied, his lean face dour, his eyes so dark they seemed black in the interior shadow of the hansom cab. Then, before Pitt could say anything further, he corrected himself. "One of the linen cupboards in Buckingham Palace. It was a particularly brutal murder."

The vehicle jerked forward, throwing Pitt back in the seat. "A prostitute?" he said incredulously.

Narraway was silent for a moment. The horse's hoofs clattered loudly, the carriage's wheels rattling over the cobbles dangerously close to the pavement edge.

"Surely that's a bad joke!" he said at last as they swung around the corner into The Mall and picked up speed again.

"Very bad," Narraway agreed. "At least I hope so. But I fear it is perfectly serious. However, if Mr. Cahoon Dunkeld proves to be wasting our time exercising his sense of humor, I shall take great joy in personally putting him in jail — preferably one of our less pleasant ones."

"It has to be a joke," Pitt said, shivering at the thought. "There couldn't be a murder at the Palace. How could a prostitute get in there, anyway?"

"Through the door, exactly as we shall, Pitt," Narraway answered. "Don't be naïve. And she was probably more welcome than we shall be."

Pitt felt a little stung. "Who is Cahoon Dunkeld?" he asked, avoiding looking at Narraway. He had a reverence for Queen Victoria, especially now in her advanced age and widowhood, even though he was perfectly well aware of her reputed eccentricities and the fact that she had not always been so popular with her people. She had been in mourning too long, retreating not only from joy but also from duty. And he had gained some personal knowledge a couple of years ago of the extravagance and the self-indulgence of the Prince of Wales, and knew he kept several very expensive mistresses. Pitt had been superintendent of Bow Street then, and the conspiracy around the Prince had cost him his job and very nearly brought down the throne. That was why Pitt was now working for Victor Narraway in Special Branch, learning more about treason, anarchy, and other forms of violence against the State.

But the thought of a prostitute in the Queen's home was different. It disgusted him, and he had difficulty concealing it, even though he knew Narraway found him plebeian amd faintly amusing for having such idealism.

"Who is Cahoon Dunkeld?" he repeated.

Narraway leaned forward a little. The dappled, early-morning sunlight of The Mall made bright patterns on the road. There was little traffic. It was not a residential area, and such horseback riders as were out would be cantering up and down Rotten Row on the edge of Hyde Park.

"An adventurer of considerable charm when he wishes, and undoubted ability, who is now seeking to become a gentleman in the more recognized social sense," Narraway answered. "And apparently a friend of His Royal Highness."

"What is he doing at the Palace at this hour of the morning?" Pitt said.

"That is what we are about to find out," Narraway snapped as they came out of The Mall in front of the Palace. The magnificent wrought-iron railings were tipped with gold. Guards were on duty wearing bearskin helmets, their red tunics bright in the sun.

Pitt looked up at the sweeping façade itself and then at the roof. He saw with a flood of relief that there was no flag flying, indicating that Her Majesty was not in residence. At the same time he was inexplicably disappointed. He was quite aware that Narraway would find it gauche of him, but Pitt would like to have caught another glimpse of Her Majesty Queen Victoria. In spite of all common sense, there was a quickening of his heartbeat. Even inside the hansom cab he sat straighter, lifted his chin a little, and squared his shoulders.

If Narraway noticed, he did not allow himself even the slightest smile.

They swung round to the right, heading for the entrance where tradesmen and deliveries would go. They were stopped at the gate. Narraway gave his name, and immediately the guard stepped back and saluted. The cabdriver, startled into respect, urged his horse forward at a newly dignified pace.

Ten minutes later Pitt and Narraway were being conducted up the wide, elegant stairs by a manservant who had introduced himself as Tyndale. He was of slight build but he moved with suppleness, even some grace, although Pitt judged him to be well into his fifties. He was courteous enough, but quite obviously distressed beyond any ability to maintain his normal composure.

At any other time Pitt would have been fascinated to think that he was inside Buckingham Palace. Now all he could think of was the enormity of what lay ahead of them. The magnificence of history meant nothing.

Was this an idiotic practical joke? Tyndale's pallid face and stiff shoulders said not, and for the first time since Narraway had made his extraordinary statement in the hansom, Pitt considered the possibility that it might be true.

They were at the top of the stairs. Tyndale walked across the landing and knocked on a door a little to the left. It was opened immediately by a man of much greater height than he, with broad shoulders and a dark face of remarkable dynamism. He was severely balding, but this in no way diminished his handsomeness. His gray hair must once have been black because his brows still were. His skin was burned by sun and wind to a deep bronze.

"Mr. Narraway has arrived, Mr. Dunkeld," Tyndale said quietly.

"Good," Dunkeld replied. "Now please leave us, and make sure that we are not interrupted. In fact, see that no staff come up onto this floor at all." He turned to Narraway as if Tyndale was already gone. "Narraway?" he asked.

Narraway acknowledged it, and introduced Pitt.

"Cahoon Dunkeld." The big man held out his hand and shook Narraway's briefly. He ignored Pitt except for a nod of his head. "Come in, close the door."

He turned and led the way into the charming, highly overfurnished room. Its wide, tall windows overlooked a garden, and beyond them the trees were motionless billows of green in the morning sun.

Dunkeld remained standing in the middle of the floor. He spoke solely to Narraway. "There has been a shocking event. I have never seen anything quite so . . . bestial. How it should happen here, of all places, is beyond my comprehension."

"Tell me exactly what has happened, Mr. Dunkeld," Narraway responded. "From the beginning."

Dunkeld winced, as if the memory were painful. "From the beginning? I woke early. I . . ."

Deliberately Narraway sat down in one of the large overstuffed chairs covered in wine-colored brocade. He crossed his legs elegantly, if a little rigidly, at the knees. "The beginning, Mr. Dunkeld. Who are you, and why are you here at this hour of the morning?"

"For God's sake . . . !" Dunkeld burst out. Then controlling himself with obvious difficulty, body stiff, he sat down also and began to explain. He had the air not of having grasped Narraway's reasoning so much as being given no choice but to humor a lesser intelligence. His fingers drummed on the arm of his chair.

"His Royal Highness, the Prince of Wales, is deeply interested in an engineering project that may be undertaken by my company, and certain of my colleagues," he began again. "Four of us are here at his invitation in order to discuss the possibilities — the details, if you like. Our wives have accompanied us to give it the appearance of a social occasion. The other three are Julius Sorokine, Simnel Marquand, and Hamilton Quase. We have been here two days already, and the discussions have been excellent."

Pitt remained on his feet, listening and watching Dunkeld's face. His expression was intense, his eyes burning with enthusiasm. His left hand, gripping the chair arm, was white at the knuckles.

"Yesterday evening we celebrated our progress so far," Dunkeld continued. "I assume you are a man of the world, and do not need to have every detail drawn for you? The ladies retired early. We sat up considerably longer, and a certain amount of entertainment was provided. The brandy was excellent, the company both relaxing and amusing. We were all in high spirits." Not once did he glance at Pitt as he spoke. He might have been as invisible as a servant.

"I see," Narraway answered expressionlessly.

"We retired between one and two in the morning," Dunkeld went on. "I awoke early — about six, I imagine. I was in my robe, not yet dressed, when my valet came with a message that he had received over the telephone. It was a matter His Royal Highness had asked to be informed of immediately, so, in spite of the hour, I took it to him. I returned to my room, shaved and dressed, had a cup of tea, and was on my way back to see His Royal Highness further about the matter, but passing the linen cupboard in the passage I saw the door slightly open." His voice was harsh with tension. "That in itself, of course, is of no interest, but I became aware of a curious odor, and when I pulled it wider . . . I saw . . . probably the most dreadful thing I have ever seen." He blinked and seemed to need a moment to compose himself again.

Narraway did not interrupt him, nor move his gaze from Dunkeld's face.

"The naked body of a woman, covered in blood," Dunkeld said hoarsely. "There was blood all over the rest of the linen." He gulped air. "For a moment, I could not believe it. I thought I must have taken more brandy than I had imagined and become delirious. I don't know how long I stood there, leaning against the door frame. Then I backed into the corridor. There was no one else in sight."

Narraway nodded.

"I closed the door." Dunkeld seemed to find some comfort in remembering the act, as if he could at the same time close the horror from his inner vision. "I called Tyndale, the man who called you. He is the principal manservant in this guest wing. I told him that one of the women from the previous evening had been found dead, that he must keep all servants from that corridor; serve breakfast to the other guests in their rooms. Then I asked for the telephone and called you."

"Is His Royal Highness aware of this event?" Narraway asked.

Dunkeld blinked. "Naturally I had to inform him. He has given me full authority to act in his name and get this ghastly tragedy cleared up with the utmost haste, and absolute discretion. You cannot fail to be aware of the scandal it would cause if it became public." His eyes were hard, demanding, and the very slight lift in his voice suggested he needed reassurance of both Narraway's intelligence and his tact. "Her Majesty will be returning next week, on her way from Osborne to travel north to Balmoral. It is imperative that your investigation is entirely accomplished before that time. Do you understand me?"

Pitt felt his stomach knot, and suddenly there was barely enough air in the room for him to breathe. He had been here minutes, and yet he felt imprisoned.

He must have made a slight sound, because Dunkeld looked at him, then back at Narraway. "What about your man here?" he asked abruptly. "How far can you trust his discretion? And his ability to handle such a vital matter? And it *is* vital. If it became public, it would be ruinous, even affect the safety of the realm. Our business here concerns a profoundly important part of the Empire. Not only fortunes but nations could be changed by what we do." He was staring at Narraway as if by sheer will he could force some understanding into him, even a fear of failure.

Narraway gave a very slight shrug. It was a minimal, elegant gesture of his shoulders. He was far leaner than Dunkeld, and more at ease in his beautifully tailored jacket. "He is my best," he answered.

Dunkeld looked unimpressed. "And discreet?" he persisted.

"Special Branch deals with secrets," Narraway told him.

Dunkeld's eyes turned to Pitt and surveyed him coolly.

Narraway rose to his feet. "I would like to see the body," he announced.

Dunkeld took a deep breath and stood up also. He walked past Pitt and opened the door, leaving them to follow him. He led the way along the corridor with its ornately plastered and gilded ceiling, and up another broad flight of stairs. At the top he turned right past two doors to where a young footman stood at attention outside a third door.

"You can go," Dunkeld dismissed him. "Wait on the landing. I'll call you when I need you again."

"Yes, sir." The footman glanced with anxiety at Narraway and Pitt, then did as he was told, his feet soundless on the carpet.

Dunkeld looked at Narraway, then at Pitt. "What do you normally do? Chase spies? Uncover plots?"

"Investigate murder," Pitt replied.

"Well, here's one for you." Dunkeld opened the cupboard door and stood back.

Pitt stared at the sight in front of him. At his elbow Narraway gasped as his breath caught in his throat. The older man gulped and put his hand to his mouth, as if afraid he might disgrace himself by being sick.

It was not surprising. The woman lay on her back and was obscenely naked, breasts exposed, thighs apart. Her throat had been cut from one side to the other and her lower abdomen slashed open, leaving her entrails bulging pale where they protruded from the dark blood. One leg was raised a little, knee bent, the other lay slack, foot nearly to the floor. Her long, brown hair had apparently been pulled loose from its pins in some kind of struggle. Her blue eyes were wide open and glassy, her mouth gaping. There was blood everywhere, spattered on the walls, soaked into the piles of sheets, daubed across her body, and pooling on the floor. Even her hands were scarlet.

Pitt stared at her less with revulsion than with an overwhelming pity for the gross indignity of it. Had it been an animal the callousness of it would have offended him. For a human being to die like that filled him with a towering anger and a desire to lash out physically and strike something. His breath heaved in his chest and his throat convulsed.

Yet he knew he must keep calm. Intelligence was needed, not passion, however justified. Someone had done this to her. And since this was a royal residence, guarded day and night, it had to be someone within the Palace walls. He found himself shaking at the desecration of the woman's body, of life, and of the Queen's home. He steadied himself with difficulty and tried to still the churning of his stomach.

Why? Surely only a man bereft of reason would do such a thing anywhere, let alone here?

Narraway cleared his throat.

Pitt turned to him. He was white around the lips and there were beads of sweat on his skin. Pitt guessed he had never seen such grotesque violence and degradation before. He should say something that would soften the horror, but his mind was empty. Perhaps he did not want to. One should feel sick, stunned, torn apart by such things.

Instead, he turned away and moved into the cupboard, stepping carefully to avoid standing in the pooled blood. It seemed to be all over the place: thick, dark gouts of it, scarlet only where it was smeared and thin.

He touched the woman's arm. It was cold

and the flesh was growing stiff. He guessed she had been dead for at least six hours. It was now half-past eight in the morning, which meant she had been killed by half-past two, at the latest.

"What is it?" Narraway gulped as if his throat were constricted.

Pitt told him.

"I think we know that," Narraway said hoarsely. "She arrived here yesterday evening, and presumably was seen by several people up until one o'clock." He turned to Dunkeld. "I'm sorry to ask you, but would you look at her face, please, and tell us if you recognize her?" Then he swiveled round to Pitt again and his voice was jerky, losing control. "For God's sake, man, put something over the rest of her! The cupboard's full of sheets. Use one!"

Pitt took one from the top shelf, far away from the body, and opened it up. With some relief he spread it over her, right up to her neck, deliberately covering the fearful gash in her throat.

Narraway stepped back to allow Dunkeld past.

"Yes," Dunkeld said after a few moments. "Yes, that is one of the women from last night's party."

"You are certain?"

"Of course I'm certain!" Dunkeld shouted. Then he gasped, put his hand over his brow and pushed his fingers back over his scalp as if he had hair. "For the love of God, who else could it be? I don't look at prostitutes' faces. She's ordinary enough. She was hired for her . . . her skills, not her looks. Brown hair, blue eyes, like a hundred thousand other women."

Pitt looked at her again, this time just at her face. Dunkeld was right; she was ordinary: pleasant features, clear skin, slightly crooked teeth. He guessed she had been in her early thirties. She had been handsomely built, with full breasts, small waist. That was very probably more where Dunkeld's attention had been. He was right; who else could she be but one of last night's prostitutes? She was certainly not one of the guests, and a maid would have been reported missing and identified by one of the other staff.

"Thank you, sir," he said aloud. He reached forward and closed her eyes.

"Can't we move her?" Dunkeld demanded. "This is . . . obscene. One of the women might find her, by accident. And we've got to have maids back here to change the linen, clean the rooms. Let's put her somewhere decent, and get this cleared up. It would be very nice to keep it secret, but

21

the staff will have to know. You'll have to question them."

"In a little while," Pitt replied.

"I asked Narraway!" Dunkeld raised his voice again, temper flaring.

Narraway stared at him, eyes cold, his face almost expressionless. When he spoke, his voice was fully under control. "Mr. Dunkeld, Inspector Pitt is an expert in murder. I employ him because I trust his knowledge and his skill. You will do as he tells you, otherwise I regret that we will not be able to accept the case. You can call in the local police. In fact, now that we are aware of it, we will be obliged to do so ourselves."

Dunkeld searched Narraway's face. His eyes were savage. He was hot with rage at being cornered. It was obviously a situation he had not been forced to endure in a long time. But he saw no wavering whatever, no fear in Narraway and no mercy. He yielded with sufficient grace to maintain his dignity, but Pitt had no doubt whatever that he would await his time for revenge.

"Look all you wish, Pitt," he said grimly. "Then attend to it. Can you arrange for a mortuary van discreetly, disguised as a delivery of some sort?" His expression made it plain that the inquiry was as to his competence, not a request for his help.

"Once I have learned all I can," Pitt answered him, "I will ask Mr. Tyndale to have the cupboard cleaned up."

"See to it." Dunkeld turned on his heel and strode away, leaving Narraway to follow him, and Pitt to do whatever he wished.

Pitt took the sheet off the body again and dropped it in the corridor, then looked once more at the scene in the linen cupboard, trying to visualize what had happened. Why had they been here at all, this woman and whoever had killed her? With what? A knife of some sort; the slashes were clean-edged as far as he could see through the blood.

He looked around, felt between all the stacked and folded sheets, on the floor, under her body, then he did it again even more carefully. There was no weapon, and no evidence that someone had wiped it here before removing it: there were no smear marks on any of the sheets he could see, only spatters and deep-soaked stains.

And where were her clothes? She would hardly have come here naked, no matter how wild the party. Prostitutes gave only what they were paid for; it did not normally include even kissing, let alone running around without clothing. But then he had never dealt with those who catered to such an elevated clientele as this. Still, the question remained: Where were her clothes? She had certainly arrived at the Palace in them.

He studied the body again, looking for marks, scratches or bruises, pinches, anything to indicate whether she had taken her garments off herself or they had been torn from her while alive, or stripped off after she was dead.

The wound in her stomach was more jagged than the one in her throat, as if it had been made through something resistant, like cloth. It would be difficult to strip a lifeless body that was heavy, limp, and covered in blood. Why on earth do it? What could it be about her clothes that mattered so much? Something that would identify her killer?

Once the heart stops beating, blood gradually stops flowing, even with wounds like these. From the amount of blood on the sheets and the floor, she had to have died here. What was she doing in a linen cupboard? She was an invited guest, sanctioned by the Prince himself. She had no need to hide.

Unless she had left the Prince, already asleep or in a drunken stupor, and gone to earn a little extra money? Or possibly simply to enjoy herself with someone else, someone without a better place in which to be private? The obvious answer was one of the servants.

Still, Pitt could see no sense to it. Why had he then killed her? Had she threatened him with exposure? Would anyone care? Not a servant, unless his job were at risk. Would the Prince dismiss a servant for using the same prostitute he had used himself? What about one of the guests? Hardly, since their wives had gone to bed knowing the nature of the party they left. They might be hurt, angry, revolted, but no woman in such a position would expose herself to ridicule and, worse than that, public pity by drawing attention to her husband's habits.

Pitt considered the possibility of a servant again. Perhaps one had been pressured into the theft of some small, valuable object, but killed his tormentor rather than fall into such a trap? No, that would not do. It did not answer the violence of the crime, the slashes across both throat and stomach. And who went to an assignation carrying the kind of knife that had done this damage?

There was nothing more to learn from this scene. He could sketch it quickly into his notebook to prompt his memory, then call a mortuary van and give them Narraway's instructions to come and collect the body for the police surgeon.

He was on his way back down the stairs to find Narraway when he met Cahoon

Dunkeld on the landing.

"Where have you been?" Dunkeld demanded, his face dark. "For heaven's sake, man, don't you realize this is urgent? What's the matter with you?"

Pitt's temper rose. Was it guilt, embarrassment, or fear that made Dunkeld so ill-mannered? Or was he simply an arrogant man who saw no need to be civil to those he considered inferior?

"Come on!" Dunkeld said abruptly. "His Royal Highness is waiting to see you." He started up the stairs. "I assume you have made arrangements to have the body removed so the staff can clean up the cupboard and we can begin to get back to normal? With all your staring, did you find anything to indicate who this maniac is?"

Pitt ignored the question and kept up with Dunkeld, pace for pace. They were of equal height, although very differently built. Dunkeld was muscular, heavy-shouldered. Pitt was gangly, inelegant in any fashionable sense, and yet he had a certain grace. He took more care of his clothes now than he had done in the past, but he still put too much into his pockets, with the result that they bulged and poked, very often weighing down one side of his coat. He was clean-shaven, but most of the time his hair was un-

26

ruly and too long.

It took several minutes to reach Narraway waiting outside the door of the room where presumably the Prince of Wales would receive them.

Pitt's anger evaporated and he found himself suddenly intensely nervous. He had met the Prince before, at the end of the Whitechapel matter, but he did not expect to be remembered. At that time all attention had been on Charles Voisey, the man who had apparently saved the Throne at such great personal risk. But Voisey was dead now, and the whole issue was history.

Narraway turned as they arrived, his face bleak, his mouth a thin line. He met Pitt's eyes questioningly, but Dunkeld allowed them no time to speak to each other. He walked straight up to the door and knocked. It was answered immediately and he opened it and went in, closing it behind him just as Narraway stepped forward.

Narraway swiveled on his heel. "Anything?" he demanded of Pitt.

"Observations that make no apparent sense," Pitt replied. "Why —"

He got no further. The door opened again and Dunkeld ordered them in.

Narraway went first, Pitt on his heels. They both stopped a couple of yards inside. It was a high-ceilinged room like the others, ornately furnished with much gold and dark red, and highly polished wood. The Prince of Wales was standing in the center of the floor, a portly, middle-aged man with a full beard. He had unremarkable features except for pale eyes a trifle down-turned at the outer corners. This morning his skin was blotchy, the whites of his eyes bloodshot, and his hands very definitely shaky.

"Ah!" he said with evident relief.

"Your Royal Highness," Dunkeld said immediately. "May I present Mr. Narraway of Special Branch, and his man, Pitt. They are here to attend to the unfortunate matter of last night, and to get it cleared up as soon as possible. The . . . evidence . . . is already being removed. Mr. Tyndale seems to be keeping the servants calm. They know only that there was an incident during the night and someone was hurt. I'm not sure how much more they need to know." He looked at Narraway, his eyebrows raised slightly.

Narraway bowed his head for a moment then looked across at the Prince.

The Prince cleared his throat and had difficulty finding his voice. "Thank you. I am obliged you came so quickly. This whole thing is unutterably dreadful. Someone is quite clearly insane. I have no idea —"

"It is their job to find out, sir," Dunkeld said so smoothly it was barely noticeable that he had interrupted. "If it cannot be completed today, one of them may need to remain overnight. If I —"

"By all means." The Prince waved one hand, his face flooded with relief. "Anything. Deal with it, Dunkeld. You have my permission to take whatever steps are necessary." He looked at Narraway. "What do you require?"

"I don't know, yet, Your Royal Highness," Narraway answered. "We need to learn more about exactly what happened. May I take it for granted that no outsider could possibly have come or gone without the staff and the guards being aware of it?"

Dunkeld answered, but addressing the Prince rather than Narraway. "I have already taken the liberty of inquiring, sir. No one entered or left, other than those we already know of, and who had permission."

There was a moment's silence in the room as the implication of that became perfectly clear.

"It appears it must be one of the servants, sir," Dunkeld said to the Prince. "Mr. Narraway will find out which one, and do all that is necessary. I strongly believe we should continue as close to normally as possible. If we are fortunate, the ladies may never need to know the details."

"I should be very grateful if the Princess of Wales did not need to know," the Prince said quickly. "She is bound to speak to Her Majesty. It would be . . ." He swallowed and a fine beading of sweat broke out on his skin.

Dunkeld looked at Narraway. "His Royal Highness has made his wishes clear: You are not to distress the Princess with this tragedy. Perhaps if you begin immediately with the servants, you may solve it all quite quickly. Someone may even confess."

"Yes," the Prince of Wales agreed eagerly, looking from Dunkeld to Narraway. "Or others may know who it was, and the whole thing can be dealt with today. And we shall get back to the matter at hand. You appreciate it is of the utmost importance to the Empire. Thank you, Mr. Narraway. I am most obliged." He turned to Dunkeld, his voice warming. "And thank you, my dear fellow. You have been a true friend. I shall not forget your loyalty or your steadfastness." He seemed to consider the matter finished. His air was one of dismissal.

Pitt's mind was teeming with questions. Who had arranged for the dead woman to come, how, and from where? When were the arrangements made? Had these particular women been here before, or to any other place to meet with the Prince, or his friends? But how could he ask these things now when clearly Dunkeld was all but ushering them out the door? He looked at Narraway.

Narraway smiled very slightly. "Your Royal Highness, which is of the greater importance, speed or discretion?"

The Prince looked startled. The fear flooded back into his face, making his skin pasty and his jaw slack. "I . . . I cannot say," he stammered. "Both are imperative. If we take too long, discretion will be lost anyway." Yet again he looked to Dunkeld.

"For God's sake, Narraway, are you not capable of both?" Dunkeld said angrily. "Get on with it! Ask the servants. Ask the guests, if you have to. Just don't stand here making idiotic and pointless remarks."

Narraway's cheeks flushed a dull red with anger, but before he could retaliate, Pitt took the opportunity to ask his question. He looked at the Prince of Wales. "Sir," he said firmly. "How many women — professional — guests were there?"

"Three," the Prince said instantly, coloring.

"Were any of them already known to you from any previous . . . party?"

"Er . . . not so far as I am aware." He was

discomfited rather than embarrassed, as if the questions puzzled him.

"Who arranged for them to come, and how long ago?" Pitt continued.

The Prince's eyes opened wide. "I . . . er . . ."

"I did," Dunkeld answered for him. He glared at Pitt. "What has this to do with anything? Some madman lost control of himself and took a knife to the poor woman. Who she is or where she came from is irrelevant. Find out where everyone was, that's the obvious thing to do, then you'll know who's responsible. It hardly matters why!" He swiveled round to Narraway. "Don't waste any more time."

Narraway did not argue. He and Pitt left, Dunkeld remained.

"Mr. Dunkeld is certainly making himself indispensable," Narraway said drily when they were twenty feet along the corridor and out of earshot. "We'd better begin with the servants, for which we shall need Mr. Tyndale's assistance. What did you learn from the linen cupboard?" They reached the stair head and started down.

"Where were her clothes?" Pitt asked. "She can't have gone in there naked. Why did he take them away? Wouldn't it have been far easier to leave them? What was it about them that he wanted, or that he dare not let anyone else see?"

Narraway stopped. "Such as what?"

"I have no idea. That's what I would like to find out. How was she dressed? Who did she oblige? The Prince, presumably. Who else?"

Narraway smiled, and then the amusement vanished like a light going out. "Pitt, I think you had better leave that part of your investigation until such time as it should become unavoidable."

"Suddenly it's my investigation?" Pitt raised his eyebrows. He started down again.

"I'll make the political decisions, you gather the evidence and interpret it." Narraway followed hard on his heels. "First we must find Tyndale, acquire a list of all the staff who were here last night and whichever guards were on duty for any entrance to this part of the building. And search for the dead woman's clothes," he added. "Or some signs as to how they were disposed of."

Tyndale was very obliging, although his manner made it apparent that he deplored the suggestion that a member of his staff could be responsible for such a barbaric act. He could not fight against the conclusion because he could not afford to, but neither did he accede to it.

"Yes, sir. Of course I will make available

every member of staff so you may interview them. But I insist upon being present myself." He met Pitt's eyes with acute misery.

Pitt admired him. He was a man caught in an impossible situation and trying to be loyal to all his obligations. Sooner or later he would have to choose, and Pitt knew it, even if he did not.

"I'm sorry . . ." Narraway began.

"Of course," Pitt agreed at the same moment.

Narraway turned his head sharply.

Tyndale waited, embarrassed.

"I shall welcome your assistance," Pitt said, looking at neither of them. "But it is imperative that you do not interrupt. Do you agree?"

"Yes, sir."

"Then we will begin with whoever admitted the women when they arrived," Pitt directed. "And go on through who waited on them through the evening until someone saw the other two leave. Did they ask after the third? What explanation was given?"

"It would be Cuttredge who let them in, sir, and Edwards who saw them out," Tyndale answered. "I already asked Edwards, and he said he thought at the time that the last one must have been staying until morning. He's . . . not very experienced."

"That never happens?" Pitt asked.

The muscles in Tyndale's face tightened. "No, sir, not with a woman of that class."

Pitt did not pursue it. "Then if we could see Cuttredge first, and after him, whoever took them to . . . wherever they went. And any staff that waited on them later on. And I need to have her clothes, if they can be found."

"Yes, sir."

When Tyndale had gone Pitt considered apologizing to Narraway for countermanding his orders, then decided against it. It was a bad precedent to set. There was no room for protecting position or deferring to rank. The price of failure would descend on them all.

Tyndale returned with Cuttredge, who was a man of very average appearance but entered with a certain dignity; he answered all their questions without hesitation. He described letting the women in with only the very faintest distaste, and a military precision as to where he had taken them and at what time. He had not noticed their faces. One street woman was much like another to him. It was obviously part of his duty that he disliked, but did not dare express that.

"And you did not see them leave?"

Pitt asked.

"No, sir. That would be Edwards. I was off duty by that time."

"Where were you?" Narraway asked, leaning forward a little in his chair.

Cuttredge's eyes widened. He glanced at Tyndale, then back again. "In bed, sir! I have to get up before six in the morning."

"Where do you sleep?" Narraway asked.

Cuttredge drew in his breath to answer, then quite suddenly realized the import of the question and the blood drained from his skin. "Upstairs, where the rest of the staff do. I . . . I never left my room." He drew in his breath to say something further, then gulped and remained silent.

"Thank you, Mr. Cuttredge," Pitt excused him.

Cuttredge remained seated, his hands grasping each other. "What happened? They're saying she's dead . . . one of the women. Is that true?"

Tyndale opened his mouth and then closed it again, remembering Pitt's warning.

"Yes, it is," Pitt answered Cuttredge. "Think carefully. Did you hear anything said, an altercation, a quarrel, perhaps an arrangement for her to see someone else after the party? Even a suggestion that she already knew someone here, or they knew her?"

36

"Certainly not," Cuttredge said instantly.

Narraway hid a tight smile.

"Not necessarily professionally, Mr. Cuttredge," Pitt pointed out. "Had she been here before?"

Cuttredge glanced at Tyndale, who nodded permission to answer.

"No," Cuttredge replied. "That I do know. The arrangement wasn't made by any of us. It was . . . it was Mr. Dunkeld."

"Indeed. Thank you." Pitt excused him again, and he left.

The next man to be seen was Edwards, who had let out the two other women. He was younger, slimmer, and, in spite of the circumstances, rather confident, as if his sudden importance excited him. He said he had noticed nothing unexpected, and he did not look to Tyndale for support. He reported that both women seemed cheerful, definitely a little drunk, but not in any way afraid or alarmed. Certainly neither of them had suffered any injury. He himself had gone to bed when most of the clearing-up had been done and the main reception room at least was ready for the morning.

"Close to two o'clock, sir, or as near as I can recall," he finished.

"And you went to bed yourself?"

"Yes, sir."

"Did you pass anywhere near the linen cupboard on your way up to your quarters?" Narraway put in.

Edwards was deeply unhappy and now consciously avoiding Tyndale's eyes. "Yes, sir, I did. I walked along that very passage. I shouldn't 'ave. We're supposed to go the long way round, but it was late and I was tired. It's hard work making certain everything's right. Bottles, glasses, cigar ash on the good rugs an' all. Stuff spoiled. It's no five-minute job, I can tell you."

"Don't you have maids to help?" Narraway asked him.

Edwards looked aggrieved. " 'Course we do, but not at that time o' night. An' it's still my job to see it's right. All the furniture back in its places, marks washed out, everything smelling like new again. So the ladies who are guests come down in the morning an' can't even smell there was a party, never mind see the dregs of it around."

Pitt wondered if any of the women were fooled, or if it simply allowed them the dignity of pretending they were. There were occasions when blindness was wise.

"You passed the linen cupboard," he prompted.

"I didn't see or 'ear nothing," Edwards told him quickly.

"Or smell anything?" Pitt asked.

Again Tyndale moved uncomfortably, and with an obvious effort forbore from interrupting.

Edwards drew in his breath and bit his lip. "Smell?" he said shakily. "What would I smell? You mean . . ." He could not bring himself to say the word.

"Blood," Pitt said for him. "It has a sweet, ironlike smell, when there is so much of it. But I imagine if the door was closed that would be sufficient to conceal it. The door was closed, wasn't it? Or was it ajar? Think back, and be very careful to answer exactly."

"It was closed," Edwards said without thinking at all. "If it'd been open I'd 'ave seen it. It opens that way, the way I was going." He took a deep breath. "Was she . . . was she in there then?" He gave an involuntary shudder, betraying more vulnerability than he had meant to.

"Probably not," Pitt replied, although the moment after he had said it, he thought perhaps he was wrong. She had almost certainly been killed before that, and from the amount of blood, she had obviously been killed in the cupboard. But if Edwards were right and the door had been closed, then someone else had opened it between two o'clock when Edwards passed, and six or so when

Dunkeld found the body.

Edwards also could prove neither that he had gone to bed nor that he had stayed there.

"He must be lying about the door being closed," Narraway said as soon as Edwards was gone.

"Or the latch is faulty," Pitt answered. "We'll look at it, Mr. Tyndale."

"No, sir, it's perfectly good," Tyndale replied. "I closed it myself . . . after . . . after they took the body away."

They spoke to the rest of the male staff as well and learned nothing of use. No one had found the dead woman's clothes. Tyndale ordered tea for them, and the housekeeper, Mrs. Newsome, herself brought it up on a tray with oatmeal biscuits.

They stopped long enough to drink the tea and eat all the biscuits. Then they interviewed the menservants of the four visitors, this time without Tyndale present, because they were not his responsibility. They gave the same unhelpful result.

Mrs. Newsome brought more tea, and this time sandwiches as well.

"One of them must be guilty," Narraway said unhappily, taking the last of the roast beef sandwiches and eating it absentmindedly. "She didn't do that to herself. And no woman would do that to another, even if she could."

"We'd better speak to all the female staff," Pitt said resignedly. "Somebody is lying. Even the smallest slip might help." He would have liked another sandwich, but there was only ham left now, and he didn't fancy it. "I'll get Tyndale to fetch them."

It took a great deal of patience to draw from them very little indeed. No one knew anything, had heard anything, or seen anything. There were tears, protests of innocence, and a very real danger of fainting or hysterics.

"Nothing!" Narraway said in exasperation after they were all gone. "We haven't learned a damn thing! It could still have been anyone."

"We'll start again," Pitt replied wearily. "Somebody did it. There'll be an inconsistency, a character flaw somebody knows about." He was repeating it to comfort himself as much as Narraway. Impatience was a fault in investigation, sometimes a fatal one.

He turned to Tyndale. "Where do the guests' servants sleep?"

"Upstairs in the servants' quarters," Tyndale replied. He looked exhausted, his skin blotched on his cheeks, the freckles standing out on the backs of his hands resting on the tabletop. "We've plenty of room for them. All guests bring their own personal servants."

"Maybe they'll remember seeing or hearing something. Do they eat with the Palace servants?"

"Not usually," Tyndale responded. "They're not really part of Palace discipline. We have no control over them." He said it wearily, as if with long memory of unfortunate incidents.

"Please get them back here, one at a time."

They began with Quase's man, who said only what he had said before. The second to come was Cahoon Dunkeld's man, florid-faced and sunburned like his master. He stood to attention.

"Came down the servants' stairs, sir?" he said to Pitt's question. "No, sir. Not possible, sir, unless it were after two in the morning. I was up an' about myself, sir. Pantry at the end o' that corridor, right opposite the bottom o' the stairs. Was up there getting Mr. Dunkeld an 'ot drink, sir. Bit of an upset stomach, 'e had. In an' out, an' along that corridor, I was, right from the time 'e came up to bed."

"An upset stomach?" Narraway's eyes opened very wide.

The man looked uncomfortable. "Yes, sir. If you'll pardon my saying so, sir, His Royal

Highness can 'old 'is drink rather better than most. Mr. Dunkeld doesn't like to let 'im down, so 'e keeps pace, like, but times are 'e pays for it. Best prevent that, if you can. Spot o' the hair o' the dog as bit you, if you get my meaning?"

"That's usually the following morning!" Narraway said tartly.

The man pulled his mouth into a grimace. "I got me own remedies, sir. Duty of a gentleman's gentleman to know these things. I couldn't see the door to that cupboard 'cos it's round the corner from the pantry, but I could see the servants' stairs, an' I'd stake me oath no one came down that way. Not before 'alf-past two in the morning. An' just Mr. Edwards went up."

"You said two!" Narraway said sharply.

"Yes, sir. I waited another 'alf hour, in case Mr. Dunkeld needed me again. 'Ad a cup o' tea meself. No point in just getting to sleep, an' 'aving to get up an' go back down again."

"Are you sure?"

"Yes, sir." He still stood straight as a ramrod. "An' in case you're thinking as it was me as killed that poor creature, Mr. Dunkeld'll swear for me, sir. Didn't 'ave time, nor any idea, to do summink like that."

"Thank you," Narraway said thoughtfully, his face bleak and pale. "That'll be all."

"Yes, sir." He withdrew gratefully.

Narraway looked at Pitt. "I am afraid it begins to look as if this party of His Royal Highness's will require a great deal more investigation. If what Edwards and Dunkeld's man say is true, then the conclusion cannot be avoided that one of the guests is a madman."

CHAPTER TWO

Elsa Dunkeld awoke to find Bartle, her lady's maid, standing at the foot of the bed with a tray in her hands. The curtains were already opened and the sun streamed in, lighting the unfamiliar room. It was a moment before she remembered where she was. She had slept poorly, troubled by dreams of empty corridors, through which she was looking for someone she never found. They were there in the distance, and then when she approached, they turned to face her and were someone else, strangers she fled from.

"Good morning, Bartie," she said, sitting up slowly. She saw that the tray was set not for morning tea but for breakfast. She had not wished for breakfast in bed, but perhaps that would be pleasanter than facing the others again so soon.

"I'm afraid it isn't a very good day, Miss Elsa." Bartle set the tray down on the table beside the bed to leave Elsa room to arrange

45

herself comfortably. She had been with Elsa since before her marriage to Cahoon Dunkeld seven years ago, and never doubted with whom her loyalty lay. She was in her fifties, broad-hipped, sensible but with a startlingly fresh sense of humor. Mostly she kept her opinions to herself, which, considering what they were, was just as well.

"I don't suppose it will be any worse than yesterday," Elsa replied with a slight smile, pushing her hair back off her brow. "We can manage it for a week."

"I'm afraid today will be a lot worse," Bartle said grimly. "You'd better take a sip or two o' that tea." She placed the tray on Elsa's lap and poured from the pot without being asked to.

"Why? Is Mr. Dunkeld in an ill temper?" As soon as Elsa had said it she regretted being so frank. She should keep her fear to herself.

"Not as far as I know, ma'am," Bartle answered, pulling her lips tight. "In fact, full of 'imself. Taking charge of everything."

That was unusual candor, even for Bartle. For the first time it occurred to Elsa that there was something really wrong. "What is it?" she said nervously. "What's happened?" She imagined some romantic intrigue. The first and most obvious one that came to her mind concerned Cahoon's daughter by his first marriage, Minnie Sorokine. Minnie was in her late twenties, tall and slender, yet with a voluptuous grace. She was not conventionally beautiful; instead, she had an air of daring and glamour about her that was more exciting than mere regularity of features or flawlessness of complexion. It suggested passion and originality, a challenge to master. There was something unsatisfied in her that gave her a restlessness many men found attractive. Eight years ago she had married Julius Sorokine. This fact was so painful to Elsa that she couldn't bear to dwell on it, and yet neither could she fully leave it alone. Minnie and Julius's wedding had happened just before Elsa had married Cahoon, although Elsa was ten years Minnie's senior. Family obligations had delayed the point where Elsa was able to marry, which in fact had not been a hardship because there had been no one she truly loved. But then she met Julius, and of course that was far too late. By then he was her son-in-law, and there was no hope at all for any other relationship between them, just a dream that there could have been something infinitely, passionately better than this! Her life could have had laughter in it, kindness, the sharing of joy and pain, the trust and the inner gentleness that is love.

But Minnie had not found it in Julius, or she would never have indulged in that brief, white-hot affair with Julius's half-brother, Simnel Marquand.

"What is it, Bartie?" Elsa said more abruptly. "Stop fussing with the things on the dressing table and tell me." She took a second sip of her tea, steadying herself.

Bartle put down the tortoiseshell-backed hairbrush. "The gentlemen had a . . . a party last night," she said stiffly. "It seems one of the trollops they had in got herself killed . . . in the linen cupboard of all places." She sniffed. In spite of her words, her face was crumpled with pity. "I can't imagine what the stupid creature was doing there. Although I suppose they have to do whatever they're paid for, poor things."

"Killed?" Elsa was incredulous. The cup nearly slipped out of her hand. "What kind of an accident can you have in a linen cupboard, for goodness' sake? You must be mistaken."

"It wasn't an accident, Miss Elsa," Bartle explained miserably. "They've got the police in. That's why everyone's having breakfast in bed. The Prince has asked everyone to stay in their rooms until it's been seen to."

"That's absurd." Elsa struggled to grasp

the meaning of what Bartle had said. "No one here would kill anybody, and surely the Palace, of all places, cannot be broken into?"

"No, miss. That's what's so bad about it," Bartle agreed, waiting for Elsa to understand.

"It must have been an accident." Elsa's mind raced to think what could have happened. She had gone to bed early, as had the other three women, to avoid the appearance of even knowing about the party. "That's the only thing possible. It's ridiculous to get the police in."

"Shall I lay out the green and white muslin, Miss Elsa?" Bartle asked.

"If the woman is dead, I should wear something darker," Elsa replied.

"She was a street woman, miss. And you're not supposed to even know about her," Bartle pointed out.

"She's still dead," Elsa retorted.

Bartle did not reply, but went on laying out the expensive morning gown of printed linen and muslin. It had a deep collar heavily frilled with lace and ribbons, and more lace down the front and at the sleeves. A wide, dark green ribbon tied around the waist and fell on the first tier of the skirt. The middle tier was plain green linen, the third heavily gathered muslin again. Cahoon was generous, and of course he expected his wife to look both beautiful and expensive. It was a reflection upon him. He had married Elsa because she knew how to conduct herself, to say the right things, and use the correct form of address for everyone. She was an excellent hostess. Her dinner parties never failed. She had a gift for knowing exactly who to invite with whom. And she never complained. That was part of the bargain between them.

"Bargain" was a terrible word to describe a marriage, and yet, tacitly, that is what it had been, in spite of the turbulent physical beginning. And that was past now. Emotionally she bored him, which both hurt, because it was humiliating, and was a kind of relief, because she no longer desired him either. He was intelligent, commanding to look at, and he certainly afforded her a life of luxury, travel, and conversation with most interesting people — men who invented, explored, dared, and governed all over the Empire.

Elsa knew she was envied. She had seen the quick fire of interest in other women's eyes, the flush to the skin, heard the altered pitch in their voices. She had enjoyed it. Who does not wish to have what others so clearly want?

But at the end of even the most vigorous or luxurious day, even if briefly physically intimate, at heart she was alone. She and Cahoon did not share laughter or dreams. She did not know what hurt him or moved him to tenderness, nor did he appear to know it of her. What twisted the knife in the wound was the fact that he did not wish to.

Would life with Julius have been any different? It was a sudden, bitter thought that if he did not love Minnie, maybe then perhaps he was not capable of loving anyone.

It was a long, frustrating morning alone. She did not go to the withdrawing room for the guests' use until shortly before luncheon. The walls were lined in vivid yellow brocade exactly matching that of the sofas and the seats of the elegant, hard-backed chairs. The enormous windows, stretching almost to the height of the ornate blue-and-white ceiling, were curtained in the same shade. The mantel was also white, with tall blue lamps on either end of it, giving the whole room a delicate, sunny feeling. The carpet was pale blue and russet. The only darker tones were the surfaces of the tables in the center and against the wall, where one might rest a glass.

Elsa found only Olga Marquand there, wearing a plum gown that did not flatter her dark looks. It should have been warming to her sallow complexion, and yet somehow it failed. Nor did its severe line lend her any suggestion of softness. A gathering, a drape, an additional tier of skirt might have helped.

Olga was a little above average height and very slender. With more confidence she would have been elegant, but looking at her now, Elsa realized how little Olga had the spirit to fight. She did not brazen it out and make people believe that her square shoulders and angular grace were more interesting than the more traditional curves of someone like Minnie. She had high cheekbones and a slightly aquiline nose. Her brow was smooth and her black hair swept back from it with unusual classic severity. Her dark eyes were hooded. At their first meeting Elsa had thought Olga uniquely beautiful. Now she seemed beaky, and cold.

Olga turned as Elsa entered the room. "Have you heard anything more?" she asked quietly. Her voice was good, even rich. "Who is it who died? Why is everyone being so secretive?"

"My maid said it was one of the . . . the women from last night's party," Elsa replied, keeping her own voice low as well.

Olga raised her arched eyebrows. "What did she do, fall downstairs blind drunk?" Her voice was raw with disgust, though perhaps it was pain. Elsa could only guess how she felt about her husband associating with such women, even if it was only to please the Prince of Wales. Perhaps he thought he had no choice, if they were to ensure the Prince's support in their bid to gain the contract for a railway right from Cape Town to Cairo, like a spine to all Africa. Did Olga understand that, or did it hurt too much for her to care?

Elsa looked at her and thought how different they were. She realized with surprise that she was not repulsed by the thought that Cahoon should have indulged himself with either the brandy or the women. She would have, in the beginning, but not now. Olga cared to the point where she could not keep from betraying the pain of it, even in front of others. It was more than self-possession or dignity, or a trespass on her pride. She still loved Simnel, in spite of everything.

Olga was staring at her, waiting for a reply. She was angry, perhaps because Elsa was not hurt as she was, or maybe because it was Cahoon who had arranged the evening.

"In the linen cupboard, I believe," Elsa said aloud.

"You must be mistaken." Olga was derisive. "How can you kill yourself in a linen cupboard? Did she suffocate in a pile of sheets?"

"I gather it was worse than that, but I don't know how."

Olga tried to hide her shock. "You mean somebody did it deliberately? That's absurd. Why would anyone bother?" There was an infinity of contempt in the final word.

You are wearing your unhappiness too openly, Elsa thought. It does not make you more attractive. Aloud she said, "I don't know. But men do a lot of things for reasons I don't understand."

"Including having women like that to a party!" Olga added bitterly.

Liliane Quase entered in a swirl of pale golden-green skirts, light, airy, and feminine. She was beautiful in an abundant way. She had creamy skin, dark auburn hair, and eyes of golden brown. She was just a little too short to have real grace, but most of the time she disguised it with cleverly cut gowns that suggested more height than she had. Today the line of the gathered second tier was lower than usual, sweeping outward and making her legs seem far longer. Another woman would notice the artifice, but a man would not.

Elsa found herself smiling very slightly. She also knew that Liliane wore a higher heel to her shoes and had learned to walk in them very gracefully. She must have practiced a long time.

"For goodness' sake, it's necessary to humor the Prince of Wales, Olga!" Liliane said impatiently. "It's probably largely harmless, a bit of showing off. It's all very silly, but it's even sillier of you to allow yourself to be offended by it. You give it more importance than it deserves." She looked around for some form of aperitif, and saw nothing. "Women who keep taking offense are very tiresome, my dear. Nothing bores a man faster. Take my advice and pretend you don't care a fig. In fact, better than that, don't allow yourself to care."

Olga drew in her breath to make a stinging retort, then apparently could not think of one. "Elsa is hinting that she was murdered," she observed instead.

Liliane swung around to regard Elsa with surprise. "Who is saying such an idiotic thing?" Her voice was perfectly steady, but her eyes were bright and her gaze unnaturally firm. "Murdered how?"

"I don't know," Elsa admitted. "But she was found in the linen cupboard."

"The linen cupboard!" Liliane exclaimed. "By whom, for heaven's sake? Probably some stupid maid in hysterics. I dare say the wretched girl was with child and tried to abort herself. I expect they'll get it cleared up, and we can all get back to what matters. There is a great deal to discuss yet to ensure that His Royal Highness is fully aware of all the facts."

"I'm sure he knows the map of Africa as well as we do," Olga told her. "It's really quite simple. Cape Town is on the coast of South Africa, which is British anyway. After that the railway would go up through Bechuanaland, then the British South Africa Company territory. There is only the stretch between German East Africa and Congo Free State that is foreign, then we are into British East Africa. Sudan might be tricky, but then there's Egypt, which is British, and we are in Cairo. It isn't largely the diplomatic issues that are the problem." She dismissed them with a jerk of her hand. "It is the engineering. Let the police clear up whatever happened to this woman in the cupboard. It's totally absurd for such a thing to hold up discussion of a railway that will change the face of the Empire. There must be prostitutes dying every day, somewhere or other."

"This is not 'somewhere or other,' " Elsa pointed out. "It is a linen cupboard in Buckingham Palace, not twenty yards from my bedroom door, or yours, for that matter."

"My dear," Liliane said with elaborate patience, "it is as irrelevant to you as if it were in China! For goodness' sake forget about it, and concentrate on being charming to His Royal Highness. It's probably not good manners even to mention such a thing, let alone be seen to be disconcerted by it."

"Positively vulgar!" Minnie said from the doorway. "A guest should never appear to find anything odd, no matter what it is. Good morning, Elsa, Mrs. Marquand, Mrs. Quase." She looked superb. Her morning gown was a rich golden yellow with a long, two-tiered skirt that swayed when she moved and had ribbons at her throat and wrist. The bloom of youth was in her skin, her eyes were bright, and she had a kind of concentrated energy so delicately controlled that she seemed to be more alive than any of the others. It was an inner excitement, as if she knew something they did not. Elsa sometimes wondered if that were so.

"I suggest we don't refer to it," Minnie added, moving toward the door into the dining room. "Where is everyone else?"

"It is more than a misfortune in domestic arrangements," Elsa said tartly. Minnie's callousness annoyed her, as did everything else about her at one time or another. Minnie's father's intense admiration for her was almost a fascination, as if she were a reflection of himself. But most of all, of course, the spur to her dislike was that she was Julius's wife.

"No, it isn't," Minnie contradicted her with a slight shrug. "People do die. It can't be helped. It is rude to make much of it. I should be fearfully embarrassed if one of my maids died vulgarly when I had house-guests."

"Of course you would," Julius agreed, coming in from the hall. "Dying vulgarly is a privilege exclusive to the upper classes. Servants should die decently in bed."

"Don't be witty, Julius," Minnie snapped. "It doesn't become you. Anyway, she wasn't a servant, she was a . . ."

"Where should they die, my dear? In the street?" he inquired languidly.

She opened her eyes very wide and stared at him. "I have no idea. It is not a matter I have ever considered." She swung round, elegantly turning her skirt with a little flick, and walked away into the dining room.

Julius glanced at Elsa, a faint, rueful smile on his face, and then sighed and followed after his wife.

Elsa felt her throat tighten and her heart lurch.

Then the moment was broken by Simnel

coming in. Although he was Julius's half-brother, they were not alike. Julius was taller and broader at the shoulders, and Elsa could see a greater imagination and more vulnerability in the line of his mouth than in Simnel's. But then she was more certain of her emotion than of her judgment. Perhaps that was only what she wished to see.

"What on earth is going on?" Simnel asked, looking around. "Who are the men asking questions and sending the servants into hysterics? I just saw one of the maids with tears streaming down her face, and she ran from me as if I had horns and a tail."

Cahoon came in practically on his heels. "There's been an ugly incident," he answered, as if the question had been addressed to him. "One of last night's whores was murdered. Regrettably we have to have the police in, but if they do their job properly, they may clear it up within a day or so. We must just keep our heads and go on with our work. Shall we go in to luncheon." That was an order more than a suggestion. "Where is Hamilton?"

Elsa disliked the use of the word *whore*. It sounded so pitiless, particularly when her husband was being brutally frank. She had despised the women when they were alive, but now that one of them had been mur-

59

dered she felt differently. It was uncomfortable, even disconcerting, but for the sake of her own humanity, she told herself that she needed to observe their common bond more than their differences.

Cahoon went into the dining room ahead, leaving her to follow, with Olga beside her. The Prince of Wales was obviously not joining them, so there was little formality observed. They each took the places at which they had sat the previous day, the women assisted by servants.

This room also was magnificent, but too heavy in style for Elsa's taste. She felt dwarfed by the huge paintings with their frames so broad as to seem almost a feature of the architecture. The ceiling stretched like the canopy of some elaborate tent, with the optical illusion of being arched. It was beautiful, and yet she was not comfortable in it. Certainly she did not wish to eat.

The soup was served in uncomfortable silence before Hamilton Quase joined them, taking the one empty chair without comment. He was tall and slender, and in his late forties. He had been handsome in his youth, but his fair hair had lost its thickness. His face was burned by the sun and marred by an absentminded sadness, as if he had forgotten its exact cause, or possibly chosen to forget it.

Liliane looked at him anxiously. The footman offered him soup but he declined, saying he would wait for the fish. He did accept the white wine, and drank from the glass immediately.

"You'd expect a place like Buckingham Palace to be safe, wouldn't you!" he said challengingly. "How the devil can a lunatic break in here? Can anyone walk in and out as they please?"

"Nobody walked in," Cahoon told him. "Or out."

Hamilton set his glass down so violently the wine slopped over. "God! You mean he's still here?"

"Of course he's still here!" Cahoon snapped. "He was always here!"

Hamilton stared at him, the color draining from his face.

"You're frightening the women," Julius said critically to Cahoon. He glanced around the table. "Nobody broke in, and nobody will. One of the servants completely lost control of himself and must have hit her, or strangled her, or whatever it was. It's a tragedy, but it's none of our business. And there is certainly nothing for us to be afraid of. The police will deal with it."

Hamilton raised his glass in a salute to

Julius, and drank again.

Liliane relaxed a little and picked up her fork.

"Knifed her," Cahoon filled in as the butler placed the fish in front of him. "Cut her throat and . . . and her body. I'm afraid this is going to be unpleasant."

"How do you know?" Simnel asked with more curiosity than alarm. He glanced at Minnie, and then back at Cahoon.

"I found her," Cahoon said simply.

Elsa was startled. The wineglass slipped in her fingers and she only just caught it before it spilled. "I thought she was in a linen cupboard!"

"What on earth were you doing in a linen cupboard so early in the morning?" Julius asked with a very slight smile. "Or at any time, for that matter."

"The door was open," Cahoon told him tartly. "I smelled it."

Liliane wrinkled her nose. "If we must have this discussion at all, could we at least put it off until after we have finished dining, Cahoon? I'm sure we are grateful that you seem to be taking charge of things, but your zeal has temporarily overtaken your good taste. I would prefer to have my fish without the details."

"I'm afraid we are not going to escape all

of the unpleasantness," Cahoon said drily. "The servants are bound to be useless for a while. Some of them may even leave."

"One of them needs to," Julius pointed out.

Elsa wanted to laugh, but she knew it was out of fear rather than amusement, and wildly inappropriate. She choked it back, pretending to have swallowed badly. No one took the slightest notice of her.

"It makes you realize how little you know people," Olga murmured.

"One doesn't know servants," Minnie corrected her. "One knows *about* them."

"If they knew about him, they would hardly have employed him." Julius looked at her coolly.

"I imagine they thought they did." Cahoon began to eat again. "None of us know as much about people as we imagine we do." He glanced around the table, his eyes for a moment on each of them. "We have all known one another to some degree for years, but I have no idea what dreams are passing through your mind, Julius. Or yours, Hamilton. What do you wish for most at this moment, Simnel?"

"A peaceful luncheon and a productive afternoon," Simnel replied instantly, but there was a touch of color in his cheeks and he did not meet Cahoon's eyes, still less did he look at Olga.

Elsa knew he was thinking of Minnie. Probably they all did. She stole a very quick glance at Olga, and saw the pallor of her skin and the pull on the fabric of her dress as it strained across her hunched shoulders. For a hot, ugly moment she hated Cahoon for his cruelty.

Minnie was concentrating on her plate, the shadow of her eyelashes dark on her cheek. She seemed to glow with satisfaction.

"Slashed with a knife?" Elsa said aloud. "Whoever takes a carving knife to an assignation in the linen cupboard? It doesn't make any sense!"

"Cutting a whore up with a carving knife doesn't make any sense wherever you do it, Elsa," Cahoon said abruptly. "We aren't looking for a sane man. Surely you realize that?"

She felt humiliated, but she could think of nothing to say that would rebut his remark. Of course she knew it was not a sane thing to do. It had been an impulsive observation.

Oddly, it was Hamilton Quase who defended her. "Someone who is sane enough to pass as a Palace servant probably appears sane in most things," he said with a casual air, as if they were discussing a parlor game.

"If he were running up and down the staircases with wild eyes and blood on his hands, someone would have noticed."

"Providing they also were sober," Olga said waspishly. "And not doing much the same! Were any of you sober enough last night to have noticed such a thing?"

"Unkind, my dear," Hamilton responded, picking up his glass again. "You should not remind a man of his lapses, especially in front of his wife."

"She is the one person with whom they are quite safe," Cahoon responded, looking across the table at Liliane.

Liliane's eyes were very bright and there was a touch of color in her cheeks. She too seemed to search for something to say, and not to find it. For a moment a shadow crossed her face with possibly hatred in it. Then, as if the sun had returned, it was gone. "Of course," she said with her lovely smile. "Are we not all loyal to family and friends? Such a thing is hardly worth remark."

Julius applauded silently, but none of them missed his gesture.

Minnie shivered. "It's a horrible thought." She looked at her father, shrugging her shoulders elegantly, avoiding everyone's eyes but his. "I hope they find him very soon."

"Don't make any assignations with servants in the linen cupboard in the meantime," Julius told her. "You should be safe enough."

Cahoon froze, his face red. "What did you say?" he demanded, his voice like ice.

Julius paled slightly, but he held Cahoon's eye and repeated his words exactly.

Cahoon leaned forward, knocking a water glass over and ignoring the mess on the table. Elsa knew she should intervene, but she was afraid of Cahoon when he lost his temper. She tried to speak, though her mouth was dry and her throat tight.

"You are speaking of my daughter, sir!" Cahoon said loudly. "You will apologize to her, and to the rest of us, or I will horsewhip you!"

"No, sir," Julius corrected him. "I am speaking of my wife. I think sometimes you forget that. And undoubtedly sometimes she does."

For once Minnie blushed.

Cahoon's face was still red, his eyes blazing.

"Calm down and don't be an ass," Hamilton Quase said calmly and with a delicate derision. "Nobody is fooled by any of this. We are all afraid. There's a madman loose in the Palace, and he may be downstairs socially, but there is no bar on the stairway and he can come up anytime he wishes, as demonstrated by the fact that the wretched woman was found in the cupboard on our landing. Please heaven, let's hope this policeman is up to his job and takes the man away as soon as possible."

Cahoon turned to regard Hamilton coldly. "Do you have any idea what you are talking about, Hamilton? I saw the woman's body! It was like nothing you have ever imagined. Or perhaps you have? How long were you in Africa?"

Liliane was gripping her fish fork as if it were a weapon, her knuckles white. She stared at Cahoon, hatred in her eyes. "Long enough to show courage and resolution in the face of tragedy, Mr. Dunkeld, and to know how to help people rather than make things worse by losing his temper and his judgment," she said loudly. "How long were you there?"

Hamilton looked at her with some surprise, and a sudden, overwhelming tenderness in his eyes. Then he turned to Cahoon.

Elsa wondered what they were talking about. She could see Julius's eyes widen, and a faint flush on Hamilton's face. They were referring to something specific. They knew it. She, Minnie, and Olga were completely confused.

Slowly Cahoon sat back in his chair.

Elsa found herself shaking with relief.

The servants, who had stepped back, resumed their silent duties, and one by one everyone began to eat again.

Elsa's mind raced. What had Cahoon been referring to? It had been an attack on Hamilton somehow, and Liliane had leaped in to protect him, as she seemed to do so often. From what? What was she afraid of? According to Cahoon, a woman of the streets had been murdered here where they were guests, and everyone was afraid. But were they all afraid of the same thing, or was it different for each of them?

The main course was served. Cahoon introduced the subject of the great railway again. The men all contributed from their various skills and fields of knowledge as to the difficulties they might face and how they should be overcome.

Simnel was a financier, brilliant at attracting funds at the most excellent rates. What he had to say was in many ways dry: lists of bankers and wealthy men who would be willing to invest. It was the wealth of his knowledge and his memory for detail that impressed. He knew not only everyone's worth, but their history, and, if he chose to, he could be amusing in recounting it.

He spoke mostly to Cahoon, but he included all of them. When he looked at Olga it was casual, as it was to Elsa and Liliane, no more than that. When he looked at Minnie there was a heat in his eyes, and he moved his glance quickly, as though he knew he betrayed himself.

He did not look at Julius at all. Elsa wondered if it were guilt because Minnie was his wife, or something older and deeper than that. Did he want Minnie for himself, or was it really because by taking her he was cuckolding his brother?

They moved to discussing one of the most difficult legs of the journey diplomatically, which, as Olga had said, lay between German East Africa and Congo Free State. Julius touched briefly on how it was both a political and a logistic problem. It was his art to persuade, suggest compromise, know every nation's ambitions and fears, strengths and weaknesses, so he could offer a solution that left all parties feeling as if they had had the best of the deal.

Elsa listened to him intently, and only moved her gaze from his face when she noticed Cahoon watching her, and then Minnie's smile. Julius had never once looked at her. Was he afraid in case his looks were too close, too soft? Or did he simply have no wish to? How much of what she remembered was really only imagination, her own wish, her burning hunger, and for him merely politeness, possibly even embarrassment?

Minnie was so vivid, so alive. Cahoon was watching her now, his face brooding, but his eyes bright with pleasure. He was the organizer of men and labor. He had a farsighted vision in planning the movement of machines, timber, and steel. He knew where to buy and how to ship. He was passionate about the whole vision and the excitement of it rang in his voice. He seemed to radiate energy.

Minnie turned quite deliberately to watch him.

What he was describing would be the backbone of Africa from the Cape of Good Hope, which divided the South Atlantic from the Indian Ocean, almost seven thousand miles, up across the equator, to the delta where the Nile poured into the Mediterranean. In spite of herself, Elsa was fired up by the vision too.

Lastly Hamilton spoke. He was the engineer. He could not only weigh and judge the more obvious issues, he could make leaps of the imagination laterally, create possibilities no one else had considered, solve problems, and devise new methods of doing things. He spoke well, with dry, self-deprecating humor. Was it a mannerism, as if he had been taught the vulgarity of self-praise? Or did he really have so little regard for his own abilities?

Elsa looked at Liliane, to see if she perceived it also, and saw fear without knowing of what. Then she wished she had not understood so clearly. She was guilty of an intrusion.

She was not really interested in the facts. Of course, she wished the project to succeed because it was what the men wanted. It would bring them both immense financial profit, and even more, it would inevitably bring fame and honor. She knew that was what Cahoon hungered for.

She looked at him where he sat now, his broad shoulders hunched a little as if his jacket restricted him, his face intent.

What he wanted was recognition, title. He had a compelling hunger to be ennobled, and to become part of the Prince of Wales's circle. That was the highest in the land, since the Queen had no circle anymore. She had lived in a kind of seclusion ever since Prince Albert's death more than three decades ago.

Elsa looked across the table where Minnie

71

was watching her father. There was a warmth in her face, an ease in her eyes and mouth, and yet she was still not entirely comfortable. Her concentration was too direct.

They were all pretending to be absorbed in the intricacies of the great plan, but she wondered how many of them were actually more interested in their own hungers? Why did Minnie find Simnel attractive? Was it to test her power because she could not find in her own husband the passion she longed for?

Suddenly Elsa was assailed by guilt. She imagined being in Minnie's place, married to Julius. To the outside world she would possess a happiness any woman would desire. Elsa did! Yet in reality perhaps Minnie was also alone, close but never touching in the heart or mind, nearness without intimacy. How many people lived like that?

Someone was speaking to Elsa, but she had not heard him. It was Cahoon, and he was angry that she was not listening. It showed a lack of respect. Did it hurt anything more than his vanity? He wanted her to love him, she knew that. But why? For the power it gave him? To feed his self-esteem? Or because he too ached for tenderness, someone to share his laughter and pain?

"Elsa!" His voice was sharp.

She must pay attention. "Yes, Cahoon?"

"What's the matter?" he demanded. "Are you ill?"

"No." She must think of a quick lie. "I was wondering if the policeman was having any success."

"There are two of them, and they are from Special Branch," he corrected her. "Apparently they are more discreet than the regular sort. I asked you if you would like to come with me to Cairo when we negotiate some of the details there."

Instantly she wondered if Julius would be involved. Did Cahoon mean diplomatic details, or engineering? She could not ask. And did she want to be near Julius or not? Did she want the heightened loneliness, the wondering? If she became certain that he did love her, it would fill her heart. It would be desperately sweet, overwhelming. But there was nothing that they could do about it, ever. He was married to her stepdaughter. There could never be happiness in a double betrayal.

Or she would discover that he did not love her, only desired her, as Simnel had Minnie — and, it seemed, still did — with a hunger filled with resentment because it was a kind of bondage. This only triggered more emptiness within. Did she want to know if he was shallower than she thought, worth less? Or even worse, that she herself was?

"Elsa, take command of yourself!" Cahoon snapped. "Do you want to come or not?"

"Yes, of course," she answered, because she could think of no excuse. Or perhaps it was because she could not let go of the chance to spend time with Julius, whatever the cost. All reason was against it, and yet she had chosen to do it unhesitatingly.

She used to feel as if she and Minnie were a world apart from each other, so different there was no possibility of understanding between them. Perhaps she was wrong, and in reality she was just like Minnie, only with slightly less flair.

The afternoon was miserable. The men resumed their discussions, joined at about three o'clock by the Prince of Wales, who looked formal and very serious. Elsa spoke to him only briefly, but she could see that he was still suffering from the effects of a night of self-indulgence and then the most appalling shock. He greeted her with his usual courtesy, but did not say anything more than to inquire after her well-being and wish her a good afternoon. She could not help noticing the relief in his face when he saw Cahoon walking over toward him, smiling and with a confidence in his stride and in the set of his shoulders that suggested he was master of events. There was nothing to fear after all.

Of course there wasn't, she told herself. It was tragic for the woman concerned, and it was most unpleasant, but no more than that.

She filled in the afternoon walking in the gardens alone for a while, then played cards for an hour with Olga, who seemed to find as much difficulty as she did in concentrating. At afternoon tea she made conversation with Liliane, mostly gossip neither of them cared about. Who had said what to whom had never mattered much to either of them.

At about quarter to six Bartle came to Elsa's room to tell her that the policeman would like to speak with her.

"With me?" Elsa was startled. "Whatever for? I have no idea what happened."

Bartle's expression was grim. "I don't know, Miss Elsa. But he an' the other one've been talking to the regular servants here all afternoon. He just spoke to Mrs. Quase, an' now he'd like to see you. I think there's something badly wrong, ma'am."

Elsa opened the door to the small sitting room with more curiosity than trepidation. The man she found inside was taller than she had expected, but otherwise he appeared fairly ordinary, apart from an unusual intelligence in his eyes. He was clean-shaven. His hair was curly and too long, and she noticed immediately that his coat hung badly, possibly because the right pocket bulged with something large inside it. His shirt collar sat crookedly and his tie was too loose. He looked tired.

"Good afternoon," she said, closing the door. "I believe you wished to speak with me?"

"Yes, Mrs. Dunkeld," he replied, stepping back a little to make room for her to pass him easily and choose whatever chair she wished. "My name is Inspector Pitt."

She was surprised. His voice was excellent, deep, and with both the timbre and the enunciation of a man of education, which he could not be, or he would not be employed in such an occupation. Everyone knew that except in most serious command, police were from the lower social orders. Even the better servants frowned on them.

She sat down in one of the smaller wing chairs and adjusted the skirts of her afternoon gown. "I cannot help you," she said politely. "I know very little of the Palace. This is the only time I have been here, and it is only two days since I arrived."

"Yes, I know that, Mrs. Dunkeld." He took the seat opposite her, which was upright and less comfortable. "Are you aware of what happened here last night?"

She noticed that he looked concerned, as if he were obliged to tell her something she would find distressing. She wanted to put him at ease. "Yes, I am. One of the women who came to the party yesterday evening was murdered."

He looked surprised that she could be so blunt about it. She wondered if he had been afraid she did not know what manner of women they were.

"You have been questioning the servants all day, to find out who is responsible," she added. "I hope you have been successful. The reason we are His Royal Highness's guests concerns a matter of the greatest possible importance. It would be far better if the gentlemen were all free to continue with their business without further distress." She chose the words to be as tactful as possible, leaving open the suggestion that there was pity for the dead woman as well as inconvenience involved. She could not tell from his face if he understood that. There was a flash of humor in his eyes that could have meant anything. It disconcerted her because she could not read him as swiftly as she had imagined she would.

He looked at her steadily, a very slight

frown between his brows. "The prostitute that the Prince had chosen for himself was found in the linen cupboard this morning," he told her. "I'm afraid she was completely unclothed, and she had been slashed to death with a knife."

Elsa was stunned. For a moment she found it hard to breathe. Cahoon had mentioned a carving knife, but she had thought he was being deliberately brutal. From this quiet man with his bulging pockets and his steady eyes, quite suddenly the woman's death had a reality that was shocking. She started to speak, and then had no idea what she wanted to say.

"We have questioned all the servants," Pitt continued, "and found that none of them could be responsible."

For a moment she did not understand. "You mean someone broke in?" she said incredulously. "But we are in the Palace! That could not happen. Or are you saying it was one of the guards? I find that hard to believe. Are you certain?"

"No one broke in, Mrs. Dunkeld. The guards can account for one another. This is the sort of crime that a man commits alone."

"You mean it was . . . ?" She did not wish to use the words necessary to explain herself. Why had she supposed the murder had been committed merely out of anger? Given the occupation of the woman, it could be assumed that she had earned her fee. "Poor creature," she added, imagining what it must have been like. Involuntarily her mind flew to occasions of intimacy with Cahoon when she had been aware of her own helplessness, and frightened of him, even physically hurt. He had taken pleasure in her pain, she was sure of that now. It had excited him.

"I'm sorry." The policeman was apologizing to her. Had her face been so transparent? She felt the heat rise up on it. Please heaven this man mistook it for modesty. She was allowing him to unnerve her. Cahoon would find that contemptible.

"I am quite capable of facing facts, Mr. Pitt," she said sharply. "Even if they are unpleasant. I have not lived my entire life in the withdrawing room."

If he understood her, there was no reflection of it in his expression, except perhaps a flash of pity. "No one broke in, Mrs. Dunkeld. I am afraid that leaves no possibility other than that it was one of the guests."

She had thought herself already stunned. This was beyond belief. "You mean one of us?" Her voice was high-pitched; she refused to accept the thought. "That's absurd!" Even as the words spilled out, she knew it was not absurd. All kinds of people have passions that lie beneath the disciplined surface, until some fear or hunger makes them momentarily ungovernable. Usually it is violent words that break through, or something beautiful or precious is smashed to pieces in rage. What prevents it from being a human being? The conventions of society and the fear of punishment. All human life must be regarded as sacred, or one's own may be endangered as well. But do women who sell their bodies for others to use count as human life in the same way? If they did, could one buy them in the first place?

He was watching her.

"I have no knowledge that could be helpful, Mr. Pitt," she said as steadily as she could. "As you must already know, the gentlemen remained at the party, and we retired early. I did not see anyone again until my maid woke me this morning and told me there had been a tragedy, and we were requested to remain in our bedrooms."

"Do you know at what time your husband retired?" he asked.

He must be aware that they had separate rooms. This was a perfectly usual thing for the wealthy, but not, she imagined, for the class to which he belonged.

"No, I don't," she answered. "Perhaps if

you ask the other gentlemen, they will be able to tell you." Not counting the Prince of Wales — and that he should be guilty was unthinkable — there were only four of them: Cahoon, Julius, Hamilton, and Simnel. What this policeman was saying seemed inescapable, and yet it was also ridiculous. He did not know them, or he would not even imagine it.

But how well did she know them? She had been married to Cahoon for over seven years, lived in his house, sometimes intimately, at other times as strangers, misreading each other, saying the same words and meaning different things. She knew his mind. He was lucidly clear. But she had never known his heart.

Hamilton Quase was charming when he wished to be, but Liliane was obviously afraid for him. She leaped to defend him as if he were uniquely vulnerable. Memories flashed into Elsa's mind of looks between Liliane and Julius, a sudden pallor on Hamilton's face, and a smile on Cahoon's, then a thinning of the lips, an unnatural change of subject.

"I would help you if I could, Mr. Pitt," she said, struggling to sound resolute and in control. "This is an appalling thing to have happened, for all of us, but of course mostly for the poor woman. I retired a little after nine. I have no knowledge of what happened after that. You will have to ask my husband, and the other gentlemen."

"I have done, Mrs. Dunkeld," Pitt replied. "Each says that after the . . . entertainment . . . was finished, he retired alone. Except Mr. Sorokine. He says he left them early, and they all confirm that he did, as do the servants. Unfortunately, since he did not share a room with Mrs. Sorokine, or see her again until morning, that is of little value to us in excluding him."

She felt her face burn. "I see. So you know nothing, except that it was one of us?"

"Yes. I am afraid that is exactly what I mean."

She could think of no reply, not even any protest or question. The silence lay in the room like a covering for the dead.

CHAPTER THREE

On the day the murder was discovered at the Palace, Gracie Phipps had been the all-purpose maid at the Pitts' home for nearly eight years. She was twenty-one now and engaged to marry Police Sergeant Samuel Tell-man. Gracie was intensely proud of working for such a remarkable man as Pitt. She had no doubt whatever that he was the best detective in England.

When she began in his service, she had been four feet ten inches tall and could neither read nor write. She had not considered the possibility of ever doing either. However, Charlotte Pitt had offered to teach her. Now Gracie could not only read newspapers but even books and, more than that, she enjoyed it. She had also grown a whole inch and a half.

She was reading in her bedroom with the attic windows open to the rustling of leaves and the distant sounds of traffic, when there was a knock on the door. She was startled. It was dark outside and must be late. She had lost count of time in the adventure on the pages.

She stood up quickly and went to answer the knock.

Charlotte was on the landing, still fully dressed but with her hair rather less than tidily pinned, as if she had put it back up again in haste.

"Yes, ma'am?" Gracie said with a flutter of alarm. "Is something wrong?" Her mind went instantly to Pitt, having been called out in an emergency early that morning. There had been no message from him since. "Is Mr. Pitt all right?"

"Yes, perfectly, I believe," Charlotte said with an oddly rueful smile. "Mr. Narraway, from Special Branch, would like to see you. He has something to ask you." Her expression softened. "Please feel perfectly at liberty to answer him as you wish to. Whatever you say will be acceptable to me, and I shall see that your decision is respected."

"Wot . . . wot's 'e gonna say?" Gracie asked with panic rising inside her. She knew Narraway was Pitt's superior. He was a strange man, quietly spoken and elegant in a lean, very dark sort of way. But Gracie had seen hard men in the East End of London where she had grown up, men who carried knives and knew how to use them, whom she would not have backed in a fight against Mr. Narraway. There was something in him only a fool would challenge. Except when he looked at Mrs. Pitt. Then he was just as human and easily hurt as anyone else. Gracie thought she might be the only one who could see that. It was odd what people missed sometimes. "Wot does 'e want wi' me?" she said again.

"Come down and you'll find out," Charlotte told her. "I'm not carrying a message down to the head of Special Branch to say you won't see him!"

Gracie thought about her hair, which was straight as rain, screwed up in a knot at the back of her head, and her dark blue dress, which was more than a little crumpled. She would be putting a clean one on tomorrow anyway, so she had not bothered about sitting on it.

"Just as you are." Charlotte must have read her thoughts. "He will mind a few wrinkles far less than he will mind waiting."

That was alarming. Gracie smoothed her skirt once, ineffectively; her hands were shaking. Then she followed Charlotte down to the landing, past the bedroom doors of Jemima and Daniel, the two Pitt children, then on down the next flight to the hall.

Narraway was waiting in the front parlor. He looked extremely tired. His face was lined and his thick, dark hair with its sprinkling of gray was definitely less neat than usual. He was apparently too restless to sit down.

Gracie stood to attention. "Yes, sir?"

Charlotte closed the door and Gracie hoped to heaven she had remained inside, but she dared not look round to find out.

"Miss Phipps," Narraway began, "what I am about to tell you, you will keep with the same absolute discretion you do all things you learn in this house. Do you understand me?"

"Yes, sir! I know what discretion is," Gracie said indignantly. "I don't talk about things to no one wot in't their business."

"Good. Mr. Pitt was called this morning because there has been a murder at Buckingham Palace, where the Queen lives. Although she is not there at the moment, fortunately. However, the Prince of Wales is."

Gracie stared at him speechlessly.

"A prostitute was knifed to death," Narraway continued. "And her body was left in the linen cupboard in the guest wing, where there are presently eight people staying. They are on extremely important business with His Royal Highness."

"An' Mr. Pitt's gonna find out 'oo killed 'er," Gracie finished for him. "Don't worry, sir. We can take care of things 'ere."

"I'm sure you could, Miss Phipps." Narraway nodded very slightly, the briefest possible flash of humor in his eyes. "However, that is not what your country requires of you."

Charlotte let out her breath with a sigh.

Narraway colored faintly, but he did not turn to look at her.

"Wot d'yer mean, 'my country'?" Gracie asked, completely bewildered. "In't nothing I can do."

"I suggest you get to the point, Mr. Narraway," Charlotte cut in at last. "If I may say so, you are wasting time, and it is late."

Narraway looked uncomfortable. There had been a distinct edge to Charlotte's voice, and Gracie was sorry for him. Her awe of him vanished. She had heard it said that no man was a hero to his valet. Perhaps he wasn't to any servant who could read emotions in him that were so oddly vulnerable.

"Wot is it yer'd like me to do, sir?" she asked gently.

A flash of gratitude crossed Narraway's face for an instant, then vanished. "I would like you to take temporary employment at

Buckingham Palace, Miss Phipps. The position is already secured for you, as a general between-stairs maid. No one will know that you are really working for Special Branch, assisting Mr. Pitt, except Mr. Tyndale, who is in charge of the servants in that wing. It is a difficult job, and possibly dangerous. One of the guests there is a murderer. We need someone whose skill and discretion we can trust absolutely, and I have no man at all who could pass himself off as a servant. He would be found out in half an hour. You would not. Pitt says you are observant and trustworthy. It will be for only a few days at the most. We have to solve this crime before Her Majesty returns from Osborne."

He looked at her very steadily. "If this becomes public, the scandal will be appalling. Will you do it? You will report to Mr. Pitt and do whatever he tells you, to the letter."

"You don't have to, Gracie," Charlotte interrupted quickly. "It's dangerous. This man has already killed a prostitute, by cutting her throat. You are quite free to say no, and no one will think less of you."

Gracie's voice trembled. "That in't true, ma'am. We'll all think less o' me. Specially I will. I got ter go an' 'elp Mr. Pitt."

"And Her Majesty," Narraway added.

Gracie squared her shoulders and stretched

to her full height of almost five feet. "An' that poor cow wot were killed. 'Oo's gonna get justice for 'er if we don't, eh?"

Narraway swallowed and cleared his throat. There was only the slightest trace of a smile on his face. "No one, Miss Phipps. We are greatly obliged to you. Will you be so good as to pack a bag with whatever you require? Uniforms will be provided for you. I shall wait and take you tonight. The sooner you begin, the better."

Gracie turned at last to look at Charlotte fully, to try to make certain from her eyes rather than her words that she really wished her to go.

"Please look after yourself, Gracie," Charlotte said softly. "We shall miss you, but it won't be for long."

"What about the laundry then?" Gracie said anxiously in a last grasp for safety.

"I'll get Mrs. Claypole to come in an extra day," Charlotte replied. "Don't worry. Go and help Mr. Pitt. I think he may need you far more than I do, just at the moment."

"Yes. O' course I will," Gracie agreed, her heart beating suddenly high in her throat. "Observant and trustworthy," he had said. That burned like a flame inside her.

An hour later Gracie was in Buckingham

Palace being introduced by Pitt to Mr. Tyndale. They were in the housekeeper's room,
but Mrs. Newsome herself was absent. She
was not to know Gracie's purpose here. Only
Mr. Tyndale was to be aware of it, and that
delicately balanced situation was going to require some skill to maintain. At the moment
Mr. Tyndale was explaining Gracie's duties
to her, and the basic rules of behavior to be
followed by servants.

"This will be entirely different from any
other post you may have held," Mr. Tyndale
said carefully, seeing her ramrod-straight
back and figure so small that all dresses had
had to be taken up to prevent her from tripping over the skirts. It obviously took him
some effort to conceal most of his disbelief
that she could really be here on behalf of
Special Branch.

"Yes, sir." She had no intention of telling
him that she had come to the Pitts when she
was thirteen and had never worked for anyone else. He was not so very big himself, and
he too squared his shoulders and walked an
inch or two taller than he really was.

"You will not speak to any of the guests
unless they first speak to you, do you understand?" he continued gravely.

"Yes, sir."

"And in no circumstance at all will you

speak in the presence of His Royal Highness, or, if she should come through to dine with the guests, the Princess of Wales, or to any other member of the household. And that includes ladies- or gentlemen-in-waiting."

"No, sir."

"You will perform ordinary household duties such as sweeping, dusting and polishing, fetching and carrying as you are asked. You will wear your cap and apron at all times. You will speak to the menservants only as necessitated by your duties, and there will be no giggling, flirting, or generally making a nuisance of yourself —"

"Miss Phipps is here from Special Branch, Mr. Tyndale," Pitt cut across him coolly. "She needs instruction regarding Palace etiquette, not in how to conduct herself with dignity. You might remember, sir, that you require her assistance in this unfortunate matter, and she requires and has a right to expect your protection as she helps me to learn the truth as rapidly and discreetly as possible."

Tyndale colored. "You may count on me, Inspector," he said stiffly. "If I offended you, Miss Phipps, I apologize. Ada will show you to your room. I have seen to it that you do not have to share. I imagine that might have made your task more difficult."

"Thank you, Mr. Tyndale." She was indeed very grateful. It was going to be hard enough to take orders all day without having to share a bedroom as well. She realized with a jolt how accustomed she had become to doing her duties as she pleased. It seemed like a very long time ago that she had first come to the Pitt house, a scruffy and awkward child needing to be taught almost everything. Now fully in charge, able to read and write, and engaged to be married, she was on the brink of becoming a thoroughly respectable woman.

She turned to Pitt. " 'Ow do I tell yer if I larnt summink, sir?"

"I'll find you," Pitt promised. "And . . . thank you, Gracie."

She gave him a huge smile, then, aware of how inappropriate it was, she turned on her heel and went out into the passage to wait for Ada, who would show her up to bed.

Ada proved to be a pretty girl with flaxen blond hair and clear, fresh skin. She regarded Gracie with only a mild interest. The look on her face suggested that she thought anyone so small and thin was not going to prove a threat to her place in the hierarchy, nor was she likely to be a companion of much fun.

"Come on, then," she said briskly, in one phrase establishing her superiority in the order of things.

The narrow bedroom, actually designed to accommodate two people, was right at the top of the stairs. It was quite well appointed, and the window looked out over a vista of treetops toward the distant roofs of the city. Gracie thanked Ada, and as soon as the door was closed behind her, unpacked her meager belongings to put away in the chest at the bottom of the bed. She was barely finished when there was a knock on the door again. A different maid, who introduced herself as Norah, brought a dark uniform dress, which looked to be the right size, and a freshly starched cap and apron, handsomely trimmed in lace.

"I'll call you at six," she said cheerfully before leaving and closing the door behind her.

But tired as Gracie was, sleep was almost impossible. She lay on one side, then the other, then on her back staring up at the ceiling. She was in Buckingham Palace! She, Gracie Phipps, was on a special mission for Mr. Pitt. Someone had knifed a prostitute to death in a linen cupboard in the guest wing a couple of floors down from where she lay, and she was to help him solve the case. How on earth was she going to do that? Where should she even begin?

She had not had time to tell Samuel about it, and perhaps she shouldn't anyway, not until it was over. But what a story she would have then! She could imagine his face as she described it. She'd wager a week's money he had never been inside Buckingham Palace in his life.

All the same, she would rather have told him now. He was a good sleuth, really good. He would have done this far better than she. But he despised being in service. They had had lots of arguments about it. She thought it was just silly pride to prefer being cold and hungry, living in some rot-smelling rooms and drinking water from a well that might not even be clean, just to say for yourself whether you came or went. Better to have a warm room, good food every day, and be as safe as anybody is, at the price of being told what to do.

Everybody had to obey rules, no matter who you were. They were just different sorts of rules. He couldn't see that. Stubborn, he was. But then she wouldn't really want him much different, even if more sensible. She smiled in the dark as she thought of him. She would be able to tell him all about it soon. She would make notes, just to remind herself — about the Palace, not the detecting.

That was secret from everybody — except Mr. Pitt, of course.

She must have finally gone to sleep because she was jolted awake by a knock on the door, and a moment later Norah was standing by her bed with a candle in her hand. She waited until Gracie actually climbed out and stood up in her nightgown, bare feet on the floor.

"Can't 'ave yer late on yer first day," she said cheerfully, and, satisfied, turned to leave. "Breakfast's in the servants' 'all at 'alf-past six. Don't miss it or yer'll be 'ungry."

Gracie thanked her, then she poured the water she had fetched the night before. She set about getting ready, as well as she could, in both body and mind.

The uniform dress was a trifle large, especially around the waist, but with the apron tied it looked very smart. It was perfectly ironed, with not a suspicion of a crease, and the lace was as good as a lady's. The cap felt uncomfortable, but when she peered at herself in the small glass on top of the chest of drawers, she was surprised how much she liked the look of it. She was self-conscious, but rather pleased all the same.

The servants' hall was less grand than she had imagined it, and considerably more utilitarian, but then she had never worked anywhere but in the Pitts' house. Her visions of large and wealthy establishments was based solely upon Charlotte's sister's house, where she had stayed briefly several years ago. The Palace was somewhat similar, and that was in a way comforting. The large beams across the ceiling were also hung with dried herbs, and there were polished copper pans and utensils on the farther wall.

There were a dozen other people there, including Ada, who was pretty and very smart in a clean black dress, which flattered the curves of her figure. Her lace-edged apron was tied tightly around her waist. Gracie was shown her place at the table and joined them silently. Mr. Tyndale stood at the head, Mrs. Newsome at the foot. Mr. Tyndale waited a moment while everyone composed themselves, then he offered the daily prayer. He hesitated before the end, and Gracie, with her eyes closed, wondered if he was going to mention the dead woman, but had changed his mind.

They all obediently sat down and were served with porridge, then toast and jam and tea. She had expected more conversation. Were they always as subdued as this, or was it because of the murder? How much did they know about it? She watched them guardedly as she ate, trying not to be observed doing so.

"Is them police still 'ere?" one of the maids asked nervously.

" 'Course they are!" a dark-haired footman told her. "They're gonna be 'ere till they find which o' the guests killed 'er, aren't they!" That was a challenge, not a question.

"An' 'ow are they goin' ter do that, then?" Ada asked him. "Nobody saw it, or we'd know already, wouldn't we!"

"I dunno!" the footman said sharply. "I in't a policeman, am I! They gotta 'ave ways."

Gracie plunged in. "I 'spect they'll ask questions."

"Well, you don't 'ave ter worry." The footman grinned. "It weren't none of us. One o' the gentlemen's gentlemen was up 'alf the night, an' 'e swears as none of us came down the stairs."

"You watch yourself, Edwards," Mr. Tyndale said warningly. "You're a bit too free with your comments."

"Sorry, Mr. Tyndale," the footman apologized quickly, but he was looking at Gracie under his lashes.

"Of course it wasn't one of us," Mrs. Newsome added. "Nobody ever entertained such an idea."

"I entertained a few ideas," Ada said under her breath.

"I beg your pardon?" Mrs. Newsome put down her knife and regarded Ada coldly.

"I wouldn't entertain the idea, ma'am," Ada replied with practiced innocence.

Someone giggled.

"Am I going to have to require you to leave the table?" Mrs. Newsome said frostily.

"No, ma'am," Ada whispered.

The rest of the meal was concluded in silence. Finally they were told they might leave. Gracie excused herself, aware that both Mr. Tyndale and Mrs. Newsome were watching her, although for entirely different reasons.

It was Ada's task to look after her, tell her what to do and show her where to begin. Either she was fortunate or Mr. Tyndale had seen to it that she was employed in the guests' area of the wing rather than the kitchens or the laundry. First they collected all the appropriate brooms, brushes, pans, dusters, and polish they would need, then went up the stairs to begin.

"We gotta clean the sitting room and the bedrooms," Ada told her. " 'Course, we gotta be sure as the guests in't in there, nor their maids neither."

"Do they all have their own maids?" Gracie asked.

Ada gave her a withering look. " 'Course

they do! Where d'yer come from then?"

Gracie wished she had bitten her tongue before she spoke. She changed the subject very quickly. They were in the long upstairs corridor. She looked around in awe, not quite sure what she expected. It was spacious, with a higher ceiling than anywhere she had been before, and all decorated with elaborate gilded plaster, but other than that it was not unusual. There were no crowns in the plaster molding, no footmen in their dark livery and white gloves waiting for orders; in fact, no one else at all. It was completely silent. One of the doors was narrower than the others.

"Is that the cupboard there?" she asked in a whisper.

Ada gave a convulsive shudder. "Yeah. We can't go inter it, thanks be ter Gawd. I'd faint at the thought, I would. But it means we gotta bring all the linen up fresh from the laundry every day, which is all more work." She looked Gracie up and down. "You in't never seen nothing like the work there is 'ere. We gotta do the sittin' room first, before any o' them gets up an' wants it."

She started walking again. "Come on, then! The gentlemen was in it last night an' we never got to finish it 'cos o' bein' asked questions all day by that police. Scruffy lookin' object 'e is, an' all. Must 'ave a wife wi' two left 'ands, by the look of 'is shirt collar. Still, I s'pose 'e were clean enough, an' that's more'n 'e might a' bin."

Gracie resented the slur on Pitt's shirts bitterly, but she could hardly say so. She had ironed them herself, and they had been perfect when he put them on.

They were in the sitting room now and Ada looked around critically. "Smells summink awful, don't it? It's them cigars Mr. Dunkeld 'as. I dunno 'ow 'is wife stands it. 'E must taste like dirt."

"I don't s'pose she's got no choice," Gracie replied. Pitt did not smoke and she was aware of the heavy, stale odor here. It was a beautiful room, floored with ancient wood worn rich and dark with time and polish. Rows of huge, gold-framed portraits and still-life paintings hung on the walls. There was a magnificent fireplace with an ornate, carved, and inlaid marble mantel and a considerable number of heavy sofas and armchairs. There were small wooden tables here and there for convenience, and their polished tops were as bright as satin, except for the odd one soiled by wet glasses or ash. There was also ash in several places on the carpet, and at least one stain as if something dark like wine had been spilled.

Ada noted Gracie's stare. "You should've seen it the night o' their 'party,'" she said with a curl of her lip. "In't nothing now." She drew in a sharp breath. "Well, don't stand there gawpin' at it! Get on wi' cleanin' it up."

"Wot is it?" Gracie asked, looking at the stain, her imagination racing. Wine? Blood?

"That in't none o' your business!" Ada snapped. "You work 'ere, Miss Pious. Yer gotta learn ter keep yer opinions ter yerself an' don' ask no questions. There's two sets o' rules in life: one for them, an' one for us, an' don't you never forget it. Don't matter wot you think. Understand?"

Gracie drew herself up stiffly. Already she did not like Ada, but that was unimportant. She was here to help Pitt, and Mr. Narraway. "I don't care 'ow it got there," she said coldly. "I gotta know wot it is ter get it out proper. Is it wine, or coffee, or blood — or wot is it?"

"Oh." Ada looked somewhat mollified. "That's 'is nibs' favorite chair, so it'll be brandy, I 'spect. Soap an' water'll do most things, baking soda for smells, an' tea leaves for general dust an' stuff."

"I know that," Gracie said with dignity, then instantly regretted it. She might need Ada's help later on. It almost choked her to apologize. "Not that I in't grateful ter be

101

told," she added. "I wouldn't want ter do it wrong."

"Yer wouldn't, an' all," Ada agreed heartily. "Mrs. Newsome'd 'ave yer! An' don't dawdle around. We in't got all day. They won't all be stayin' in their rooms till luncheon today. We got catchin' up ter do."

Gracie bent obediently and set about lifting stains, sweeping up ash, polishing wood and marble, while Ada spread the damp tea leaves all over the rugs to absorb the dust, and then swept them all up again.

Gracie looked at the fireplace. It was tidy enough because there were no fires necessary in sitting rooms at this time of year, but the marble did not look clean. Should she say so, or would it be viewed as criticism of Ada's skills?

"Wot yer staring at?" Ada demanded. "Won't do itself!"

"Is that good enough?" Gracie gestured toward the marble.

"It'll 'ave ter be," Ada replied. "Takes a day or two to do it proper. Got ter leave the paste on. Can't 'ave that when we got guests."

"Wot d'yer do it with?" Gracie asked.

Ada sighed impatiently. "Soap lees, turpentine, pipe clay, and bullock's gall. Don't yer know nothing, then?"

"I do it with soda, pumice stone, an' chalk

mixed wi' water," Gracie replied. "Comes up straightaway."

"Ain't you the smart one!" Ada was clearly annoyed. "An' if it stains it worse, oo's gonna get the blame, eh? This is Buckingham Palace, miss. We do things the right way 'ere. Don't you touch that fireplace 'ceptin' wi' wot I tell yer. D'you 'ear me?"

Gracie swallowed. "Yes."

"Yer do all the light mantels, an' make sure yer do 'em proper," Ada said, pointing to the glass over the gaslamps. "I want 'em like crystal, right? No marks, no smears, no scratches. An' if you break one yer'll pay for it out o' yer wages . . . fer the next year!" She stood with her arms folded, watching until Gracie picked up the cloth again and began to work.

Gracie knew she had made an enemy. It was a bad start. Her mind raced as to what on earth Mr. Narraway thought she could do to help Pitt. She knew very well that over a length of time servants learned a lot about their masters, or mistresses. You saw faults and weaknesses, you learned to know what people were frightened of, what they avoided because they could not face it, and what made them laugh. You certainly knew who they liked and who they did not. It was easy with women. How a woman dressed and how long she took to do it, how many times she changed her mind, told you all kinds of things.

But was that any use?

A servant could watch people in unguarded moments. Having a servant in the room was regarded as being alone. But how long would she have to spend coming and going, fetching things, cleaning and tidying up, before she saw or heard anything that mattered?

It was a horrid realization, being as unimportant as a piece of furniture. It meant people didn't care in the slightest what you thought of them. She imagined what Samuel would say! Charlotte Pitt had never treated her like that.

But one of these wealthy and important men was a lunatic who mutilated women and left them bleeding to death in cupboards. She felt shivery and a little sick at the thought. Like a picture flashing before her mind came the memory of finding that terrible body in Mitre Square. She had never been so frightened in her life. That was ripped open too, like the other Whitechapel victims. Why did anybody do something like that?

" 'Urry up!" Ada said peremptorily. "We gotta be out of 'ere before anyone wants ter use it, an' we ain't nowhere near finished yet. Get them dirty dusters up, an' them glasses. Make sure there in't no rings left on the tabletops, or Mrs. Newsome'll 'ave yer skin."

"There's a scratch on the top over there," Gracie pointed out, indicating an elegant Sheraton table.

"Yeah. Done it the other night when their tarts was 'ere." Ada's voice was sharp with disapproval. "Dunno why they can't just keep 'em in the bedroom. In't like they could sing, or nothin'."

"Do you like working here?" Gracie said quickly.

Ada looked surprised. "'Course I do! Meet some very good sort o' people. Never know where it could take yer, if yer lucky and play yer 'and right."

"Where could yer work better than 'ere?" Gracie was amazed.

"Not work, yer dozy cow!" Ada said in disgust. "Yer wanter work all yer life? I wanter marry someone with a nice steady job an' 'ave an 'ouse o' me own. No one ter tell me when ter get up an' when ter go ter bed."

It was on the tip of Gracie's tongue to say, "I'm going to marry a policeman! And not just a constable, a sergeant." Then she realized she could never say that here. A pity. It would stop Ada's patronizing air quickly enough.

"Wot is it?" Ada asked her, staring, duster in her hand.

"Yeah." Gracie let her breath out. "I see wot yer mean. One o' them guardsmen'd be nice."

Ada laughed. "They're gentlemen, stupid! Yer a daft little article! Where d'yer come from, then? Yer better lookin' out fer a delivery boy, or summink o' that sort. When yer finished 'ere yer can sweep the stairs. Then yer can fetch the linen up from the laundry, so we can change all the beds when we do the rooms. An' don't 'ang about. There in't no time ter waste."

"I'm coming." Gracie was amazed how much she resented being ordered around. She had not expected it to be so difficult. Maybe Samuel had something after all. But freedom came at a very high price. And she was here to help Pitt, and to work for her country.

Perhaps the bedrooms might yield some piece of information, although she could not think what it would be. How on earth could she learn anything useful? What would be useful anyway? How would she recognize it if it were there? And what would happen to Pitt if they failed?

However, she had very little time to spare

to do more than clean up, dust, tidy, straighten, and fetch linen for Ada. It was hard work going up and down the stairs, and there was a rigid hierarchy among the servants in which she was at the very bottom, which Ada never allowed her to forget. In spite of the fact that she was twenty-one, and therefore very senior for a maid, on this occasion she was passing herself off as far less, and it pinched a little that it was without any difficulty at all. Narraway had told Mr. Tyndale both her real age and that which she was assuming, and he had not argued. She was the newest here, and that was what counted. Ada enjoyed her power and made the most of it. She must have been new once, and she was making sure of her repayment for every indignity she had suffered.

Gracie was on her way up with a pile of towels she could hardly see over the top of when Edwards caught up with her and offered to carry them for her. "No, thank you," she declined.

"Independent, are we?" he said with a slight edge of offense in his voice.

She avoided his eyes, not wanting to see what might be in them. "Not really," she said steadily, climbing the steps by touch more than sight. "Can't afford ter get the wrong side of anyone on me first day."

"An' what if I think you're being standoff-ish?" he asked. "Too good to take a bit of an 'and from someone?"

"You wouldn't be so daft!" she said sharply, hoping to heaven it were true. She didn't need trouble from an amorous foot-man. "Yer know Ada better'n that, even if yer don't know me." She promptly tripped over the bottom step of the next flight, and he grabbed at her arm to steady her. "Thanks," she said tartly. "Now don't get me on the wrong side o' nobody, please."

"Ada's gone downstairs," he replied. "I'll 'elp yer put these in the rooms, so yer don't fall over yer feet again."

"Yeah? An' if one o' them ladies comes into 'er room, 'ow are yer goin' ter explain that then, eh?" she said quickly. "Don't yer get caught up 'ere on this landin', or them police is goin' ter ask yer 'ow often yer come up 'ere when yer in't supposed ter!"

That silenced him smartly, and she was re-lieved to see him go back down the stairs again, leaving her alone to place the towels. Since Ada was gone, she had a little more time. She must make use of it.

She was quick in the women's rooms. Mrs. Quase's bedroom was very feminine. She had lots of perfumes and decorative combs, pretty handkerchiefs, silver-backed brushes, creams and ointments in crystal jars. Gracie imagined a woman very keen to preserve her beauty. She could not resist a quick look into the wardrobe, and estimated enough money spent on dresses to pay a score of maids for a year. From what she could see, her frocks were all immaculately cared for.

Mr. Quase's room was different. There was no smell of perfume in it, rather more like leather and boot polish. The surfaces were very tidy and there was a case for papers. She touched it and found it locked.

Mr. Dunkeld's room also had a case in it, larger than Quase's, and it was locked as well. There were expensive cuff links and collar studs in a small bowl. They looked like gold. His shaving things were expensive also, and he had silver-backed brushes for hair and clothes, a silver-handled shoehorn, and an engraved silver whisky flask with a pigskin case on the dresser. He was obviously a man who liked to have expensive possessions and show off a little. The room still smelled vaguely of cigar smoke, for all Ada's attempts to get rid of it. They would have to come back with more lavender and beeswax polish. What a waste of time!

She noticed also that he had seven books on the shelf, all to do with Africa. She would like to have looked at them, but she could not risk being caught.

Mrs. Dunkeld's room had no trace of the smoke. It smelled of lily of the valley, cool and clean, not sweet like Mrs. Quase's room.

She went down for more towels and came back up again.

Mrs. Sorokine's room was remarkable for the scarlet robe splashed across the bed and the strings of pearls and crystals flung on the dressing table amid a profusion of hair ornaments and jars of cream and perfume. Fearing she might come back any moment, because the room looked so interrupted, Gracie dared not stay. She placed the towels and left.

Mr. Sorokine's room was a surprise, largely because of the number of books, and none of them was about Africa, as far as Gracie could see. There was one on the bedside table with a marker in it. She picked it up and looked at the title: *The Picture of Dorian Gray.* She opened it at random and started to read. She was immediately so absorbed in the strength of the words, the evil and passion in them, that she did not hear the door open. The first she was aware of him was when he spoke.

"Can you read it?"

She was so startled the book slipped out of her hand and fell to the floor. "I'm sorry!"

she said too loudly, feeling the heat scorch up her face.

He bent and picked it up, being careful to straighten the pages. "Can you?" he asked again.

She stared at him in horror. He was a tall man, handsome, with a broad brow. He had strong features, but not insensitive. Somehow, she would have expected his eyes to be brown, not the gray they were. She nodded. It was not a matter of not lying to him so much as not denying the gift Charlotte had given her.

He smiled. "What did it say?"

"It were about wanting to be beautiful always," she answered, gulping. "An' young."

He looked satisfied, as if her answer pleased him. "I'll leave it on the table," he told her. "Then you can look at it again. You can put the towels on the dresser."

She had left them in a heap on the bed. Her face still burning, she picked them up and put them where they should be. Then, with hands shaking, she fled into the corridor.

Without looking at anything at all, she replaced the towels in Mr. and Mrs. Marquand's rooms, and gathered up all the old ones. She staggered down to the laundry with them, occasionally dropping one or two and having to go back and pick them up, awkwardly, dropping others as she did so.

Downstairs in the laundry finally she dumped the lot of them in one of the big wicker baskets and decided to take a look around. If anyone found her here, she could easily say she was looking for soap or bran or any of a dozen other things. It was part of her duties to be familiar with all the cleaning materials available. She saw plenty of bran. Charlotte had shown her how to use that to clean stains out of good fabrics. There was white spirit — probably gin — for the same purpose; also soap, pumice, chalk, turpentine, pipe clay, flowers of sulfur, black rosin, several large lumps of yellow wax, laundry blue, and fresh-made starch. Below that were bottles labeled for oxalic acid, salts of sorrel, sal ammoniac, and gum arabic.

She changed her mind about attempting to help with laundry and decided to do some detecting instead. She pulled out the other wicker laundry basket and opened it up. Her heart beat violently and her stomach lurched. It was full of sheets, white, with scarlet splashes fading into brown. They were soaked, spattered, and smeared with blood. At the edges it was dull and dried, but in the middle the stains were still red and when she touched her fingertip to them they

112

were damp. Poor woman. There was so much of it! She must have bled and bled. Gracie was a little numb at the thought. What would make anybody do such a thing? And here, of all the places in England.

But then a lot of this was not really as she had thought it would be. It was the Queen's house. It should be different from everywhere else in the world. And yet the dust and the ring marks on tables, the dropped ash, the scuffs on the floor, were exactly like anyone's house. Except that Pitt would have picked up after himself, and since he could not afford to replace his carpets and tables — he had had to save up to buy them in the first place — he would have taken more care of them.

One of those men really had killed that woman. Why? What kind of rage made you do something like that? Did they think they could get away with it? She had already realized that the servants here protected people from having to pay for reality the way most people do. Would they hide even this? Was that part of the job description? Were they paying you not only for your time and your obedience but for your conscience as well? She could just imagine what Samuel would say about that!

But would it help you if the law came after

you? That was a totally new thought. Did Pitt have any real power here? If not, why would they pretend with nice words that they wanted him to expose the culprit ready for prosecution, only then to cover it up and deal with it themselves? She knew the answer: because they couldn't find out without him. Perhaps they needed his brains but not his honesty. How would they make him keep silent about what he knew? Did he face a danger he knew nothing of?

She was cold now, even though it was steaming hot down here, and the air was full of the smell of soap and washing soda. What could she do to help him? Should she warn him? Would that be good, or only make it worse?

She started to look through the sheets again, deeper into the basket. This might be her only chance to examine them before they were washed. They were of a quality she had never felt before: fine and soft, their threads so fine they could have been silk. And she could smell the sickly odor of the blood.

They were all stitched with tiny holes along the seam at the hem. She had seen people do drawn thread work like that. It took hours. It was beautiful. Some of them had other embroidery on as well. The two very best had what looked like a *V* and an *R*, in satin stitch, and a little crown. Victoria Regina. It could only mean one thing: The Queen's sheets had been in the cupboard where the poor woman was killed! But they were drenched in blood, soaked in it! And they were crumpled. They had been lain on, in fact they had been slept in. The blood was smeared and marked more lightly, as if transferred from someone's body who had rolled in it.

Gracie galvanized into movement. She must hide them where they could not be found, then go to fetch Pitt. She had no idea what this information meant, but someone was lying pretty badly, because this made no sense at all. Who had stolen the Queen's sheets, and used them, and for what? To carry the poor woman's body, to cover it up, to hide it for a while?

She had the sheets in her hands when she heard footsteps on the stairs and one of the maids giggling. Then Edwards the footman's voice was quite clear, cajoling, wheedling.

"C'mon, Ada! You know you want me to!"

Gracie had never been in that position herself, but she knew exactly what he meant. What she did not know was whether he was right, and Ada was perfectly willing. Either way, Gracie's presence here would make an enemy for life of at least one of them, most likely both. And she was doing badly enough with Ada as it was. She found herself hot with embarrassment that she might accidentally witness something she would very much rather not.

"Cheeky!" Ada said warmly. "I don't know nothin' o' the kind! You fancy yerself way too much, Mr. Edwards, an' that's a fact."

"Not 'alf as much as I fancy you!" he retorted. " 'Old still, then!"

They had not seen Gracie yet, but a couple of steps farther down into the laundry and they would. Worse, they would realize that she had to have heard them. What would she do? She was revolted at the thought of hiding in one of the baskets, full of other people's dirty sheets. She might even get marked with blood herself, and how would she explain that? But she had to have these sheets for Pitt. There was no other way out of here, just the one flight of stairs, and Ada and Edwards were already at the foot of it. If Gracie had not been so small, and bent double half behind the linen basket, they would have seen her by now.

She must hide the sheets safely: That was more important than saving herself from embarrassment, or even bullying in the future. It was only for a few days, after all! But how? What could she do to distract their attention? She stared around at the shelves with all their jars and packets, then at the big copper tubs bubbling away with the sheets and towels in them. If she opened the flue on the boiler, it would roar up quickly. There would be steam all over the place — perhaps even a small flood. She could hide the embroidered sheets, stuff them in the bran tub temporarily, and when Ada and Edwards were busy trying to stop the flood, she could come from the bottom of the stairs as if she had just arrived. It might work. It had to.

She crouched behind the basket and reached for the long wooden spirtle that was used to stir the linen around. It would be just long enough to reach the flue, if she were very careful. Her arm ached with the weight of holding it up from one end and keeping it steady. She must make no sudden moves or it might catch their notice.

Ada was giggling more loudly and Edwards was talking softly to her the whole time. If Gracie didn't do something pretty soon, this was going to get worse. The spirtle was long and awkward. There were tears of frustration in her eyes by the time she finally hit the flue open. Then the spirtle slipped out of her grip and clattered to the floor.

Miraculously neither of them took any notice. If she got caught now, Ada would never forgive her. She could not afford that. Ada hated her enough already. Gracie had wild thoughts of finishing up in the linen cupboard like the prostitute. Had she also seen something that she shouldn't have, poor soul? Was that what had got her killed? It was about the only reason that made any sense. But what could she have seen here that anyone cared about? They seemed to do anything they wanted to anyway.

Seconds ticked by. Ada was resisting, thank heaven, playing a game. Gracie had no idea where to look for Pitt. Could she ask Mr. Tyndale to find him?

Steam belched out of the copper and the lid banged up and down with the force of it. It happened a second time before Ada realized what it was and gave a yelp of horror. Edwards must have thought it was something he had done, because he laughed.

"The copper's on too 'igh, stupid!" Ada shouted, as steam billowed out and filled the room. "Come an' 'elp me get it off!"

As she plunged forward, yanking her dress straight as she went, Gracie slipped through the steam toward the stairs, then turned around rapidly, and gasped with surprise.

"Wot 'appened?" she cried out as if aghast.

"Never you mind!" Ada shouted at her. "Go and get on wi' yer own job. I'm all right 'ere. Yer swept the stairs yet? Well, do it then! Don't stand there gawpin'!"

"Yes, miss," Gracie said obediently. She scampered upstairs before the steam cleared and she was obliged to see Ada's open dress and general disarray.

Gracie realized that once someone put those sheets into the boil, no one would be able to prove a thing. She nearly asked Mags, the other between-stairs maid, if she had seen the policeman, then realized she had no explanation for wanting to know, so instead she went immediately to her alternative plan and found Mr. Tyndale.

He was alone in the butler's pantry, inspecting the silver to see if it had been cleaned to perfection. He looked very serious, frowning a little.

She knocked on the door.

He looked round with irritation, then saw who it was. "Miss Phipps? Is something wrong?" he asked anxiously.

She came in and closed the door behind her. "Yer'd better call me 'Gracie,' sir," she corrected him, feeling awkward and yet savoring a flicker of very definite enjoyment. "I gotter speak ter Mr. Pitt, very urgent, but there in't no way I can ask anyone where 'e is. I found summink as could be very important. Can yer 'elp me?"

"Yes, of course I can. What have you found?" He was clearly worried.

She shook her head. "I gotter tell Mr. Pitt."

Tyndale was embarrassed. He obviously felt foolish for having asked, and then been rebuffed.

Now she was sorry for him, and perhaps a trifle foolish also for making him uncomfortable. He might remember it and not be the ally she needed. She swallowed hard. This could be the wrong judgment, but regardless of that she had better be quick. "Can I ask you summink, sir?"

He was still guarded, uncertain of the correct protocol with her. She was a servant, and yet she was not. "Certainly. What is it?"

"The sheets with *V R* stitched on 'em, an' a little crown . . . does anybody get ter sleep on them 'ceptin' 'Er Majesty, like?"

"Where did you see those?" he asked sharply.

"In the laundry."

"That's impossible! Her Majesty is at Osborne, and no one else uses them. Thank you for telling me. I shall find out what has happened and put a stop to it."

"Yer mustn't do that, sir!" She all but grasped hold of him, getting her hand as far as to touch his sleeve before she snatched it away. "It's a clue, or least it may be. Yer gotta keep it a deadly secret till Mr. Pitt says yer can tell. It's a murder, Mr. Tyndale. Yer can't tell nobody nuffin'."

He looked pale. "I see."

At that moment there was a sharp rap on the pantry door, and a moment later it flew open and Mrs. Newsome stood in the entrance. She was a good-looking woman in an agreeable, ordinary way, but now her face was flushed and her eyes were hot. "What are you doing in here, Gracie Phipps?" She looked from Gracie to an obviously uncomfortable Mr. Tyndale, now also coloring deeply with both anger and embarrassment.

"She came . . ." he started, and then floundered badly.

Mrs. Newsome's face tightened, her eyes hard.

Ridiculously, Gracie thought of Ada and Edwards on the laundry stairs, and felt the heat in her own cheeks. She must rescue Mr. Tyndale. The idea was absurd, and revolting, but it was abundantly clear what Mrs. Newsome thought. And Mr. Tyndale was only in this situation because he was helping Gracie. He might care what Mrs. Newsome believed of him, but even if he didn't, he would care bitterly about being thought to behave inappropriately with a brand-new serving girl less than half his age.

Gracie lied with ease. "I came ter give 'im a message as the policeman'd like ter see 'im, ma'am."

"Really," Mrs. Newsome said coldly. "And why did he ask you to deliver such a message?"

" 'Cos I were there, I 'spect," she said, her eyes wide.

"Indeed." There was no light whatever in Mrs. Newsome's face. "Well, in future, Gracie, you will get about your duties without speaking to policemen, and you will not come into the butler's pantry, or into any other room, and close the door. Do you understand me? It is completely inappropriate."

"Yes, ma'am. I mean, no, ma'am, I won't." Gracie swallowed her anger and her dignity with quite an effort.

"I told her to close the door, Mrs. Newsome," Tyndale suddenly found his voice. "I did not wish other staff to be hearing a message from the police. It is distressing enough having them here at all. Everyone is upset."

Mrs. Newsome's face expressed disgust that was almost comical. "Do you imagine I am unaware of that, Mr. Tyndale?" she said scathingly. "While you are here counting the knives with Gracie, I am trying to find Ada; assure Mrs. Oliphant that she will not be murdered in her bed; persuade Biddie that she cannot leave, at least until the police tell her she can, and she'll get no character from me for leaving us in the lurch. I am also trying to stop Norah from having hysterics, and make sure someone dusts the hall and at least gets a start with the ironing." She picked at a stray wisp of hair across her brow and poked it back into its pins savagely, making the whole effect worse. "And in case you have not noticed," she went on, "one of your serrated-edged meat knives is missing. You should have twenty-four." Less flustered, she would have been a comely woman, and not as old as Gracie had at first assumed.

Suddenly Gracie was aware of a vulnerability in her that almost took her breath away. Mrs. Newsome was jealous. It was absurd, and desperately human. She cared for Mr. Tyndale.

"I had better go and see what the policeman wants," Tyndale said unhappily. "I . . . I know it is difficult. Please do your best, Mrs. Newsome. And I know one of the knives is missing. I shall speak to Cuttredge about it." He closed the drawers in which the knives sat in their green baize slots, and locked it with one of the keys from his small, silver chain. Then he walked past both women and went out to look for Pitt.

Gracie and Mrs. Newsome stared at each other. The silence grew increasingly awkward.

"May I be excused, please, ma'am?" Gracie said at last, her mouth dry. She wanted intensely to escape the emotion in the room. She must not allow Mrs. Newsome to know how much she had seen. She would never be forgiven for it.

"Yes." Mrs. Newsome straightened her skirt automatically, her own much larger key ring jangling. "Of course you may. Is Ada looking after you, showing you what to do?"

"Yes, thank you, ma'am." She would say nothing about what Ada was really doing in the laundry, or that Ada was something of a bully. It was difficult to think that Mrs. Newsome could be so blind! But one did not tell tales.

"Good. Since it is eleven o'clock, you may go to the kitchen for a cup of tea."

"Thank you, ma'am." Gracie bobbed rather an awkward curtsy. It was not something she was used to doing; Charlotte would have found it ridiculous.

Along the corridor, in the huge kitchen with its Welsh dressers of crockery and copper pans on the walls, rafters hung with herbs, Cuttredge was sitting in one of the hard-backed chairs. Mrs. Oliphant, the cook, was in another opposite him. There was a teapot on the table, several clean cups, and two plates of fruit cake.

"I reckon it were stole!" Rob, the boot boy, said with a shrug. "Yer won't never find it."

"Nonsense!" Mrs. Oliphant retorted sharply. "You keep a still tongue in your head, boy, or you'll go to bed with no dinner!"

He bit his lip, but his expression said he knew a lot he dared not say.

"Well what, then?" Mrs. Oliphant demanded. "Who stole it? You saying one of us is a thief?"

" 'Course I in't," he said indignantly, his round eyes widening. "Why'd anyone 'ere take a knife for? Can't sell it, can yer, not one dinner knife."

"It was probably dropped," Cuttredge put in.

Mrs. Oliphant ignored him. "Well, there's no one else, unless you think one o' those wretched girls took it?" she said to Rob. "They weren't nowhere near the dining room, you stupid boy! Dinner was all cleared away before we took 'em up. You don't feed tarts like them. What are you thinking of?"

"There was the old feller," Rob said stubbornly.

"What old feller?" Mrs. Oliphant challenged. " 'Ere you. Gracie, that your name? Well, sit down, girl. Pour yourself a cup o' tea. Cake's fresh. Oh, come on!" She snatched the pot and a clean cup and poured it for Gracie impatiently. She pushed it across at her, and one of the plates. "Look like a twopenny rabbit, you do. Put a bit o' meat on your bones, girl. Next thing they'll accuse us o' starvin' you." She turned back to Rob. "What other one? What are you talking about?"

He blanched, so that his freckles stood out like blotches onhis skin. "I mean the old feller what come wi' the big box, Mrs. Oliphant."

"What old feller?" she said with disbelief. "What are you talking about?"

Gracie stopped with her cup halfway to her lips.

"The man wot came 'ere a bit after midnight wi' that box o' books come for Mr. Dunkle, or wot's 'is name," Rob answered her.

Mrs. Oliphant's wispy-fine eyebrows shot up. "You sayin' as that old man what delivered the books pinched one of our knives and took it with 'im?" she said with disbelief. "Whatever for?"

"I dunno, do I!" Rob said indignantly. " 'Cos it come from the Palace, I s'pose. You should 'ear some o' the things I get asked ter nick fer people."

"You take a pinch o' dust, my boy, an' your feet won't touch the ground!" Mrs. Oliphant said furiously. "I catch you, an' I swear you'll eat off the mantelpiece fer a week, an' glad of it."

Rob rubbed his behind as if it were already aching. "I said I were asked, I din't say as I took nothing!" Now he was really offended. "Was me as told yer the knife were gone. You're ungrateful, that's what you are."

"Don't you speak to me like that, you cheeky lump!" she said hotly. "You forget yourself, Rob Tompkins. You let Mr. Tyndale catch you talking nonsense an' he'll wash your mouth out with soap, he will, lye soap an' all!"

"Then you tell 'im the old fellow took the knife!" he charged her.

" 'Ow do I know?" she demanded. "You stop crying an' drink your tea before I throw it away!"

He snatched the cake before she could remove the plate.

"You better have the last one too," she said. "Go on! Take it! Another twopenny rabbit if ever I seen one."

He grinned at her, showing gappy teeth.

"Where'd yer see 'im?" Gracie asked as casually as she could, her mouth dry. At last she was learning something.

"Don't encourage 'im!" Mrs. Oliphant warned.

Gracie shrugged. "Sorry. 'E's probably nobody."

"Yeah 'e is so!" Rob insisted. "Bit taller'n me, 'e were, wi' scruffy white 'air an' dirty face. Edwards knows — 'e 'elped the fella carry it. 'E were down 'ere while they was unpackin' the box, before 'e takes it back out again. Cup o' tea, I s'pose. 'E come past Mr. Tyndale's pantry an' out o' the kitchen through the side door inter the yard. S'pose 'e went back ter the cart 'e come in. But 'e went past the pantry, I swear!" He looked at Gracie, hopeful of support.

"An' how do you know?" Mrs. Oliphant asked. "What were yer doin' out o' yer bed at that time of night? Stealin' cake, I'll wager!"

"I come fer a drink o' water!" Rob said with self-conscious righteousness.

"Down them stairs?" Gracie asked doubtfully.

" 'E sleeps in the scullery," Mrs. Oliphant explained.

Rob nodded, smiling. "Nice an' warm in there."

Gracie refrained from pointing out that

there was also a tap in there — but not cake.

"Stupid," she said, sipping her tea. "Fancy stealin' a table knife! In't even any good. Why don't 'e take a kitchen knife, if 'e wanted one?"

"Them table knives is special for meat," Mrs. Oliphant told her. "Shave your face with them, yer could. Believe me!"

Gracie finished her tea with difficulty, heart pounding, then thanked Mrs. Oliphant and excused herself as swiftly as she dared. She was going so hastily she almost ran into Pitt on the stairs.

"What is it?" he asked her with an edge of urgency in his voice. "Mr. Tyndale said you wanted to see me. Something about sheets."

"I found 'em in the laundry," she said breathlessly, no louder than a whisper. "I 'id 'em in the bran bin. They're 'Er Majesty's sheets. They got *V R* and a crown on 'em, an' they're all soaked in blood."

"From the cupboard," he said calmly. "They took all the sheets down to see which ones they could save."

"But *V R* means they's 'ers!" She stared up at him, exasperated at his obtuseness. " 'Er own, like! An' they weren't folded like the rest of 'em in the cupboard, sir. They bin slept in! They was all creased and rankled up."

Pitt looked very grave. "Are you certain, Gracie?"

" 'Course I am! It din't make no sense, but I'm certain sure for positive," she was emphatic. "An' that in't all. There's a table knife missing, one o' the real sharp ones for cutting meat. Rob, the boot boy, says he saw an old man 'ere wot brought a big box, about midnight, an' then took it away again."

"When?" Pitt asked. "The night of the murder? Where?"

"Downstairs, going past the butler's pantry and out into the yard," she replied. " 'E came wi' a big wooden box. Edwards 'elped him carry it."

"How big was the box?" Pitt said immediately.

"Dunno. But I can ask."

"No," he said quickly, grasping her arm. "Don't ask. It doesn't matter. See if you can find out if anyone else saw him, and how long he was here. Just possibly the woman's death has nothing to do with the guests here after all." He smiled suddenly, a glowing look, full of hope.

Gracie grinned back at him, satisfied she had helped him, really helped. Maybe even helped the Queen herself. Suddenly the scrubbing and the obedience were worth it. She heard footsteps below, and went on up the steps with light feet, leaving Pitt to go down.

CHAPTER FOUR

Pitt received Gracie's information with a surge of optimism. He paced the room he had been given, turning it over in his mind. If it could be proved that the old man the boot boy had seen entering the Palace with the box delivered to Cahoon Dunkeld was guilty, then the case could be closed with no worse scandal than a certain laxity on the part of the guards who had allowed him in. But even that was something for which they could hardly be blamed. He had come because he was a carter delivering a box belonging to one of His Royal Highness's guests. And if he had taken one of the dinner knives, the sudden opportunity presenting itself, then he had not arrived armed, or with the intent to commit murder.

So how on earth had he found the prostitute and persuaded her to go with him to the linen cupboard? What had happened to her clothes? No one had yet found them. And more than that, if he were a lunatic seeking a victim at random, why not one of the maids he met in a corridor?

He must have known the prostitute and deliberately sought her out. By the time he had gone upstairs he already had the knife, taken from downstairs because the dinner plates had long since been removed from the dining room.

It was imperative that they find out more about the woman: her nature, her background, even her other clientele. The crime could be personal after all. He must contact Narraway and tell him. Perhaps after all there was an escape from the appalling conclusion that the murderer had to be one of the guests.

He turned on his heel and went immediately to Tyndale to ask him for permission to use the telephone. Permission granted, he called Narraway and told him the latest development and the necessity of finding out as much as possible about the woman. Then he sent for the footman, Edwards, and questioned him again.

"This box that was delivered for Mr. Dunkeld between midnight and one o'clock on the morning of the murder," he began.

Edwards looked uncomfortable but his gaze did not waver. "Yes?"

"Can you describe this carter?"

Edwards chewed his lip, moving his weight from one foot to the other. "Didn't really look at 'im. I was too busy carryin' that box up the stairs. 'E 'ad the back end of it."

"How large was it?" Pitt asked.

" 'Bout three feet long, maybe four, an' . . ." Edwards gestured with his rather large hands, describing the shape of an ordinary luggage chest, broader than it was deep. "Like that."

"Heavy?"

" 'Bout like yer'd expect with books an' papers."

"Lot of books?"

"Dunno, forty or fifty maybe. Don't carry books very often."

"Where did you put it, at what hour of the night?"

"In the sittin' room next door to 'ere. Can't 'ardly take it to 'im at midnight, can I? 'E could be doin' anythin'!" The shadow of a leer touched his mouth and then vanished again. "As it was, 'e was there anyway, like 'e was expectin' it. An' 'e told us to come back for it in ten minutes or so. Seems the carter wanted 'is box back."

Pitt found himself disliking the young man intensely.

"Describe as much as you saw of the

carter," he ordered.

Edwards shrugged. "Din't really see 'is face. Oldish, stooped over. Had a hat on, jammed down 'ard, an' a coat with a collar. Half-mitts on 'is hands, probably for drivin' the horse. Weren't that cold."

"What was the cart like?"

"Don't know."

"Four wheels, or two?" Pitt insisted.

"Four."

"And the horse?"

"Dunno. Pale. A gray, I suppose."

"And did you go back in ten minutes?"

" 'Course I did!"

"Where did you go in the meantime?"

Edward's eyes widened. "You think he could 'ave done it?"

"Could he?"

Edwards looked reluctant. "Don't see how. 'E were only in the place a few minutes. An' 'e went downstairs an' out the back, then in again. Was the murder real gory, like?"

Pitt winced with distaste, remembering the woman's torn entrails, pale in all the blood. "Yes."

"Then I don't see as 'e could. 'E was clean as a whistle," Edwards replied unblinkingly. "Not even any dirt on 'im, let alone blood."

"You're certain?" Pitt's hopes sank.

"Yes, sir. Ask Rob, the boot boy, 'e'll say

the same thing."

"What was the boot boy doing up at that time of the morning?"

"Lookin' for a piece of cake, most likely. Always eatin', 'e is."

"But Mr. Dunkeld was waiting for you, you said? Where?"

"On the stairs. Told us not ter take it any further up, we might waken the ladies. Said it was books 'e needed in a hurry, an' we was ter put it in the room there off the passage, an' 'e'd take 'em out, an' we was ter come back and take the box away. Carter never went up to where the linen cupboard is," he added.

"And you went back for the box and the carter took it again?"

"Yes. Bleedin' heavy box it was too. Must've been teak, or somethin' like that. Couldn't see at that time o' night in what light there was."

"And it was midnight, no later?"

"Yes."

"Thank you. For now you can go."

Reluctantly, Pitt was forced to abandon the idea that the carter could have killed the woman. He was back again to the inevitability that it had to have been one of the guests of the Prince of Wales.

He was on the next landing, weighed down

with a sense of disappointment he knew was unreasonable, when he met Cahoon Dunkeld coming up.

"Ah, afternoon, Pitt," Dunkeld said briskly. "His Royal Highness would like to see you." He frowned. "For heaven's sake take that rubbish out of your pocket, man. And straighten up your cravat. You look as if you've slept in your shirt! Doesn't your housekeeper have an iron, or a needle and thread?"

Pitt knew he was untidy, and had never cared until now, but the insult to Charlotte stung him like a hot needle. He ached to be just as rude in return, but he did not dare to. Only for short stretches of time, an hour or two at most, did he forget that he was in Queen Victoria's palace: he, the son of a gamekeeper who had been deported to Australia for stealing from his master's estate. He was never certain who knew that, and who did not. If he were to retaliate, he always half expected the stinging contempt of the rejoinder.

Shaking with anger he took the handful of objects out of his coat pocket and redistributed them as evenly among his other pockets as possible, then straightened his cravat.

Dunkeld made no comment but his expression was eloquent. With a shrug of exasperation, he led the way to the room where the Prince of Wales was waiting. To Pitt's deep annoyance, he followed him in.

Pitt stood to attention. He knew better than to speak first or to stare around at the ornate ceiling and the magnificent pictures that almost covered the walls.

The Prince was dressed in a linen suit of a nondescript color. He was neatly barbered and looked considerably better than the last time they had met. His eyes were less blood-shot, and though his skin was a trifle mot-tled, it was more likely from a lifetime of in-dulgence than a single drunken night and the devastating shock of murder.

First he thanked Dunkeld, then looked ap-praisingly at Pitt.

Pitt felt uncomfortable, like livestock at a market, but he remained motionless.

"Oh, hello . . . Pitt, isn't it?" the Prince said at last. "Is everybody giving you the assis-tance you need?"

"Yes, sir, thank you," Pitt replied.

"It's not an inquiry for your health, man," Dunkeld growled. "What progress have you made?"

Pitt was not an equal, and he was acutely aware that he could only lose by behaving as if he were, no matter how Dunkeld provoked him. He smiled. He could be utterly charming, when he wished. "It was an inquiry for my professional needs," he said calmly. "His Royal Highness's help is necessary for our success, and I am grateful for it."

The Prince glanced at Dunkeld, a cold, puzzled look, then back at Pitt. "Well taken, sir," he said quietly. It was a reminder to Dunkeld not to assume too many liberties. Pitt glanced at Dunkeld's face and saw the burning humiliation in it, for an instant, and wished that he had not. Worse, he knew Dunkeld had understood it.

"I am quite satisfied, sir, that none of your domestic staff could be guilty." Pitt forced himself to speak gravely, addressing the Prince. "Two people were where they could observe the servants' staircase at the relevant time. No one came or went."

"And one of those two couldn't have done it?" the Prince said hopefully.

"No, sir. One of them was Mr. Dunkeld, and the other was his manservant."

The Prince swiveled to stare balefully at Dunkeld. "You didn't say so!" he accused him.

Dunkeld stood his ground, the anger momentarily vanished. "I did not realize it was the relevant time, sir. I assume Mr. Pitt has worked that out somehow?"

The Prince turned to Pitt, his eyes cold.

"Yes, sir," Pitt answered. "The woman was last seen alive sometime between midnight and one o'clock, and from the rigidity of the body when we found it, she must have died before half-past two in the morning, when Mr. Dunkeld's manservant left the landing and could no longer observe the bottom of the staircase up to the servants' sleeping quarters."

Dunkeld shifted his weight from one foot to the other, tense and impatient.

Pitt ignored him. "I learned of an old man who came into the Palace with the delivery of a box for Mr. Dunkeld," he went on. "But he was observed for all except a few minutes, which would not have been long enough to commit this crime."

The Prince's rather protruding eyes widened. "Wouldn't it? Are you certain?"

"Yes, sir. Also his hands and clothes were clean of any blood."

The Prince paled visibly. Perhaps Dunkeld had given him some idea of how much blood there had been. Now he turned to Dunkeld again. Pitt would like to have asked to leave, but he did not dare to. He was ashamed of himself for yielding to the pressure. This was his profession, and Dunkeld was no one of importance to Special Branch. He held no office in the Palace, only the power of his personality and the need the Prince seemed to feel for his presence. What was the Prince afraid of? Scandal? Another crime? Or that something hideous would be exposed? Did he know who it was, and dared not say?

Pitt felt a loathing for his own helplessness.

"Sir," he said firmly. "We are left with the only conclusion possible, which is that one of the gentleman guests here killed this unfortunate woman."

"Oh, no!" the Prince said immediately, shaking his head several times. "You must be mistaken. There is some alternative you have not investigated. Dunkeld, explain it to him!" He shrugged, as if Pitt were a problem Dunkeld should deal with.

Pitt clenched his fists at his sides, nails biting into his palms. This time he must not allow Dunkeld to dominate him. He drew in his breath to speak, but Dunkeld cut in before him.

"I'm sorry, sir," Dunkeld said very softly to the Prince. "But he is right. It pains me very deeply to say so, but it can only have been one of us. That is what is so very terrible about this situation." His face was tense. His eyes seemed almost black in the shadows of the room in spite of the fact that the sky was vivid blue beyond the velvet-curtained window.

The Prince stood frozen, his eyes wide, his hands half raised helplessly. "But we trusted these men!" he said with dismay. "They are outstanding, all of them! We need them for the railway!" He turned again to Dunkeld, as if he might offer some explanation that would make the situation different.

"I don't know, sir," Dunkeld said unhappily. "I could have sworn for all of them myself."

"You did!" the Prince said with sudden petulance.

Dunkeld's face tightened. "I did for their intelligence and their skills, sir. And for their reputations."

The Prince's expression tightened in irritation. "Yes. Yes. I'm sorry. Of course you did. I wish we could have had Watson Forbes. He would have been the perfect man. Do you think we could still persuade him? If . . . if the worst happens and we find" — he took an awkward, suddenly indrawn breath — "if we lose someone?"

Dunkeld bit his lower lip. "I doubt it, sir. But of course I will try. Forbes told me unequivocally that he has retired from his African interests."

"If I asked him personally?" the Prince asked, staring at Dunkeld.

"Of course I am sure he would do anything

within his power to please you, sir. We all would," Dunkeld replied, but there was no warmth in his voice. He made the remark merely to placate, and Pitt could see that, even if the Prince could not. He looked temporarily mollified. "But I fear the reason he has forsaken all his African interests stems back to the death of his son," Dunkeld went on as though an explanation was necessary.

The Prince was puzzled. "Death of his son? What happened? Surely that is not sufficient to make a man of his skill and resource abandon the work of his life?"

"It was his only son," Dunkeld's voice dropped even further, "and he died in dreadful circumstances nine years ago. Poor Forbes was very shaken by it. I heard tell that it was he who found the young man, or what was left of him." There was a look of distaste on his face and his mouth turned down at the corners. "It was crocodiles, or something equally nightmarish. I wasn't in Africa myself at the time. My son-in-law, Julius Sorokine, was there. And I believe Quase and Marquand were too. And Forbes's daughter, Liliane. It was before she was married." His mouth tightened. "You can hardly blame Forbes if he has settled his affairs there and does not wish to return, particularly with the very people he must as-

sociate with the bitterest tragedy in his life."
His voice quite gently insisted that the
Prince observe the decencies of such a loss.

His Royal Highness appeared resigned. He
would not abide being thwarted by people,
but circumstances, he knew, he could not
fight. The rituals of death had to be observed. He had survived his mother's
mourning for three decades and never even
penetrated the shell of it.

He looked back at Pitt as if he had suddenly remembered his presence. "This is a
very unhappy situation," he said, as though
Pitt might not have understood what they
had said. "I would be obliged if you could be
as tactful as possible, but we have to know
who is responsible. It cannot be left."

Pitt had no intention whatever either of
abandoning it or of conceding defeat. The
Prince's manner was patronizing, and it
pained Pitt like a blister, but there was nothing he could do to retaliate. He thought of
the night's indulgence and the appetites that
had precipitated it. Both men here had been
perfectly happy to buy the use of the
woman's body for the evening, under the
same roof as their sleeping wives. The callousness of it revolted him. And now it was
the fear of scandal and the inconvenience
that moved them to concern. The Prince at

least had possibly even been intimate with the woman, caressed her body, used her, and the next morning she had been found hacked to death. They were annoyed because a man bereaved of his only son had withdrawn from business in Africa and did not wish to assist in building their railway.

The magnitude of it, the power of those mere individuals, the sheer arrogance stunned him. And it frightened him that men so childlike should have such power.

"It will not be left, sir," he said stiffly. "It was a hideous crime. The woman's throat was cut, her abdomen torn open, and her entrails left hanging." He saw the Prince shudder, and he felt some satisfaction as the color drained from his skin, leaving him pasty and with a film of sweat on his brow.

Dunkeld sighed to indicate he found Pitt crude and more than a little tedious, but that he had not expected better.

"Really!" he said wearily, turning to the Prince. "I apologize, sir. Pitt is . . . doing his best." Quite obviously he had been thinking that he was of an inferior social class, roughly the same as the dead woman. Only the implication was that while she had quite openly been a whore, and fun in her own way, Pitt was a prude and utterly boring.

Pitt's temper soared. It was only the look

of slight amusement on Dunkeld's face when it was toward Pitt and averted from the Prince that held him in check from lashing back.

"Mr. Dunkeld is quite right, sir," he said instead. "But it is an extremely delicate matter. Naturally all the gentlemen say they were in bed, but considering the manner of the evening's entertainment, their wives cannot corroborate that."

"Menservants?" the Prince asked with a moment of hope.

"All the gentlemen dismissed them, sir, except Mr. Dunkeld."

"Oh. Yes, I forgot. Well, there must be something you can do! What do you usually do in cases like this?"

"Ask questions, look at facts, at evidence," Pitt replied. "But not all murder cases are solved, especially where women of the street are concerned." He clearly wanted to add "and their customers," but knew he would never be forgiven for it. It was not worth the few moments' satisfaction; worse, it would be highly unprofessional. He must rescue himself now, before anyone else spoke. "But people who are lying usually trip themselves up, sooner or later," he went on a little too quickly. "Crimes like this do not happen without some event first that stirs the murderer beyond his ability to control his obsession."

"And you'll look for that?" the Prince said dubiously.

Pitt felt the color hot in his face. Put like that it sounded completely ineffectual. He forced himself to remember the number of cases he had solved that had at one time or another appeared impossible. "And other things, sir." He forced himself to smile, and it felt like a baring of his teeth. "But I should be grateful for any assistance you could offer, any insight. I appreciate that speed is of the greatest importance, as well as discretion."

Two spots of dark, angry color appeared on Dunkeld's sunburned cheeks, but even he dared not contradict Pitt now. The air was electric in the room. One could believe that, beyond the tall windows, a summer storm was about to break.

"Yes," the Prince agreed unhappily. "Quite. Of course, any help at all. What is it you wish to know?" He did not look to Dunkeld, but Pitt had the impression that he was preventing himself from doing so only with a conscious effort.

Pitt knew he might never have this chance again. "Were there any disagreements at all, either between the guests, or between guests and the women? Candor would be of the greatest service, sir."

The Prince seemed quite relieved to answer. "Sorokine was in a poor temper," he replied. "He wasn't rude, of course, just discourteous in his unwillingness to join in. He seemed preoccupied."

Pitt forbore from suggesting that possibly he did not enjoy such entertainment and was unable to disguise the fact.

As if reading his thoughts, Dunkeld interrupted. "Before you imagine any finer feelings on his part, Inspector, Sorokine is a man of the world, and quite capable of enjoying himself like a gentleman. I believe he had had some altercation with his wife, and with his brother, Simnel Marquand. He is my son-in-law, but I admit, his temper is uncertain."

"And the other gentlemen participated more wholeheartedly?" Pitt asked.

"Certainly," the Prince answered without hesitation. He smiled for a moment before the memory clouded with the horror of the morning. "Yes," he repeated.

"You all retired at what hour?" Pitt pressed.

The Prince's face registered distaste. It was a tactless question, indelicate. Pitt was aware of it and of the discomfort in the room. But he had no intention of catering to this sudden sensibility. Their delicate feelings were for themselves, as if they had been observed in some bodily function by a prurient stranger. Perhaps that was pretty close to the truth. He waited.

"I did not look at my pocket watch," the Prince said coldly. "I imagine it must have been something after midnight. Sorokine went earlier."

"I see. Each of you with a separate woman?"

"Naturally!" the Prince snapped. He seemed about to add something more, then changed his mind. The color was still hot in his face.

"Which of you was with the woman who was killed, sir?" Pitt asked.

"I was," Dunkeld answered quickly.

Pitt knew it was a lie, both from Dunkeld's face and from the Prince's. It was an absurd moment, and equally it was irretrievable. He saw the Prince's flash of gratitude and then his mortification in Pitt's recognition of it, as if he had been caught in an act of cowardice.

"I see," Pitt said quietly, forcing his expression into blandness, without the amusement and the contempt he felt, although it was difficult. "And how long did she remain with you, Mr. Dunkeld?"

"I didn't time it!" Dunkeld said with a flare of temper. "And before you ask, I have no idea where she went. Presumably to one of the others, and her death."

"We know from Edwards, one of the footmen, what time the other two women left," Pitt pointed out, "and what time the third woman must have died, from the time she was last seen and the state of the body."

"Then, as you implied before, it must have been Sorokine, Marquand, or Quase," the Prince said with total despondency. "I suppose you had better find out which one. Thank you, Dunkeld. I appreciate your discretion and your loyalty. You may go . . . er, Pitt."

Pitt bowed his head and went out into the corridor, closely followed by Dunkeld.

As soon as they were beyond possible earshot Dunkeld caught him by the arm and swung him round, almost knocking him against the wall. "You incompetent fool!" he snarled. "That is the future King of England you were talking to as if you were some self-righteous maiden aunt. Who the hell do you think you are to patronize him with your working-class prudery? Do you have any idea what a fool you make of yourself? No one expects you to behave like a gentleman, but at least have the wit to keep your moral judgments to yourself. Your manners belong in the gutter, where presumably most of your trade is."

"Yes, it is," Pitt replied between his teeth. Dunkeld's face was less than a foot from his, and he could feel the heat of the man's rage physically and smell his skin. "But I find gutters run in the most unexpected places." His eyes did not leave Dunkeld's.

Dunkeld swung his right shoulder back as if to strike him, then seeing Pitt's unflinching gaze, he changed his mind. Suddenly he smiled, with an ugly curl of the lip. "If I were in your place, I should want to use this opportunity to better myself and earn the gratitude of my future sovereign, so my sons could find a more honorable occupation," he said between his teeth. "Perhaps they could even escape such employment as the police, clearing up other people's filth. And my daughters might marry tradesmen rather than their employees. But obviously you have neither the wit nor the vision for that."

He let go of Pitt's arm at last. "You're a fool. If you really are the best Narraway has, God help the country. Go and get on with your questions. I suppose it would be pointless telling you not to offend anyone?"

"It would be a waste of time giving me orders at all, Mr. Dunkeld," Pitt said a little hoarsely. "I answer to Mr. Narraway, not to you." He walked away, refusing to straighten his jacket from the way that Dunkeld had left it.

But as he went down the corridor he could not stop Dunkeld's words beating in his mind. Had his sense of disgust sounded self-righteous? Had he shown it where a better man would not have? He did not like Dunkeld, and he had been unsophisticated enough to allow the man to see it, and no doubt the Prince of Wales as well. And obviously the Prince not only liked and trusted Dunkeld, he seemed to be relying on both his judgment and his loyalty.

Pitt could have shown loyalty as well, and some sympathy for a man who had unwittingly invited into his home — or more accurately his mother's home — a man who had turned out to be a lunatic. If he had, he would have earned the Prince's gratitude, and taken the next step up the ladder toward being a gentleman.

Never mind whether he owed that to his children. Every man wants his sons and daughters to have more than he had. Unquestionably he owed it to Charlotte. She had been born into a financially comfortable and socially respected family. Her sister, Emily, had married Lord Ashworth, and on his death inherited his fortune. Her son had all his father's privileges to inherit. Charlotte had married Pitt, and her son would have the best education Pitt could afford for him, but nothing else.

Dunkeld was right; he could have given Charlotte more than that for her children, even for himself, and had allowed his pride and anger to stop him. He was startled by his own selfishness, and sick that it had taken Dunkeld, of all people, to show it to him.

He was in one of the main corridors now. It was vast compared with his own house. How could he possibly feel so shut in, almost imprisoned, in such a place? He should be proud to be here at all, not longing to escape.

He must learn all he could about the guests, including Dunkeld himself. Narraway was investigating the facts: reputation, financial standing, ambitions, friends, and enemies. Pitt must explore their natures, their angers and fears, their knowledge of one another. One of them had slashed a woman to death. Underneath the courteous, intelligent exterior there had to be a madman driven by a hatred so bestial he could not control it even within the Palace walls.

Pitt spoke to Hamilton Quase first. He was obliged to draw him from a conversation with Marquand, but he could not find Julius Sorokine, and he was not going to address Dunkeld again so soon.

He had something of a plan. It was not enough to give him confidence, merely a place to begin. He sat in a large armchair in the room Tyndale had given him. He was facing Hamilton Quase in one of the other chairs. Quase crossed his legs elegantly and waited. He looked tired, his eyes bloodshot and his skin, beneath the darkening of sun and wind, was mottled by too much drink. He kept his hands still in his lap, but Pitt thought that were he to hold them more loosely, they might tremble.

"Will you describe the party to me, Mr. Quase?" Pitt began bluntly. "From the beginning. Who arranged it? Whose idea was it?"

Quase looked slightly surprised. "You don't think the murder of that unfortunate woman was planned, surely? Why on earth would anyone do something so . . . so stupid? And dangerous." He had a good voice, stronger than one might have expected from his slightly unsteady air.

"What do you think?" Pitt returned.

Quase's eyebrows rose even higher. "I've no idea who did it, if that's what you are asking."

Pitt smiled very slightly. "If you did know, why would you not have told me?"

Quase smiled back with a sudden flash of humor. "Is there some kind of penalty for the first one of us to answer a question? Do we lose?"

"Lose what?"

"The struggle, the battle of wits," Quase replied.

"Then I have won," Pitt told him.

"Oh . . . yes." Quase smiled back. "I answered you. Does it feel like a victory?"

"Not at all. Why would we be battling? Are we not on the same side?"

"That depends upon how far we go," Quase answered. "I don't know who killed the woman, or why. I suppose I wish you to find out, but there are answers that I would not like."

"There will probably be answers that no one likes," Pitt agreed. "Murder affects far more than the murderer and the victim." He leaned back a little, as if relaxing in his chair. "We all have loves and hates, and secrets. That doesn't affect the questions I have to ask, and go on asking until I know who killed her, and can prove it."

Quase looked at him with mild amusement. There was something else in his eyes, which Pitt found too complicated to read, but it was a kind of unhappiness, as if an old wound were aching again. "Then you had better begin," he said quietly. "I warn you, I have absolutely no idea who killed her, and still less why. She seemed a perfectly harmless sort of tart."

"Did she?" Pitt was feeling his way carefully. It was an odd investigation. The victim was someone who was a stranger to all of those who could possibly be guilty of killing her. No one admitted to ever having seen her before. "What was she like?" he asked. "For that matter, what was her name?"

Quase frowned, but there was a crooked smile on his lips. "Sadie, I think. I didn't actually . . . er . . . speak to her, if you like? She was not here for my amusement, except most indirectly."

"Whose?"

Again Quase was slightly surprised. "His Royal Highness's, of course."

"Why was she especially for him?"

"Actually, she seemed intelligent," Quase said frankly. "She had quite a ready wit. Not cruel at all, just very quick. She could read and write, and she had a considerable knowledge of men and of human nature. I mean emotional as well as the more obvious aspects."

"A courtesan rather than a whore?" Pitt

asked. He should have expected that.

"Elegantly put," Quase agreed. "Yes. She wasn't actually particularly pretty. I've certainly seen many prettier. Good skin and eyes, but otherwise very ordinary. It was her personality, her laugh, her suppleness of mind as well as body. And she sang very well. She really was entertaining." A sadness passed over his face, and for a moment it was as if his attention was far away.

Pitt winced, wondering how much of what he was saying was the truth and what the omissions were. Perhaps it was the things he was not telling that would have been the most revealing.

"Poor creature," Quase said quietly. "She was so alive."

Pitt breathed in and out slowly, suddenly struck by the belief that Quase was speaking not of this woman, but of some other. He dismissed it as fantasy. He must be more tired than he thought. It was getting toward late afternoon and he would not go home tonight; perhaps not tomorrow either. "You observed her very closely," he said at last.

"What?" Quase looked up.

"You observed her very closely," Pitt repeated. "She must have been in the room for some time, and spoken quite a lot."

"No. Just an impression."

Quase was lying.

"You had seen her before?" Pitt asked. "Perhaps purchased her services on some other occasion? Please don't deny it if it is true. It will not be too difficult to find out, and then a great deal of other information would emerge as well." The threat was veiled but perfectly clear.

Quase smiled broadly, but his eyes were pinched with hurt. "A waste of your efforts, Mr. Pitt. I have many vices. I am a moral coward at times. I debase myself to serve men who have higher office than I and lower morality, and I know it. Certainly I drink too much. But I do not frequent the whorehouses of London, or of anywhere else. As you may have noticed, I have a very beautiful wife." He drew in his breath and let it out with a sigh of pain. "And unlike some men, I find that quite sufficient."

Pitt believed him. Some sense of delicacy prevented him from pursuing the subject. "I understand Mr. Sorokine went to bed early also. Is that correct?" he asked instead.

A flash of appreciation lit Quase's eyes and then vanished. "Yes. And alone, if that is what you are asking. Whether he remained alone or not I have no idea."

"So there were three women for Mr. Marquand, Mr. Dunkeld, and His Royal Highness," Pitt concluded.

"It would appear so," Quase agreed. "I stayed up until they retired, which was around midnight. What happened after that I have no idea. As far as I am concerned the women earned their fee by being extremely entertaining company and making a somewhat plodding evening pass with pleasure."

"A plodding evening?" Pitt raised his eyebrows.

"His Royal Highness, when sober, can be heavy going," Quase told him with a flicker of a smile. "And when drunk, even heavier. A bit like plowing a field after a week's rain. Dunkeld is a bully, as you may have observed. Marquand is good enough, I suppose, although I find his rivalry with Sorokine rather a bore. They are half-brothers — I assume you knew that. Sorokine himself can be rather a bore because he is absorbed in his own problems, which he wears heavily. And before you ask me, I don't know, but I assume they are largely to do with his wife, whose behavior with Marquand is outrageous."

"And would not tell me if you did," Pitt added.

"Precisely," Quase agreed.

"So it was an enjoyable evening? No quarrels? No tension as to who should have which woman?"

Quase laughed outright. "Between whom, for God's sake? His Royal Highness took what he wished, Dunkeld would choose between the other two, and Marquand would have what was left. If you really need me to tell you that, then you haven't the wits to find out what the menu was, let alone who killed that poor creature!"

"It is not only what I learn, Mr. Quase, it is who tells me, and how," Pitt retorted, then immediately wished he had not. He had defended himself, and thus betrayed his need to do so. Too late to pull it back. "Thank you. Would you ask Mr. Marquand to come, please?"

Five minutes later Simnel Marquand came in and closed the door behind him. "I really can't help you," he said before he had even crossed the floor. He sat down, less gracefully and less comfortably than Hamilton Quase. He was a good-looking man with an intelligent and sensual face. He dressed well, but without that effortless elegance of a man who, once having understood fashion, can follow it or ignore it as he pleases.

"I did not see the poor woman after I went to bed," he explained. "And I have no idea what happened to her. I didn't see anyone around in the corridor, and I understand you have already accounted for the servants.

It seems inexplicable to me." He spoke as if that were the end of the matter.

"It seems so," Pitt agreed. "And yet it must be simply that we have not found the explanation. The facts are inescapable. Three women came for the evening, two left, and the third was found dead in the linen cupboard. The servants are accounted for and the only other person to come beyond the kitchen and be alone even for a few moments was the carter who helped the footman carry Mr. Dunkeld's box up the stairs. He was alone for only a matter of minutes, and was not upstairs in the bedroom corridor. Also, he had not a spot of blood on him when he left. If you had seen the poor woman's body, you would know that could not be the case with whoever killed her."

Marquand was pale, his body unnaturally still. It obviously disturbed him that Pitt was so graphic. He had strong hands, slender but with square tips to the fingers. Just now they were clenched with an effort to stop them trembling.

"I did not kill her, and I have no idea who did," he repeated.

Pitt smiled. "I had not been hopeful that you could tell me, Mr. Marquand. But you could describe the party of that evening."

"It was just a . . ." Marquand began, then

stopped. "Yes, I imagine you have never attended such a . . . an evening?"

"No," Pitt agreed soberly. The sarcastic observation was on his tongue, and he refrained from making it only because he had to. "Presumably the ladies retired to bed early, and then the . . . women were conducted in?"

Marquand's lips tightened and a very slight color stained his cheeks. "You make it sound vulgar," he said critically.

Pitt leaned back. He could not get Olga Marquand's dark, sad face out of his mind. And yet that was foolish. She was probably quite used to these arrangements and would surely know that accommodating the Prince of Wales was largely what her husband was here to achieve.

"Then explain it to me," he invited.

Marquand's eyes opened wide. "For God's sake, man, are you envious?" he said in amazement. "I can assure you, you could have had as much fun at a singsong at your local public house! More at a good evening in the music halls, pleasures which are not open to His Royal Highness, for obvious reasons. The ladies retired, not that they wouldn't have stayed, if society permitted such liberty. We drank, probably too much, sang a few songs, told some very bawdy jokes, and

162

laughed too loudly."

Pitt imagined it. "Are you telling me that you all went to bed separately?" he inquired, not bothering to keep the disbelief out of his voice.

"No, of course not," Marquand snapped. "The Prince took the woman who was later found dead. Sarah, or Sally, or whatever her name was . . ."

"Sadie," Pitt supplied.

"All right, Sadie. I took Molly and Dunkeld took Bella. I never saw the others again. Are you sure that one of the other women could not have killed Sadie? In a jealous rage, or some other kind of quarrel, possibly over money? That seems quite likely."

Pitt decided to play the game. "Is that what you think could have happened?" he asked.

Marquand stared at him. "Why not? It makes more sense than any of us having killed her! Do you think one of us took leave of our senses — for half an hour, hacked the poor creature to bits — then returned to bed, and woke up in the morning back in perfect control, ate breakfast, and resumed discussions on the Cape-to-Cairo railway?" He did not bother to keep the sarcasm from his voice.

"I would certainly prefer it to be one of the other women," Pitt conceded. "Let us say, for the sake of the story, that it was Bella. She left Mr. Dunkeld's bed, crept along the passage awakening no one, happened to run into Sadie, who had chanced to have left the Prince's bed, stark naked. They found the linen cupboard and decided to go into it, perhaps for privacy. Then they had a furious quarrel, which fortunately no one else heard, and Bella, who happened to have had the forethought to take with her one of the knives from the butler's pantry, cut Sadie's throat and disemboweled her. Fortunately she kept from getting any blood on her dress or her hands or arms. Then she quietly left again, with Molly, whom she had found, and was conducted out of the Palace and went home. Something like that?"

Marquand's face was scarlet, his eyes blazing. Twice he started to speak, then realized that what he was going to say was absurd, and stopped again.

"Perhaps you would tell me a little more of the temper, the mood of the evening, Mr. Marquand?" Pitt asked, aware that his tone was now supremely condescending. "Was there any ill-feeling between any of the men, or they and one of the women?"

Marquand was about to deny it, then changed his mind. "You place me in an invidious position," he complained. "It would

164

be preposterous to imagine that the Prince of Wales could do such a thing. I know that I did not, but I cannot prove it. Dunkeld was presumably with the other woman, Bella, except when he went to unpack his damned box of books, and it seems he can prove it." The inflection in his voice changed slightly, a razor edge of strain. "My brother, Julius, retired early and alone. He did not wish to stay with us, and did not give his reasons. The Prince of Wales was not pleased, but it fell something short of actual unpleasantness."

"Mrs. Sorokine is very handsome," Pitt remarked as casually as he could. "Probably he preferred her company to that of a street woman."

The tide of color washed up Marquand's face again. "You are extremely offensive, sir! I can only assume in your excuse that you know no better!"

"How would you prefer me to phrase it, sir?" Pitt asked.

"Julius went to bed in a self-righteous temper," Marquand said harshly, hatred flaring momentarily in his eyes. "His wife did not see him until luncheon the following day."

Pitt was disconcerted by the strength of emotion, and embarrassed to have witnessed it.

"Did he tell you this, or did she?" he asked.

"What?" The color in Marquand's face did not subside. "She did. And before you ask me, I have nothing further to say on the subject. Julius is my brother. I tell you only so much truth as honor obliges me to. I will not lie, even for him."

"I understand. And of course Mrs. Sorokine is your sister-in-law," Pitt conceded. Actually he did not understand. Was Marquand's anger against his brother because he had placed him in a situation where he was forced to lie or betray him? Or was it against circumstances, the Prince and his expectations, even Dunkeld for engineering this whole situation? Or his own wife for making him feel guilty because he attended the party, and perhaps enjoyed it?

Pitt elicited a few more details of fact, and then excused him. He then asked to see Julius Sorokine, even though he had left early and would apparently know far less than the other men.

Julius came in casually, but there was an unmistakable anxiety in him. He was taller than his brother, and moved with the kind of grace that could not be learned. His ease was a gift of nature. He sat down opposite Pitt and waited to be questioned.

"Why did you leave the party earlier than

everyone else, Mr. Sorokine?" Pitt asked bluntly.

The question seemed to embarrass Sorokine, and it flashed suddenly into Pitt's mind that perhaps rather than spend at least some of the time with one of the prostitutes his father-in-law had provided, he had been with another woman altogether, of his own choosing. Perhaps that was why the handsome Minnie Sorokine had been confiding in her brother-in-law.

"Did you have an assignation with someone else?" Pitt asked abruptly. "If so, they can account for your time, and it need not be repeated to your wife."

Julius laughed outright, in spite of his discomfort. It was a warm, uncompromising sound. "I wish it were so, but I'm afraid not. I was totally alone. Even my manservant cannot account for more than the first half hour or so, which cannot be the relevant time, since the women were all still at the party."

"Why did you leave early?" Pitt asked. "Were you ill? You seem well enough today."

"I was perfectly well," Sorokine replied. He looked self-conscious. "I simply preferred not to indulge in that kind of pleasure."

Pitt's eyes widened a little, not certain if he was leaping to unwarranted conclusions.

Sorokine understood him instantly and blushed. "I have a certain regard for a woman who is not my wife," he said a little huskily. It obviously embarrassed him. "I would prefer that she did not see me drinking and fornicating with prostitutes. I care for her opinion of me." He lifted his eyes and stared at Pitt with surprising candor.

"I apologize," Pitt said, then felt foolish. He was doing no more than his job, and the thought had been a brief idea discarded. But he would remember that about Julius Sorokine. It was another layer of the complicated emotions that lay between these people. Was he referring to the gorgeous Mrs. Quase, whose husband drank too much and spoke so disparagingly of himself?

It would be easy enough to understand. Or the unhappy Olga Marquand, elegant, stiff, and withdrawn, his brother's wife? Or was it Elsa Dunkeld, as remote as an undiscovered country, where everything there was still to be found? He would be a brave man who would abandon Cahoon Dunkeld's daughter and try to take his wife!

He looked carefully at Sorokine's face and did not see that kind of courage in it. The strength was there, but not the fire, nor the resolve.

Pitt asked him a few more questions, but

learned nothing that seemed to be of value. Finally he excused him and sent for Dunkeld again.

"Well?" Dunkeld asked as he closed the door. "Have you achieved anything, apart from insulting the Prince of Wales and disturbing everyone else?" He did not sit down but remained standing, towering over Pitt, who had not had time to rise to his feet.

Pitt remained seated, deliberately trying to appear relaxed. "The large box that arrived for you shortly before Sadie was murdered," he said calmly, crossing his legs comfortably. "What was in it, and where is it now?"

"What?" Dunkeld's voice rose angrily. "You called me away from my meeting to ask me that? Have you discussed anything at all as to who killed the wretched woman?" He leaned forward. "Have you completely lost your grasp, man? Have you any idea what has happened? Someone has murdered a prostitute in the Queen's residence! What does it require to spark you into some action? One of these men, God help us, is a maniac."

Pitt leaned back slowly and looked up at him. "I assume you mean one of the other three: Marquand, Sorokine, or Quase?"

Dunkeld looked a little paler. "Yes, regrettably, of course I do. Do you know of any alternative?"

"What was in the box?" Pitt asked again. "You were apparently expecting it? Why did it come at that hour of night? Carters don't usually deliver at midnight."

Dunkeld sat down at last, leaning forward with his elbows on his knees. "Books," he said gratingly. "Mostly maps of the regions of Africa with which we are concerned. Yes, I was expecting them. They are extremely important to the work we plan to do."

"Then why did you not bring them with you?" Pitt asked.

"I sent for them from a dealer!" Dunkeld snapped back. "If I had had them in my possession when I came, then of course I would have brought them with me! Are you a complete fool?"

"And whoever sent them to you delivered them at midnight?"

"Obviously! I don't know why it took him so long. What the devil has that got to do with the woman's death?"

"I don't know what anything has to do with it yet. Do you?"

Dunkeld controlled his temper with clear difficulty. "No, of course I don't, or I would tell you. You obviously need every scrap of help you can find."

"As I remember it, Mr. Dunkeld, it was you who called us," Pitt replied.

Dunkeld's face darkened dangerously. "Why you arrogant, jumped-up oaf! You are a servant. You are here to clean up other people's detritus and keep the streets safe for your betters. You are the ferret that decent men send into holes in the ground to hunt out rabbits."

"Then if you want your rabbit hunted and you are incapable of getting it out yourself," Pitt said icily, "you had better employ the best ferret you can find, and give it its head. Otherwise the rabbit will escape and you will be left standing over an empty hole."

Dunkeld stood up slowly. "I shall not forget you, Pitt." It was blatantly a threat.

Pitt rose to his feet also. They were of equal height, and standing too close to each other for civility or comfort. But neither would move. "I shall probably forget you, sir," he replied. "I meet many like you, in my field of work." He smiled very slightly. "Thank you for answering my questions. I don't think I need to ask you about the . . . party . . . you organized for the Prince of Wales. I have several rather good accounts of it already."

Dunkeld spun round on his heel and slammed the door on his way out.

■ ■ ■

It was after six o'clock and Pitt was sitting in the same room again, mulling over the impressions he had gained from the four men. He was wondering if he should ring the bell and ask whoever answered it if he could have a cup of tea, when there was a tap on the door.

"Come in," he said with surprise. Gracie was not supposed to contact him so openly, and he could think of no one else who would approach him.

But when the door opened it was not Gracie who stood there, but an elegant woman in her middle years. She was beautifully dressed in the height of fashion in very dark silk, tiered from the waist down and with a slight train. There was expensive lace at her bosom and a cameo at her throat, which Pitt estimated would have cost as much as a good carriage.

He rose to his feet, certain she must have mistaken the room.

"Good afternoon," she said courteously. "Are you Inspector Pitt?"

"Yes, ma'am." It seemed ridiculous to offer to help her. She was obviously very much more composed than he.

She smiled slightly. "I am lady-in-waiting

to the Princess of Wales. Her Royal Highness would be greatly obliged if you would attend her. I can accompany you now." It was phrased as if it were a request, but quite clearly he could not refuse.

"Of . . . of course." His mouth was dry. His mind raced as to why she would want to see him, and what he could say to her. The first thought was that Dunkeld had reported him for rudeness. But why would the Princess of Wales summon him rather than the Prince? What kind of lie could he possibly think of to avoid telling her of the situation he was investigating? How much did she know anyway? He had heard that she was severely deaf. Perhaps she knew nothing and wanted to ask why he was here. What should he say?

He followed the lady-in-waiting obediently. She led him a considerable distance through wide, high-ceilinged corridors until they came to what was apparently their destination. She knocked and then went in without waiting for an answer, signaling Pitt to follow her.

The room in which he found himself was richly overfurnished like the others he had seen, high-ceilinged and crusted with plasterwork gilded and painted, but he did not even glance at it. His total attention was focused on the woman who sat in the tall chair by the window, a tea tray on the carved table in front of her. It was set for three. There were tiny sandwiches on a plate and very small cakes cut to look as if they had wings poised above the whipped cream. There were also fresh scones he could actually smell, a dish of butter, one of jam, and one of clotted cream. He swallowed as if tasting them. He had not realized before how hungry he was.

"How kind of you to come, Mr. Pitt," the woman at the window said graciously. Pitt had heard that Princess Alexandra was beautiful, but he was still unprepared for the perfect skin, the flawless features in spite of her being now well into her middle years.

What did one say to a deaf princess who would one day be queen? Did it matter? Would the lady-in-waiting help him? Should he raise his voice, or was that inexcusable, regardless of her hearing?

He gulped. "It is my honor, Your Royal Highness." Was that too loud?

She was watching him closely. What was she going to ask?

"Please sit down," she invited, indicating the chair opposite her. "Would you care for tea?"

Should he accept, or was the invitation merely a form of politeness? He had no idea.

Did she know how rude he had been to the Prince?

"Please accept," the lady-in-waiting said quietly, from a step or two behind him. "Her Royal Highness wishes to speak with you. The tea will be very agreeable."

"Thank you," Pitt said more gently. "Thank you, ma'am." He sat down, aware of being clumsy, as if he were all arms and legs, as uncoordinated as if he were still an adolescent.

The lady-in-waiting poured the tea. It was very hot, obviously only just brought in, and the fragrance of it was delicate but unmistakable.

"You have a very difficult task, Mr. Pitt," the Princess observed, taking a small cucumber sandwich and indicating that he should do the same.

"Yes, ma'am," he agreed. He took a sandwich carefully, wondering if he could possibly stretch it to three mouthfuls.

"Have you met all His Royal Highness's guests?" she inquired. She had fine eyes, intelligent and very direct.

"Yes, ma'am." He must add something more. He was sounding stupid. "I have spoken more to the gentlemen this afternoon. I am not sure if the ladies can tell me much." How much did she know? He must be desperately careful not to tell her anything she had not already heard. That would be appalling.

"You may be surprised," she said with a very slight smile, amusement fleeting and then gone. "We observe more than you think."

He had no idea how to answer her, and he did not think it polite to take another bite of the sandwich.

She sipped her tea. "You may find that they also have been quite aware of tensions, likes and dislikes, and of rivalries."

"I will ask them, ma'am," he promised, although he thought it a useless exercise.

"You are thinking that they will be too loyal to their husbands to tell you anything that could be of use in this unpleasant matter," she went on.

The last piece of the sandwich went down his throat the wrong way, probably because he drew in his breath at the same time. He found himself coughing and the tears coming to his eyes. He was making a complete fool of himself. It was a kind of nightmare.

"Take a sip of tea, Mr. Pitt," she suggested gently. "It will no doubt be better in a moment. Do not try to speak and make it worse, please. I quite understand. I have noticed a few small nuances of character myself, which you may find of help."

He thought that so unlikely as to be impossible. What could she conceivably know of the ways of prostitutes, or the more violent elements in men's nature? He could not say so because courtesy forbade it, and he was still afraid of choking if he tried to speak.

She smiled a little absentmindedly, as if her attention was already engaged in marshaling her thoughts. "I have noticed that Mrs. Sorokine has a certain air of wanton glamour about her that does not seem to hold her husband's eye at all," she said with devastating candor. "I do not think he is affecting indifference. I saw no signs of it in him. If he looked at anyone unobtrusively, it was at his stepmother-in-law, Mrs. Dunkeld."

Pitt cleared his throat. "You are very observant, ma'am."

"I have plenty of time," she said ruefully, but the calm expression in her face barely changed. "When you are deaf, people do not talk to you a great deal. It is too much trouble to make themselves understood. Few realize how much of understanding comes from seeing a person's face, and watching them while they speak. You might be surprised how often the eyes and the lips give different messages."

He knew she was right. That was very often

how he sensed that someone was lying, even before he knew the facts. "And what did you observe in the others, ma'am?" he asked.

She frowned slightly. "I beg your pardon?"

He repeated the question more slowly and a little more loudly. He could feel his face color with the awkwardness of it. He felt as if he came across as faintly condescending, although he did not intend to be.

"Oh." This time she understood. "Mrs. Marquand is very unhappy. Watch her face in repose. She alternates between anger and misery. And Mrs. Quase is frightened. Her hands are always fiddling with something."

"And Mrs. Dunkeld?" he asked.

Obviously she had not heard him. "And Mrs. Dunkeld," she went on, "is afraid of her husband, which is quite different. Mrs. Quase is, I think, afraid for Mr. Quase. Although what she believes may happen to him I do not know. Mrs. Dunkeld never looks at Mrs. Sorokine. I think perhaps she does not dare to, in case her eyes betray her."

"You are extremely observant, ma'am," he said sincerely.

"Please drink your tea." She gestured toward the tray. "It is far less pleasant cold. And try a scone or two. It is not impolite. I requested them for you and shall be disappointed if you do not enjoy them."

He dared to smile at her. "Thank you, ma'am."

She smiled back in a suddenly charming gesture. "You see, I would make a better detective than you think. Mr. Dunkeld does not like Mr. Sorokine. I do not hear what he says, but I see his eyes. Even though he laughs, it is not a laugh of warmth or of pleasure. He is an angry man."

"Do you know why, ma'am?" Pitt asked.

She did not hear. "My husband likes him, but I do not. I think he is using His Royal Highness in order to obtain something he wishes for. Not that that is unusual, of course. One must expect it. However, the Prince sometimes thinks better of people than I believe is justified. He imagines that those with whom he enjoys his leisure time are more of a like mind with him than they really are."

Pitt had a glimpse of loneliness that was terrible, a world where no one was equal and no one dared speak the truth if it would not please you. You would always be floundering in a sea of lies. "I'm sorry," he said with intense feeling.

She must have understood from the movement of his lips. "You have a gentleness in you, Mr. Pitt. Please remember how that poor woman died, and that whoever it is you are looking for has no pity at all, for her or for you."

He was stunned into silence.

"Do have some cream with your scone," she offered. "It adds greatly to the pleasure."

"Thank you, ma'am," he accepted. He felt obliged to take it, with considerable gratitude. It was delicious.

"We are all naturally very disturbed," she went on, as if answering some comment he had made, although in fact he had his mouth full. He wondered if she had even the faintest idea what had really happened, of the violence, the hostility involved. "No one can be expected to carry on as usual," she continued. "But we must make an effort. It is part of our duty, do you not think?"

"Yes, ma'am, if at all possible." He swallowed and made the only reply he could. He could hardly disagree with her.

"All sorts of little things have to change, of course. Do you care for some more tea? Eleanor, my dear . . ."

The lady-in-waiting poured it before Pitt could answer.

"Thank you," he said quickly.

"It is gracious of you to spare me the time," the Princess went on. "I am sure you are much occupied. Of course, it could be something to do with the railway, but I confess I do not see how. They all seem very keen on it, except perhaps Mr. Sorokine. He made some remark, but I am afraid I did not hear all of it. But there was doubt in his face, I remember that, and the others were all annoyed with him. So much was clear."

She took a scone herself and covered it with jam and cream. "What time was the poor creature killed, Mr. Pitt?"

Pitt froze. So she knew!

"In the early hours of the morning, ma'am. Before half-past two."

Beside him the lady-in-waiting stiffened.

Alexandra saw it. "Oh, do be realistic, Eleanor," she said briskly. "I am deaf, certainly, but I am not blind. I know perfectly well what the party was all about. What I don't know is why the bath was still warm."

"I beg your pardon?" Pitt said before he realized the impropriety of it.

"The bath was warm," she repeated, offering him another scone. "The cast iron holds the heat from the water for a while afterward, you know. Otherwise it is quite cold to the touch. It was still noticeably warm at eight o'clock. I touched it myself."

"Which bath, ma'am?"

"His Royal Highness's, of course. But his valet did not bring water up. Do have more

181

cream over that. It makes all the difference."

Pitt took it from her quite automatically,
his brain racing, his fingers almost numb.

CHAPTER FIVE

While Pitt had begun his investigation that morning, Narraway had traveled by hansom cab to Westminster and the House of Commons. He wrote a brief message on a card, saying that he wished to consult on a matter of the most extreme urgency, and asked one of the junior clerks to take it to Somerset Carlisle, wherever he might be. Then he waited, pacing the floor, glancing every few moments at each doorway of the vast antechamber to see if Carlisle was coming. Every footstep alerted him, and even though he knew many of the members who crossed the antechamber on their way from one meeting to another, he chose to remain near the wall and meet the eyes of none of them. His work was better done if he moved in the shadows and few could actually say exactly what he looked like or who he was.

It was about twenty minutes before Carlisle appeared. He was soft-footed on the stone-flagged floor, thinner than he used to be, and not quite as straight of shoulder. But he had exactly the same gaunt, ironic face with heavy brows and quick intelligence, and the air as if no joke could be lost on him.

"What is so urgent that it brings you out into the open?" he said in a low voice. To a passerby he would be no more than acknowledging Narraway's presence, as one would a constituent come on business.

"I need information," Narraway replied with a slight smile.

"How surprising." Carlisle was amused rather than sarcastic. "About what?"

"The Cape-to-Cairo railway."

Carlisle's brows shot up. "And this is sufficiently urgent to call me out of a meeting with the Home Secretary?"

"Yes, it is," Narraway replied. He saw Carlisle's skepticism. "Believe me, it is."

"It will take decades to build," Carlisle pointed out, facing Narraway now. "If they do it at all. I cannot think, offhand, of anything less important."

"I need to know about the issues, and the people involved," Narraway told him. "Today. And even that may be too late."

"But you expect me to tell you the truth." Carlisle made it obvious that he did not believe Narraway. There was an irritation in his face, as if he felt Narraway was lying to him in order to use his skills. It was uncharacteristic of him. He was not a vain or short-tempered man.

"If I tell you, then it must be alone, not overheard, and if possible, not observed either." Narraway yielded in order to save time. This was an ugly case. Because of the Prince's involvement, they had to tread a great deal more delicately than in most instances of violence or threatened anarchy. A scandal uncovered could do damage impossible to predict. One never knew where it would end.

"Let us go up Great George Street to Birdcage Walk," Carlisle replied. "When we are free of Westminster, you can tell me what it is you need to know, and I'll give you any information I have. But I warn you, the entire project is only speculative. Cecil Rhodes would certainly back it, and that means a good deal. Highly ambitious man. You're not mixed up with him, are you?"

"No," Narraway said wryly. "At least I doubt it. This is much more immediate."

"I suppose you know what you are talking about, but I'm damned if I do!" Carlisle remarked with a gesture of resignation. "But I'll listen. Come on." He led the way out to the street and slowly up the hill away from the river with its traffic of pleasure boats, barges, and ferries until finally they were all but alone on Birdcage Walk. The green expanse of St. James's Park lay to their right, trees rustling in the slight breeze, and promenading couples totally uninterested in anyone but each other.

Narraway began at last. He had no idea if the murder had anything to do directly with the proposed railway or any of its diplomatic ramifications. The motives might be of ambition or personal greed that sprung from the power and the profits to be won. Or it could be simply that one of the men involved was a madman, and the time and place of his act a hideous coincidence.

Regardless, he needed to learn all he could. Carlisle was the last man to tell him, and at the same time the man he could most trust to absolute discretion.

"The Prince of Wales is interested in the Cape-to-Cairo railway," he began aloud, phrasing it as briefly as he could. "He has as his personal guests at the Palace at the moment four men and their wives: Cahoon Dunkeld, Hamilton Quase, Julius Sorokine, and Simnel Marquand."

"Planning to bid for the railway?" Carlisle asked, slowing to an amble.

"Yes. To obtain the Prince's approval so he

will favor them." Narraway matched his stride.

"That makes sense. Why is it Special Branch's concern? Is there one of them you distrust?"

Narraway smiled. "Profoundly," he said bitterly. "The problem is that I don't know which one. You see, two nights ago the gentlemen, including the Prince, had a rather wild party, with three prostitutes as guests for their entertainment. The following morning the corpse of one of them was discovered in the linen cupboard, throat cut and disemboweled. We have excluded the possibility of it having been any of the servants, and since it is the Palace, it is not difficult to exclude any intruders."

Carlisle had stopped abruptly, almost losing his balance. "What?" He blinked. "What did you say?"

"Exactly what you thought I said," Narraway replied softly. "It was not Dunkeld. He is accounted for. One of the other three has to have been responsible. I need to know which one, as quickly and discreetly as possible."

"Get Thomas Pitt," Carlisle answered, a flash of rueful humor in his eyes. "He's the best man I know of to solve a complicated murder among the gentry." He had his own reasons for knowing this. Narraway had heard it mentioned but had never inquired as to the details. This was not the occasion to begin, even if Carlisle would have told him.

"I have him there already," Narraway answered. "What can you tell me about the less obvious aspects of the Cape-to-Cairo railway?"

Carlisle was surprised. "You think it has to do with that? Isn't it just some . . . some private insanity?"

"I don't know. It seems an odd time and place for it."

"Decidedly. But I imagine real madness does not cater to convenience."

They were walking under the trees now, the smell of cut grass heavy in the air, the path easy and smooth. There was barely a soft crunch of grit under their feet and the sound of birdsong in the distance. A child was throwing sticks for a happy spaniel pup.

"That sort of madness doesn't explode without some event as a catalyst," Narraway answered him. "Some old passion woken by mockery, rejection, a compulsion exploding in the mind, a sudden surge of rage out of control."

"I know very little about any of those men," Carlisle said apologetically. "Not much that is more than common knowledge."

"Or it could be a colder and saner motive," Narraway said. "A sabotage to the talks. A long and bitter enmity. Who else could build this railway, if not these men? Who would want it stopped, and why? National pride? Political power? Tell me something I can't read in the newspaper."

Carlisle thought for several minutes. They passed from the shade of the trees and emerged into the sun again.

"I don't know of anyone else in particular who would be as good as this group, if they work together," he said at last. "Marquand is a superb financier with all the best connections. Sorokine is a better diplomat than he has so far shown. He's lazy. I don't mean he isn't good; he could be brilliant if he cared enough to stir himself. Quase is an engineer with flashes of genius, and he knows Africa. And Dunkeld is a driving force with intelligence, imagination, and a relentless will. If any man can draw it all together, he can."

"Ruthless?"

Carlisle smiled. "Unquestionably. But what use would a man be at a task like this if he were not? And you say he is accounted for?"

"Yes. Who else might achieve it?"

Carlisle thought for a moment. "A few years ago I would have said Watson Forbes," he answered. "Cleverer than Dunkeld, but perhaps less magnetic. Better knowledge of Africa. Explored a lot of it himself, all the way up from Cape Town north to Mashona-land, and Matabeleland. Knows Cecil Rhodes personally. Walked the Veldt, saw the great Rift Valley, took a boat up the Zambezi, looked at the falls there, maybe the biggest in the world. And he knows Egypt and the Sudan too. Been up the Nile beyond Karnak and the Valley of the Kings, and then on by camel as far as Khartoum. But he's returned to England now. Had enough. The man's tired. He was actually offered this project and declined it, which is how Dunkeld came to the fore."

"Why, do you know?"

"I don't, really. Lost the energy. Perhaps the climate got to him."

Narraway considered for a hundred yards or so, then turned to Carlisle again. "Any serious political enemies to the project?"

"What difference would that make?" Carlisle asked with a slight shrug. "Sorry, but I think you're looking for a man who is sane and highly intelligent almost all the time, but has a germ of madness in him that burst through a couple of nights ago. I don't see how it can have anything whatever to do with the railway. Of course, there's vast money to be made in it, eventually, and, far more than all the financial fortunes, there's honor, immense personal power, certainly peerages, fame for a lifetime and beyond. Your name would be on the maps and in the history books. For some men that's the prize above all others. Never underestimate the love of power."

They walked a few more yards in silence, Narraway turning over in his mind what Carlisle had said. The music of a hurdy-gurdy drifted faintly on the breeze.

"You might find a personal hatred among these men, although I still can't see how murdering a prostitute is going to profit anyone at all," Carlisle resumed. "Still, you are probably dealing with a man who has some sexual aberration who, in the heat of the excitement, power, and money at stake, simply lost his head and his basic insanity tore through his usual control. Perhaps the woman mocked him, or belittled him in some way."

"Nobody against the railway?" Narraway asked without expecting anything more than another denial.

"Possibly someone with interests in another country," Carlisle said thoughtfully, pushing his hands deeper into his pockets as he walked. "French, Germans, and Belgians are bound to be affected by us having such a tremendous advantage. But we have it already — this would only be adding to it. Look at a map of the world. One of your men might have financial interests we don't know about, or be bribed, I suppose. That could almost rank as treason. But what could it have to do with the murder of a prostitute?"

"No idea," Narraway admitted honestly. The more he considered it, the more it seemed as if it must be a personal madness in one of the men, which pressure of some sort had exposed. He wished the murder could have been anywhere else, then it would have been the problem of the Metropolitan Police, and not Special Branch. "None of it makes any sense," he said. "What do you know about these men personally?"

"Very little," Carlisle replied with a grimace. "At least of the nature that would be of use in this. What an awful mess! As if the Prince's reputation were not dubious enough!"

"Who does know?" Narraway persisted. "Who will answer me honestly and ask no questions?"

"Lady Vespasia," Carlisle said without hesitation.

Narraway smiled. "You do not surprise

me. Thank you for your time."

Carlisle nodded. He knew better than to request that Narraway keep him informed. They turned and together walked back through the dappled shade as far as Great George Street.

Narraway returned to his office briefly and gave instructions regarding other matters. Pitt telephoned him from the Palace, giving Sadie's name and asking for as much information about her as possible.

Narraway dispatched two of his men to investigate, then set out to look for Lady Vespasia Cumming Gould.

It took him nearly four hours to finally speak to her. Vespasia had been the greatest beauty of her time, and even in old age she maintained the features, the grace, and the fire that had made her famous. She had added to them even greater courage and wisdom, curiosity, and passion for life.

She was not at home, but, knowing who Narraway was, her maid had informed him that her ladyship had gone to luncheon with her niece. However, afterward they would visit the exhibition of paintings in the National Gallery, and could no doubt be found there. Accordingly, Narraway walked from one room to another there, looking hopefully at every fashionable lady who was a little taller than average and carried herself with that perfect posture required when balancing a particularly heavy tiara on one's head.

The instant he saw her, he felt foolish for having wasted more than an instant looking at anyone else. She was wearing a simple street costume exquisitely cut in silk, of a soft shade of blue-gray, and a smaller hat than had recently been in vogue. The brim was higher, showing her face. It was less dramatic, except for the fact that it had a very fine veil, which not so much concealed as accentuated the beauty of her skin, the character and mystery of her eyes.

Beside her was a woman in her early thirties with a flawless fair complexion. She was wearing a delicate shade of water green, which, on a less animated person, might have been draining, but on her was most becoming. At the moment Narraway saw them she was laughing and describing some shape that amused her, outlining it with gloved hands. It was Charlotte Pitt's sister, Emily Radley. For a moment, Narraway was reminded of a warmth he had experienced only from the edges, as an onlooker, and he felt a surge of envy for Pitt, because he belonged.

Narraway thought of Pitt in the Palace,

finding it strange, overwhelming. He would certainly make errors in his social conduct and be embarrassed. His sense of morality would be offended. His illusions and even some of his loyalties might be broken, if this case forced him to learn more about the Prince than he had already. But Pitt knew what he believed, and why. And that was another thing Narraway envied in him.

He pushed the thoughts out of his mind and walked over to stand where Vespasia could see him.

"Good afternoon, Victor," she said with interest. "Emily, do you remember Mr. Narraway? My niece, Mrs. Radley."

"Good afternoon, Mr. Narraway," Emily said quietly. She was not quite beautiful, but the vitality in her appealed even more, and the arch of her brow, the line of her cheek reminded him again of Charlotte Pitt. "I hope you are well?"

"Good afternoon, Mrs. Radley," he replied. "I am very well, thank you, but unfortunately I have to ask Lady Vespasia's help with a confidential matter. I apologize for such an ill-mannered intrusion. I would avoid it if I could."

Emily hesitated, then recognized that she had no graceful alternative, even though her eyes betrayed a burning curiosity. "Of course." She gave him a dazzling smile. She turned to Vespasia. "I shall meet you at the carriage in . . . shall we say an hour?" And without waiting for a reply, with a swirl of skirts, she was gone.

"Your problem must be urgent." Vespasia took Narraway's arm and they moved slowly toward the next room. "Is it to do with Thomas?"

He heard the edge of anxiety in her voice. "Pitt is quite well," he said quickly. "But we are dealing with a case of such delicacy that I dare not mention it, except that it has to do with the Prince of Wales. I need your assistance."

"You have it. What may I do?" She did not raise her voice or alter her tone.

He knew it would disappoint her that it was merely information he wanted, and he regretted it. In the past she had involved herself in cases more daringly, and shown considerable flair. "There are several people I need to know more about than I can ask easily, and with the speed and discretion I require," he told her.

"I see." She looked away so he could not see her silver-gray eyes, or read the emotions in them.

"There has been a murder," he confided as they came into the next room. "The victim is a woman of the streets, but she was found in a residence where even her presence would cause a scandal, let alone her bloodied corpse in the linen cupboard."

Vespasia's silver eyebrows rose. "Indeed? How unfortunate. Who is it you suspect?"

"It has to be one of three men." He named them.

"I am surprised," she confessed.

"You think none of them capable?"

She smiled. "I think none of them foolish enough, which is not the same thing at all."

"What can you tell me of them, in the way of gossip, scandal, or anything else that may be of interest?"

"You mean of relevance," she corrected him. "I am quite capable of reading between the lines, Victor."

He was pleased that she should use his Christian name, and aware that it was ridiculous it should make such a difference to him. "What can you tell me?" he asked.

"I should be surprised if it is Julius Sorokine," she began thoughtfully, speaking almost under her breath. "He is a young man perhaps too handsome for his own good. Much has come to him easily, though not personal happiness, I think. He has not extended himself because he has had little need. He has no temper and not the kind of vanity that lashes out against denial. He is too lazy, too much on the periphery of life, nor has he so far the emotional energy necessary for violence." She looked a trifle sad as she said it, as if he had disappointed her.

If someone had asked her, would she have said the same of him: "too much on the periphery of life?" Refraining from violence not through self-mastery but through emotional indolence? He had loved, and betrayed, but it was a long time ago. As always, he had chosen duty over passion.

No, that was not true. Passion was far too strong a word for what he had felt. The choice had not torn his heart. He remembered it with a certain shame, but not agony.

Vespasia was watching him, waiting for his attention to return.

"And Marquand?" he prompted.

"It is possible," she conceded. "He is Julius's half-brother, elder by a year or two, and driven by a certain jealousy. Of course Julius married Cahoon Dunkeld's daughter, Wilhelmina. I believe she calls herself Minnie. A girl with a great talent to attract masculine admiration, which she exercises freely. What the unkind may call a troublemaker."

"And what would you call her, Lady Vespasia?" He concealed a very slight smile.

"An unhappy young woman who is having

a prolonged tantrum," she replied without hesitation. "Too much like her father."

"And what would you say of him?"

"You did not include him," she pointed out.

"Only because his whereabouts are accounted for."

"Perfectly capable of killing anyone," she said without hesitation. "But far too intelligent to do so. If he is guilty, I would say he lost his temper, which is considerable, and did so more by accident than design."

"You do not cut a woman's throat in the linen cupboard by accident."

Her eyes widened only very slightly. "No, that is true. Then I doubt it was Dunkeld. If you had told me he beat his wife, I should have believed you."

"Why?"

"Because he is a man who takes his possessions very seriously."

"I see. That leaves Hamilton Quase."

"A very civilized man," she observed.

"Too civilized for violence?"

"Certainly not! The most outwardly civilized are the most capable of appearing to be something different from reality. I am quite sure you know that as well as I do." There was a slight reproof in her voice.

"I apologize," he said sincerely.

"Thank you. If Mr. Quase were to have done such a thing, I believe he would have had a reason for it that seemed to him to be adequate. But he is a man who takes risks and will pay highly for what he wants."

"Really!" He had put Quase down as a man who dreamed rather than acted, finding most of his reality at the bottom of a bottle. "And what does he want?" he asked.

"A few years ago I should have said it was Liliane Forbes," she said. "Now, of course, I do not know. Perhaps it has not changed."

"He is married to her," he observed.

"There is more to possessing a woman than the legality of marriage, Victor," she corrected him. "Quase was very much in love with her, or else he would not have behaved as he did over her brother's death. A very messy affair. If Eden Forbes had lived, Liliane would very probably have married Julius Sorokine, and a great many things would be different."

Now he was genuinely interested. "Watson Forbes's son?"

"His only son."

"What happened to him?"

She frowned, her voice dropping even lower as they stood in front of a large, very ugly portrait of a woman. "The details are very unclear," she answered. "He died in

Africa, boat overturned in a river. Hippopotami, crocodiles, or something of the sort. Watson Forbes was shattered, as was Liliane. It was Hamilton Quase who dealt with the whole, very miserable matter. Kept it as discreet as possible, saw to the funeral and so on. Liliane had been in love with Julius, but after a decent period of mourning, she married Quase instead."

"Gratitude?" Narraway inquired. "And if Quase rose to the occasion, and Sorokine did not, perhaps she chose the better man?"

"Possibly."

"You don't think so?"

She smiled at him. "I think she paid a debt of gratitude, but that is only a supposition. I don't know."

"How do you know so much about it? Were you there?"

"In Africa? Good gracious, no. It holds no enchantment for me," she replied. "But I have an excellent friend, Zenobia Gunne, who has explored in all manner of places, including long stretches of the Congo and Zambezi rivers, certainly in much of Southern Africa. It was she who told me."

"Nobby Gunne," Narraway said with a smile, remembering a remarkable woman who was unafraid of lions, elephants, tsetse flies, or malaria, but still able to be cut to the quick by disloyalty and wounded by the suffering of others. "If she says that is what happened, then I will take it as so."

"It is of very little use, though, I fear," Vespasia said unhappily. "I know a little of the wives, but it is only trivial: matters of fashion and spite, who said what to whom, where love or dreams may have led. I cannot imagine that any of it was toward murder in a linen cupboard, no matter whose. It seems a preposterous story to me."

"It is preposterous," he agreed. "But regrettably true. Somerset Carlisle suggested that Watson Forbes was the greatest expert in the practicalities of the proposed railway, both diplomatically and with regard to engineering."

"After Cecil Rhodes, you mean?" she said, amusement touching her lips. "I imagine Mr. Rhodes, with his boundless ambition and love of Empire, will be a keen backer of this project?" She started to move on from the picture. "As Prime Minister of Cape Colony, it will be vastly in his interest. All British Africa will be open to him by land as well as by sea. He would be a better friend than enemy."

"I'm sure that is true," Narraway agreed, following her closely. "But I can't imagine any way in which he will be involved in this tragedy in London."

"I cannot see why anyone would be," Vespasia said unhappily. "I think you will find it is a madness that is quite personal and could as easily have happened anywhere else, once the passion that ignites it is disturbed."

They walked past a few more portraits, only glancing at the faces, then made their way to the entrance. They had been together almost an hour. He escorted her to her carriage where Emily was waiting. He thanked her both for the information and quite genuinely for the pleasure of her company, and he thanked Emily for her patience.

Half an hour later he alighted from a hansom cab in Lowndes Square to call upon Watson Forbes. He had already ascertained by telephone that he would be received.

The house was elegant, with all the marks of unobtrusive wealth, a man who is comfortable with his possessions and does not need to display them except for his own pleasure. The outer doors were of carved teak, oiled and gleaming. The parquet flooring in the hall was Indian hardwood in various shades of rich brown. The paintings were quiet: Dutch canal scenes, domestic interiors, light on water, a furled barge sail, a face in repose, a winter scene all blues and grays on the ice.

It was not until he was in Forbes's study that Narraway saw the paintings of grasslands with an elephant standing motionless in the heat and the strange, flat-topped acacia trees in the distance. There were many carved animals in ivory and semi-precious stone. One entire wall was lined with books, nearly all of them leather-bound. On the well-used desk was an ostrich egg and a box covered with what looked like crocodile skin.

Watson Forbes was a solid man with thick hair that had once been dark but was now paling almost to white, leaving black brows and a sun-darkened complexion. He had a long nose and a neat, chiseled mouth, which was surprisingly expressive. It was a powerful face, and highly individual. Narraway had heard that he was close to seventy, but he rose easily to his feet and came forward to greet the Special Branch man with interest.

"How do you do? You said in your conversation on the telephone — wonderful invention — that you need expert information on Africa. I know only parts of it, but whatever knowledge I have is at your disposal. Please," he gestured to include the several leather-covered chairs, inviting Narraway to take his pick. "What is it you wish to know?" He sat down in the chair opposite. "Whisky? Or do you prefer something more exotic? Brandy, perhaps? Or sherry?"

"Not yet, thank you," Narraway declined. "Do you know Cecil Rhodes?"

Forbes smiled. It lit his face, altering the severity of it, but the look in his dark eyes was guarded. "Certainly. One cannot do serious business in British Africa and not know him."

"And Cahoon Dunkeld?"

"Interesting you should mention them almost in the same breath," Forbes observed. "Coincidental, or not?" Now the amusement was in his eyes also.

"Of course not," Narraway answered. Forbes's intelligence was obvious; he would be a fool to try to dupe him. He needed Forbes's knowledge and perhaps also his judgment. He must not insult him, even unintentionally. "You see a likeness? Or a contrast?"

"Both," Forbes replied. "Dunkeld has the same ambition, something of the same ruthlessness, but far more charm. However, he started his African adventures later in his life than Rhodes, and he has no brothers to help him."

"But a gifted man?" Narraway pressed. "And able to gather about him others of talent, and to inspire loyalty in them?"

"Obedience," Forbes replied, choosing his

word carefully. His eyes never left Narraway's face.

"Well liked?"

Again he smiled. "No. Why do you ask? Is this to do with the plan for a Cape-to-Cairo railway?" Forbes was now studying him quite openly. His amusement was more marked, his eyes bright. "It's not a new dream, Mr. Narraway. It may be built, but it will be a far bigger undertaking than some of its proponents believe. Have you any knowledge of the terrain it will pass through? It is farther from Cape Town to Cairo than it is from New York across the great plains of America and the Rocky Mountains to the Pacific shores, and then back again. And the climate and terrains cross extremes of equatorial jungle, grassland, mountains, desert, waterless wastes you cannot imagine." He gestured with strong, square hands. "There are diseases, parasites, poisonous reptiles and insects, plagues of locusts, and the largest beasts on earth. Africa is another world, Mr. Narraway. It is nothing like Europe at all."

Narraway heard the emotion. Forbes's voice was thick, almost trembling, and there was a passion in his eyes.

"It has a great and terrible beauty," he went on, leaning forward a little. "See a bull elephant charge! It is the most magnificent beast in the world. And intelligent! Hear lions roar in the night. Or hyenas laugh. They sound human, but insane. It chills the blood. Have you heard about the drums? They send messages over hundreds of miles, one drummer to another, as we would use beacon fires. Only, of course, their messages are much more complicated, an entire language."

Narraway did not interrupt him.

"There are scores of kingdoms," Forbes went on urgently. "Boundaries that have nothing to do with the white man: Zulu, Mashona, Hutu, Masai, Kikuyu, and dozens more. And the Arabs still trade in slaves from the interior to the coasts. There are old wars and hatreds going back a thousand years that we know nothing about."

"Are you saying that it cannot succeed?" Narraway asked. He was both awed and disappointed. Did he want Africa tamed by the white man's railway? Did he want the British Empire spreading culture, commerce, and Christianity throughout? Or was it a better dream to leave its dark heart unconquered?

He surprised himself. He loved knowledge, acquired it, traded in it, and benefited from its power. There was a kind of safety in there being something still unknown, as if dreams and miracles could still happen. To know everything was to destroy the infinite possibilities of unreasoning hope.

Did he see some reflection of this in Watson Forbes's face also, even a certain humility? Or was that only what he imagined he saw?

"No," Forbes said softly. "It may succeed one day, but I think it will be a far longer undertaking than these men are prepared for. It will need greater courage and fortitude, and require greater wisdom than they yet have."

"You know the people who could do it?" Narraway dragged his mind back to his reason for coming here.

"Of course. Africa is larger than we who are used to England can imagine, but the white men there still know one another. There are few enough of them."

"Tell me what you know of them, honestly. I cannot tell you my reasons for needing to know, but they are real and urgent."

Forbes did not argue, and if he was troubled by curiosity, it did not show in his unusual face. "Where should I begin?" he asked.

"With Cahoon Dunkeld," Narraway answered. Dunkeld was the leader, by far the most dominant personality. If there was an ordinary human person behind this crime, then surely Dunkeld's will, his cruelty, or his mistake was at the heart of it. "Is there more to say of him? What do you know of his wife?"

"Elsa?" Forbes was surprised. "Nothing much. A woman with the possibility of beauty, but not the fire. In the end she is essentially boring."

"Is he bored with her?"

"Undoubtedly. But she has certain attributes that make her an excellent wife for him."

Narraway winced.

"His daughter is a completely different matter," Forbes continued, the slightest smile moving his lips. "She is passionate, handsome, and dangerous. I cannot think why she married Julius Sorokine, who is emotionally also a bore. He is very gifted in diplomacy, has great charm when he wishes to use it, but he is lazy. He could be immeasurably better than he is, and that is his tragedy."

"And his half-brother, Simnel Marquand?"

"Oh, Simnel. He is probably at the crown of his achievements. His financial abilities are superb. He understands money better than any other man I know."

"Is that all?" Narraway asked, remembering that Vespasia had said he envied his brother. Surely not for an ability he was too lazy to use?

"Quite possibly. But then that is all they will need from him for the railway." There was still a shred of humor in Forbes's face, but other emotions also: anger, regret, and also an immense power.

"And Hamilton Quase?" Narraway asked, dropping his voice without having meant to. He knew the relationship between the two men.

"My son-in-law?" Forbes's dark brows rose. "I am hardly impartial."

"I will set it against other people's opinions."

Forbes measured his words carefully this time. "He is a brilliant engineer, imaginative, technically highly skilled. Anyone proposing to build across an entire continent could do no better than to employ Hamilton."

"You are telling me of his professional skills. What of his character?"

"Loyal," Forbes said immediately. "Essentially fair, I believe. He will pay for what he wants. A hard man to read, very much out of the ordinary in his tastes, and perhaps in his dreams. He drinks too much. I am not betraying him in saying so. Anyone else will tell you the same."

Narraway remembered what Vespasia had said of Quase, and of his courage and discretion over Eden Forbes's death because he was in love with Liliane. And Liliane had wanted Julius Sorokine. It sounded as if her father's bargain with Quase had earned her the better man. Narraway hoped with considerable depth that she had acquired the wisdom to appreciate that also.

"Thank you," he said sincerely.

"Is it of any assistance to you?" Forbes inquired.

"I have no idea," Narraway confessed. "Do you believe they will succeed in building the railway, with the right backing?"

Forbes hesitated, his eyes flaring with sudden, intense feeling, masked again almost immediately. "The Queen will approve it," he said softly. "The risk will be high, in the short term, but in the medium term — say for the next four or five decades — it will be the making of men, perhaps of nations."

Narraway watched him carefully, noting the minutest shadows of his face. "And the long term?" he asked. "After the next half-century, as you judge it?"

"The future of Africa and its people?" He dropped his guard. "That will be in our hands. There will be good men who will want to teach Africa, bring it out of darkness — as they see it. God only knows if they will see it clearly." His mouth twisted a little. "And on the heels of the good men will come the traders and the opportunists, the builders, miners, explorers. Then the farmers and settlers, scores, hundreds of white men trying to turn Africa into the English suburbs, but with more sun. Some will be teachers and doctors. Most will not."

Narraway waited, knowing Forbes would add more.

"Good and bad," Forbes said, tightening his lips. "But our way, not the Africans' way."

Narraway was disturbed by the thought. "Is it not inevitable? We cannot undiscover Africa," he pointed out, but it was as if he were speaking of something already broken.

"Yes, it probably is," Forbes said flatly. "And I suppose if anyone is going to exploit it, it might as well be Great Britain. We are good at it. God knows, we've had enough experience. But I didn't step back from it for that reason. It is difficult living in harsh climates far from home. I want adventure of the mind now rather than of the body. Cahoon Dunkeld is as good a man for this as you can get. I'm perfectly happy for him to do it."

"And Sorokine, Quase, and Marquand?"

"Probably the best choices available to him."

"Why? Best for the job, or because Sorokine is his son-in-law, Marquand is Sorokine's half-brother, and Quase your son-in-law?"

Forbes flashed him a sudden smile. "I don't doubt that will have some part in it. One trusts the judgment of those whom one knows, or at least has a perception of their vulnerabilities. Do you fear that the railway is under threat of some kind of sabotage, even this early?"

"If it were, whom would you suspect?" Narraway asked him.

"Ah. Is that what you really want?" Forbes eased back in his chair a little.

"And if I do?"

"If there is another group of men as appropriately gifted, I am not aware of it. If you have any real basis for fear, then you should look to some of the other countries with major interests in Africa. You might begin with Belgium. Congo Free State is vast, and rich in minerals. King Leopold has boundless ambition there." He made a steeple of his fingers. "The other major participant is Germany. Any railway would have to cross the territory of one of them, or acquire a line of passage between the two. But I assume

213

you can read a map as well as I can?"

"I've looked at it, certainly."

"That may be where Sorokine's skills come in. He is a diplomat with many connections and far more intelligence than his somewhat casual attitude suggests."

"Thank you. You have been most courteous." Narraway rose to his feet.

"A suitably equivocal remark." Forbes rose also. "If there is anything else I can do, don't hesitate to call again."

Narraway returned to the Palace and found Pitt in the room they had given him, the windows wide open and the warm evening air blowing in. He was eating a supper of cold roast beef sandwiches. Narraway was instantly struck by how tired he looked. He seemed to have none of his usual energy.

"Anything?" Pitt asked with his mouth full, before Narraway had even closed the door.

"Interesting," Narraway replied, walking over and sitting in the other chair. The sandwiches looked good: fresh bread and plenty of meat. He realized he had not eaten all day. Still, these were Pitt's, not his, and superior rank did not excuse ill manners. "Not certain if it means much. How about you?"

"Gracie's about the only one who has achieved anything," Pitt said ruefully. "And it doesn't seem to mean much either. You've got men inquiring about Sadie?"

"Yes. Too soon to expect anything yet."

"I know. I'm not sure if it matters anymore. Probably not."

Narraway looked around for the bell. "Do you think they'd fetch me some?" He eyed the sandwiches.

"Have some of these," Pitt offered. "But there's no more cider. Maybe you'd prefer ale anyway?"

"Cider's fine, but I'll send for some myself, thank you," Narraway answered, and rose to pull the bell rope. "What did Gracie learn?" He was disappointed. He had had an intense and perhaps unreasonable hope that Pitt would either have learned or deduced something profound. His skill at solving complicated murders was one Narraway had come to value, and he had no intention of allowing the Metropolitan Police to have Pitt back again. He would use his influence, plead the safety of the realm from anarchy or foreign subversion, whatever it required to keep him.

He was placing pressure on Pitt to succeed now, and he was aware of it. It was harsh, but they could not afford to fail. Was he asking too much?

Pitt finished his sandwich before answering. No one hurried to the summons of the bell, but then they knew whose room it was, and no doubt guests took precedence.

"Two badly bloodstained sheets in one of the baskets in the laundry," Pitt answered, watching him.

Narraway was baffled. Pitt was stating the obvious. Was he overwhelmed by where he was? "Where else would you expect to find them?" he asked. "I imagine most of the sheets from the linen cupboard are there. At least all they think they can save."

"They had the Queen's monogram on them." Pitt looked at him with a frown, his eyes puzzled. "Not the Palace, the Queen personally. And they had been slept on. They were crumpled and the blood was smeared."

"God Almighty, Pitt!" Narraway exclaimed. "What are you saying? The Queen's at Osborne."

"I know that," Pitt replied steadily. "I've been thinking about it ever since Gracie showed them to me, and I don't know what it is I'm saying. Somebody used the Queen's sheets on a bed that was slept in, or at any rate used, if you prefer a more exact term, and somebody bled on them, very heavily."

Narraway's mind raced. "Then she can't have been stabbed in the linen cupboard! She was killed somewhere else, and put there afterward. That makes some sense. Why would she have gone willingly to the cupboard anyway? Whoever killed her put her in a place he thought would not incriminate him. We should have realized that before."

"Bodies don't bleed a lot after they're dead," Pitt pointed out. "Heart stops."

"But it doesn't stop instantly. There could still be blood," Narraway argued.

"Nothing like as much as we found in the cupboard. She must have been alive when she was put in there." Pitt's face was twisted with pity and an anger Narraway had rarely seen in him, and was the more moving for that.

"Ripped her belly open in the bed, then carried her naked along the corridor and slashed her across the throat, then left her to bleed to death in the cupboard," Narraway said very quietly. "By the way, have we found her clothes yet?"

"No," Pitt replied.

Narraway shivered. "What in God's name are we dealing with, Pitt?"

There was a knock on the door.

"Come in!" Narraway said savagely.

The door opened and Gracie's diminutive figure stood on the threshold. She looked different and even smaller in

Palace uniform.

"Come in," Narraway repeated, more civilly this time. "Can you get me a supper like Pitt's, roast beef sandwich and a glass of cider?"

"I'll ask Cook, sir," Gracie said, closing the door behind her. "But I come because one o' the maids found the missing knife." She spoke to Pitt, not Narraway. "An' it's got blood on it, sir. Even a couple of 'airs, little ones." She colored faintly. She could not bring herself to be more exact than that.

"Where?" Pitt stared at her. "Where did they find it? Who did?"

"Ada found it. In the linen cupboard, sir."

"But we searched it!" Pitt protested. "There was no knife there!"

"I know that, sir," she agreed. "Someone gone an' put it there, jus' terday. We got someone 'ere in this palace 'oo's very wicked. Mr. Tyndale's got the knife, sir. I'll go an' get yer some sandwiches, an' a glass o' cider." She turned round and went out, whisking her skirt, which was at least two inches too long for her, leaving Pitt and Narraway staring at each other.

CHAPTER SIX

Elsa sat in front of her bedroom mirror, stiff and unhappy. Everyone was afraid. On the day the body was discovered they had been so shocked they had taken a little while to absorb the horror of what had happened, but with the second day the reality of it was far more powerful. The gangling policeman with his overstuffed pockets was asking questions. They were always courteous; questions that only afterward did you realize how intrusive they had been.

It seemed absurd, like something senseless out of a nightmare where none of the pieces fit, but at last they were realizing that it had to have been one of them who had killed the woman. No one dared say it. They had talked about all kinds of things, making remarks no one listened to, and gossip in which, for once, no one was interested.

She stared at her reflection in the glass. It was pale and familiar, horribly ordinary.

It was impossible to sleep properly, but even the little rest they had had meant they had woken with a far more painful clarity. They were trapped here until the policeman found a solution, and one of them was destroyed forever. Or perhaps they would all be. How did you survive the fact that someone you knew, perhaps loved, could kill like that? Was that who they had always been underneath? You had just been too stupid, too insensitive to have seen it?

She was in love with Julius. Or she was in love with the idea of love, the hunger for it that was a gnawing ache inside her, as if she were being eaten from within. She didn't know Julius, not really.

She shuddered as Bartle laid out her gown for the evening. It was exquisite: the sort of smoky blue that most flattered her cool coloring, and was trimmed with black lace. Minnie could get away with the hot scarlets and appear wild and brave. Elsa would only look like a failed imitation. Cahoon had told her as much. He had often compared her to Minnie — never to her advantage. This was in the shades of dusk, or the twilight sea that she had once felt to be romantic. Now she simply found it drab.

She obeyed patiently as Bartle assisted her into first the chemise, then the petticoats, and finally the gown itself, then she stood still while it was laced up as tightly as she could accommodate without actual discomfort. It was wide at the shoulder with the usual exaggerations of fashion, and low at the bosom. It had a sweeping fall of silk down the front, and pale ruches at the hem. The bustle behind was very slight but extraordinarily flattering. The color made her skin look flawless, like alabaster, and her eyes a darker blue than they really were.

Then she sat again, motionless while Bartle dressed her hair. It was long and thick, dark brown with warmer lights in it. The jewels that Cahoon was so proud of would come last.

It was preposterous to be preparing for dinner when that woman had been hacked to death, and they could not escape the fact that one of the men at the table with them had done it. But neither could they put off the occasion without arousing a suspicion they could not afford. The Prince was dining with them, and of course the Princess. Lord Taunton was the guest. He was a financier Simnel had been courting, who had specific interests in Africa. His support would be of great importance, possibly even necessity. He had never married, so he would bring as his companion his younger sister, Lady Parr, who was recently widowed. Her husband had left her with a fortune of her own, and she was handsome in a rather obvious way. She certainly had admirers — Cahoon among them. Elsa had seen the flash of hunger in his eyes, the way he had once looked at her.

The evening would require great fortitude and the sort of self-mastery that even the strongest woman would find taxing. They would all have to hide their fears. There must be no frayed tempers, no hint of anxiety. Taunton must believe that all was well, that they were full of optimism and faith in the success of the new and marvelous venture.

"There you are, Miss Elsa," Bartle said, clasping the sapphire necklace around her throat. "You look lovely."

Elsa regarded her reflection. She was tired and too pale, but there was nothing she could do about it. Pinching her cheeks would bring a little color, but only for a very short time. It seemed a pretense not worth making.

She thanked Bartle and sent her to inform Cahoon that she was ready.

A moment later she heard the door close and saw his reflection in the glass. He examined her critically, but seemed satisfied. He said nothing, and they went down the stairs together in silence.

Olga and Simnel were already waiting, standing in the yellow sitting room with its illusion of sunlight, two or three yards apart from each other. She wore a gown of dark green, darker than the emeralds at her ears and throat. It was hard and too cold for her. It leached from her skin what little color there was, and its lightless depth made her look even more angular. Her lady's maid should have told her so. Perhaps she had, and been ignored. There was not the warmth or the softness about her that one would wish to see in a woman.

She turned as Elsa and Cahoon came in and acknowledged them with nervous politeness. "Do you know Lady Parr?" she asked Elsa.

"I have met her on several occasions," Elsa replied, realizing as she spoke how much she did not like Amelia Parr. She had no idea why. It was unfair and unreasonable. "She is very pleasant," she lied. She felt Cahoon glance at her and knew that her face betrayed her.

"She is said to be very interesting," Olga continued. "I hope, I must admit. I would find it hard to think of anything to say this evening."

No one needed to ask her to clarify what

she meant.

Hamilton and Liliane came in. He appeared to have already drunk a considerable amount of whisky. There was too much color in his face and a mild, slightly glazed look in his eyes. Liliane kept glancing at him as if to reassure herself that he was all right. She herself looked superb. Her shining amber hair and gold-brown eyes were richly complemented by the bronze of her gown, trimmed with elaborate black velvet ribbons. She made Elsa feel as dowdy as a moment before she had considered Olga to be. To judge from the appreciation in Cahoon's face, he was of the same opinion.

More words of apprehension and encouragement were exchanged, then the door opened again and Minnie swept in. She was vivid as a flame in hot scarlet, her dark hair piled gorgeously on her head, adding to her height. Her skin was flushed, and her bosom a good deal more accentuated than Elsa would have dared to copy, although she was easily as well endowed by nature. But curves had little to do with Minnie's allure; it lay in her vitality, the challenge given by the boldness of her stare, the grace with which she moved. There was a constant air of risk and bravado about her as if she were always on the edge of something exciting.

"Good evening," Olga said quietly. No one answered her.

Minnie smiled, ignoring Julius, two steps behind her. "Ready to sail into the attack?" she said brightly. "Are you ready to be charming to Lady Parr?" she asked Cahoon, then, before he could answer, she turned to Elsa. "Or perhaps you had better do that. It will confound her completely, especially after your last encounter." She gave a small, meaningful smile.

Elsa knew exactly what she was referring to, and felt the heat burn up her cheeks, but she had no defense. She ached to be able to belittle Minnie, just once to tear that glowing confidence to pieces. She might despise herself afterward, but it would be wonderful to know she could do it.

"And Papa can bewilder the Princess of Wales, while Simnel and the Prince talk to Lord Taunton," Minnie went on. "It really doesn't matter what you say to the Princess. She will pretend to be interested, and not hear a word of it." She shot a withering glance at her husband. "Perhaps we should let Julius talk to her?"

The innuendo was so sharp for a moment no one responded.

Elsa felt fury rise up inside her. Cahoon had often told her she should remain silent at such moments, but the words rose to her lips. "A good idea," she agreed sharply. "He knows how to conduct himself and exercise loyalty and good manners. He will not embarrass her by showing off."

"Of course not!" Minnie retorted instantly. "He will be utterly predictable."

"To whom?" Elsa snapped back. "You couldn't predict rain with a thunderstorm."

Minnie looked her up and down, a faint curl on her lip. "If it is a cold, gray day and has rained all morning, I can predict that it will rain all afternoon!" she said with arched eyebrows and a cool, pitying look at Elsa's gown.

Elsa longed for something crushing to say, something that would hurt Minnie just as much, but nothing came. There were times when what she felt for Minnie was close to hatred.

Julius was smiling. Was it to hide pain, or had he simply not understood her implication? Or was that what he did to conceal embarrassment? "Have you ever seen a dry lightning storm?" he inquired of nobody in particular. "You get them sometimes in summer. Spectacular, and rather dangerous. In Africa they can set the grassland alight and the fires consume thousands of acres."

"How destructive," Olga murmured uncomfortably.

"Yes," he agreed. "But the new growth afterward is marvelous. There are some plants whose seeds only germinate in the extreme heat." He looked very quickly at Elsa, his eyes soft for an instant, then away again. Or did she imagine it?

Minnie was temporarily confused, aware she had been bettered, but not certain how it had happened. She smiled dazzlingly at Simnel. "I think storms can be rather fun, don't you?"

He was uncomfortable, as if somehow guilty, but he could not drag his gaze from her.

Olga moved even farther away from him, her face almost colorless. Her body was all angles, as if she might be clumsy enough to knock over ornaments balanced on the side tables. Had she any idea how naked her feelings were?

Elsa looked at Julius and saw the pity in his face. For an instant it was the most beautiful thing she knew. He was utterly different from Cahoon. Cahoon had no patience with the weak. Mercy was an impediment to the march of progress. She had heard him say so many times, and inside herself she had longed to protest. What about the beautiful, the funny, the kind, which might also be vulnerable?

She was afraid of Cahoon. She knew it with a sort of sickness that made the thought of eating repulsive. How could she get through the evening without fumbling, dropping knives and spoons, making stupid remarks because her mind was on the woman in the cupboard, and the knowledge that one of these men had killed her? Was it Simnel, because he lusted after Minnie and loathed himself because he could not control it? Did he imagine that killing some poor woman who awoke the same in him would make anything better? Or Hamilton Quase, for God knew what reason? Because he was drunk and frightened and suddenly lost all sense? Perhaps the woman had laughed at him. Elsa tried to imagine it. It was pathetic and disgusting. She hoped profoundly that that was not true. She refused to think it could be Julius. That was unbearable. What a pity it could not have been Cahoon.

What a terrible thought! How could she have allowed it into her mind? She had lain in his arms. Once she had even thought she loved him, imagined awakening in him a tenderness toward her he had felt for no other person in his life.

How naïve! The only person he had ever loved was Minnie, and even that was equivocal. She was too like him, too strong to be controlled, and he resented that.

The footman announced that dinner was about to be served. They all trooped after him from the guest wing to the magnificent state dining room hung with portraits of past members of the royal family, framed in ornate gold. It was far too big for such a gathering and Elsa wondered why the Prince of Wales had chosen it. The red curtains and carpet warmed the almost cathedral-like vault of the pale golden walls and domed and fretted ceiling. Still it dwarfed them, and the table seemed lost in its enormity. The chandeliers glittered; the light on the silver and crystal was blinding. The white mantel and white tablecloth were as virgin as snow. The scent of lilies on the table reminded her of a hothouse. Everywhere there were more footmen in livery, gold buttons gleaming, white gloves immaculate.

The Prince and Princess of Wales welcomed them. She looked magnificent in cream and gold and blue, blazing with diamonds. She was a beautiful woman, with classic features; calm, remote, and slightly bemused.

Elsa curtsied and smiled, and wondered how much the Princess was aware of anything going on around her. It must be a purgatory to be deaf, never knowing quite what was happening, like seeing everything through thick glass. See but never hear, know but don't touch, never quite understand. How often do people get frustrated and simply not bother trying to communicate anymore?

Did she even know that there had been a murder? Probably not. Perhaps she always lived on the edge of everything.

Lord Taunton and Lady Parr were shown in and presented, then introduced to everyone else. She was dressed in plum-colored silk. It was very rich and complimented her skin, though it clashed hideously with Minnie's scarlet. It amused Cahoon. Elsa could see it in his face.

Dinner was announced and they went to the table in exact order of precedence, the Princess of Wales on Lord Taunton's arm, followed by Elsa and Cahoon. She saw the flash of discontent in his eyes. He would like to have been in Taunton's place, but he had no title, no status except that of money, and all the money in the world counted for nothing here.

Next came Hamilton and Liliane, Simnel as elder brother, with Olga, then Julius with Minnie, and lastly the Prince of Wales with Lady Parr.

The first course of julienne soup was served, or alternatively fillet of turbot and Dutch sauce, or red mullet. Elsa ate very sparingly. She knew there would be entrées of meat or fowl, then a third course of heavier meat, possibly including game, maybe venison at this time of year. Then there would be a fourth course, probably some kind of pastry dish — fruit pies, tarts, custards — and lastly a dessert of grapes or other fresh fruit, and after the meal, cheese.

It would drag on for hours before the ladies would withdraw and the gentlemen pass the port and cigars. The gentlemen would talk of Africa and the railway; the ladies, if they spoke at all, would simply gossip.

If the gentlemen rejoined them, Lady Parr would flirt with Cahoon, and the Prince. Minnie would flirt with Simnel, and with the Prince, of course. Liliane would be clumsy; Olga would grow more and more wretched. Elsa would try to think of something to say, and end up being boring, and utterly predictable, as Minnie had said so damningly of Julius.

And yet one of them had murdered the woman in the cupboard.

The footman poured white wine for her.

Was it possible that whoever it was, his wife

really had no idea? How could you live with a man, take his name, lie in his bed, and know so little of him? Nothing that really mattered, such as what he believed, what frightened him or what he longed for. But then no one else knew what she really cared about either, only the trivial things she said.

She must be careful not to drink the wine and eat too little. She would become tipsy. There was nothing uglier than a drunken woman: loud, indiscreet, desperately embarrassing.

Did one refuse to know what one's husband was really like because it would be unbearable? One lived on dreams. Of what? Not wealth, certainly not fame or extraordinary beauty. Not power. What power did a woman have except to influence others because of her example? Dreams of being loved, by someone you could both love and trust in return. Someone you admired, who could make you laugh, make you feel as if the world were better, brighter, and wiser because you were in it. Someone you liked?

Lord Taunton was speaking to her. She replied politely, meaninglessly. The fish was served, and curried lobster or fricandeau brought in, and of course more wine.

If you could not have love, then perhaps the other great need was to do something of value. Many people looking at this glittering table with its burden of food, its women dressed in silks and jewels, its beauty, comfort, and wealth would envy everyone here. The men Elsa could understand — they were all excited, faces eager, planning and dreaming of a railway that would stretch the length of a continent, seven thousand miles of it. It would change the Empire, and the world. Probably in centuries to come it would be regarded as one of the wonders of human achievement.

But what did she do? She had no children. She had married too late for that. She wanted for nothing material. She was fed, clothed, and housed. She had health and the respect of others, because she was Cahoon's wife. She had contributed nothing whatever.

She stared around the table and considered if there was anyone here whose life she really affected. Was anyone wiser, braver, or kinder because of her? She did not need to ask the question; the answer was already there. It would never have risen to her mind if there were anything at all to affirm it.

Minnie was laughing. She was as vivid as the flame-colored silk of her dress. The air around her seemed warm. Was Julius really in love with her, and his indifference was only a pretense, a shield to hide the hunger inside him for her to love him as much?

Elsa felt so sick she could hardly swallow, and the thought of another mouthful nearly made her gag. Perhaps Minnie was only flirting with Simnel in order to make Julius jealous. Was it a game between them?

How much would Elsa care if Cahoon flirted with someone? Not at all, except for the wound to her self-esteem because he so openly preferred someone else. He was talking now about timber for railway ties and steel for the rails themselves. He was speaking to Lord Taunton, but his eyes kept straying to Lady Parr. Was that a courtesy to give her the illusion of being included? No. He was smiling at her, his eyes warm. Elsa knew that look. So, apparently, did Amelia Parr, from the satisfaction in her face.

Why did one love one man and not another? Was there really anything noble or beautiful in Julius that was not in Cahoon, or did she imagine it was because she wanted there to be? She tried to think back to every time they had spoken, his visits to her home in company with Minnie. What had he said or done that had captivated her, made her see in him a sensitivity, an impression of tenderness, of strength to do something better than seek his own profit?

He was talking to Lord Taunton now. Simnel was watching him, waiting for the moment to interrupt. Under the assumed courtesy there was an anger inside him. His hand was clenched on his knife and he ignored the lobster on his plate.

"The biggest difficulty may be the Congo," Julius was saying. "King Leopold has dreams of extending Belgian dominion in Africa. The price he will ask for passage could be enormous."

"For heaven's sake, Julius!" Simnel said impatiently. "The railway will benefit all Africa. And if Leopold doesn't grant access to it, then go through German East Africa. They're far more reasonable. You talk as if Leopold were the only one we could deal with. Do you expect everything to drop in your lap for nothing?" There was a light of bitterness in his eyes and his shoulders were stiff under the black fabric of his jacket.

"I don't expect it for nothing, Simnel," Julius replied, emotion hard in his voice also, as if this were not a new argument, merely the resumption of an old one in a different form. "But there are prices that are fair to pay, and some that are too high for the value you receive."

"You deal with the diplomacy," Simnel told him. "Leave the finance to me, or to Lord Taunton. You were never any good with money." He seemed about to add something more, but bit it back.

"I was referring to diplomatic price," Julius replied. He sounded tired, as if the whole project were too heavy, too much trouble, and something in him was disillusioned by it.

Simnel was obviously controlling his temper with difficulty. Elsa thought that if they had been alone there would have been a blazing quarrel, Simnel attacking and Julius defending himself, perhaps inadequately. Was that a lack of courage? Cahoon, for all his faults, had never been a coward. She pushed the plate away from her, only an inch or two — there was nowhere else to place it.

The footmen cleared away the course and brought the next: roast saddle of mutton, haunch of venison, or boiled capon and oysters, all accompanied by vegetables.

Cahoon was talking to Lady Parr. Elsa thought how charming he could be, how intense his power and intelligence. She remembered falling in love with him and being so excited, so flattered when he asked her to marry him. Would her marriage have become just as hollow if it had been to Julius instead? Did he talk to Minnie, trust her, share his ideas or his dreams with her, make her laugh, allow her into his disappointments or his pain?

She picked at the boiled capon on the plate and looked across at Minnie. Simnel was staring at her, but she was looking at her father, frowning, as if something puzzled her and she were trying in vain to identify it.

At the other end of the table Liliane was laughing. It looked so easy. She was very beautiful with those amazing gold-brown eyes. Only because Elsa knew her did she hear the edge to her voice, and see how often her glance strayed to Hamilton, who was allowing the footman to refill his glass too often and beginning to look even more glazed. If he must drink so much, he should eat more. Maybe someone was going to have to help him later in order to prevent an embarrassment when he tried to stand up. It would be humiliating, impossible to pretend one had not seen.

There was another burst of laughter. Under cover of its sound Cahoon glared across the table at her. "Do your duty!" he mouthed angrily. "Don't be so weak!"

She felt the color burn in her cheeks. The charge was true. She waited until she had heard enough of Lady Parr's conversation to join in, then did so with concentrated good manners. She did not like the woman at all. Her face was handsome, but coarse; her lower lip was too full. The very effort of addressing her with enthusiasm took her entire concentration. They spoke of art, of the recent regatta at Henley, of mutual acquaintances, safe things of no importance to either of them.

Yet another course was served, this time roast grouse and bread sauce, vol-au-vent of greengages, fruit jelly, raspberry cream, custards, and fig pudding, and naturally more wine.

After it came dessert. The gentlemen did not care for it and the ladies had already eaten more than was comfortable. Elsa was watching to see the Princess of Wales nod very slightly to Lady Parr to indicate that it was time for the ladies to withdraw.

Elsa was tired with the effort of pretense, and she saw the same moment of surrender, and the lift of the head and forced smile again in Olga.

Minnie swept by, her skirt swirling, her pale shoulders smooth, skin gleaming against the scarlet silk. She was twice as alive as any of them, watching, listening to everything as if not a gesture would pass by her unnoticed. She seemed to be filled with an insatiable curiosity that excited not only her mind but her emotions. In a hideous instant Elsa wondered if Minnie actually knew what had happened to the woman in the cupboard, and who had done it. Then she dismissed the idea as absurd. It was just Minnie showing off, being the center of attention as usual.

Olga straightened her shoulders and followed after her, but there was no swagger to her walk and she did not look to either side of her, as if just for the moment she could not bear to meet anyone's eyes.

Liliane glanced back before the drawing room door closed. Elsa thought she was taking one more glance at Hamilton to reassure herself that he was still upright, or even catch his eye and warn him. Then Elsa realized it was at Julius that Liliane was looking, and there was anger in her face, just for a moment, and an unanswered pain, as if he had denied her something.

Elsa's head was spinning. Lady Parr was saying something and she had no idea what it was. Liliane and Julius had been in Africa at the same time, before either of them were married. It had been at the same time as Eden Forbes had died.

They took their seats, all watching the Princess of Wales. Elsa was invited to sit next to her. It was going to be hard work, but for some reason the Princess seemed to wish her to.

"Your husband is a very commanding man," the Princess observed conversationally, but she was watching Elsa's face as she spoke. Perhaps that was how she guessed at people's replies: She read the emotion when she could not distinguish the words.

Elsa smiled. "Yes, he is, ma'am." She inclined her head in agreement. "And he cares passionately about this project." She kept her sentences short.

"Of course," Alexandra said with humor in her voice. "It has much to offer."

Did she mean to Africa, to the Empire, or to Cahoon personally? Had she read in his face how hungry he was for recognition, a seat in the House of Lords, and all the social honor that that would bring him? She must be used to being courted for her position, not for herself. For that matter, had she any idea how many women the Prince flirted with, touched intimately, even slept with? Or did she refuse to look because it was unbearable?

How much would Elsa be wounded in mind and heart if she knew Cahoon had made love to Lady Parr? Not much; only revolted if he came back to her afterward. And if she were honest, she thought perhaps he would not. That was a strange kind of rejection too, a sort of loneliness half wanted, half painful.

Alexandra was asking something again. Elsa thought how difficult it must be always having to be the one to initiate every conversation, but one did not speak to royalty until they spoke first. She could not help, much as she wished to.

"You will miss your husband when they begin to build," Alexandra went on. "Or will you go to Africa yourself?"

"I don't yet know, ma'am," Elsa replied.

"I hear Africa is very beautiful," Alexandra continued.

Elsa must make an effort. She could see the look of open contempt on Minnie's face.

"You should go," Minnie said suddenly. "It would give you something to talk about. It is such a bore to have nothing whatever to say." She knew that with her face turned toward Elsa, Alexandra would not hear her.

"Frightful," Elsa said tartly. "Especially to those who insist upon saying it just the same."

Alexandra turned to look at Minnie in time to see her face flame red. She seemed to understand as well as if she had heard. "It seems a shame to miss an adventure," she said quietly.

"She has nothing to keep her at home," Minnie added. She did not say that Elsa was childless, but it was implied. Minnie herself was childless, but still young enough to change that.

"I imagine you will be going," Olga said suddenly to Minnie. "You will certainly want to follow the men!"

Minnie arched her eyebrows. "I beg your pardon?" she replied icily, but there was a hot flush in her cheeks still.

Lady Parr's face flickered with amusement.

"Do you wish me to repeat it more loudly?" Olga inquired.

At home Minnie would have stormed out, as she had an impulsive temper like her father's. Here, she was forced to remain.

"I imagine it will be necessary to begin in both Cairo and Cape Town," Alexandra murmured, as if she had heard none of the last exchange. "You know Cape Town, do you not, Mrs. Quase?"

"I have a slight acquaintance, ma'am," Liliane answered. "I'm afraid I don't know Cairo at all."

"I thought you knew Cape Town quite well." Minnie looked puzzled. "Papa said you had lived there. Was he mistaken?"

Liliane faced her squarely. "He probably told you that my brother died there," she replied, her voice trembling so slightly it was barely discernible. "Or perhaps it was your husband who told you. He was in the area at the time."

"Julius never tells me anything," Minnie replied. "But then I dare say you know that. You knew him before I did." She frowned. "Although it does seem odd that he should not have mentioned it at all."

"Perhaps you were simply not listening?" Elsa suggested.

"I suppose he told you?" Minnie retorted. "You are always listening. I don't know what you expect to hear. Or perhaps it doesn't matter, just so long as it is something."

Elsa looked at her gravely. "I am sure you would like to reconsider that remark," she observed. "You cannot have meant it." She allowed her gaze to wander to Alexandra, then away again quickly.

Suddenly Minnie understood and the blush spread from her cheeks down her neck to her bosom, but there was of course no elegant way for her to explain that she had meant Elsa's vanity, not the Princess's deafness.

For the first time in the evening, Olga laughed. It was a rich, extraordinarily pleasant sound, more attractive than Minnie's higher, louder voice.

There was another half hour of chatter,

gossip, polite nothingness, before the gentlemen rejoined them. Cahoon was in charge, talking so earnestly with the Prince it seemed an effort for them to even acknowledge the ladies. They returned almost immediately to their conversation.

Simnel and Lord Taunton were obviously discussing finance, the language of which was sufficiently esoteric, and therefore they had no need to be particularly discreet. Hamilton came in last, walking so close to Julius it was not difficult to guess that Julius was both steering him and preventing him from falling over.

Liliane saw them and started to rise, then sank back again, biting her lip. To have gone to him would have made the situation even more apparent. She sat silently, her face tense, avoiding everyone's eyes.

"I feel we are a great step closer," Cahoon said with a smile. He looked at Taunton. "We have certainly received both support and excellent advice. I look forward to being in Africa again. I can almost feel the sun on my skin, the heat, the dust, the smell of animals." He looked at Lady Parr and then at Alexandra. "Africa is unlike any other place on earth, ma'am. It is almost as if one were carried back to the dawn of creation, when everything was new and barely finished.

There is an energy to it that stirs the blood and fires the brain." This last was to Lady Parr only. "You would love it!"

She smiled at him, the vision of it lighting her eyes. "I will." It sounded more like a promise than a mere remark.

Elsa caught Alexandra's eye, but neither of them spoke. Perhaps such understanding was better without words.

"It's not all . . . glamour." Hamilton spoke with a slight slur. "It's also dirty and as hot as the stones of hell. Except, of course, when it's wet. Then it's more like being boiled alive."

"I dare say we wouldn't go into the jungle," Olga filled the silence that followed. She turned to Liliane. "Isn't Cape Town very pleasant?"

"The climate is most agreeable," Liliane replied, looking from Olga to Hamilton and back again. "I should rather like to see Cairo. Wouldn't you, Julius?"

"Julius doesn't care about any of them," Simnel put in before Julius could reply. "He'll probably be riding around the capitals of Europe being charming, eating the best food, drinking the best wine, and in no danger of getting dirt on his boots, never mind fever or snakebite or charged by a bull elephant. But he won't see a million stars across the sky, or hear lions roar in the night." He said it with a smile, but there was anger behind the smoothness of his voice.

"Most of the banks are in London, Zurich, and Berlin," Julius pointed out. "Your boots shouldn't suffer too much there. Or your appetite. Perhaps there are some good banks in Rome, or Milan? Lombardy has always been good for money also. And Italian food is marvelous. Their boots are pretty good as well."

"I'll accept your advice; you always have only the best," Simnel replied. There was something in his face that suggested his remark covered far more than the subject at hand.

Julius turned away.

Cahoon looked at Lady Parr. "Of course, Africa is dangerous. Some fearful things happen there. But then they happen in London also. Every place that man ventures has its darkness."

Liliane was staring at him, her eyes unmoving. Elsa had stared at spiders in the washbasin with just that feeling inside her. What you fear may be hideous, but at least if you watch it, you will know when it jumps.

"I never imagined Africa being steeped in misery and exploitation, degraded, as parts of London are," Lady Parr said to Cahoon.

"Surely it is, as you say, more primal, less tired and corrupted?"

Cahoon looked across at Hamilton, who was slumped a little crookedly in his chair. "What do you think, Quase? You have spent more time in Africa than any of us."

Hamilton opened his eyes wider, and with something of an effort he focused on him. "I think there are barbarians everywhere," he answered, enunciating his words with exaggerated care. "It's just that the veneer is thicker in some places than others."

"Of course it's different from Europe," Liliane said quickly. "That doesn't really mean anything."

Lady Parr looked at her with surprise, waiting for an explanation. When she realized she was not going to receive one, her gaze returned to Cahoon.

"What makes you say that, Hamilton?" Cahoon asked curiously, his expression innocent in a way Elsa knew was false. What was he looking for? Hamilton was drunk, his face crumpled with pain, and Liliane was obviously frightened for him. Why? What had happened in Africa? Something that was still an open wound, a danger even now? No. It must simply be that Liliane's brother had died in Africa. Elsa wished she could stop Cahoon's cruel probing into the matter. But Cahoon had never shrunk from cruelty if he thought it served his purpose. He had often told her that you could not build anything worthwhile if you were afraid to destroy what was taking up its place.

Everyone must have been aware of the emotion in the room, but Taunton and his sister, and probably the Princess of Wales, were unaware of the woman who had been murdered in the cupboard, and that one of the men who were guests here had to be responsible: the husband of one of these women. And did that woman know, or even guess?

"What makes you think that, Hamilton?" Cahoon repeated.

Hamilton blinked as if he had forgotten the question, but there was fear in his eyes, and disgust.

"Oh, of course," Cahoon said, seeming to remember something at last. "You're thinking of that awful murder. The poor woman who was slashed to death in Cape Town. Throat cut, and . . . and other things. I heard about it. That was appalling. You were there then too, weren't you, Julius?"

They all turned to look at Julius.

"Yes," he said simply. He seemed about to add something, then changed his mind, as if it were true, but pointless to express.

"It can happen anywhere," Liliane said a trifle too loudly. "Even in Africa they never had anything worse than the Whitechapel murderer, right here in London."

Hamilton shuddered violently.

"Another brandy?" the Prince of Wales offered. He looked embarrassed and unhappy, but was trying to mask it.

"No," Liliane answered too rapidly. "Thank you, sir."

The Prince looked at Hamilton, then sighed and turned to Cahoon. "Perhaps it is a man's country, at least to begin with. I envy you the chance to be in at the very foundation of such a world-changing enterprise. It seems comparatively tame to remain here at home. One cannot build real happiness in life totally upon safety."

"We can do without one adventurer more or less, sir," Cahoon replied. "We have only one future king."

Julius smiled. Hamilton shivered again, his hands clenched. Simnel looked at Julius, the emotion in his face unreadable. Lady Parr regarded Cahoon with open admiration.

Elsa wished the evening were over, but knew they had at least two more hours, more probably three, before anyone could retire. No one could leave before the Prince and

Princess of Wales.

It was nearly midnight when Alexandra invited Elsa to accompany her to one of the galleries that held some of her favorite pictures. Elsa had no interest in pictures at the moment, but apart from the fact that one did not refuse a princess, she was grateful for the escape. They excused themselves and rose.

Elsa walked beside the Princess through magnificent rooms, walls covered with the great masterpieces of Europe throughout the centuries. It was a visual history of the dreams, the life, and the characters of half a millennium of Western civilization. In spite of herself, Elsa was drawn into it.

"A somewhat unusual evening," Alexandra observed with a smile, catching Elsa's eye for a moment as they stood before a dark, moody Rembrandt, all gold light and flesh tones against an umber background. Next to it was a cool Vermeer, morning light on blues and grays, and clarity so sharp one could see the grain in the stones of the floor.

"I'm sorry," Elsa apologized. "We are all at odds with one another." She could not give the real reason. "They care so much about the project."

"Of course they do," Alexandra agreed.

"There is very much to win, or lose. But I imagine it is the other unfortunate event that is really disturbing them and, I think, awakening old fears connected to the new ones."

Elsa stared at her, her mind racing, trying to deduce whether the implication was accidental or not. Could she possibly know?

Alexandra smiled bleakly. "Did you imagine I was unaware of it? My dear, that man Pitt would not be here and allowed to ask such questions were there not something very badly wrong. I'm so sorry. It must be wretched for you."

Elsa struggled for something appropriate to say, and found nothing. They walked in silence from that gallery to the next one, and the one after.

"If you would care to look at these a little longer, I am sure there is no reason why you should not," Alexandra said at last. "I fear I should return and speak to Lady Parr again. Not that she would mind in the slightest if I didn't, but duty requires it."

"Thank you," Elsa accepted gratefully. Her mind was whirling, and the further respite was intensely welcome. She needed time to be alone. Her thoughts were chaotic, kept in turmoil by emotion. She was frightened because it had to be Simnel, Hamilton, or Julius who had killed the woman in such an appalling way. Someone she had stood next to, exchanging polite chatter, had torn a woman apart, a woman whose name she did not know, whose whole life she knew nothing about, except the sordid manner in which she earned money. How much choice had she had in that?

They were all imprisoned here until the police found the answer. What if they didn't find it? They couldn't stay here indefinitely. Would they let them all go? With that hanging over their heads forever? It would be unbearable to live with. Had the police the power to keep it secret? That was a cold, terrifying thought. A woman could come in here, be butchered like an animal, and nothing would ever be said! That kind of power should not exist.

And yet how could they make it public, and allow three men to live with that type of scandal for the rest of their lives.

She was looking at the dark, passionate Spanish face in a Velázquez portrait when the sound of footsteps jerked her back to where she was. Please heaven it was a servant of some sort, someone she would not have to speak to. Resolutely she kept her face turned toward the picture. Whoever he was was close to her.

"You can feel his emotions, can't you?"

252

he observed.

It was Julius. It was the first time she had been alone with him in a year. She could remember the last time exactly. It had been after dinner at the new home Cahoon had bought in Chelsea. They had been in the conservatory. The smell of leaves and damp earth had hung in the air, warm and motionless, like a tropical jungle.

She cleared her throat. She was shivering. "Yes." Should she go back to the party now? It would be cowardly. She loathed the coward in herself even more than in others. She wanted to stay, even if they did not speak to each other. "There is a Rembrandt in the next gallery. Different sort of face altogether."

"Self-portrait?" he asked.

"Yes, yes, I think so. It would be hard to see yourself honestly enough for a painting to be worth doing, wouldn't it." It was not really a question, simply a remark to fill in the silence, and prevent anything personal from being said.

"Yes," he agreed. "To catch the weakness, the indecision, the thing that's pleasant but shallow. Willfulness would be easier. Or appetite."

"More attractive?" she asked, thinking of Minnie. What about herself? Did she find

Cahoon's passion and will more exciting than Julius's less forceful nature? Was she afraid that behind the strong bones of his face there was essentially a man without the hunger or the courage to fight for his dreams? Or without dreams at all? But why should she expect of him what she seemed to lack herself?

He had not answered.

"Is it?" she pressed him. "Is that what we like to see?" Then as soon as the words were out she did not want him to answer. But if she spoke again, stopping him from doing so, she would always wonder what he would have said.

"Not on my own walls," he answered. "I would rather have something with truer beauty, someone you feel would smile at you, if they could move." He hesitated. "And I would rather have mystery, the feeling that there is something I have yet to learn, perhaps would never entirely know, because it might change in time, grow, as living things do."

She was burning and cold at once, her heart pounding, her hands chilled. "I would like something with a warmth I could trust," she said. Was that too obvious? Was she being as clumsy and predictable as Minnie had said she was?

Julius was so close she could smell the faint odor of soap and clean cotton, and the heat of his skin.

"Perhaps we all would." His voice was not much more than a murmur. "How much of what we see in a face is really there?"

"Not always very much," she admitted. "If we could read them with any skill we wouldn't make so many mistakes. We see what we want to."

"And we change," he added. "We find what we were looking for, and discover that we don't like it after all." He touched her shoulder a moment with his hand, then dropped it away again.

She wanted to turn round, face him, look into his eyes. That was a lie. She wanted infinitely more than that, and it would be a disaster, something too wonderful to forget, or too empty, too revealing of disillusion ever to heal. She must change the subject, however violently.

"What was Cahoon talking about before? Was it like this poor woman here?" Her voice sounded too harsh.

"Yes, pretty much." He did not step away.

"Is he . . . suggesting it was the same person who did it?"

"Yes, I think so. Particularly since he was in Europe at the time, so it couldn't have been him. And Eden Forbes is dead."

"Liliane's brother? Why did you mention him? What happened to him anyway? She's never spoken of it." Elsa had not meant to, but she sounded frightened and accusing.

"I don't know," he answered. "I believe it was crocodiles. He was in a boat that capsized. Stories were a bit garbled, and everyone was very shocked. From what I heard, Hamilton did a lot to help. Watson Forbes was there, and Liliane, but they were devastated by it. I was actually a couple of hundred miles away up-country when it happened."

She tried to imagine it, and deliberately stopped. "I'm not sure if I would like Africa. Not that I have to go. I don't think Cahoon will care whether I do or not, and I'm certainly not necessary."

"We don't have the contract yet," he pointed out.

She was surprised. "Don't you think we will?" Failure was not something she had seriously considered. Cahoon never failed, and he wanted this more passionately than anything else in his life. But that had been before the murder.

Julius answered slowly, concentrating on each word. "I suppose that depends on what the policeman finds." There was irony in his voice, and pity, and fear. He would have been a fool to possess less. She was glad to hear it; at least he felt something.

"And I'm not as certain that the railway will be an unqualified asset as I used to be. There are other factors. I thought I knew as much as I needed to, now I'm not sure. What about a generation from now — or two? The internal boundaries in Africa are all very fluid. What if they change? If only one country opposes the British Empire, we become desperately vulnerable. And even if we can safeguard the project, militarily or through treaty, what will it do to Africa itself?"

"Give it a unity," she replied immediately. She did not understand why he was concerned. "Isn't that good? We did the same in India."

"India already had a degree of unity," he pointed out. "Africa doesn't. It has far more changes in climate and terrain, in race, culture, and religion. Maybe it's all better tied together by a British railway, but I'm far from certain of that. I've been wondering if east to west, inland to the sea, might be far more practical, not only physically but morally."

Elsa was amazed, and in spite of her resolution not to, she turned to face him. "Have you said so?"

"No. I'm not certain, and Cahoon isn't listening anyway. He considers anyone who questions him to be committing an act of betrayal." A half-smile touched his lips. "But you know that."

She did know it. She realized that it must be so plain that he had seen it even from outside. There was no answer to give.

"I think I should return," she said. "I have been gone rather a long time. I would rather do it before I need to give explanations."

"Of course. I'll follow in a few minutes. I'd like to look at this portrait a little longer."

She moved away without looking at him again. He had not touched her again, and she felt alone, somehow incomplete because of it.

Cahoon followed her to her bedroom and closed the door hard behind him. He dismissed Bartle, who was waiting. "Your mistress will pull the bell if you're wanted," he said brusquely.

Bartle went out, head high, shoulders stiff. Elsa stood facing him.

"You didn't know about that, did you?" he demanded, a slight curl of amusement on his lip. "You thought this was the first time he'd done it."

"I don't know what you're talking about."

She played for time. She was afraid of his temper. He had struck her before, although never where anyone would see the marks. Always it had been because of her coldness, as he saw it, her lack of fire or passion, the ways in which she fell short of his wishes and her duty as his wife. Was it Minnie he was comparing her with, or Amelia Parr?

"Whoever killed the damn woman in the cupboard, Elsa!" he shouted. "For God's sake, stop pretending! Haven't you the courage to face the truth about anything at all?" His disgust was palpable. "You live in a world of insipid dreams, all the edges of passion or pain blunted. Well, you're going to have to face reality now." He moved closer to her, six inches taller than she, and massively more powerful. She could smell the cigar smoke and the brandy on his breath.

"I don't know the truth," she said with as much composure as she could muster, refusing to step backwards. "If you do, then you should tell the police."

"I will, when I can prove it. Although I don't know what that local clod of a policeman will do about it, unless the Prince tells him. Incompetent ass!"

"The Prince or the policeman?" she asked with an edge of sarcasm. She was tired of being complacent, whatever the cost. She despised herself for it, although she would have to pay later.

His eyes widened. "You think perhaps the Prince of Wales is an incompetent ass?" he said quietly.

"How on earth would I know?" she retorted. "He drinks too much and he seems to do whatever you advise him to. Do you admire that?" It was a challenge.

"He's probably bored sick with his tedious wife," he snapped back. "Only the poor devil can't escape — ever. Unless she dies."

She felt cold, as if suddenly she had walked into icy rain and been wet to the skin by it. He was staring at her, amused, enjoying it.

"So he has parties, and hires women from the street to come and entertain him," she said without the force she had wanted because she was shivering. "Poor man. No wonder you are sorry for him. I am sorry for her. She must be so ashamed for him."

He knew exactly what she meant, and the rage flared in his eyes. He swung his arm back, and then changed his mind. "I suppose you'd just run to Julius, and tell him I beat you! I wasn't in Africa when that other woman was killed, Elsa. He was! Have you considered what he might do to women when he can get away with it? Not quite the dream you had, is it?"

"You have no idea what my dreams are, Cahoon. That's one place you can't reach. You never will."

"Do you really imagine I want to?" His black eyebrows rose incredulously. "Insipid is a word that hardly does them justice. Like a blancmange, pale and tasteless. You bore me to death, Elsa." He turned away, then, when he reached the door, swung around to face her again. "Julius may never win anything but toleration from Minnie, because the law doesn't allow a woman to leave a man for adultery, if he ever raises the courage or the manhood to commit it — a fact you would do well to remember. You owe me everything you have: the food in your mouth, the clothes you stand up in, and your loyalty — at least in public. If you forget that, I will destroy you. Julius can't save you, and he won't try. If he wanted you, he'd have done something about it before now, which if you had either courage or honesty you would have realized. He has plenty of excuse to put Minnie away, if that were his choice. It isn't. Face it. All he wants you for is to irritate me."

"He seems to have succeeded," she said, her voice like ice. "You have lost control of your temper — again."

"No I haven't," he contradicted her. "If I

had, you would be senseless on the floor."
He went out and closed the door hard.

She went to it and turned the key in the lock, then sank onto the bed and wept.

CHAPTER SEVEN

Gracie had taken the bloodstained knife to Pitt, who had immediately seen the significance of it. Someone had placed it there after they had searched the cupboard on finding the body. That meant it could only be someone living right here in this guest wing of the Palace. Had they done it to get rid of it, in case Pitt caught them with it, or so he could find it and blame someone else? That was probably what Pitt was thinking of right now. Gracie scrubbed the laundry floor. Ada liked to give her the heaviest, wettest work to keep her aware of her position at the bottom of the hierarchy, just in case she forgot.

Gracie thought of the Queen's bloodstained sheets as well. It didn't seem to make any sense. Would Pitt manage to find out who did it, and, even more than that, prove it?

Her brush moved a little slower. What if he

didn't find out? That thought frightened her. She didn't know what they would do to him, but she understood power, and anger, and fear. Surely even the people here would not be able to cover up a scandal like this. Or maybe they would think they had to. She could remember five years ago when the Whitechapel murderer had struck. There had been anger in the streets then. A lot of it in the East End had become very ugly. Anarchists and republicans had turned against the Queen. There had been talk of getting rid of her and setting up a new kind of government, without a monarchy any more. There had even been crazy talk that someone in the royal family had had a hand in it. That was really daft. One of the first things you did in detecting was to find out where people were. She had known that for years.

But she also knew how stupid people could be repeating things that a moment's thought would have told them couldn't be true. Anger doesn't need much food to grow. Poor and hungry people have more feeling than sense. She had grown up in the East End and she knew her own beginnings, even if she had left them behind for Keppel Street and was now busy on her hands and knees scrubbing the floor of the Queen's laundry.

She wiped the last yard and fetched fresh

water to begin in the morning room, excusing herself to Biddie, who was busy ironing petticoats.

She started to scrub again.

Those three women the Prince had here were the same sort as the ones the Whitechapel murderer had attacked. So was this murder a similar attempt to try to destroy the Crown? Did Pitt know that? Or was he being used without realizing it, to break open another scandal? The thought made her so angry she bruised her fingers on the sides of the scrubbing brush and caught a bristle under her nail.

She was sitting on the floor in the corner out of sight, trying to pick the splinter out when she heard footsteps in the passage and then a rustle of fabric as skirts brushed the sides of the door. It sounded like silk. A maid's plain cotton dress made no sound. She ignored the piece of bristle and moved a little forward to see across the passageway.

It was a deep, plum-pink silk, and very wide. That would be Mrs. Sorokine — she liked such hot colors.

The silk moved farther inside and a moment later the sound of Minnie's voice proved her correct.

"I wonder if you could iron this for me?" Minnie asked. "I've gotten it rather crumpled, and I don't want my maid to know how careless I was."

Biddie was startled. She let the iron slip out of her hand and it struck the ironing table with a thud.

"I'm sorry," Minnie apologized. "I didn't mean to make you jump. I think we are all very frightened at the moment."

"Yes, ma'am," Biddie said automatically. " 'Course I'll do it. You just leave it 'ere an' I'll bring it up ter you."

"I don't mind waiting a few moments," Minnie replied. "I don't want you to have to come all the way upstairs again."

Biddie started to say it was no trouble, then bit the words back.

Gracie was curious. Such consideration did not seem in character for Mrs. Sorokine. She remained where she was, listening. The floor could wait.

"I don't blame you for being frightened," Minnie went on conversationally. "I am too. I know the culprit has to be someone that probably we both saw, and on the night it happened. Maybe we even spoke to them."

"Oh, ma'am! It doesn't bear thinking of!" Biddie said softly.

"But you can see why I'm concerned, I'm sure," Minnie said warmly. "My own husband is one of the people they suspect."

"I'm really sorry, ma'am," Biddie said in a hushed tone, as if she had just realized the enormity of the crime. "I'm sure you'll find it in't 'im."

"Are you?" From Minnie's tone it was a question, not in any way a challenge. "How can you be? Do you know where he was? I suppose you must have seen a lot, maybe more than the police thought to ask you." Her skirts rustled a bit as she leaned forward. "You were up and down the stairs most of the evening, weren't you?"

"Yeah, I s'pose we were." There was awe in Biddie's voice and there was no movement of the iron. It must be quite cool by now, and she had not changed it for the hot one on the stove.

"What were they like, the three women?" Minnie asked. "I didn't even see them."

Still sitting motionlessly, Gracie saw Biddie's skirt give a twitch as she shrugged her shoulders. "Ordinary enough, ma'am. You shouldn't 'ave ter know about them things."

"Oh, please!" Minnie begged. "I won't tell anyone you said so. I just need to know. There are only three men suspected, one of them is my husband. Please!"

Biddie must have looked at Minnie's face, because she relented. "Well, they was women from one o' the bawdy 'ouses, not off the street, like. Clean an' all. At least far as yer can know. An' dressed quite decent when they come."

"But they were . . . professional?"

"Oh, yeah. Yer can tell that by the way they talked."

"You've seen them before?" Minnie pressed.

Gracie was getting a crick in her back, but she dared not draw attention to herself by moving.

"Not them in particular," Biddie answered after apparently having thought for a moment. "But ones like 'em."

"Does Mr. Tyndale know them?" Minnie was not yet satisfied.

Biddie giggled. "Not Mr. Tyndale, ma'am. 'E don't approve of it something terrible, but it'd be more'n 'is job's worth ter say so. It don't do ter let anyone think as yer've got opinions."

"No," Minnie agreed. "Of course it doesn't. Who finds these women, then?"

"Oh, ma'am . . . I . . ."

"Are you telling me you don't know?" Minnie was incredulous. "Somebody must have taken them in and upstairs, and then told somebody they were here. Otherwise they could have been anyone."

"Oh, they was 'oo they said, ma'am!" Bid-

268

die responded instantly.

"Who said so?"

"Mr. Dunkeld, ma'am."

"I see." There was profound emotion in Minnie's voice. It was husky, almost choked. Was that what she had wanted to prove, or to disprove? "And when the two of them left, who took them out? And what about the old man who helped carry the box up?"

"When the two o' them went they looked much the same," Biddie told her. "Bit used, like, wot yer'd expect. A good few drinks the worse for wear, but not 'urt or nothing."

"And the old man," Minnie urged. "What did he look like? Was he strong? Might he have attacked her, do you think? Was he rough-looking?"

Biddie's voice was gentle. "I'm real sorry, ma'am, but 'e looked like 'e were too old ter be up ter such things. An' the way I 'eard it, 'e took the box up an' came down again to his 'orse, then straight back up to fetch the box when it were empty. I'm real sorry, but that won't 'elp yer, ma'am, much as I wish it would."

"That's all right. Thank you," Minnie said, moving again, from the rustle of her skirts. "I'm very obliged for your help. Please don't repeat our conversation to anyone."

"No, ma' am," Biddie promised. There was

a swish of silk and a moment later Biddie swore. "Stupid article!" she said in exasperation. "She din't even taken 'er linen with 'er after all!"

Gracie stood up, relieved to move at last. "I'll take it up to 'er as soon as I've finished this. I'm nearly done."

"Ta," Biddie said sincerely.

Quarter of an hour later Gracie was on the guest landing with Minnie Sorokine's chemise neatly folded, but there was no answer at her bedroom door, which was locked. Norah, in the pantry, had no idea where she was, but thought she had gone back downstairs.

"Again?" Gracie asked her. "Are yer sure?"

" 'Course I'm sure," Norah said indignantly. "Ever such an odd one, she is." She was putting away the tea canisters after filling them: Darjeeling, Earl Grey, China. "Not a beauty like Mrs. Quase, but yer can't miss that Mr. Marquand prefers 'er. Can't keep 'is eyes off 'er, Ada says. An' Mrs. Sorokine don't seem ter care. Askin' me about buckets an' mops and carryin' things around in the middle o' the night. As if I'd know! An' now she's gone downstairs ter ask Timmons about it."

"About wot?"

"About 'oo was cleanin' up, fetchin' an' carryin' bits o' broken china an' buckets o' water an' cloths an' brushes an' things! In't you listening?"

Gracie stiffened. "When?"

"The night that poor creature were killed in the cupboard, o' course!"

"Then they was cleanin' out the cupboard," Gracie concluded. "Isn't that clear enough?" She thought of the knife. " 'Oo was it, anyway?"

"No, it weren't the cupboard!" Norah replied smartly. "Too clever by 'alf, you are, missy! The policeman done that 'isself. This were way along the other wing, near the Prince and Princess's own rooms, an' the Queen 'erself, o' course. But 'ers is further off again. Maybe they was tryin' ter get rid of anyone knowin' that tart 'ad bin along in the Prince's room. Dunno why! That policeman may not be as sharp as they are, but 'e in't stupid! 'E knows fine where she were. An' don't ask me wot the china were, 'cos I dunno."

"That's what Mrs. Sorokine was trying to find out?" Gracie's mind raced. What on earth was she imagining?

"That's wot she said. Now do you want me to give that to 'er when she comes back, or not?" She gestured to the chemise.

"Yes . . . please. I'll go and find her to tell her it's 'ere." And Gracie passed it to her, then turned on her heel and went to see if she could learn what Minnie Sorokine was looking for, her mind racing with ideas. Why was she asking? What did she suspect? It made no sense.

She had to ask three people before she nearly ran into Minnie herself, talking quietly to one of the footmen. Gracie stopped only just before either of them saw her, and hid behind a curtain to listen. She felt foolish, but she dared not miss the opportunity.

"What kind of china?" Minnie was saying, her voice sharp with excitement.

Walton, the footman, obviously thought she was so unnerved by the murder that she had taken leave of her judgment. "Just china, ma'am, like a dish or a bowl. No harm, we've got plenty. 'Course, it's a bad thing when something gets broken, but it happens now an' again."

"Did one of the maids break something?" she asked.

"Must have," he reasoned.

"A bucketful?"

"Got to carry broken pieces in something, ma'am."

"You could get a whole tea service in a bucket!" she pointed out. "Who broke it?

Don't they have to own up?"

"It wasn't a tea service, ma'am, it was just about as much as a good-sized dish. An' I don't know who broke it."

"Which dish was it?"

Gracie could see Walton's face. He looked totally bemused. "I don't know, Mrs. Sorokine. Sort of blue, with some gold on it, and white, I think."

"Do you have a service like that?" There was something like excitement in Minnie's voice now.

"Not that I can think of. But we must, or it wouldn't be broken, would it?"

"Thank you very much." Minnie's voice sounded frightened, full of raw-edged emotion.

As Gracie saw her swing round she scrambled ridiculously behind the curtain, only just in time to avoid being seen if Minnie had turned. Only she did not turn, she swept back along the corridor at a pace Gracie could not have kept up with unless she had run, and that would have drawn so much attention to her that it would end all her usefulness here.

She lost Minnie and came face-to-face with Mrs. Newsome.

"If you have nothing to do, girl, go and help in the kitchen," Mrs. Newsome said tartly. "There are plenty of dishes to wash. No wages for daydreaming."

"Yes, Mrs. Newsome." Gracie had no choice. And there was nothing more to learn in the laundry anyway. She went to the kitchen and did as she was told.

By lunchtime she was exhausted, and knew she was wet and crumpled. What would Samuel think of her now? And she wasn't even learning anything useful! She could not work out what Minnie thought she had found.

Gracie ate her cold mutton, pickle, and mashed potatoes, keeping her eyes on her plate. Her mind raced: broken china that didn't fit any of the tea services, buckets of water carried up and down stairs; descriptions of the street women — why had Minnie Sorokine asked about these things? They were ordinary enough. Did she really think she had discovered something?

Yes, of course she did. It was in her voice, in her eyes, in the way she raced along the corridor. But was it something to do with the murder, or just whatever romance she was planning? Was it something to prove her husband's innocence?

Later, when Gracie was tidied up and her dress changed, with a clean apron on to carry up extra sandwiches for afternoon tea, she saw Minnie Sorokine again. This time she was standing in the gallery in a beautiful muslin afternoon dress with frills on it like foam and cerise pink ribbons. She was quite obviously flirting with the Prince of Wales, who stood in the sunlight flooding in through the bay windows. He was looking at her and smiling. She was asking him something and he was happy to answer, except once when Gracie saw a swift frown and then a moment's awkwardness.

"Snooping again, are you?"

Gracie swung round to see Ada standing no more than a yard away, a look of satisfaction in her face. Gracie felt the color rush up her cheeks because she had no answer to save herself.

"Eavesdropping on your betters," Ada went on. "Well, if yer out ter learn 'ow ter flirt, yer couldn't do better than watch that one! I never seen as good. But she's out o' your class. Yer get caught watchin' 'Is 'Ighness an' you'll be out before night, I can assure yer." She said that with obvious pleasure. "But yer in't goin' ter get me thrown out fer not watchin' you proper, so one more time yer cross me, miss, an' I'll tell Mrs. Newsome wot yer like. It's my turn ter carry out the slops. Yer'd like ter do them for me as a favor now, wouldn't yer?"

However much she might dislike it, Gracie had no choice but to agree. She was here to learn all she could that might help Pitt, not to carve herself a career at the Palace. She went obediently and worked at fetching all the slops and emptying them, washed out all the bowls and jugs, then had to change into another clean dress and damp down and re-press the first one.

She was late for supper and Mrs. Newsome told her off in front of all the others.

"You're going to have to learn to keep up, Phipps," she said coldly. "You can't be coming to table late like this. It is discourteous and it inconveniences everyone. You must learn to fit in. It's not always easy, but if you cannot manage it, then you are not right for this position. Perhaps you are a little too old to accommodate yourself."

Gracie felt the anger boil up inside her as everyone along both sides of the table turned to stare at her. She ached to be able to tell them she had no intention of staying here any longer than was necessary to help Mr. Pitt and Mr. Narraway. But of course she could say nothing. To defend herself would betray a confidence that would make her role unbelievable. She drew in breath to apologize, the words all but choking her under Ada's triumphant gaze. In that instant it became a rock-hard certainty that Ada was doing this precisely to get her dismissed. Ada saw Gracie as some kind of threat. She must have sensed a strength of will in her, because it was certainly not her looks. As even Samuel had said, she was the size of a rabbit.

In spite of the danger, Gracie felt a surge of elation.

"You are being too quick, Mrs. Newsome," Mr. Tyndale said with an edge to his voice. "The circumstances are unusual at the moment. Everyone is frightened and shocked by what has happened —"

"Phipps was not here when it happened," Mrs. Newsome interrupted him. "She cannot use that as an excuse."

"It was not Phipps who raised the issue, Mrs. Newsome." The color was high in Mr. Tyndale's face now also, and his hand on the table was clenched. "It was I. Before you spoke, I was about to say that none of the staff is behaving as usual. I have noticed several other irregularities. But with the police questioning people, and guests who are plainly under a great burden of anxiety, and even greater fear than ours, we cannot expect the same standard of conduct from anyone as we would at any other time."

Mrs. Newsome opened her mouth, and then closed it again. Her lips were white, her eyes burning with anger and embarrassment. He had curbed her, quite sharply, in front of the junior servants. Judging from the silence all around the table, that was something that had not happened before. Gracie was surprised to feel so uncomfortable for her.

"Continue with your supper," Mr. Tyndale ordered, and one by one they all picked up their knives and forks again and began to eat, conscious of every movement, every sound. No one spoke, not even to ask for the salt or the teapot.

Gracie's mind raced. She had seen Ada's look of anger and puzzlement, and she knew it would not be long before she worked out how to launch another attack. Next time it might even compromise Mr. Tyndale. He had been unwise, at the very least, to expose his position as Gracie's defender, and Ada had unquestionably noticed it.

Mrs. Newsome would not forget that either, and both Gracie and Mr. Tyndale would probably have to pay. This rivalry, anger, and manipulation was something she had not even thought about before. In comparison, Keppel Street seemed an island of peace, nothing to do but tasks she was used to and knew she did well. No one to answer to most of the time, and when there was, it was only Mrs. Pitt, who, in spite of being born into gentry, never gave herself airs.

Gracie wondered if she would be as happy as Mrs. Pitt when she married Samuel! It would be a totally new experience and she would lose all the little things she was familiar with. She was taken aback to realize that as well as excited, she was also a little afraid, even sad.

Of course, if Mr. Pitt did not solve this horrible crime, then everything might change, probably for all of them. And if it did, would Gracie be able to leave them at all, even to marry Samuel? It would seem like a desertion. She might even have to stay and work without any pay, just her food. Not that she would mind that; it would be fair.

Gracie finished her rice pudding and declined another slice of bread and jam. When they had all put down their knives or spoons, she rose and waited a few moments to see which way Mr. Tyndale was going, then followed after him. She hoped everyone else assumed she was going to apologize.

She caught up with him in the pantry. She wanted to close the door, but she remembered the speculation that had caused before and left it ajar. She spoke very quietly. This was desperately awkward, and she had to do it immediately, before she lost her nerve.

"Mr. Tyndale, sir," she began, "I'm very grateful that you stood up for me, 'cos Ada's making things right awkward, which is why I were late. But you didn't ought ter, 'cos yer can't tell no one why I'm 'ere, an' being the way they are, they're gonna think summink else, wot in't fair." She took a deep breath. "You gotter stay 'ere, sir, but I don't, so it don't matter wot they think o' me."

He looked embarrassed. She was suddenly terribly sorry for him. This place and the people in it were his whole life, the reason he believed in himself. Perhaps he had found some way to come to terms with the things he disapproved of: the strange women who came at night, for what reason he must know; the guests he might not care for, either for their manners or their purposes in being here. Many of them would take advantage, and there would be nothing he could do.

And now there was murder, and he still had to try to keep it all quiet and everything working as usual. Would he even be thanked for it? Thanks could mean a lot, in fact it could mean almost everything.

"But I am grateful," she added in the prickly silence. "Wouldn't 'a done for me to tell everyone as Ada made me do 'er job wi' the slops, which is wot made me late. An' please don't say nothin'! I'll sort 'er."

He looked desperately uncomfortable. "Have you . . . have you learned anything?" His voice caught in his throat.

"Best you dunno, sir," she replied.

"Would it be helpful if you were to serve at dinner tonight?" he asked.

"Serve? You mean like at the table?" she was horrified.

"Yes. They are not dining until late. You still have at least two hours. Would it help you to observe?"

"I . . ." She hated to admit it. "I dunno as I know 'ow ter do it, sir. Not . . . not wi' silver dishes an' all them glasses an' all."

"You won't be asked to serve the wine," he assured her. He looked better, and he had the upper hand again. "Just the vegetables, and clear away. The footman will serve the wine and the soup. Would it help?"

"If someone's as mad as all that, yer'd think yer could see it, wouldn't yer?" she said thoughtfully. "Mrs. Sorokine's bin goin' around all day askin' things. Mr. Tyndale, sir, do you know if someone broke a dish, all blue and white china, wi' a bit o' gold in it? One from upstairs, I mean? She were askin' like it mattered."

He looked concerned. "Yes, I am aware of that. She asked me also. I tried to discourage her. It seems I did not succeed. Who was she asking?"

"Walton. 'As it got summink ter do with the murder, sir?"

"No. No, you have quite misunderstood. There isn't such a dish here. The matter has to do with some unfortunate behavior of a quite different nature," he said firmly, watching to see if she believed him. "It is His Royal Highness. Leave it absolutely alone. Do you understand me, Miss Phipps? I am most desperately serious."

She was astounded, and a little frightened as well. She realized for the first time the delicacy of the balance Mr. Tyndale needed to keep between his own beliefs and those of the man and the class he served. Did he even see the absurdity of it? How difficult was it for him to explain to himself, and justify, when it was late at night and he was alone in his room? Did he question, waver? Then count the cost?

He blinked under her gaze. "Do you understand me, Miss Phipps?" he said again.

"No, sir," she replied. "But I'll do like you say."

The door swung wide open and Mrs. Newsome was there again, her face white apart from two spots of color in her cheeks.

"Phipps —" she started.

"If you have something to say, Mrs. Newsome, then you had better say it to me," Tyndale cut across her abruptly. "Phipps was reporting a certain matter to me, which I shall relay to the police. The fewer people who know of it the better. It may turn out to mean nothing, but we must see. You will keep this entirely to yourself." That was an order; there was no possibility of misunderstanding this time. Was he repaying her for showing him up in front of the other staff at the table?

"Indeed," Mrs. Newsome said unhappily. She turned from Tyndale to Gracie. "Phipps, there is a considerable amount of rubbish in the still room after the party. No one got round to cleaning it up. Go and do so, and while you are there, you can scrub the floor."

"I want her to help at table this evening," Mr. Tyndale said.

"She's not fit to, but if that's what you want, then she can do so. After she's scrubbed the still-room floor," Mrs. Newsome rejoined. "Don't stand there, girl! Go and do as you're told!"

It was a messy and quite difficult job. The room was cluttered with all manner of rubbish, as Mrs. Newsome had said, and in the early-evening heat Gracie could hear the irritating buzzing of flies. She hated the big, lazy things circling round anything dirty or sticky, settling and laying eggs on the surfaces. She gave a little shudder of distaste, and went to fetch a bucket of water and some baking soda to help it get back a decent smell.

It took her half an hour of cleaning and scrubbing and washing down and repiling up again before she came to the bottles where the flies were. They were old wine bottles, by the look of them, and expensive too. The labels were ornate and in soft colors, like old parchment. She picked one up and looked at it. A fly buzzed out of the neck and zoomed away.

"Ugh!" she said disgustedly. "Must be very sweet." She looked at the label. She could not read all of it, but she recognized the word *port*. That would be for the gentlemen to drink after dinner. She had heard about that. Could be terribly expensive. She put it to her nose experimentally and sniffed a little. It was sweet, like sugar and salt, and a bit like iron. Certainly not anything she would want to drink. It was revolting! Wonder if that one was bad. Could wine go bad?

She picked up another, and tried it very gingerly. That smelled entirely different, and very nice indeed, like real wine she had tasted before. She went back to the first one and tried again. It was just as horrible. There were eight empty bottles and she tried all of them. Five were lovely, three disgusting, all the same, with the sickly sweet, ironlike smell.

She tipped one up and poured out a few drops onto the back of her hand, then smeared it gently over her skin. A fly returned and settled on her. She shook it off violently. She put her finger to the red stain and spread it a little farther across her hand. Then she knew what it was — blood.

She tipped up the others that smelled the same, and got a little trickle of blood out of each one, mixed with the lees of the wine. Why would anyone put blood into a wine bottle? What kind of blood — animal or human?

She stood up so quickly she nearly overbalanced and had to reach out and grasp onto a broom handle to hold herself up. She was a little dizzy, but there was no question in her mind what she must do: hide the three bottles that had held the blood, and then go and tell Pitt. No one else must know. She would feel ridiculous if it were something to do with a special recipe of the cook's, but far more so if it had something to do with that poor dead woman someone had butchered, and she did nothing about it. Nobody deserved to end up that way, no matter who they were.

She went back to Mr. Tyndale and told him she had to speak to Pitt straightaway. Ten minutes later she was standing in front of Pitt.

He looked tired and worried. His hair was even more unruly than usual and his shirt collar was crumpled. It seemed no one was looking after him. She noticed it all, and it brought a stab of both sorrow and guilt to her, but it was not important compared with the bottles in the still room.

"Are you all right, Gracie?" he asked as soon as she had closed the door. "Tyndale said the other servants are making things difficult for you."

"In't nothing as matters, sir," she said, surprised that Tyndale should have told Pitt. "I came about summink I found wot could be . . . I dunno. Mebbe I'm bein' a bit daft meself, but it don't seem right, or make no sense."

A flicker of hope lit his eyes. "What is it?"

"I were scrubbin' out the still room an' I found eight empty bottles wot 'ad 'ad port wine in 'em," she replied. "Five of 'em smelled like wine, real nice, an' three of 'em 'ad flies all around, an' smelled different. I tipped 'em out, an' they 'ad blood in 'em."

"Blood!" He was stunned. "Gracie, are you sure?"

"Yes." She frowned. "Could the cook 'ave mixed blood an' wine ter make summink? A sauce, or summink like that?"

"Three bottles of port! I don't think so." He shook his head. "And why put the blood into the port bottles anyway? Wouldn't she have mixed it in a bowl or a pan?"

"Yer gonna ask?"

"Yes, I am! Where are the bottles now?"

"I 'id 'em." She told him exactly where. "D'yer know anything else, sir?" She would never have asked him such a thing even a month ago.

"Not much," he admitted, defeat flattening his voice in spite of an obvious effort to keep it up. "It could still have been any one of the three men. Dunkeld told me where he heard of the prostitutes and that he took them on recommendation of an acquaintance. Never saw them before. Mr. Narraway's been looking into it to see if anything about them would help. He questioned the two women still alive, but they never saw or heard of any of the men before, and Sadie had said she didn't know them either. They talked about it on the way here."

"A man wot in't mad don't kill tarts," she

said flatly. "Don't care enough, for a start. Why would 'e? Don't make no sense. But someone smashed summink I thought were one o' 'em dishes with a stand on, made o' blue, white, and gold china. But Mr. Tyndale says as they in't got any like that." She frowned. "I over'eard it were done upstairs an' taken down in a bucket, all in tiny bits. Someone were goin' up an' down wi' buckets o' water too, but when I asked Mr. Tyndale about that 'e got all white an' quiet an' told me it was 'Is Royal 'Ighness be'avin' badly. Said I weren't never ter think of it again, never mind say nothin'. But I know about it 'cos Mrs. Sorokine were askin' Walton today, an' got ever so excited about it when she 'eard. Kind of excited an' upset at the same time."

Pitt frowned at her. "Mrs. Sorokine?"

"Yes. She's detectin', sir, I'd swear to it, but I dunno if it's got anythin' ter do with the murder, or jus' 'er own life, wot's nuffin' like it should be."

Pitt smiled twistedly. "You've noticed!"

"Can't 'ardly 'elp it, can I?" she retorted. "If a parlor maid threw 'erself about like that, twitchin' 'er skirts an' 'er be'ind, she'd get 'er notice for bein' loose."

"The rules for ladies and parlor maids were never the same." He stood up. "Let's go and find these extraordinary bottles of blood. You're right, it doesn't make any sense at all. But there isn't much about this whole disgusting affair that does."

An hour later Gracie was back in her best uniform with clean and starched white lace-edged cap and apron, and lined up with the other servants for Mrs. Newsome to inspect her, showing her hands back and front. Her hair had so many pins in it she felt as if she had a helmet on underneath her cap, but she was sure no stray piece would escape to make her appearance less than perfect. Her boots were also inspected and found spotless.

"Dunno wot for," Ada said as they went out to begin their duties. "Yer skirt's so long no one even knows yer got feet, let alone boots. I never seen such a skinny little rabbit as you are."

"Well, I seen scores like you!" Gracie retorted. "Ten a penny, up an' down any street, an' on it too! Too much chest, an' all. Everybody else can see yer got feet, they're big enough, but I lay odds yer can't see 'em yerself!"

"I'll wash yer mouth out wi' lye, yer cheeky bint!" Ada hissed under her breath. "No man in't never gonna fancy you! Not unless 'e's one o' these wot likes little kids!"

"Then I'm safe from Edwards, in't I?" Gracie retorted. " 'Cos 'e likes 'em big an' blowsy, fat enough ter be 'is ma!"

Ada reached her hand back as if to take a wide swing and hit Gracie on the side of her face, then realized that Biddie was looking at them, and changed her mind. "I'll get yer, yer little bitch!" she said half under her breath.

"No yer won't," Gracie responded in the same tone. "Or I'll tell wot I saw in the laundry the other day, when it all got fogged up. Weren't only the copper as was steaming, were it!"

"I'll say yer lying!" Ada spat back. "They'll believe me, 'cos nobody likes you! I'll say it were you 'oo was teasin' Edwards, an' then Mrs. Newsome'll get rid o' yer for sure! She's only waitin' fer the chance."

"No they won't believe yer," Gracie hissed back at her. " 'Cos like yer said, nobody'd fancy me. They all know Edwards is after you. An' you're after Cuttredge. An' 'e's gonna believe me. So you keep yer mouth shut an' all, an' leave me alone!"

They reached the dining room and Ada was obliged to hold her peace. She was fuming, but she was also beaten, at least until she thought of a way of retaliating.

The guests came in and took their seats.

Footmen in livery held doors, Gracie and the other women servants stood in the anteroom and waited, but she could see through the gap in the doorway. The guests looked marvelous, all bright colors of silk, velvet, and lace and glittering with jewels. Gracie was dazzled by white necks and bosoms; she had never seen so much skin even when she had a bath.

Mrs. Sorokine was wearing yet another burning shade of pink, so hot you'd think you could cook dinner over it. She looked excited, her dark eyes glittering as she turned from one person to another, ignoring her husband. Her eyes went up and down Mrs. Marquand's thin body in its dark blue gown, which made her look even more bony, then on to Mr. Marquand, who was looking back at her, smiling. He was a bit pink too, as if warming himself in the glow of her dress. Gracie wondered if the real quality went on like this a lot of the time, or if it was only these ones. Maybe she could work up the nerve to ask Mrs. Pitt one day.

Mrs. Quase was wearing a strange shade of brownish gold with a plunging neck at the front, though nobody seemed to be noticing it much. She was very beautiful.

Mrs. Dunkeld wore a soft, cold lavender gray, which oddly enough made her skin

look warmer. She was beautiful too, in a la-
dylike sort of way. She looked unhappy, and
her eyes met those of everyone except her
husband's, and Mr. Sorokine.

Gracie was directed to go back down to the
cellar and ask Mr. Tyndale to fetch another
two bottles of the white wine. When she returned it was almost time to take away the
soup plates.

"Be careful!" Ada warned, her eyes bright
with anticipation. "You drop any o' that on
someone's dress an' you're finished!"

Gracie went into the dining room already
shaking and afraid she would trip over her
own feet — or worse, her too-long skirt —
and send the dishes right across the floor.

She accomplished her duty with fierce
concentration, aware that Ada would be only
too delighted if she had a disaster. Then she
assisted as the fish was served, and stood
back watching while it was eaten. It smelled
delicious. No one considered her to be
eavesdropping, because they did not notice
her at all.

First she watched Cahoon Dunkeld. There
was a power in him that drew her eyes as if
there were something in his mind, his
strength of will, that dominated them all. He
was talking about Africa, and the great railway they were going to build, and how it

would be the backbone of the whole continent.

"And of course His Royal Highness will give you his support, won't he, Papa?" Mrs. Sorokine said with conviction. She sounded so sure that it was not really a question.

"I expect so," Mr. Dunkeld replied. "But we shouldn't take it for granted. That would be foolish, and insulting."

Gracie thought he said that for the benefit of the Prince, in case someone should repeat it back to him.

"But aren't you his friend?" Mrs. Sorokine pressed. "I would think, from the way you have helped him in this ghastly business, he would be forever grateful to you." There was a funny, bright edge to her voice as she said that, and her eyes never left his face.

"This ghastly business, as you put it, would not have happened if we weren't here," Mr. Sorokine pointed out. "Apparently one of us killed her. No one is going to be grateful for that."

"Oh, do be quiet!" his wife said impatiently. "He was the one who wanted the women here. Papa simply arranged it for him." She turned back to her father. "Didn't you?"

"Couldn't we discuss something else?" Mrs. Quase interrupted with irritation. "At least over dinner."

"Why?" Mrs. Marquand asked suddenly. "Whatever we talk about — the weather, fashion, gossip, politics, even Africa — we are all thinking about it! I look at the table-cloth, and I think of the sheets in the linen cupboard where she was killed. I look at the meal on my plate and think of the blood!"

"It's fish," her husband told her. "Stop indulging your imagination, or you'll end up in hysterics. Have a glass of water." He held up his hand. "Somebody, fetch her a glass of water!"

Gracie stepped forward, picked up the crystal water jug, and poured a wineglass full. She gave it to Mrs. Marquand, who took it with a startled gesture and drank a couple of sips before putting it down.

Gracie retreated to the wall again, hoping to resume her previous invisibility.

"He still relies on you, though, doesn't he, Papa?" Mrs. Sorokine took up the previous conversation as if nothing had happened. "I think there will be no question of his complete support."

"Let us hope so," Mr. Dunkeld replied. He did not look as pleased with her as Gracie would have expected. After all, she was in a way complimenting him.

"There is no one else with better credentials," Mrs. Quase said with forced cheerfulness. "In fact, I'm not sure there is really anyone else at all."

"There will always be other offers," Mr. Sorokine pointed out. "But I agree, they are not nearly as good."

"I expect they'll try, though, don't you?" Again Mrs. Sorokine was looking at her father. "The Prince of Wales's support will make all the difference, won't it?"

"Obviously!" Dunkeld said with considerable sharpness. "That is what we are here for. You do not need to keep repeating what is already obvious."

"We can hardly be complacent." Mrs. Dunkeld spoke for the first time. "After all, however good we are at building railways, apparently one of us killed that poor woman."

"She was a street whore, Elsa," Dunkeld said brusquely. "Don't speak of her as if she were some poor girl attacked on her way to church."

Mrs. Dunkeld looked at him with a sudden flare of fury in her blue eyes. "So were the victims of the Whitechapel murderer. They'd have hanged him just the same, if they had caught him."

Mrs. Quase gave a gasp. Mrs. Marquand was ashen.

Mrs. Sorokine raised both her hands in

mock applause. "Oh, bravo, Stepmother! That's the perfect remark to season the fish course! Now we shall feel so much more like choosing game. What is it, pheasant in aspic, jugged hare, or a little venison perhaps? Nothing like talk of a good hanging to improve the appetite."

"Yours anyway, it would seem!" Mrs. Dunkeld shot back at her. "It is idiotic to sit here and talk of the plans for a railway the length of Africa when one of us is a lunatic who kills women, and the police are here and not going to leave until they find out which one of us it is."

"We are all powerfully aware of that," Dunkeld said freezingly, his face set hard. "It appears to have escaped your intelligence that we are trying our best to have a civilized meal and behave with some dignity until such time as that is. Always assuming that idiot policeman is capable of doing anything more than sitting in his chair and asking endless, stupid questions. He doesn't appear to be any further forward than he was the morning he arrived."

Gracie was so furious she almost choked on her own breath, perhaps partly because she had a terrible fear that Mr. Dunkeld was right about Mr. Pitt's lack of progress. They had as evidence the Queen's sheets, the knife, the bottles, and knew about the broken dish that wasn't supposed to exist, and buckets and buckets of water, but none of it made any sense. She ached to be able to snap back at him that they wouldn't know anything about what progress Pitt was making anyway, until he was ready to arrest someone, but she could do nothing but stand there against the wall as if she were a bundle of clothes on a peg.

Almost unbelievably, it was Mrs. Sorokine who said what Gracie wanted to say. "He might know all kinds of things, Papa. He would hardly be likely to tell us. After all, we are the suspects."

"Only if he's a fool!" Dunkeld snapped at her. "I wasn't even in Africa when the first woman was killed, which I shall remind him, if he is idiotic enough to suspect me. And no woman could have done such a thing."

Hamilton Quase put his wineglass down with a shaking hand, slopping some of it over, even though it was half empty. "You seem to be assuming it was the same person. I don't know why! It doesn't have to be. Unfortunately slashing prostitutes to death is not a unique propensity."

"Straining coincidence a little far, don't you think?" Dunkeld's face was twisted with sarcasm. "Exactly the same way, with the same three men present? Even Pitt could get far enough to see the unlikelihood of that. But if he can't, then I shall have to give him a little assistance."

"Perhaps you should tell him who the Whitechapel murderer is at the same time?" Quase suggested bitingly. "The whole country would be glad to know. Except whoever it is, of course."

"That's irrelevant," Mr. Marquand observed contemptuously. "None of us were in London in the autumn of 1888."

"Except Papa," Mrs. Sorokine said. "You were here, because I was too, and I saw you. We all knew what happened to those women, everybody did." She smiled dazzlingly, her eyes too bright. "And in case you think that is irrelevant, my point is that when something hideous happens, people get to know about it, and could copy it closely enough, if they were sufficiently insane, or sufficiently evil."

"I have finished all the fish I desire to eat." Mrs. Quase laid her implements on the plate and turned toward Gracie. "Would you remove my plate, and begin to serve the next course? You have no need to fear interrupting the conversation. It is finished."

"Yes, ma'am," Gracie said obediently.

"And get me some more wine," Mr. Quase

added, holding up the almost empty bottle so she could see the label.

"No! Thank you," Mrs. Quase cut across him. "We have sufficient. Just clear away the plates."

"If my wife doesn't want the wine, she doesn't need to have it." Quase swiveled in his chair unsteadily until he was facing Gracie. "I do. Fetch it. Take this, so you get the right one." He thrust the bottle out toward her.

Mr. Sorokine stood up and took it from him. "Just clear the dishes," he told Gracie. "The footman will bring whatever wine we are having with the next course. It may be red, or at least something different."

Gracie took the bottle, relieved at being rescued. "Yes, sir." She turned to give it to Ada just beyond the door, then began to collect the plates with Biddie's help.

By the time she had taken them to the kitchen and returned, the next course was served and they were all eating again, or pretending to.

Mrs. Sorokine seemed too excited to do more than take the occasional mouthful. She went on making oblique remarks to her father, as if deliberately baiting him. Sometimes he ignored her, once or twice he responded sharply, almost viciously.

Gracie saw Mrs. Dunkeld flinch, as if the barbs had been directed at her. There was an unhappiness in her face in repose, a kind of stillness as if she were concentrating on mastering pain. It made Gracie wonder how much she was afraid, and whether it was all for herself or for a tragedy that had yet to happen and could overtake them all. Did she actually have some idea which of the men sitting at the table around her had done this nightmarish thing?

When Mrs. Sorokine was not looking at her father, her eyes flashed to Simnel Marquand. Gracie did not see her once look at her husband. What did that mean? That she did not want to, or that she did not dare?

Olga Marquand remained almost silent.

The course was cleared and the roast beef served, then the puddings, and lastly the biscuits, cheese, and fruit. Gracie managed to fetch and carry without dropping anything or getting anything seriously wrong until the very end, when Ada bumped her elbow and she sent a pile of dirty plates crashing down the stairs. Nothing was broken, but Gracie spent the next half hour cleaning it up and washing the stains out of the carpet.

"Uppity little cow!" Ada observed with satisfaction as she walked around her, lifting her skirts aside with care.

With difficulty, Gracie refrained from reaching out and tripping her. At the moment her mind was busy trying to understand the chaotic emotions she had seen at the dinner table and attempting to decode what Mrs. Sorokine had really meant when she was talking to her father. Gracie was quite certain it had to do with the questions she had been asking all day. She had deduced something, and she was trying to tell them all, perhaps to frighten someone into an action that would betray him.

It was a dangerous thing to do, but there seemed to be something in Mrs. Sorokine that was starved for excitement, however dangerous, or even morally wrong.

Or else maybe it wasn't excitement, but fear, hidden as well as she was able to, because the man who had done this was someone she loved. Was that why she could not look at her husband?

Perhaps she was brave, and very honest, even at such a cost.

Gracie fetched, carried, and cleaned, still thinking of it. It all made Ada pretty unimportant: just irritating and rather grubby, like the flies that buzzed around the bottles once full of blood.

CHAPTER EIGHT

Pitt had a restless night. He disliked being away from home. He missed Charlotte acutely. Since joining Special Branch, he could no longer tell her the details of his cases, which meant she was unable to help in the practical ways she used to when he dealt with simple murders. All the same, her presence, her belief in him, made him calmer and stronger.

The pieces of information Gracie had brought him were extraordinary. They must mean something, and yet he could make no sense of them. He had asked the cook about the port bottles, and she had confirmed that Mr. Dunkeld had brought them as a gift for the Prince. They had contained port of a quality far superior to any that would ever be used in cooking. They had been served at table for the gentlemen. He did not mention the blood. Whatever warnings he gave, she would be bound to tell someone — probably everyone.

He had made inquiries about the broken china, but received no reply. They all disclaimed any knowledge. Similarly, everyone said the Queen's sheets must have been put in the linen cupboard by mistake, and no one seemed to understand that they had been slept on. They simply denied the possibility.

When he finally drifted off to sleep, it was into a tangle of dreams. The glory of Buckingham Palace was mixed with the stink and terror of the back alleys of Whitechapel, where those other fearful corpses of women had been found.

He woke with a start, his heart pounding, and sat upright in bed, for a moment at a loss as to where he was. There was a wild banging on his door. Before he could answer, it swung open and Cahoon Dunkeld staggered in, his face ashen gray in the light from the corridor.

Pitt scrambled out of bed and instinctively went to him. The man looked as if he were about to collapse. Pitt grasped him by the shoulders and eased him into the single chair.

Cahoon drooped his shoulders forward and buried his head in his hands. Whatever had happened, he seemed shattered by it.

Pitt lit the gaslamp and turned it up, and then waited until Cahoon regained control of himself.

When at last he sat up, his face was blotched where his fingers had pressed against it and his eyes had a fevered look. He was so fraught with emotion his body was rigid and he could not keep his arms still, as though he were desperate to do something physical but had no idea what or how.

He rubbed his hand over his brow and up over his head. His knuckles were bruised; one was torn open.

"It's Minnie," he said hoarsely. "She was behaving erratically all day, but I thought she was just seeking attention, as she does. She . . . she needs to be admired, to draw people's eyes, occupy their thoughts. Her husband is . . ." His jaw clenched and for several moments he was unable to continue.

Pitt thought of completing the sentence for him, to prompt him to go on, but decided the issue was too grave to misdirect. He waited, motionless.

Cahoon took a shuddering breath. "At dinner she kept raising the subject of the dead woman in the cupboard. I told her fairly sharply to be quiet about it. I thought she was afraid, and losing control of herself. Oh God!" His chest heaved and he seemed to clench all the muscles of his upper body.

Pitt began to be afraid. "What has happened, Mr. Dunkeld?" he demanded.

Slowly Cahoon raised his head again and stared at him. "During the night I thought about what she'd said. I was awake. I've no idea what time it was. I went over and over it, and I began to wonder if she knew something. She told me quite openly that she had been asking a lot of questions of the servants, and discovered what she wanted to know. I . . . I didn't believe her." He seemed desperate that Pitt should understand him. "I thought she was showing off."

"What has happened, Mr. Dunkeld?" Pitt said more urgently, leaning forward a little. The man in front of him was obviously laboring on the borders of hysteria. He was an adventurer, an explorer used to commanding other men. When the body in the linen cupboard had been found it was he who had taken charge, deciding what to do, supporting and comforting the Prince of Wales. Whatever it was that had driven him to this point must have shaken him to the core. Had he discovered that the murderer was close to him, in his own family? Then it must be Julius Sorokine. Minnie, as his wife, knowing his nature, even his intimate tastes and habits, had suspected him. Pitt had always found it hard to believe that a woman of any intelligence at all — and honesty — could be married to such a man, and have not even a shadow of doubt, of fear.

The tears were running silently down Cahoon's cheeks.

Pitt touched his shoulder gently. He did not like the man — he could not afford to forget the threats he had made, or his pleasure in the power to do so — but at this moment he was aware only of pity for him.

"I became afraid for her," Cahoon said, his voice half choked. He rubbed his hand over his face again, spreading a fine smear of blood across it from the cut on his knuckle. His cheeks were swollen. "I . . . I went to warn her. I wanted her to be careful. I don't know what I thought she would do!" He stopped abruptly.

"Did you warn her?" Pitt demanded. "Did she tell you what she knew? You can't protect him, whoever he is! Don't you . . . ?" Pitt's words died on his lips. Cahoon's eyes held such horror it froze him. "What happened?" he shouted.

"I found her," Cahoon whispered. "She was lying on her bedroom floor, her throat cut, her . . ." He shuddered violently. "Her gown was ripped and her . . . her stomach torn open and bleeding. Just like . . . oh God! Just like the whore in the cupboard. I was too late!"

There was nothing to say. Pity was so inadequate a response that even to attempt it was an insult. Pitt was drenched with guilt. If he had done his job sooner, more intelligently, more accurately, this would not have happened! Minnie Sorokine would still be alive. He expected Cahoon to tell him that, even to lash out at him physically from his own pain. The blows to his body could scarcely hurt more than the self-condemnation in his mind. Minnie had been so burningly alive, and Gracie had followed her around, asking the servants about the broken china, and the buckets of water. From the answers she had deduced what had happened — and Pitt was still fumbling without an idea in his head! He was stupid, criminally incompetent. He could see no end to the darkness of his guilt.

Cahoon was talking again. "I went to tell Julius . . . her husband. It seemed the natural thing to do."

"Yes?" Pitt could only imagine the man's grief.

Cahoon was staring at him. "I found him in his bedroom. He was up, half dressed, even so early. He just stared at me." Cahoon began to tremble. "His eyes were wild, like a lunatic's, and there was blood on his hands and face, scratches, tears in his skin. I . . . I knew in that moment that it was he who had done that to her. I couldn't bear it. I . . . I lost all control and I beat him . . . God knows why I didn't kill him. I only came to my senses when he was lying on the floor and I realized I was beating an unconscious man. Somehow the fact that he no longer even knew what I was doing to him robbed me of the rage long enough for me to regain mastery of myself."

Pitt imagined it. They were both big men, physically powerful. Julius was younger, but taken by surprise he could have lost the advantage. Nevertheless, Pitt understood now what the torn knuckles and the bruises still swelling and darkening on Cahoon's face meant. It had been a hard fight, even assuming it was brief.

"Where's Sorokine now?" he asked softly. He felt no blame for Cahoon. If it had been Pitt's own daughter, Jemima, he would have torn the man apart.

"Still senseless on the floor, I imagine. But I didn't kill him, if that's what you're afraid of." Cahoon smiled bitterly, and winced at the pain in his jaw. He put his hand up tentatively. "I think he loosened a tooth."

"Go back to your own room, Mr. Dunkeld," Pitt told him. "I'll go with you. You had better awaken your wife and I'm afraid you will have to tell her what has happened. Shall I send for her maid? Get tea, or brandy? Would you like one of the other women to be with her? Mrs. Marquand, or Mrs. Quase? To whom was she closer?"

Cahoon stared at him. "What?" His eyes seemed unfocused.

"Someone must inform Mrs. Dunkeld," Pitt said again. "If you don't feel well enough, then somebody else can. I will, if you wish, but I am sure in those circumstances, Mrs. Dunkeld would prefer to be up and dressed."

"She was not Minnie's mother," Cahoon said flatly. "Call who you want. What about Sorokine?"

"I'll call Mrs. Quase to be with your wife, then I'll go and see Mr. Sorokine. Go back to your own room. Would you like someone to be with you?"

"No. No, I'd rather be alone." Cahoon rose to his feet very slowly, swaying a little, and Pitt cursed the fact that he had no sergeant with him to whom he could delegate other tasks.

He walked along the silent corridor beside Cahoon as far as his own bedroom, and left him there. Then he retraced his steps quickly to Hamilton Quase's room and knocked abruptly on the door.

There was no answer. Perhaps he had

drunk too much the night before to come to his senses easily. Pitt had no recourse but to go directly to Mrs. Quase. It was not something he wished to do.

She answered after only a few moments. She was wrapped in a silk robe and her glorious hair was loose around her shoulders.

"Yes?" she said anxiously.

"Mrs. Quase, I am sorry to disturb you. I tried to waken Mr. Quase, but —"

"What is it?" she cut across him. "Tell me."

"I am afraid Mrs. Sorokine is dead. Mr. Dunkeld is profoundly disturbed, too much so to inform Mrs. Dunkeld, or to be with her. I must see Mr. Sorokine, and it may take me some time. I regret having to ask, but will you please tell Mrs. Dunkeld, and be with her?"

All the blood left her face, her hand flew to her mouth. "You . . . you mean Minnie . . . was killed?"

"Yes. I'm afraid so." As soon as he had said it he realized he should not have done so when she was standing. She swayed and grasped hold of the handle of the door, leaning against it, trying to support herself.

"Have I asked too much of you?" he said apologetically. "Should I call Mrs. Marquand?"

"No! No," she protested. "I shall go to Elsa

immediately. But that's foolish. I'll call my maid to bring tea for both of us. Then I'll go. I shall be perfectly all right. How absolutely dreadful. One of us is raving mad. This is worse than any nightmare."

He apologized again, thanked her, and went to Julius Sorokine's room. He wondered for a moment if he should at least look at the body first, then realized that the rooms would connect, and if Julius were returning to his senses, there was no way of preventing him from changing such evidence as there was, or even further desecrating the body. Pitt needed help, but there was no one he could trust, or who had seen death with such violence and tragedy before.

He did not knock, but opened the door and went straight inside.

The scene that met his eyes was exactly what he expected from Dunkeld's description. A slender bedroom chair was splintered and lying sideways on the floor. A robe, which might have been on the back of it, was stretched across the carpet. Even the large, four-poster bed had been knocked a trifle off the straight, as if someone heavy had collided hard against it. A tall dresser of drawers was also crooked, and the silver-backed brush set, box of cuff links and collar studs, which had presumably been on top of it, lay scattered on the carpet. Julius Sorokine him-self lay on the floor on his face. He was wearing trousers and a shirt and no jacket. He was motionless.

Pitt closed the door behind him and walked over. He bent down and touched Julius's neck above the collar. The pulse was strong and steady, and even before Pitt straightened up, Julius began to stir.

"Sit up slowly, Mr. Sorokine," Pitt told him.

Julius rolled over, opening his eyes. He stared up at Pitt with obvious confusion. "What are you doing here?" he asked, his voice gravelly. He coughed and sat up, wincing with pain. His face was bruised and there was a heavy gash across his cheek, blood smeared on his lip and chin. His hair was tousled. However, unlike Cahoon, he had already shaved, possibly in cold water, since there was no sign of his manservant having been here.

"What happened, Mr. Sorokine?" Pitt asked him. "Please stay sitting on the floor." He made it sound like an order. He was afraid that if Sorokine got to his feet, he could easily start another fight. He was at least as tall as Pitt, and judging by the grace with which he had moved previously, very fit.

Julius blinked. Then memory rushed back.

"God! Minnie!" He started to get up.

Pitt put out a hand and pushed him back again, so that he rolled a little, off-balance. "What happened, Mr. Sorokine?"

Julius shivered. "Cahoon came storming in here, eyes blazing like a madman, snarling something about Minnie, and took a swing at me." He touched his face and drew his fingers away, covered in blood. "Knocked me over against the bed. When I got up again, I asked him what the devil was the matter. He just shouted something else indistinguishable and hit me again. This time I saw it coming and hit him back. I knocked him against the dresser and everything went flying." He shook his head, then winced. "I thought that might bring him to his senses, but it didn't. He seemed to be completely off his head." He looked totally bewildered.

"He came back and hit me," he went on. "First with his left hand, which I ducked, then he caught me with his right. We struggled a bit more. It was ridiculous, like two drunks in an alley. He must have got the better of me, because the next thing I remember was a hell of a blow, then you talking to me." He blinked. "What's happened to Minnie? We made the devil of a row. She must have heard us! Did she call you? That's stupid. I'm not going to lay charges. He's my

313

father-in-law, God damn it!"

Pitt could almost have believed him. "I'm sorry, Mr. Sorokine, but your wife is dead."

Julius looked as if Pitt had hit him again. "What?"

Was it possible he had some kind of mental aberration where he had no idea afterwards what he had done? It would explain why no one had realized his guilt before; he did not even know it himself.

"I'm sorry," Pitt said clearly. "Mrs. Sorokine is dead."

"How?" Julius demanded. "It wasn't Olga, was it? Poor woman." He closed his eyes again, drew in his breath as if to say something further, then changed his mind and looked up at Pitt, waiting for the answer.

"No, sir. No woman did to her what Mr. Dunkeld described. I'm afraid I'm going to have to lock you in here until I can contact Mr. Narraway again and have more men brought. I'll have one of the Palace servants bring you something to eat, and possibly see if you need medical help."

"Me?" Julius seemed not to grasp what Pitt had said.

"Yes. Mr. Dunkeld said you had those injuries on your face before he came in."

"Injuries?" He put his hand up again to his lip as if he had forgotten the pain and the

314

blood. "No, I didn't. I told you, he came in here and hit me!" Then the color fled from his face and he got to his feet so swiftly Pitt lurched backward away from him.

"God Almighty! You think I killed her!" Julius said, aghast. "I haven't even seen her since last night." He swung round. "Is she . . . ?"

Pitt moved rapidly past him to block his way to the dressing room and the connecting door. "No, sir. Not yet. Don't oblige me to handcuff you to the bed. That would be most unpleasant for you."

"I didn't kill her," Julius said quietly, letting his arms fall to his sides. "And I didn't touch the other woman either, poor creature."

Pitt went back to the main door and turned the key in the lock, then he put it in his pocket and went through the connecting door, pushing the bolt home on the farther side. He did not know what to believe, but he had to follow the evidence.

In spite of what Cahoon had said, he was not prepared for the sight of Minnie Sorokine sprawled across the floor of her bedroom, her throat scarlet, her gorgeous flamingo-pink gown half torn off her, and the lower half of her torso ripped open and bright with blood.

He walked toward her, feeling sick, and kneeled down beside the billowing skirts. There could be no question as to whether she was dead or not, and not much as to what had caused it. No one could live with a throat wound like that. It was almost from ear to ear, and her head lay at a crooked angle, as if her neck itself were broken.

She was cold to the touch. He had expected her to be. She was still wearing her evening gown. Her lady's maid had not been in. He would have to inquire as to why not, but he assumed it was a matter of discretion. She would come if she were sent for, and, if not, maintain a tactful absence.

Pitt forced himself to look at the mutilations. The throat wound was worse than Sadie's, but the slashing of the lower abdomen was considerably less. In fact there was almost a hint of decency about it. The cut was higher up, less overtly sexual, and her bosom had not been exposed at all. Was that because some part of Julius's brain had remembered, even in his madness, that this woman was his wife? The thought was repulsive, and peculiarly painful. Not that Pitt had never before known killers that he had liked, even understood.

But there was nothing understandable about killing Sadie. None of the men had ever seen her before. And now this! No wonder Cahoon Dunkeld had been half out of his mind with horror and grief. Julius was fortunate Dunkeld had not killed him. Had he been a slighter man, less fit, perhaps he would be dead now also, not simply locked up.

Pitt sat back on the carpet and considered what he should do. He must get in touch with Narraway, obviously; send for him to come to the Palace at once. It seemed as if the case was at an end, although there must be a great deal of evidence to collect. For what? They could hardly have a public trial of two murders at the Palace! Could it qualify as a state secret, because of where it had happened? Or would they decide that Julius Sorokine was hopelessly insane, and lock him away without a trial at all? That would be the obvious thing to do.

Even so, the evidence must be conclusive. No doctor of any honor would pronounce him mad except as proved by the fact that he had killed two women. If it seemed just as reasonable that it was actually someone else responsible, then there was nothing against him at all. All his other behavior was above reproach, even morally, let alone legally.

But considering the issues, no doubt a doctor would be found who would not be too squeamish in examining details, and who would be easily enough persuaded.

Pitt could not allow that. His own conscience found it unacceptable. If Julius Sorokine were to spend the rest of his life locked away in an asylum for the criminally insane, then Pitt must be satisfied beyond any doubt that was even remotely reasonable that it was he who had killed the women.

He could not leave Minnie's body sprawled where it was without first making an accurate diagram of it, of the mutilations and the exact nature of them. He must also search and describe the rest of the room. There was probably nothing that would tell him anything beyond the obvious: She had come up in order to retire, and someone else had entered the room either after her or before. It was almost certainly her husband. They had quarreled and ended fighting, literally.

He looked at her again and saw more clearly now that there were bruises on her face. They were little more than marks, since she had died very shortly afterward. But there were also scratches on her hands and lower arms, as if she had struggled to defend herself. That would account for the scratches on Julius's face and hands, which Cahoon had said he had seen as soon as he had gone into Julius's bedroom, and before he had attacked him himself.

With shaking hands Pitt drew her as she lay. It was out of proportion and the lines were uncertain, because he could not stop his trembling. Then he sketched the room roughly. It was difficult to tell if anything was seriously out of place; perhaps the maid would know. He would have to ask her. Nothing was broken or torn, except a small crystal bowl whose pieces were in the wastebasket. There was no glass on the floor. The breakage could have happened at any time since the basket was last emptied — presumably yesterday morning.

It seemed indecent to leave Minnie here, but there was nowhere else he could put her until Narraway came. It had been different with Sadie. Cahoon had had her moved to the ice house, almost as if she were a side of beef: an action that was distressing but highly practical. The police surgeon would be given both bodies later.

He took the top sheet off the bed, which had not been slept in, and laid it over her. Then he went out into the corridor, taking the key with him, and locked the door from the outside.

He went downstairs, found Tyndale, and asked permission to use the telephone. It was fifteen minutes before he made contact with Narraway. He was alone in the butler's pantry with the door closed.

"What is it?" Narraway said eagerly.

"There's been another murder," Pitt replied. He heard Narraway's breath drawn in sharply. "Mrs. Sorokine," he went on. He was oddly out of breath. "In her own bedroom. Otherwise it is almost exactly the same. Done roughly the same time of night. Found by Dunkeld. So far it appears most likely that it was her husband."

Narraway was silent for several moments. "I'm surprised," he said at last. "Although I shouldn't be. It had to be one of them. Is that your judgment, Pitt, that it was Sorokine?"

It was not his judgment, it was facts forced on him. "I'm not certain yet. I've locked him in his room. We'll have to prove it."

"Of course we'll have to prove it! Why, in God's name? Why would he kill her where he's bound to be found out? Is he raving?"

"No. He seems perfectly sane, just stunned."

"Admit anything?"

"No."

"I'll be there in an hour, or less if I can."

"Yes, sir."

Pitt hung up the instrument and left the

pantry to where Tyndale was waiting for him, pale-faced.

"There has been another death," Pitt said bleakly. "Mrs. Sorokine. She is in her bedroom. Obviously you will tell the maids not to enter it, without giving them any reason. Similarly you will not enter Mr. Sorokine's room. He is locked in it, for the time being."

Tyndale struggled for a moment to keep his composure. His hands were clenched together and shaking. "I'm very sorry, sir. This is dreadful. Have you informed His Royal Highness? He will be very relieved that you have solved the problem, even if it is a tragic resolution."

Pitt had not even thought of the Prince of Wales, but clearly he would have to be told. However, that task should not be left to Cahoon Dunkeld.

"No," he said unhappily. "Will you arrange for me to do that, please? As soon as possible — in fact immediately. In the circumstances there cannot be anything of more urgency."

"Yes, sir, certainly," Tyndale agreed. He straightened his coat quite unnecessarily, and left. Fifteen minutes later he returned and conducted Pitt through the magnificent corridors and galleries to the same room where the Prince had received Pitt before.

This time he looked quite different, almost comfortable: a benign middle-aged gentleman with unusually courteous manners. He was dressed in a pale linen suit and his face had a healthy glow.

"Good morning, Pitt," he said warmly. "Tyndale tells me that this wretched problem is solved. Terrible tragedy. But I am delighted, my dear fellow, that you have got to the bottom of it so quickly, and with what has to be regarded as the utmost discretion. Dunkeld was quite right to call in Special Branch." Then his face filled with consternation. "Oh my God! Of course Mrs. Sorokine was his daughter. I had quite forgotten. How perfectly terrible! He must be quite ill with grief. I shall send him my own physician, in case there is anything he can do. Is there anything else? What can I offer?"

"That is most compassionate of you, sir," Pitt replied. It was impossible to mistake the pity in the Prince's face, or in the entire attitude of his body. "But I think for the moment there is nothing. I have sent for Mr. Narraway, and we will deal with the matter as quickly as possible. Once we have established beyond doubt that it is Mr. Sorokine who is responsible, I imagine the best thing to do will be to have him declared insane, and incarcerated where he can do no further harm."

"The man's a . . . a . . ." The Prince was lost for words savage enough to say what he felt.

"Madman, sir," Pitt finished for him.

"Monster!" the Prince corrected Pitt.

"Yes, sir, it would seem so. But I think we do not wish the world to know that. It would be better for all if we agree it is insanity, an illness of the mind, and treat him accordingly. A trial would benefit no one."

"A trial." The Prince was clearly alarmed. "Good heavens, no! You are quite right, of course. Put him away. Best thing altogether."

"As soon as we are certain."

"Certain?" The Prince's eyebrows rose. "My dear fellow, there can hardly be any doubt. Cahoon himself suspected him, you know? But of course he was loath to believe it. His own son-in-law. What a fearful thing."

Pitt was surprised. "He didn't tell me he suspected Sorokine. Why? Did he know something he kept from us?"

The Prince looked embarrassed. "I am afraid you will have to ask him, if you feel that it still matters. But surely now he has been proved hideously right, and paid such a price for it, there can be no purpose served by pointing that out to him?"

"No, sir. I would much rather that you told me," Pitt urged.

"I can't. A matter of honor," the Prince said blandly. "I gave my word, you see, and that is the end of it. I'm sorry. But surely in the circumstances it doesn't matter anymore? Sorokine left the party early on the night the other poor creature was killed. He must have stabbed her also. I cannot tell you what a relief it is to have the matter ended, and so completely, before Her Majesty returns. I am obliged to you, Mr. Pitt. I shall not forget it. Thank you for coming to tell me personally."

It was a dismissal, and there was nothing for Pitt to say further that would not be argumentative and, in the circumstances, inexcusable. He thanked the Prince and withdrew.

Half an hour later he met Narraway, and took him immediately to see the body of Minnie Sorokine.

Narraway stood on the carpet and stared down at her, his dark face crumpled with unhappiness. "It looks the same," he said miserably. "But it's not! One was a professional whore, the other was his wife."

Pitt frowned. "She flirted very openly with Simnel Marquand, Sorokine's half-brother."

Narraway stared at him incredulously. "Enough to provoke this? Are you saying it is some kind of moral judgment on whoring?"

"No, I'm not. Mrs. Sorokine spent a great deal of yesterday going around asking various questions of the servants," Pitt told him. "Gracie followed her and heard most of it. It seemed to be about people's comings and goings on the night of the first murder, including in particular a broken dish of blue, white, and gold that nobody knows about, and Tyndale says doesn't exist."

"What in hell are you talking about, Pitt? You're rambling, man!

Pitt kept his temper with some difficulty. He was tired, his head ached, and suddenly he was very cold. The walls of the Palace, with all their ornately framed works of art, closed in on him. He was trapped here.

"I don't know," he said stiffly. "Mrs. Sorokine spent all day asking questions, and seemed to be very satisfied with the answers. And when Gracie asked Tyndale about it, she was told pretty abruptly that she should leave the matter alone. It concerned private misbehavior of the Prince of Wales, and was irrelevant to the murder of the prostitute."

Narraway stared at him. "On the same night?" he said dubiously. "Having a busy time, wasn't he!"

"I rather gathered he went to bed with one of the women, and fell into something of a drunken sleep," Pitt said. "Perhaps he didn't. Do you think we need to know?" He was hoping profoundly that Narraway would say they did not. "Surely it's the same piece of unfortunate behavior — unfortunate in Tyndale's eyes. He's a bit stiff."

"Where does the broken plate come into it?" Narraway asked. "So the Prince broke a plate! What of it?"

"Tyndale says there is no such plate. He is adamant."

"Perhaps it was a vase, or an ornament of some other kind?" Narraway suggested.

"And Tyndale really imagines Gracie doesn't know what kind of assignation it was with those women?" Pitt said incredulously. "He knows she is with us."

Narraway ignored him and looked down at Minnie's body again. "That's a fearful blow across the neck. Very violent. Looks as if he's almost severed her spine. Did you find the knife?"

"No. We need to search his room."

Narraway stiffened with a jerky tightening of muscles, then relaxed again. "Well, if he kills himself that may be just as well. We can't ever let him go free. But you should have looked, all the same. Now we'll have to be extremely careful going in to see him."

Pitt cursed his stupidity for not having searched Sorokine's room. Yet it was not a thing he had wished to do alone, with Sorokine in there with him. He would be far too vulnerable. He produced the key, and he and Narraway went out and along the corridor.

Julius was lying on the bed staring at the ceiling, but he could not conceal the tension in him, or the fear. The blood had dried on his face and the scratches were sharp, the bruises darkening painfully. He sat up, staring at them.

Pitt allowed Narraway to speak.

"Where are your clothes from last night, Mr. Sorokine?"

Julius blinked. "My suit is in the wardrobe and my shirt's in the clothes basket, along with my personal linen. There's no blood on them, if that's what you are looking for."

"And the knife?" Narraway asked. He sounded completely unperturbed, but there was a flicker of anxiety in the muscles of his neck and jaw.

"I have no idea," Julius told him. "I did not kill my wife." He looked at Pitt. "Do you think she knew . . . what happened to her? Did she suffer?"

Narraway drew in his breath, then let it out again.

"No," Pitt answered. "She fought, but it looks as if there was only one blow to the neck, and that killed her."

Julius winced.

"She was asking questions of the servants yesterday," Narraway continued. "What did she tell you she had found out?"

Julius looked puzzled. "I don't know. At dinner she made a lot of oblique remarks to Cahoon, as if she expected him to understand." His voice rose a little as though it were an effort to force it through his throat. "Are you saying that is why she was killed? She worked out who had murdered the woman in the cupboard?" He sat up straighter.

"Can you think of another reason?" Narraway asked.

Julius hesitated only a moment. "No." His face was filled with grief — not agony, but a kind of deep, quiet pain.

Pitt looked at him and was brushed with a fear that if he were truly mad, then it was an invisible insanity, a rage that refused to show through the veneer of what seemed to be a reasonable, even decent man. How could one know? How could one judge or guard against it? Anyone could have the madness to kill just behind the smile. One's best friend!

"Pitt, search the dressing room for the knife," Narraway ordered. "Or any clothes with blood on them, or tears." He remained standing, facing Julius, who still sat on the bed. He could not afford to turn his back on him, however calm he seemed.

But an hour later they had found nothing suggesting violence of any kind. He had apparently fought with Minnie, and cut her throat and her abdomen, without getting even a spot of blood on his shirtsleeves. There was no ash in the fireplace to indicate anything destroyed.

"He must have stripped before he went into her room," Narraway said when they were alone in the corridor again, tired and defeated. "Which seems singularly premeditated — and sane."

"Or it isn't him," Pitt argued.

Narraway chewed his lip. "This is still very ugly," he said almost under his breath. "Whatever the result, we're going to have to treat it as madness, and have whoever it is put away quietly." His voice was suddenly passionate and afraid. "But so help me God, Pitt, we have to have the right man. Apart from the injustice of it, we can't afford to leave the real one free."

Elsa's first reaction had been one of horror and pity at the waste of life. She sat on her bed, rigid with misery. She knew she had not ever truly liked Minnie. The relationship had been uneasy from the outset. Elsa had replaced Minnie's dead mother, at least socially, if not in Cahoon's affections. Not that he ever mentioned his first wife, and certainly he never made comparisons, or spoke of her with grief. She should have found that strange, but at the time she had been so fascinated by his power and the weight of his emotion, she had been flattered that he wanted her at all. And he had, then. But how quickly he had grown tired!

Minnie had seen that, and understood it. The coldness between Elsa and Minnie had become one of mutual contempt on one level, a degree of tolerance on another. It was a situation from which neither could escape. For survival, it was best to make as little trouble as possible.

And then there was Julius. Elsa was no longer sure about anyone else's emotions. This ghastly week had shaken every certainty she had. Looking at them all around the dinner table yesterday evening she had realized she had very little idea what any of them truly cared about, loved or hated, longed for, wept over. Olga's isolation and self-disgust were simple, at least on the surface. But why did she not fight back? Had victory become pointless to attempt? Was her pallor and weariness disillusion rather than defeat?

Simnel's infatuation with Minnie was not hard to understand. She had had fire and passion, laughter compared with Olga's misery. But were any of these attributes anything more than patterns on the surface? Was Minnie's fire only appetite? And Olga's chill only a result of the pain of rejection freezing her? She had barely even mentioned her children, as if she had no more heart to fight with the weapons she had.

Liliane was obviously terrified that Hamilton would drink too much and let slip some awful secret, either his own or someone else's. Was it about the murder of the other woman in Africa, so much like the ones here? She protected him as if he had been one of her children rather than her husband.

And Julius. That was the blow that left her numb. She could not accept that he had murdered Minnie, destroyed all that fierce will, that hunger and greed for life, whatever the cost. Minnie had been selfish, even cruel, but she had been as bright as a fire. To have snuffed her out seemed almost a crime against nature.

Elsa felt a searing pity for Cahoon. He had looked bruised to the heart when he had told her how Minnie had died, as if he had lost part of himself. She wanted to reach out to his agony but it was closed hard and tight inside him, and he turned away from her. Moments later he had actually left the room and she had stood alone, bewildered, bruised by rejection, and desperately sad.

She did not want to speak to anyone else, and yet to remain sitting in her room alone seemed even worse. She stood up and walked over to the window. She stared out at the heavy, summer trees, barely seeing them. Who had done this? It could not be Cahoon. Minnie was the one person he loved. She could remember a score of times she had seen them together sharing a joke, an idea, the kind of instant understanding from half a sentence that people have when they are truly close. She had never known it herself. Her father had been a distant man who did not see women as friends, only as beings of comfort, dependency, warmth, obedience, and virtue.

Minnie had been nothing like that. She was hungry, selfish, brave, and strong, like her father. Cahoon fought with her, but he admired her. If he could have found a woman like that to marry, he would have been happy.

Was it Simnel, struggling to free himself from his uncontrollable fascination with

Minnie who had finally killed her? It had led him to betray the wife he had once loved in a different way, not only privately but, because he could not conceal it, publicly as well. Olga must have seen it every day, during every mealtime at the table: the pity and the impatience in the eyes of her friends because she did not know how to fight back.

Elsa was cold, in spite of the sun coming through the window. Had Olga fought back at last?

No. That was ridiculous. If Minnie had been killed in the same way as the street woman, then it had to have been a man who had done it. Except that if Elsa could think of copying the original murder, then couldn't Olga, or anyone? Could a woman be driven to that kind of fury by jealousy?

It wasn't simple jealousy, not a matter of hating someone for having what you did not, or even hatred for taking it from you. It wasn't love that had robbed her, it was the heat of physical need, the raging appetite that destroyed both judgment and honor. It had consumed Simnel like a disease.

Most of all it might have been the humiliation, the destruction of belief in herself, even in love, the ultimate betrayal. How far was that from madness?

Surely Olga could not have killed the street

woman too? No. That was utterly different. There was nothing personal in it — if it had even happened. The prostitutes had been brought in to entertain, not necessarily anything more, although the possibility and the assumption of more extensive services were there.

The other thought, which was waiting on the edge of her mind, refused to be denied any longer. If Olga could kill out of jealousy and humiliation, then how could Elsa deny that Julius could too? And Julius would have the strength to kill Minnie, who was a big woman, tall and graceful with full bosom, rounded arms, and perfect poise. Olga would not have the strength, unless she had taken her totally by surprise. Julius would.

But had he cared enough to do it? Elsa had no idea, not really. She knew the outer man: the courtesy, the dry humor, the seeming gentleness, the way he met her eyes when she spoke to him. She knew intimately, passionately, what she hoped he was, dreamed he was, but what had that to do with reality? How much was she in love with something that existed only in her own mind? How much was anyone?

It is so easy to see what you need to see, perhaps it is even necessary.

What had Julius seen in Minnie? What had

he believed of her? He must once have thought she would be warm and loyal, gentle to his faults, strong to her own truths, that she had an inner core that could not be tarnished.

Or perhaps being beautiful and willing was enough? Had he an integrity that could not be broken, stained, bought, if the price were high enough?

For that matter, had she herself?

There was a knock on the door. She assumed it was Bartle and told her to come in without bothering to turn away from the window.

"I'm sorry to intrude on you, Mrs. Dunkeld, but it is necessary."

She whirled round and saw the policeman just inside the doorway.

"Oh!" She drew in her breath sharply. "Yes. Of course it is. Do you wish me to come to your sitting room?"

"Yes, please, if you are well enough. Otherwise perhaps your maid could wait with you?" he replied.

"I'm quite well enough, thank you," she accepted, following him out of the door again and down the stairs to the room he had been given. Bartle knew her too well; she did not want her here for the questions he would ask. She sat in the chair opposite him.

He apologized for having to distress her. She dismissed it. "You have no choice," she said. "We have to know who did this."

He nodded slightly. "Did Mrs. Sorokine confide in you at all yesterday, or the day before, Mrs. Dunkeld? It seems she had a strong suspicion as to who had killed the woman found in the cupboard, and was asking a great many questions."

Elsa was startled. She was about to deny it completely when she remembered how excited Minnie had been, and the way she had hinted at the dinner table that she had learned something no one else knew. She was showing off for her father. They had all heard her. Perhaps one of them had realized that she was on the brink of learning the whole truth, and exposing it.

Pitt was watching her. She must face him and reply.

"No. She made hints during dinner, but that's all they were. I didn't understand. It all sounded . . ." She was searching for the right word. "It sounded obscure to me. I thought she was just trying to be the center of attention. I'm . . . so sorry." That was an admission of guilt. She was guilty of not listening, not judging more kindly, not even trying to love Minnie.

She met Pitt's eyes, and saw more understanding in them than she wished to. She turned away, and realized that in doing so she was still betraying herself.

"Can you remember what she said?" he asked.

"It sounded like nonsense." She tried to recall Minnie's words. "It was something about china, a lot of cleaning up, and how much her father had helped the Prince of Wales. Do you think she really knew who killed the woman?" She hoped that was it, prayed that it was! Then it would be nothing to do with Julius, or Olga. Please God!

"Don't you think so?" he asked softly.

"Well . . . yes. I suppose so . . . unless it is just . . . no, that seems to be it." She was fumbling. She should be quiet. Why was she saying too much, like a fool?

"Did someone have another reason, Mrs. Dunkeld?"

She looked up at him quickly. There was compassion in his eyes. Chill struck her to the bone. Could he possibly know about Minnie and Simnel? Did he suspect Julius?

"Did they?" he repeated.

Could he already know about the affair? If she lied to conceal it, then he would know she was trying to protect Julius. It would seem extraordinary to him, suspicious. Minnie was her stepdaughter; that is where her loyalties should lie. At least she must pretend they did. And yet everyone knew of the affair. Someone would tell him, probably they already had. Pitt would know she was lying if she pretended not to know.

"From anger perhaps," she suggested. "Mr. Marquand was . . . attracted to her. How far it went I can only surmise, but it was intense, at least for a while." She made it sound so prosaic, reducing passion to a commonplace thing. "Regrettably, such things happen all the time," she added. "People do not kill over it. They may weep, or even lash out in some way or other. It's best to maintain all the dignity one can, and trust that it will pass. Regardless of that, Mr. Pitt, it was no reason to kill the prostitute who had nothing to do with our private affairs. None of us had ever seen or heard of her before. And you said that Minnie had been asking questions that led you to believe that she had some idea who killed the poor woman. Surely that is why she was also killed?"

"It does seem to be the case," he agreed. "My own inquiries tell me that she spent most of yesterday asking questions of the servants, and she appeared to have discovered something that made her very excited, as if she had found the answer."

"And . . ." Elsa gulped. "You think she confronted someone?"

"I think someone realized that she knew," he amended.

"I don't know who it was." The moment she had said it she knew she had spoken too quickly. He had not asked her. She had already said she had no idea. She felt her face burn.

He was looking at her steadily. "Mr. Dunkeld has no doubt that it was Mr. Sorokine. He confronted him and they fought. They both have injuries to face and hands."

She did not understand. All she wanted to do was stop Pitt from believing it. What could she say? If she defended Julius and blamed Cahoon, then Pitt would see her emotions quite nakedly. Was that what he was trying to do, see if Julius had killed his wife and was trying to blame Cahoon?

"If they fought . . ." she started, then realized the remark was pointless, and stopped.

"Neither of them denied that," he said. "And Cahoon says that Julius had his injuries before their fight."

She did not understand.

"I'm sorry." His voice was very gentle now, as if he pitied her. "Mrs. Sorokine fought for her life. Whoever killed her would have scratches and perhaps bruises as well."

She had to say it. The words were like a nightmare, but if she did not say them, it would be even worse. How could she out-think him? "My husband would never have killed his daughter, Mr. Pitt. He loved her deeply, far more than he loved anyone else."

"Didn't Mr. Sorokine also love his wife?" he asked.

She could not read the expression on his face now. He had gray eyes, very clear, as if he could see into the horror and confusion inside her.

"I imagine so," she said hesitantly. "One always assumes. And when it is family, even more so. I . . . I can't believe that Julius killed her."

He waited.

It was a stupid thing to have said, and yet it was true. Whatever Cahoon had seen, or said he had seen, she did not believe Julius had murdered either the woman in the cupboard or Minnie. She would not believe it; the burden of loss it would bring was more than she could carry.

"Thank you, Mrs. Dunkeld. I don't think I have anything else to ask you at the moment," Pitt said.

She had betrayed herself. He knew what she felt. She saw it in his face. She was em-

340

barrassed, as if she were emotionally naked. She rose to her feet, tried to think of something to say so she could leave with a shred of grace, but there was nothing. She went to the door and opened it without speaking again.

Changing her morning gown for one suitable for luncheon, she found herself alone with Cahoon. It was the one thing she had wished to avoid. Bartle had already left when he came into her dressing room. She swiveled around to face him. She always felt uncomfortable when he was behind her.

He looked haggard. He had aged ten years since yesterday. She felt a moment's stab of pity for him again. It would have been instinctive to have touched him, to have gone over and put her arms around him and held him, but the barrier of estrangement was too high. They had touched in the heat of physical hunger, but never in tenderness, the need of the heart or the mind.

"I'm so sorry," she said quietly.

He was watching her, his eyes so dark she could see no expression in them. "You didn't think Julius would do that, did you!" It was a challenge, not a question.

A shiver of alarm went through her. "Of course I didn't," she said abruptly.

341

"You didn't know him as well as you thought!" A flash of pleasure lit his eyes, almost of triumph.

She was cold inside, frightened that he could hate her enough to savor hurting her, even in the depth of his own loss.

She tried to look surprised. "Why? Did you imagine it then?" She must be desperate to be fighting back. She had thought of doing it before, but never had the courage.

Rage flared in his face. "For God's sake, you stupid creature, do you think I would have let him into the same house as my daughter if I had?" His voice was hoarse, almost cracking with grief.

Again the pity for him drowned out her own anger. "None of us saw it, Cahoon, or we would have done something and prevented this," she told him gently. Was he blaming himself for not having had Julius arrested before this happened? How could she tell him that it was not his fault without sounding both insincere and patronizing?

He was looking at her with that strange kind of triumph again, as if snatching some shred of victory out of the disaster. "They won't hang him, which is a pity," he went on. "They'll keep it all secret, to protect the Prince of Wales. They'll just take him to some madhouse and lock him up there for the rest of his life." There was something almost like a smile on his face, and he was watching her intently.

As if she should have seen it from the beginning, she suddenly understood with blinding clarity that he had always hated Julius. In spite of Minnie's death, he was still able to rejoice in his destruction. Elsa couldn't help but wonder if her husband had planned all this. Was the prostitute's death supposed to implicate and ruin Julius?

Why? Because Elsa loved him? Cahoon did not love her; he never had. But she belonged to him. This was not jealousy, it was hatred for having been insulted. His vanity was wounded, his right of possession injured.

Would she let him trample over her like this? Did she think Julius had butchered that woman, then when Minnie worked it out and faced him, he had killed her in the same way? If she said nothing, then she was admitting that she did, and that would always be part of her. Better to deny it, whatever it cost, than surrender the dream now.

"They will have to prove him guilty first," she said aloud.

"They will do," he replied, eyes shining again. "Cling on as long as you can, Elsa! Imagine all you like. You don't know men, and you don't know love. You never did!

Julius is a madman. Minnie had the courage to face that. But then she was always braver, stronger, and better than you!"

She looked at him and saw the hate in his face, for Julius, and for her too. In all his agony over Minnie — and she believed that — he had a joy that Julius would be destroyed as well. Perhaps it was all he had left now.

Except to destroy her too.

How would he do it? If Julius was locked in his room, he could not cut her throat and her stomach and blame him for it. But he could implicate her somehow, in something, and then put her aside, divorce her. Then perhaps he could marry Amelia Parr!

She looked at him, searched his face, and believed with ice-cold certainty that it was true. There was nothing to protect her, except her own nerve and intelligence, and a will not to be beaten.

"We'll see," she said softly. "It isn't the end yet."

CHAPTER NINE

Victor Narraway sat in the hansom oblivious of the sunlit streets through which he passed. He was more concerned with the murders in the Palace than he had allowed Pitt to know. Five years ago, at the time of the Whitechapel atrocities by the man who had come to be known as Jack the Ripper, the Queen had almost retired from public duties. The Prince of Wales's extravagance had been out of control and he was deeply in debt. The reputation of the Crown was so low that the cry for a republic was finding many to answer it. There had been ugly riots in the streets, especially in the East End, and around the Whitechapel area in particular.

Three years later, Pitt had encountered the same emotions still high with Charles Voisey's attempt at a republican coup. It had come far too close to success, and far too recently for a scandal like this not to be profoundly dangerous. There was a current of political unrest that was more serious than Pitt was aware.

The other matter that disturbed Narraway was the whole issue of the Cape-to-Cairo railway. On the surface it was a brilliant idea: daring, farsighted, and patriotic. It would unite Africa physically, accomplish new marvels in engineering and exploration, and bring culture, civilization, and possibly Christianity to new regions never before fully explored. And of course it would also be the greatest boost for trade in the Empire since the beginnings of the East India Company over a century before.

However, such a vast undertaking had negative aspects as well, and there was a gnawing doubt in his mind. It had been his habit all his life to listen to both sides of any argument, to give at least as much weight to the opinion against as to the praise. It was a practice that had proved painful, and often unpopular, but it had saved both money and life, not to mention political embarrassment.

In this case he had heard only murmurings against the scheme. These could quite easily be seen as envy or timidity for such a huge venture. He was on his way to keep an appointment to dine with Watson Forbes at his house, where there would be time to extend the conversation as far as it needed to go. He had not canceled it because of Minnie Sorokine's death, which might prove that the whole issue was Julius Sorokine's personal madness, some sexual deviation with no real relevance to the Cape-to-Cairo project at all. Some of the other possibilities were too fearful to think of. The ghost of the Ripper still haunted his mind.

Regardless of that, there were questions about the railway that troubled him, doubts that, if well founded, could damage the Empire for generations to come.

He arrived at Forbes's house and was received by the butler, who conducted him into the same pleasant room as before, with its African paintings and curios.

Forbes offered him sherry, then stood by the mantel, although the fire was not lit. The late-summer sun streamed in through the long windows, making jeweled patterns on the colors of the Turkish rug. He seemed mildly amused, his eyes bright.

"What is it I can tell you at such length, Mr. Narraway? I am not involved in this railway project. Did I not make that clear?"

"Quite clear," Narraway replied. "Therefore your views on it may be less driven by the desire for it to succeed."

Forbes smiled. "You think Dunkeld is too partisan to entertain a rational judgment?"

"Wouldn't you be, if your future and your honor depended on it?" Narraway asked.

Forbes sipped his sherry, rolling it over his tongue before swallowing. "Of course I would. It is the greatest adventure of a life-time, and more than most men ever dream of. Have you some specific fear in mind?"

"Cost?" Narraway suggested.

"Every building venture costs more than one calculated," Forbes replied with a rueful smile. "Whether it is a garden shed or a transcontinental railway. One expects it and plans accordingly. Or are you afraid it will cost more than it is worth?"

"Could it?" Narraway asked. Cost was not what he had feared at all, but he wanted to test Forbes on everything. He needed to know why, with all his African experience, he was not involved — in consultation at least.

Forbes was watching him over the rim of his glass. "No," he said simply. "The exercise of building it will bring in vast profits of all sorts: engineering, trade, timber, steel, sheer reputation. And Marquand is brilliant. All the investment money will be protected, as far as the builders are concerned. Africa has diamonds, gold, copper, timber, ivory — just to start with. Cecil Rhodes is totally behind the venture. Money will pour in." There was no doubt in either his voice or his face.

Narraway tried to read him more deeply and knew he failed. There was a reservation of some kind in Forbes, but he had no idea what it was. It could even be some personal emotion that had to do with the people involved rather than the project itself.

"Is it likely that we do not have the engineering skills?" he asked. "Much of it is relatively unknown country. Chasms will have to be bridged, mountains cut through, deserts and shifting sands crossed, hostile territory of all sorts, possibly even jungles traversed."

"It will be surveyed before they begin," Forbes replied without hesitation. "What they cannot cross they will skirt around. That may require some extra diplomatic skill, but Sorokine has it. And when he wants to, he has enormous charm. Congo Free State may prove difficult, but he won't have to bother with them if German East Africa is willing to oblige. No doubt he will play one against the other." He sipped at his sherry again. "Most of the territory is British anyway. They'll manage." The tone of his voice dipped a little. There was a sadness in the lines of his face.

Narraway moved to lean forward, then changed his mind. What was the shadow in Forbes's mind, the reservation that still troubled him?

"It sounds like a great advantage for the British Empire," Narraway said slowly. "Something that would bring benefits of all kinds, possibly far into the future. I assume we will make enemies. Belgium, France, and Germany just to begin with."

Forbes smiled. "Very likely," he agreed. "But then any advantage to one nation is a disadvantage to others. If you were afraid of offending people, you would never do anything at all. It's a matter of degree."

Narraway knew they were playing games with words. They had not touched the real issue yet. "You believe the project can succeed?"

"Yes. Dunkeld will not stop until he has done so."

"And make himself a fortune." It was a conclusion rather than a question.

There was a change in Forbes's face so small it could have been no more than an alteration in the light. "I imagine so."

"And so will the providers of timber, steel, labor, and the shipping of gold, diamonds, copper, timber, and ivory," Narraway added.

Forbes's face was motionless. He drew in his breath, then let it out with a sigh. "You want to know why I am not concerned to be involved with the railway. You think perhaps

it is more of a personal issue with Cahoon
Dunkeld? You are mistaken. I have spent
over half my life in Africa." Now there was
unmistakable emotion in his face. It was
clear in his eyes, his mouth, even the tightening of the muscles in his neck. "I love the
country. It is the last great mystery left in the
world, the one place too big for us to crush
and occupy with our smallness, trying to im-
press our image on its people and convince
them it is the likeness of God."

Narraway was stunned. The passion in
Forbes had taken him totally by surprise.

"You don't know Africa, Mr. Narraway,"
Forbes said softly. "You have never felt the
sun scorch your face and smelled the hot
wind blowing across a thousand miles of
grassland teeming with beasts like the sands
of the seashore. You haven't seen the sky
flame with sunset behind the acacia trees,
heard the lions roar in the night with the
Southern Cross burning in the darkness
above you, or put your ear to the ground as
it trembles with the thunder of a million
hoofs. Have you ever seen a giraffe's eyelashes? Or a cheetah run? Felt the terror in
your blood and in your bones when you
know there's a leopard stalking you? Then
you know how sweet life is, and how unbearably fragile." Forbes shook his head fraction-

ally, a denial so small Narraway almost missed it. "Here in England there's a glass wall between you and the taste of reality. I don't want to see the last true passion tamed by railways, and men with Bibles telling everyone to cover their bodies." He spread his powerful, elegant hands. "Play your string quintets, by all means, Mr. Narraway, but don't silence the drums simply because you don't understand them. The men who play violins have steel and gunpowder, and the men who play drums don't."

Narraway did not answer immediately. He studied Forbes's intense face, the powerful nose and curious, thin-lipped mouth, which was yet so expressive.

In the end he waited so long it was Forbes who broke the silence. "Is that what the Empire is for?" he asked. "To change everything into something we can buy and sell?"

Narraway was repulsed by the thought. It was worse than offensive, it was blasphemous. But he did not want Forbes to know that. That he should be so moved was a revelation he could not afford to make. "Exploitation?" he said calmly.

"Isn't it?" Forbes's black eyebrows rose. He was watching Narraway intensely.

"And you are against it?" Narraway allowed no more than a shred of sarcasm in his voice.

Temper flared in Forbes's face, then vanished. "A longer view," he said softly. "What will Africa be a century from now? Dominion, friend, enemy, battleground?"

Again Narraway said nothing.

"We will not be alive then," Forbes answered himself. "Is that all that matters, the basis of all judgment?"

Narraway did not answer. "But you think Dunkeld will build it anyway?" he said instead.

"Not easily, and not with my help, but yes, he will build it." Again Forbes's face was dark with emotion, but with such a conflicting mixture it was impossible to read.

Over dinner they spoke of other things. Forbes was an interesting and hospitable host, and Narraway did not arrive home until close to midnight.

In the morning Narraway was back at the Palace facing Pitt. There was a tray with tea on the table and Pitt sat opposite him. He looked weary, trapped. More than that, there was a disillusion in him that Narraway had not seen before. Suddenly he realized how being here oppressed Pitt, who had witnessed violence and degradation often enough, but never before on this level. It was not that these murders were more brutal than others, it was that they were here in a place he had considered inviolate.

Perhaps it mattered also that the victims were women, the second one not wildly unlike Charlotte, at least in class and origin. Charlotte had something of the same warmth inside her, the same courage and quick tongue. She was just gentler, and perhaps immeasurably happier.

This was breaking Pitt's ideals of his monarch, and threatening his feelings dangerously.

The ideals Narraway did not envy. He had lost his own illusions about people too long ago. Proximity had forced him into realism. It was hard to believe that Pitt had kept his naïveté so long. He must simply have refused to see what he did not wish. Narraway felt both impatience and pity for that.

Then he thought of Charlotte's face, her eyes, the curve of her mouth and her throat, and was drenched with loneliness. In that instant he would have traded all the knowledge and understanding he had in return for the innocence in Pitt that made Charlotte love him. Was it innocence or hope?

And if the fact of these Palace murders crushed that, what was Pitt going to lose?

Pitt finished his tea and set his cup down,

waiting for Narraway to speak. His eyes were dark-rimmed, his skin shadowed, and there were tiny cuts on his jaw where he had shaved clumsily. Did violent death still churn his stomach too, in spite of how well he hid it? Did he share Narraway's sense of guilt for not preventing Minnie Sorokine's death?

"Is Sorokine still locked in his room?" he asked.

"Yes. There was no alternative," Pitt replied unhappily.

"Are you satisfied he killed her?" Narraway did not want to ask, but he needed the matter closed, and Pitt's troubled face left him no choice. "Presumably she realized he had killed the first woman, and he could not afford to leave her alive because sooner or later she would betray him over it?"

Pitt spoke slowly. "That's what it looks like."

"Why aren't you satisfied?" Narraway's voice rose in spite of his effort to keep it level and under control. He was accustomed to anarchy, treason, and very considerable violence, but he had not met sexual aberration before. There was something uniquely repulsive about the intimacy of it, like the foul smell of some disease.

"There was no blood on him," Pitt spoke

carefully, as if picking his way through chaotic thoughts. "None at all, except the little from the scratches on his face. Nothing of the dark gore that came from her."

Narraway's stomach turned and he felt the chill of sweat on his skin. "He'd had all night to wash," he pointed out.

Pitt shook his head. "There was shaving water in the jug and basin, but it was all clean. Nothing in it but soap. And what about his clothes?"

"He stripped to do it?" Narraway suggested. "There was no blood on anyone the first time either. It seems to be his pattern."

Pitt frowned. "The first time he might have planned it, but the second was because she challenged him. He would hardly have told her to wait there while he stripped off, then came back and killed her!"

"Then what did he do?" Narraway demanded, frustration burning up inside him. Just as Pitt was still unfamiliar with the complexities of anarchy, so was he with the nature of murder.

"I don't know," Pitt replied. "He was distressed over her death, but he looked totally sane to me. He denied it."

Narraway was startled. "Did you expect him to confess?"

Pitt pushed his hair out of his eyes with a

clumsy hand. "It's not just what he said, it's the way in which he spoke. I don't know what I think." His brow furrowed. "There's something wrong with it, something about all of it that I haven't understood. I've racked my mind, but all I see is the break in reasoning, the place where something should be to tie it together. I'm not even sure what I'm looking for."

"Then for God's sake, think!" Narraway said desperately. "Before it's too late. We've got to make an arrest. This victim wasn't a whore, she was Dunkeld's daughter. We can't afford to be wrong. If we are, and we have to admit it, it will be the end of Special Branch. We won't ever have a case higher in the public eye than this, when it comes out. And it will."

"I won't condemn the wrong man to a life in the hell of a madhouse," Pitt told him, stubbornness setting hard in his face. "Have you ever been in one of those places? I have. He'll be gibbering mad in a year or two, even if he isn't to begin with. It would be cleaner and more humane to hang him in the first place. I can still hear the screaming of Bedlam in my nightmares sometimes."

Narraway leaned forward. "Pitt, we can't afford any more dead women, whether we make or break the Cape-to-Cairo railway.

One of those three men has murdered two women in four days. The Queen will be back here this week."

Pitt said nothing.

Narraway waited again, his mind going back to what Forbes had said about Julius Sorokine. He seemed a civilized and intelligent man, even if a little indolent — or taking some of his privileges for granted. What could possibly have happened to turn him into a creature who had cut the throats and gouged open the bellies of two women? "Something started it," he said aloud. "Find it."

Pitt looked up. "Two in four days? It started long before now. You aren't sane one day and then a raving, blood-soaked murderer the next, unless something has happened to shatter your mind in between, and nothing did. They sat around talking about the African railway and planning the future full of wealth and achievement for all of them. They flirted, specifically Mrs. Sorokine with Mr. Marquand. And Mrs. Dunkeld is in love with Mr. Sorokine."

"And he with her?" Narraway asked quickly. Was that a thread to the truth?

Pitt shrugged very slightly. "I don't know. But none of it began while they were here, and I doubt anyone learned of it for the first time either. Even if they did, it doesn't explain killing the prostitute. It's not a crime of jealousy or even betrayal — it's hatred born out of some kind of madness."

"Given that this particular insanity lies dormant most of the time, what wakens it out of control?" Narraway asked, the urgency building up inside him again. "You've dealt with madness before, people who kill and go on killing until they are caught. I know evil, but not unreason. Help me, Pitt! If I search through Sorokine's history, what am I looking for?"

Pitt sighed; there was weariness and desperation in it. "Obviously another death like these: a woman with her throat and belly slashed. Before that, for violent quarrels, irrational hatred of women, someone who belittled him, jilted him, did something that he might have seen as betrayal. An explosive temper. It will have to have been covered up very carefully. He's a diplomat. Look for someone else being blamed, or something unsolved, possibly described as an accident."

Narraway considered for several minutes. "I spoke to Watson Forbes," he said finally. "He's against the Cape-to-Cairo railway. He believes it will exploit Africa to its disadvantage, and ultimately to the disadvantage of the whole British Empire, possibly in the next century."

"Interesting," Pitt admitted. "But I can't see any connection with the murders. Can you?"

"No. They don't seem to have anything to do with the railway, just a ghastly coincidence that they exploded here in the Palace just as the railway is being discussed. But I don't like coincidences. I've seen very few real ones."

"There are other things I need to make sense of," Pitt went on. "If Mrs. Sorokine deduced from all these odd pieces of information exactly how her husband killed Sadie, and possibly why, then I want to know how she did it. They seem unrelated and nonsensical to me."

"What pieces?" Narraway asked.

"Port bottles with blood in them, a broken dish, which nobody admits ever existed, buckets of water being carried hurriedly and discreetly up- and downstairs. The Queen's own sheets slept on, and soaked in blood. How did whatever Minnie Sorokine knew of that prove to her that it was her husband who killed Sadie?"

"Who was carrying buckets of water? Not Sorokine?"

"No, household servants."

"Then what connection has it?"

"I have no idea!"

Narraway stood up. "I'll look into his past. And the others, at least where they cross."

Fifteen minutes later he was outside in the sun and the wind. An hour after that he was talking to a friend who had amassed a fortune in shipping and spent a good deal of it buying and selling gems. He knew most of the cities of the Mediterranean, both of Europe and of Africa, and of course the great diamond cutting and dealing centers of the Middle East. His name was Maurice Kelter.

"Sorokine," he turned the name over experimentally. "What is it, Russian?"

"Possibly," Narraway replied, crossing his legs and leaning back in the broad leather chair. He was at his club, where he should have been at ease. "If it is, it will be third- or fourth-generation. He is a diplomat, tall, good-looking, probably around forty."

Kelter nodded, sipping at the whisky and soda at his elbow. "Yes. I know the fellow you mean. Married Dunkeld's daughter, didn't he? Lovely-looking woman. Bit of a handful. Why are you interested in him? Has something happened?"

Narraway smiled, but it felt forced. "Things are happening all the time. What sort of thing did you think would be connected to Sorokine?"

Kelter made a little grimace. "To be frank, probably indifference. I don't think he's ever stretched himself to the best he could be. Very pleasant chap, but things have come easy to him. Position, enough money, certainly women."

"Many women?" Narraway asked quickly.

Kelter's eyes opened wider. "Possibly. Why?"

Narraway ignored the question. "Temper?" he asked.

Kelter smiled. "Not that I heard of, but . . . do you want unsubstantiated rumor?"

"If that's all you have." Narraway disliked innuendo, but that was often where lines of investigation began. "Temper?" he prompted again.

Kelter put his whisky down. "There was a particularly ugly affair in Cape Town a few years ago. Half-caste woman was murdered. Throat cut, stomach slit open. Never found out who did it. Prostitute of sorts, so it wasn't followed the way it would have been if she'd been decent, or white."

Narraway was skeptical. Could it really be so easy? "What was Sorokine's involvement with it?"

Kelter shrugged. "Don't really know. Whispers. Apparently he knew the woman, had some kind of relationship with her."

"Did the police investigate him?"

Kelter sighed. "We're talking about a half-caste prostitute on the edges of Cape Town, Narraway. Nobody investigated it. People asked a few questions. Men came and went: miners, traders, explorers, adventurers, all nationalities, ex-patriots who couldn't go home, drunks and fugitives, all sorts. It could have been anyone."

"Who said it was Sorokine?"

Kelter frowned. "Now that I think of it, I'm not certain. It was not much more than looks and nods. I didn't track it down because frankly I didn't care. There were far more interesting things going on at the time."

Narraway did not pursue it with Kelter, but there were other people he knew from whom he could collect favors, and he sought them out now. It was not easy to keep the sense of urgency out of his manner. He knew that betraying his need would open him up to being lied to, and favors done him now would earn repayment later, perhaps at a time when he could not afford it.

He walked into another crowded club room, the pungent cigar smoke in the air mixed with the smell of leather armchairs and old malt whisky. Sometimes he loved the game of question and counterquestion, perhaps partly because he was so good at it. He saw the respect in other men's eyes, the guarded admiration, and the equally guarded fear. Today he was tired of it. The constant measuring of words, even gestures, the sheer loneliness of it weighed him down. Pitt might feel trapped in the suffocating ritual of the Palace now, but it was only for a short while — days at the most. Then he would go home again to Charlotte, to warmth and kindness, to an inner safety Narraway would never have. Even if all his illusions were broken, his lifetime's loyalties destroyed, at heart Pitt could not be damaged. Nothing could touch what was safe inside him. Had he any idea how fortunate he was?

He walked round a corner and found the man he was looking for. He sat down opposite him, knowing he was intruding on a few moments of peace and also that the man dared not refuse him.

Yet if he did not play these games, what would he do? Through the long years he had developed no other skill that used his mind fully, or the sensitivities he had honed.

Welling looked up and jerked himself out of the study in which he had been lost. "Who are you after?" he asked.

"Sorokine," Narraway replied.

"Dead," Welling told him. "Good man. Died about five years ago. Surprised you didn't know that." There was a faint glimmer of satisfaction in his eyes.

"Julius Sorokine," Narraway corrected him.

Some of the pleasure died out of Welling's face. "Oh. Yes. The son. Good man too, but a bit too handsome for his own well-being. Doesn't have to work hard enough. Suppose that might change. Seemed to be putting a bit more energy into it a couple of months ago, then slacked off again."

"Slacked off?" Narraway was startled. This didn't seem relevant to the murderer in Cape Town he was looking for, but it was interesting because it made no sense. Any anomaly should be pursued. "What was he doing?"

"For God's sake, Narraway, don't treat me like a fool!" Welling said impatiently. "He's negotiating for this damn railway for Dunkeld. Talking to the Belgians and the Germans, and all the odd African lands right the way up to Cairo."

"And he slacked off? Why?" Now Narraway was really interested in spite of himself. Suddenly Sorokine was more complex than he had assumed. "Did someone else approach him?" It was an ugly thought, a kind of betrayal that was peculiarly offensive, presumably for money.

Welling smiled but his lips were turned down. "I doubt it. There's no one else in a position to rival Dunkeld, since Watson Forbes isn't interested. And Sorokine's married to Dunkeld's daughter anyway. It would be against his own interest."

"So why? Just lazy?"

Welling shrugged. "I've nothing but rumors, bits of whisper not worth a lot."

"Sabotage?" Narraway suggested. Had someone looked into the old murder and found something? Or even a second crime somewhere, and blackmailed him over it? He found that hard to believe, simply because the murder appeared to be the product of eruptions of a darkness inside the mind that no one could control, no matter what the threat.

"Sabotage is always possible." Welling misunderstood him. "Seven thousand miles of track, mostly unprotected? Pardon me, but it's a stupid question."

"Not of the track," Narraway told him. "I meant of the project in the first place."

"By somehow removing Sorokine? I suppose it's possible. But pretty short term, and hardly worth the trouble." Welling sat up a little straighter in the chair, his eyes sharper.

"What the hell are you really after, Narraway?"

"What was being said, exactly?" Narraway ignored the question.

"It's serious?" Welling blinked. "What I heard was that Sorokine was uncertain in his loyalty to the project altogether. Someone had been talking to him about lateral lines, from the center to the sea, rather than a long spine up the back of Africa. The real future of the British Empire lies in sovereignty of the sea, not of Africa. Build railways to take inland timbers, ivory, gold, and so on, to the ports. Let the nations of Africa have their own transport, independently, build it and maintain it themselves, and we'll ship the goods round the world. It's what we've always done. We've explored the world, settled it, and traded with it. Africa was never a maritime continent. Keep it that way." He was watching Narraway's face more closely than he let on, eyes half-veiled.

Narraway turned it over in his mind. At first it seemed reactionary: a denial of adventure, trade, the brilliant advance of engineering the Cape-to-Cairo railway would be. Then he realized that it was not denying new exploration or building, simply the scale of it. There would still be new tasks, but laterally, east to west rather than south to north.

The difference that mattered was that the railway would belong to the multitude of nations concerned, not to the British Empire.

Ships would be the key, not trains. And the British had been masters of the sea since the days of Nelson and in maritime adventure since the defeat of the Spanish Armada in the time of Queen Elizabeth. British ships traded in every port on earth and across every ocean.

"And Sorokine was listening to this?" he said aloud.

"So I heard," Welling replied. "But he might have told the man to go to the devil, for all I know. How did you get to hear of it? And why do you care? Is the Cape-to-Cairo railway Special Branch business?"

"No," Narraway said honestly. He would need Welling again. Lying to him would destroy future trust. "It's to do with the man, not the project. At least I think it is. Do you know Sorokine personally?"

"I've met him, can't say I know him. Why?"

"Is he a womanizer?"

"He's probably had his share. He's a good-looking man. Doesn't have to try very hard." He was looking at Narraway curiously now. "Are you thinking of that damn business in Cape Town with the prostitute? There was no proof it was him, just gossip, and I think honestly you could trace most of that back to Dunkeld."

"Why would Dunkeld say it if there were no foundation to it? Sorokine's married to Dunkeld's daughter," Narraway pointed out.

Welling sighed. "Sometimes you're so devious and so damn clever, you miss what a more emotional man less occupied with his brain would know instinctively. Dunkeld is possessive, especially of his daughter. Sorokine was taken with her to begin with, then he got bored with her. No emotional weight."

"Sorokine, or Minnie Dunkeld?" Narraway asked.

Welling smiled. "Probably both of them, but I meant her. To love or hate is excusable, but a woman like her is never going to forgive a man for being bored with her, whoever's fault it is. It would do you a lot of good to fall in love, Narraway. You would understand the forces of nature a great deal better. If you survived it." He pulled a silver case out of his pocket. "Do you want a cigar?"

"No thank you." Narraway had difficulty mastering his sense of having been somehow intruded upon. "Do you think Sorokine had anything to do with the woman in Cape Town?" he asked a little coolly.

"No." There was no doubt in Welling's face. "Whoever did it was raving mad. If he's still alive, he'll be foaming at the mouth by now, and certainly have done it again, probably several times." The unlit cigar fell out of his mouth. "God Almighty, is that what's happened?"

"Don't oblige me to arrest you for treason, Welling," Narraway said softly, a tremor in his voice he would prefer to have disguised. "I rather like you, and it would make me very unhappy."

"I doubt it is Sorokine." Welling was rattled. He picked up the cigar to give himself a moment more before he answered. "I don't think he has the temperament. But I've been mistaken before."

Narraway tried to think of other questions to ask, something that would indicate a further line of inquiry. A woman had been killed in Africa, and the method was apparently exactly the same as that used in the Palace. He knew Welling was watching him. He would be a fool to underestimate his intelligence.

"Tell me more about the crime in Cape Town," he asked.

Welling shrugged. "Prostitute, half-caste with the best features of both races, as so often happens. Fine bones of the white, rich color and graceful bearing of the black, but wanted by neither side. Made her money where she could, and who can blame her? No one wanted to marry her: too white for the blacks, ideas above her station. Too black for the whites, can't take her home to the parents, but too handsome not to lust after."

Welling lit the cigar and drew on it experimentally. "Ended up on the floor in a bawdy house, her throat cut and her belly slit open. Nobody ever knew who did it."

"But Sorokine was there?"

"He was in the area, no more than that. So were a lot of white men."

"It had to be a white man?"

"Apparently. It was a place that didn't allow blacks in."

Narraway said nothing. It was ugly, equivocal, and inconclusive. It was also disturbingly like the present crimes. Finally he thanked Welling and left.

Over the course of the day, he made a few more inquiries to see if he could learn of any other murders of women in the same pattern, anywhere connected with Sorokine, Marquand, or Quase. He heard stories, possibilities. There were always noted crimes in large cities or in settlements on the edges of wild places where there are many men and few women. Nothing matched exactly, although several could have been close enough. Julius Sorokine's name did not arise.

Lastly he went back yet again to Watson Forbes. It was late in the evening and it was discourteous to impose on him. Nevertheless, he did not hesitate to do so.

Forbes was polite, as always. "You look tired," he observed. "Have you eaten?"

"Not yet," Narraway confessed.

Forbes rang the bell and when the servant answered, sent him for cold beef, horseradish sauce, and fresh bread and butter. "Perhaps tea would be better than whisky?" he suggested.

Narraway would have preferred whisky, but he accepted the tea. Forbes was right, it would be wiser. They spoke of trivial things until the food came and the servant had withdrawn.

"I presume you are still concerned with the railway?" Forbes said when they were alone. "I know of nothing else useful I can tell you. I have been more than frank with my own opinion."

"Indeed," Narraway agreed. He swallowed. "I spoke with someone else who favored lateral lines, east and west to the coastal ports, rather than north and south. Said Britain's historic power lay at sea. We should enlarge on it, and allow Africa to develop itself."

Forbes's eyes opened a little wider, but it was a very slight movement, almost as if he did not wish it seen. "Really! A little . . . conservative, but perhaps he is right. It doesn't sound like a great adventure. An old man, I assume?"

Narraway smiled. "You think it is an old man's vision?"

"Isn't it?"

"I think he saw it as the vision of a man keen to build on what we have, both physically and morally, rather than risk it all on a new venture that might be dangerous in both regards."

Forbes smiled. "Possibly. I approve of his reluctance to carve up Africa, keeping all the important places in British hands. Did you come to tell me that?"

"No. I have heard of an incident in Cape Town from two or three people. A tragedy that might have bearing on the present."

"Dunkeld's project?" Forbes asked.

There was a stillness in the room now, a waiting.

"Possibly." Narraway had struggled with finding a way to ask Forbes for information without telling him of the present crisis. If Sorokine was proven guilty, then it would not matter. The fear of scandal would be past. The crime could be mentioned, Minnie Sorokine's death would not be hidden, but the details, and above all the place and circumstances, could and would be lied about. It might even be necessary to say that Julius was dead also.

"What is it?" Forbes asked, his voice very steady.

More lies might be necessary now. "A murder that happened in Cape Town, several years ago," Narraway answered as casually as he could.

"Really?" The silence thickened.

Narraway was about to continue, but some sense of conflict in Forbes's face made him hesitate. Forbes was struggling with a decision. Narraway finished the rest of his beef and buttered another slice of bread. He had eaten that also before Forbes finally spoke.

"Since you are concerned with Sorokine, I imagine you are concerned with the murder of a woman that, so far as I know, has never been solved."

Narraway swallowed the last mouthful. "Yes, I'm afraid so. I hear rumor of various sorts, nothing substantial, but enough to cause me anxiety."

Forbes seemed surprised. "Because of Sorokine's involvement in the railway?"

Perhaps at least an element of the truth was necessary in order to persuade Forbes to be frank. "Yes. It is possible the Prince of Wales may lend the project his support."

"Ah, I see. Now I understand why Special Branch is concerned." Forbes's expression was curiously unreadable. "I wish I could comfort you. Sorokine is definitely the best man I know of to make the diplomatic arrangements. His father was skilled and had excellent connections. I think Julius is even more so, and of course the connections are still there. A certain lack of commitment could be . . . overcome, if he chose. I think he has it in him."

"But . . . ?" Narraway prompted. Was it his imagination that there was a coldness in the room, as if the summer were already passing?

"But I cannot tell you that he was not involved in the murder of the woman," Forbes finished. "I am afraid I think it is more than likely he was. I don't know if you will ever prove it, or how you even learned of the matter. But if you did, then you had best be told the truth." He sounded resigned. "He was there, he appeared to have some connection with the woman. Africa can have strange effects on people. They can forget the laws they would keep almost by second nature in their own countries."

He drew in his breath and let it out slowly. "I have no proof, but were I responsible for the honor and reputation of the heir to the throne, I would not have him associate with Sorokine. You could not afford the scandal it would cause were the matter to be raised. I assume that it is why you asked me before if the project might have enemies? Of course it will, and they will be those men who have lived in Africa themselves. And whether they are prompted by envy, greed, altruism, or personal hatred, they will either know of it already, or they will make it their business to find out."

"Thank you," Narraway said unhappily. "I appreciate your candor."

He felt peculiarly alone and disillusioned as he left Forbes's house and walked down the front steps into the street. It was as if a great dream, something of nobility and vision, had collapsed unexpectedly, leaving him only dust.

He thought of Pitt in his room in the Palace, and how he too was facing disillusion. Would he be honest enough, brave enough to acknowledge it, if that were the truth? Part of him hoped he would not — Pitt had so much of life's true wealth already!

Then that feeling vanished, and profoundly, passionately he hoped that Pitt
would find that courage. If Narraway had
been a man of faith, he would have prayed.
There were times when one was empty and
did not have something larger and better
than oneself in which to believe.

CHAPTER TEN

After Narraway had gone, Pitt abandoned pretense and asked Tyndale to send Gracie to him. She came ten minutes later, carrying a tray of tea with three slices of buttered toast and a dish of marmalade. She put it down on the table and stood more or less to attention. She looked very small, miserable, and a little crumpled.

"Sit down," he said gently. "The tea's good, but it was only an excuse to get you here."

She obeyed. "Is it true they done 'er in like the poor thing in the cupboard?" she asked. Her face screwed up as she searched his eyes, frightened of what she would see.

For her sake he tried to conceal his own sense of panic. "Yes, almost exactly. It has to be the same person. You said she was asking questions all day."

"Yeah." She nodded. "An' I think as she knew 'oo did it. It were in 'er face, in the way she walked, gettin' more an' more excited, like, all the time. She were addin' it up an' it made sense to 'er, even if it don't ter us."

"Tell me again who she spoke to and all you know about it."

She nodded, tight-lipped. He could see her fear for him in every angle of her small body.

"I dunno everythin'," she started. " 'Cos I couldn't follow 'er all the time. She could 'ave spoke ter others as well. But she were on ter Biddie an' Norah about the sheets, an' ter Mags as well, an' ter Edwards about buckets an' buckets o' water up an' downstairs inter the other part goin' that way." She pointed vaguely. "This place is so big I in't never certain where anyone's gone ter, but it were out o' this wing, inter one o' the places we in't allowed. An' they come back wi' all them bits o' broken china."

She looked even more unhappy. "I asked Mr. Tyndale, an' 'e went all peculiar, like 'e were scared 'alf out of 'is wits. I in't never seen 'im like that, an all sort o' stiff an' proper bloke like 'im. Wot is it, Mr. Pitt? Is it 'cos 'ooever done it is mad? Is that's wot's got 'im so scared? Like the back streets 'as come inter their palace wot they thought was all safe from real life?"

"It could be, Gracie," he said. The thought had flicked through his mind, but he was surprised that she had seen it so sharply. Did it hurt her as it hurt him? Perhaps disillusion was the same, whoever you were. "But it's something more than that as well. Did Mrs. Sorokine know about the port bottles?"

She shook her head.

"I dunno. I don't see 'ow she could. 'Less someone else saw 'em an' told 'er? But I reckon if anyone saw 'em, they'd just 'ave thrown 'em out 'cos o' the flies. You wouldn't 'ardly go an' tell guests, would yer? An' she wouldn't 'ave asked, 'cos why would yer? 'Excuse me, but 'ave yer seen any old wine bottles wi' blood in 'em?'"

"All the same," Pitt said thoughtfully, "I wonder if she knew, or guessed? Or if they have nothing to do with the murder." But even as he spoke, he did not believe it. "That means premeditation," he said aloud.

"Wot?" she frowned. "'Ave yer tea, Mr. Pitt. Lettin' it go cold don't 'elp."

"No. Thank you." Absentmindedly he poured it, only marginally aware of the fragrant steam in the air. "It means it wasn't a sudden crime of madness, on the spur of the moment, like losing your temper. If somebody brought blood in bottles, then they planned it beforehand. You can't get blood into a wine bottle easily. You would have to use a funnel and pour with great care."

Gracie frowned. " 'Course," she agreed. "But 'oose blood, an' wot for?"

"A diversion," he answered. "That's all it could be. And it could be any sort of blood, an ox or a sheep, or a rabbit." He spread marmalade on the first slice of toast and bit into it.

"In't that much blood in a rabbit," Gracie pointed out practically. "Yer could get it at a butcher's. D'yer s'pose it were blood ter put on the Queen's sheets, ter scare us off lookin' too close elsewhere, like?"

He smiled. He had wondered the same thing.

"In't gonna work, though, is it?" she asked anxiously, trying to read his eyes.

"No," he answered her. "We won't stop looking for the truth, whatever it is." He saw her relax and realized the conflict of emotions crowding within her, led by the fear of disillusion. It was the pain that had tugged at the edge of his own feelings ever since arriving here. He did not wish to see the fragility of those he had grown up admiring, believing to be not only privileged but uniquely deserving of honor. In spite of all their frailties of taste and even loyalty to one another, he had still imagined in them a love of the same values as the best of their subjects. He had taken for granted the acceptance of responsibility for one's acts, good or bad, of kindness and truth, the value of friendship, and gratitude for good fortune.

She was looking at him steadily, reassured. "Wot d'yer want me ter do, sir? You got the bottles, but I can see if Mrs. Sorokine asked anyone about them?"

His first thought was of Gracie's safety. "No. You can't do that without betraying that you found them."

She stared at him, her eyes widening.

He had hurt her feelings by refusing to let her help. "You have no way of explaining except by saying that you found them," he said, wishing that he had put it that way in the beginning. "I can't afford to have them know who you are yet. And someone might work it out."

"You in't sure as 'e did it, are yer?" she said in awe.

He had not realized she knew about Julius Sorokine, but he should have. Orders had been given to Tyndale for all the staff that they must leave Julius's door locked, and food was to be delivered only by Tyndale himself, taking a manservant with him. That would go around the staff like wildfire. Suddenly they would all feel safe. The mystery was solved and the madman locked up. Gracie would have assumed the same thing.

Now she was staring at him with a clarity sharper than his own.

"If we are to lock him up for the rest of his life, we have to be certain, beyond any question," he answered, trying to convince himself. "At least I do."

She nodded slowly. "Well, if it in't 'im, then it's someone else," she said quietly. "I'll see if Mrs. Sorokine found out about them bottles or not. But more'n anything else for meself, I'd like ter know wot that blood were for, an' 'ow it got 'ere."

"Gracie, be careful!"

"You be careful, Mr. Pitt," she answered him fiercely. "If it weren't Mr. Sorokine, it's still one o' 'em guests. It in't one o' the servants, so they won't be after me. 'E may be mad as an 'atter, but 'e in't daft. An' it in't the only thing goin' on 'ere neither, sir. I don't like to say it, but there's summink 'orrid as Mr. Tyndale knows about an' 'e don't want nobody else knowin' it."

"Then don't look for it!" he said sharply. "That's an order. Do you hear me?"

She sat very stiffly. "Yes, sir, course I 'ear yer. Can I go now, then? If they in't gonner work out 'oo I am, then I in't better be 'ere longer'n I can explain, 'ad I?"

He watched her go with a sense of misgiving, as if the solution he had first grasped

383

were already slipping out of his hands, and out of control.

He took another piece of toast and ate it without being aware of the taste.

Could Minnie have confided in anyone else, perhaps asked them questions that might have indicated her train of thought? Perhaps it did not matter to the case, but it mattered to him that he understood what had happened and saw all the pieces fit together. It was more than simple hurt pride that Minnie Sorokine had organized all the elements into a clear picture and made sense of them, and he had not. As long as he did not see the connections, he would fear that somewhere there was a mistake, and the conclusion might be wrong. It nagged at his mind that they were proving a crime of uncontrollable insanity, committed with careful and intricate forethought. Were there two minds at work here?

Who would Minnie confide in, apart from her father? The men had been busy with the project, unavailable to her most of the day. She would not have spoken to Elsa; relations between them were strained.

Olga Marquand was consumed in her own unhappiness, and must have hated Minnie enough to have destroyed her herself, if she could have. That meant it had to be Liliane.

Was Liliane any less afraid now?

Pitt found her outside in the gardens alone, walking close to the flower beds. Their vividness and perfect order seemed a mockery of the agitated way she moved and the distracted look in her face under her broadbrimmed hat, which shaded her complexion from the glare of the sun.

He caught up with her, speaking when he was still two or three yards away, because he could see from her attitude that she was unaware of his approach.

"Good morning, Mrs. Quase."

She froze, and then turned slowly. In the warmth and perfume of the silent garden she was even more beautiful than in the formal setting. Her eyes were golden brown, and what was visible of her hair shone like polished copper, but lighter and softer.

"Good morning, Inspector," she replied. "Are you lost?"

"Not literally," he replied. "I was hoping to speak to you for a few moments." He was not asking permission, merely phrasing his intention courteously.

"Metaphorically?" she asked, then instantly wondered if she had used a word he did not know. She saw from his smile that that was not so. She blushed, but it would have been clumsy to apologize. She hurried on instead. "I thought you were sure it was Julius. Cahoon seemed to think so. But the poor man is really devastated with grief. I am amazed he did no more than beat Julius senseless."

She looked away from him, across the ordered clumps of flowers and the perfectly cut lawn, which was smooth as a table of green velvet. There was a gentle buzzing of bees, and now and again a waft of perfume in the sun. "We are not very civilized, are we?" she observed. "The veneer is no thicker than a coat of paint. You would be amazed what hideousness lies underneath such a commonplace thing."

"It seems Mrs. Sorokine saw through the paint very clearly," he replied. She had given him the perfect opening.

Her shoulders tightened. There was a small pulse beating in her throat. "You think that is why she was killed? She saw something in one of us that whoever it was could not live with? Or could not let her live with?"

"Yes. Don't you?" he asked.

"I suppose it is the only answer that makes sense."

Was she assuming he meant the murder of the prostitute and therefore did not say so, or was she afraid it was other things, a different secret?

"Was she always curious about people's actions and reasons?" he pressed. "The day before yesterday she was asking a great many questions, particularly of the servants."

She frowned. "Was she? I didn't know. I hardly saw her. She certainly made a lot of oblique remarks at dinner, as if she were determined to provoke someone. I thought then it was Cahoon, but obviously it was Julius."

"Did she speak to you before dinner, Mrs. Quase? Or to anyone else, do you know?"

She considered for several moments before replying. A butterfly drifted across the flower heads and settled in the heart of one. Somewhere in the distance a dog barked.

"She asked my husband if he had given the Prince of Wales any wine, as a gift," she replied. "Then she asked Mrs. Marquand the same thing."

"And had either of you, so far as you know?"

"No. I assume it was Cahoon. If it had been Julius, she would either have known the answer already, or have asked him."

So Minnie had known about the wine bottles, or else guessed their use!

"Thank you, Mrs. Quase."

She looked at him curiously. "What has wine to do with it? There is any amount of the best wine in the world in the cellars here."

"I think it was the bottles she was interested in, not the wine. Did she mention broken china to you?"

"No. Why?" She shivered. "Why does it matter now, Inspector? Isn't it all over? Poor Minnie asked too many questions, and found out something she would have been happier not to know. I know that is foolish. One can protect people one loves from some things, small mistakes, but not murder. I suppose he is mad." She looked away from Pitt, over the flowers. "I knew Julius before he met Minnie, you know. I could have married him, but my father was against it. Perhaps he was wiser than I." There was pain in her voice, surprisingly harsh.

"Was that in Africa?" he asked.

She stiffened, almost imperceptibly. Her voice was husky, so quiet he barely heard her. "Yes."

He remembered that her brother had died there. Was that the tragedy that touched her now? "And you met Mr. Quase, and married him instead," he said. "Do you believe your father had some knowledge of Mr. Sorokine's nature that decided him against your marriage?"

"He didn't say so. It . . . it was a difficult

time for us. My brother died in terrible circumstances . . . in the river." She struggled to keep control of her voice as she turned away from him. "Hamilton was marvelous. He helped us both. He dealt with the arrangements, saw to everything for us. I grew to appreciate his strength and his kindness, and his extraordinary loyalty. After that . . . Julius seemed . . . shallow. I realized how right my father's judgment was." She stood motionless, her back and shoulders rigid. "Poor Minnie, so strong, so sure of herself, so . . . so full of passion and spirit . . . and in the end so foolish."

Everything she said was true, but Pitt wondered if she had liked Minnie. There was nothing he could read in her to tell him.

"Mrs. Quase, did she say anything to you about what she learned from all her questions? I need to know."

"Why? It's over, and Minnie's dead." There was a curious finality in her voice.

"It's not all over," he corrected her. He disliked speaking to her back. He could see nothing of her expression. Was that on purpose? "I have not proved what happened," he went on. "Or why the prostitute was killed, and all sorts of other things that seem to make very little sense."

"Does it really matter?" There was fear

undisguised in her voice now.

"Yes. Don't you want to clear it all up, before you leave?"

She turned even further from him. "I imagine we will leave quite soon. I don't know how we can continue without Julius. And I expect Cahoon will hardly feel like going on, at least for some time."

"Will that grieve you very much? Or your husband and Mr. Marquand?"

She was surprised into looking back toward him. "I don't know. It was always Cahoon who cared about it most. I expect he will find another diplomat to take Julius's place."

"Did Mrs. Sorokine say anything to you about her deductions?" he asked yet again.

Her eyes cleared. "She said she knew where it had happened," she replied. "Rather a pointless remark, considering that we all know it happened in the linen cupboard. I thought she was simply trying to get attention. I'm ashamed to say that now."

"Thank you, Mrs. Quase. Did she mention broken china?"

"No." There was dismissal in her face. "But then that's hardly very dramatic, is it?" She turned away and started to walk slowly along the grass.

He did not follow her. Instead he went

back toward the entrance to the Palace again, turning her words over and over in his mind. There seemed only one possible conclusion: Sadie had not been killed in the cupboard where she was found, in spite of the blood.

But as soon as he made sense of one set of facts, it made nonsense of another. The sheets were soaked with blood, and even a lunatic would not have killed her in one place and then carried the naked, bleeding body to the cupboard.

Had she been attacked, even fatally, and then carried, perhaps rolled up in sheets, to the cupboard, in order not to have been found in a place linked to any one person? And then the Queen's sheets, in which she had been carried, were put in the laundry, in the hope they would never be found and looked at closely enough to be identified? That was beginning to make more sense.

So where had she been killed? In whose bed? Surely Julius Sorokine's. How had Minnie known?

He was back inside the Palace again. Painstakingly he spoke to all the staff Gracie had seen Minnie with the day before she died. Each one repeated what she had told him.

Minnie had followed a curious trail with

growing excitement. She had asked about sheets. She had been intensely interested in the shards of broken china, where they had come from and their color and shape. This she had apparently inquired of Mr. Tyndale, and met with a brief and dismissive answer. She had also been interested in the footmen coming and going with buckets of water. She had asked about wine, what was drunk and where it came from, yet there was nothing to suggest she knew of the port bottles Gracie had found.

The other focus of her questions had been the arrival and departure of the women, and the delivery of the large wooden box of books and papers for Cahoon Dunkeld. Exactly what had happened when, and where were the books now?

Pitt was totally confused. Three women had arrived, two had left, and the third had been found dead. The carter had never been alone and unaccounted for anywhere near the upstairs floor, let alone any of the bedrooms. What, if any of it, was relevant to Sadie's death?

He went over the facts again in his mind. The one thing that seemed to arise again and again, but of which he had no physical proof, were the shards of broken china that Tyndale had so vehemently refused to discuss with

Gracie. Something about them had frightened him even more than the presence of prostitutes in the guest wing of the Palace, even when one of them was murdered. Either it was something so precious it was beyond Pitt's ability to imagine, or else its breakage, added to the other evidence, meant something so appalling it had to be concealed at all costs.

His imagination could create nothing so disastrous. No matter how difficult or distasteful, or how absurd, he must try to find the pieces. And he must do it discreetly. Tyndale would know where they were put, and if he knew Pitt was looking, he might destroy them.

On the other hand, that might be the only way to find a score of pieces of china in a place as vast as this. Time was very short indeed. As early as tomorrow he might be forced to charge Julius Sorokine, and the case would be closed. There would be no trial, no weighing of evidence, and certainly no defense. Pitt's own doubts were the only voice Sorokine would ever have to speak for him.

That left Pitt no alternative. He was aware that Narraway was uncomfortable still questioning the evidence. As well, there was a certain kind of disloyalty in pursuing something that could embarrass the Prince, and which would without doubt rebound against Narraway himself, possibly against the whole of Special Branch. Pitt might pay for it, and he was very conscious that he might ultimately give Narraway no option but to dismiss him.

If that happened, he would find it very hard to gain another job he would love as he did this, or for which he had any capability, and no one else would keep his family. Had he the right to make them pay for his moral decisions?

If he accepted the evidence as it was and let Julius Sorokine go to Bedlam for killing the two women, a living hell of both body and mind, what would Pitt himself become? A man Charlotte could still love? Or one she would slowly grow to dislike and in the end to despise, mourning for what he had once been?

It was a high price to pay, but even as he was turning it over in his mind, he knew the decision was made. He sent for Gracie again, deliberately using Tyndale to find her.

"Yes, sir?" she said hopefully, when she came in. "Yer got suffink?"

"We have to find the broken china," he replied.

"You mean the dish, or whatever it were?

Mr. Tyndale's real scared about that." Her eyes were grave with doubt. " 'E'll 'ave seen to it as it's 'id good."

"I know. He might be the only person who knows where the pieces are," he agreed. "He won't tell me, but if he thinks I am going to search every corner of this place until I find them, then he might be alarmed into destroying them completely, ground into unrecognizable powder."

"Yer want me ter tell 'im as yer lookin' for it, an' mebbe ask 'im for it again?" she said.

"Yes, please. Tell him I'm going to get help in if I need it, because I've realized it's crucial to the case."

"Is it?"

"I don't know. Minnie Sorokine seemed to think so. And if it isn't, why hide it?" He looked at her small, curious face and realized she felt like a betrayer, tricking a man who had risked his own safety and comfort to befriend her. "I'm sorry," he added gently. "I have to be sure Sorokine is guilty. I think they'll arrest him formally tomorrow, and after that there'll be no one to speak for him. There'll be no trial."

She was very pale. "I know. They'll just put 'im in Bedlam in the filth an' the screamin'." She took a deep breath and let it out a little shakily. "I'll go an' tell 'im." She looked close to tears. She turned quickly and went out of the door, small and very stiff, in a dress that had been altered but was still too big for her. He knew he had torn her loyalties as he had his own.

He found it far from easy to watch Tyndale after Gracie had spoken to him, without it being obvious that he was doing so. Several times he had to hang back and leave Gracie to appear busy with a tray in her hands, or a mop and a bundle of laundry.

It was nearly two hours after he had asked her help before she came to him with a parcel of broken china concealed in a cardboard box, and passed it to him wordlessly. She looked white and miserable. The fact that she said nothing, expressed no recrimination at all, made it worse.

Together they walked back up the stairs to his room and put it down on the table. She stood in front of it, not even allowing him to question whether she was going to remain or not.

Very carefully he unwrapped the newspaper around the pieces and looked at the debris. It was exactly as Walton had said: small pieces of broken china, some of it not more than chips and dust, other pieces as large as an inch across. There was blue and gold paint on them in an exquisitely delicate pattern: tiny little lattice in gold, leaves and the edge of what looked like a woman's dress. The largest piece was curved as if from the side of a pedestal.

Gracie picked up a lump that was mostly white, and turned it over in her fingers. "Looks like it were the bottom, or summink," she said thoughtfully. "But why make all that fuss over a broke dish? Why 'ide it instead o' just throwin' it out like anythin' else wot's bust. D' yer think it's summink special? Royal, like?"

"I don't know," Pitt said honestly, picking up another piece, which was quite large and of irregular shape. "The painting on it is beautiful, but I don't know what it could be." He turned it over. "It seems to have a painted inside as well as outside. And that bit looks too flat for a bowl. I wonder if it's a lid? How could anyone break something this badly? It's completely smashed."

"Throw it at the wall," Gracie said, screwing her face up. "Yer don't bust summink like this by just droppin' it, even on a stone floor. An' it come from upstairs. Wood floor'd just break it ter pieces, but this is like someone trod on it, on purpose, like." She stared at it in dismay. "'Oo'd do summink rotten like that, just break a dish wot's beautiful inter little bits, on purpose?"

"I don't know, but I think perhaps we need to." Pitt pushed his fingers around the broken shards carefully, searching for anything large enough to identify. "There's not much, is there. Have you ever broken a large dish, Gracie?"

She blushed unhappily. "Yeah." She did not add any details.

"Was this how much of it was left?"

"No. Were a lot more. But I broke cups before, an' they weren't this much in bits, not the good porcelain ones. D'yer reckon as this weren't a reg'lar plate, Mr. Pitt?"

"Yes, I do, Gracie. I just can't work out what it was." He pulled out a small, round piece, three-quarters of an inch at its widest. He turned it over, looking at it carefully. It was mostly plain white, but there was a little bit of writing on one side — the letters *IMO* and what looked like an *E,* incomplete.

It was part of a word, and suddenly he knew what the word was: "Limoges." He had seen it before written on exquisite porcelain: candlesticks, chargers, vases, bowls, and figurines. Long ago in the police he had dealt with theft of such works of art.

"It was an ornament," he said quietly. He turned over the piece in his hand again. "I think this was part of the base. The name was on it. The gold was probably the rim.

The blue would be part of a picture."

"Is it very precious?" she asked, her face tight in sympathy with whoever had broken it. "Somebody's gonna lose their place 'ere 'cos they smashed it?"

"Do you think that is enough to explain Mr. Tyndale hiding it?" Pitt said instead of answering her.

She shook her head, a stiff, tiny gesture.

"It seems to have been broken the night Sadie was murdered," he went on, thinking ahead. "It has to have had something to do with it. That's the only thing that would explain why he would go to so much trouble to conceal it."

"'Ooever it belongs ter is goin' ter be pretty angry," she said seriously.

"He's not hiding it from them; they'll find out anyway," he said. "He's hiding it from us."

"D'yer think so?" She frowned.

"Yes, otherwise he could have told us in confidence, and we would have thought no more of it. Domestic breakage is hardly Special Branch business. I wonder where it came from, whose room it was in?"

"D'yer reckon as that poor cow stole it?" Gracie looked doubtful. "'Ow would she 'a got it out? Dishes in't easy ter carry without someone seein' 'em."

"Exactly," he agreed. "And why would Mr. Tyndale wish to protect a prostitute who was also a thief? I think the fact that it is broken is what matters."

"Yer gonna ask Mr. Tyndale?" She was looking at him now in intense concentration.

"Yes, I am."

Pitt spent a little more time searching for other pieces large enough to give a better idea of the shape and diameter of the plate, and formed the opinion that it was possibly a pedestal dish rather than a flat one. Some of the pieces were too thick to be part of an ordinary plate.

He put them in the box again and carried them down to the butler's pantry, where he found Tyndale with ledgers open and a pen in his hand. Apparently he was working on the cellar records. He looked up. Pitt came in and closed the door.

"What may I do for you, Mr. Pitt?" Tyndale said coolly.

Pitt leaned against the wall. "Tell me where the Limoges pedestal dish was, and how it came to be broken," he replied.

The color bleached from Tyndale's face and his voice came only with an effort. "I'm sorry, sir, but I have no idea what you are talking about. Her Majesty has literally thousands of pieces of porcelain. If one has been broken, I know nothing of it. I don't believe it was in this wing. If it were, one of the maids would have told me."

"Mrs. Sorokine knew where it came from," Pitt told him.

Tyndale looked even whiter. Pitt was afraid he was on the verge of some kind of attack, possibly his heart. "I'm sorry." He meant it, but he could not afford the mercy he would have liked. "Julius Sorokine faces a lifetime in an asylum, without trial. Before I let that happen to anyone, I am going to be certain beyond any sane or reasonable doubt that he is responsible for the deaths of these women. I am going to find out who smashed a Limoges plate the night Sadie was killed. I can do it quietly, with your help, Mr. Tyndale, or I can question every manservant in the place, and find out whatever it was Mrs. Sorokine found out, and which very likely cost her her life!"

"Her husband killed her," Tyndale told him, his voice catching in his throat. "This . . . this breakage had nothing to do with it. It's another matter altogether, and private."

"There is no privacy where there is murder, Mr. Tyndale. What was the ornament, and where was it? How did it get broken, and why did you hide it?"

Tyndale was wretched. He loathed lying

and it was naked in his face.

"It was broken by accident. I didn't hide it, I simply disposed of the pieces. There is no point in keeping them. No one could mend it. For heaven's sake, Inspector, it's shattered! It's dust!"

"I can see that. I can also see that it was Limoges, and probably very beautiful. Where was it and who broke it?"

"One of the maids, but no one is taking responsibility. I can't punish anyone for clumsiness when I don't know who it is." Tyndale looked eminently reasonable, his voice was steadying again.

Pitt had not the slightest doubt that he was lying. Minnie Sorokine had pursued this, and learned what it was. How? What questions had she asked that Pitt had not? Why had Tyndale answered her, and yet would not tell Pitt? What terrible thing had her questions made him realize?

"At what time?" he said.

"I beg your pardon?" Tyndale was putting off answering.

"When was it broken? At what time? That will tell you who did it, surely?"

"I . . . I don't know." Tyndale was flustered. "Some time the . . . the day of the death of that woman. We were all upset. I dare say we didn't notice it immediately."

"A Limoges plate was lying smashed on the floor, and the maid cleaning didn't notice it?" Pitt said with open disbelief. "I'm sorry, Mr. Tyndale, but that won't do. Where was the dish?"

"I don't know." Tyndale's face was set in refusal.

"It was a pedestal dish," Pitt said, guessing as he went. "Mostly white with a blue picture in the center, and a gold edge. I found pieces of those."

"I don't know," Tyndale repeated stubbornly.

"Then I shall ask the maids," Pitt replied. "And the footmen. Someone will have seen it. Don't they dust regularly?"

"Yes, of course they do! But . . ." Tyndale tailed off. His face was blotched; a muscle ticked in his jaw.

"Assemble the staff in the servants' hall, Mr. Tyndale. I shall speak to them in fifteen minutes. I want everyone there," Pitt ordered.

Tyndale hesitated.

"Don't oblige me to ask the Prince of Wales's assistance in this," Pitt warned.

"It doesn't have anything to do with the murder!" Tyndale protested again. "It's . . . it's a domestic matter! This is absurd."

"An ornament is smashed on the night of

a murder," Pitt said grimly. "Someone was in the room, and committed a violent and extraordinary act, perhaps of rage. I want to know which room it was, and who was there. Assemble the staff, Mr. Tyndale."

Tyndale left obediently, walking like a man under condemnation of some fearful punishment.

Pitt waited, feeling guilty. Was he really pursuing a clue that would explain the anomalies in the case and enable him to be satisfied that Julius Sorokine had killed both Sadie and his own wife? Or was he merely determined to force his will on Tyndale because he had defied him, and Pitt wanted an answer for no reason except his own satisfaction? Did he resent the fact that Minnie Sorokine could assemble these facts and deduce the truth, and he could not? Had she known some extra fact that he had not?

In fifteen minutes exactly he walked to the servants' hall and saw them all dutifully lined up, hot-faced and frightened. Gracie was at the front, probably so as not to be hidden behind taller, plumper girls. He avoided looking at her.

"A Limoges plate was broken on the night the prostitute was murdered," he said gently. "It was probably a pedestal plate, mostly white with a painting in the middle with quite a lot of blue in it and a gold rim. I don't think any of you broke it. I think it may have been one of the guests, either the one who actually killed the woman, or someone who saw what happened." That was a stretch of the truth. "I want to know which room it was in."

They all stood staring at him. No one spoke.

"Who does the dusting?" he asked.

"Me and Norah, mostly," Ada said nervously. "An' Gracie, since she come."

"Which room was that dish in?" Pitt asked.

"I dunno."

"Didn't you dust it?"

"I never seen it."

Pitt turned to Mrs. Newsome. "You are the housekeeper — aren't you responsible for works of art? Especially valuable ones?"

"Yes, I am," Mrs. Newsome said stiffly. She looked puzzled and unhappy. She was avoiding looking at Mr. Tyndale so clearly that it was obvious.

"Where was that dish kept, Mrs. Newsome?"

"I don't recall a dish like that," she said flatly.

"Did you send maids to clean up, wash and scrub a room on the morning of the murder?"

"Of course. The linen cupboard. But only after you told me to," she said stiffly.

"Before that! At the end of this wing, or into the east wing?"

"No. And the east wing is not my responsibility. I would be exceeding my authority to do that."

There was nothing else he could think of to say. They stood stiffly, shoulders back, faces carefully blank. No one was going to tell him. There was nothing for him to do but accept defeat with the little dignity left him.

He returned to his own room confused and angry. He paced the floor, trying to think of a way to force Tyndale's hand. He was certain Tyndale knew where the plate had been, and had told Minnie. The more he refused to say, the more certain Pitt became that it mattered.

It had belonged somewhere. Why were they all lying? He had not seen a flicker in the faces of any of them, even Mrs. Newsome. Was there any point in asking Gracie to speak to them? Were there any tiny pieces embedded in a carpet, or into the wood of the floorboards, between the cracks? Might Gracie even have seen it already, without recognizing what it was?

He went to the bellpull and was about to ring it, when another thought occurred to him. His hand froze, fingers stiff, still clinging to the pull. Maybe they were not lying. Perhaps they had not seen it because it was not in any of the rooms they cleaned. What if it had been in the Prince of Wales's own rooms?

A furious quarrel, a hysterical woman, china smashed. It would have to be concealed — at any price. Is that what had happened? Perhaps Sadie had refused to do something that was asked of her, or been unable to? The Prince was drunk. He had lost his temper and lashed out. And what? Killed her? Cut her throat with one of the dining room knives, and then gone on slashing at her?

Had he been so drunk he had then passed out, then woken up in the morning beside the bloody corpse, and sent for Cahoon Dunkeld to help him?

There was a knock on the door and Pitt whirled round as if it had been a shot. He steadied himself, breathing in and out slowly, his heart pounding. "Yes?"

Gracie came in and closed the door behind her. She stood still, leaning against the knob, staring at him. " 'E din't tell yer, did 'e?" she said softly. "Wot does it mean, Mr. Pitt? They in't lyin'. Nobody knows, fer real. Wot's goin' on?"

"I think it means it was in a room they don't go into," he replied, his mouth dry. "Mr. Tyndale knows where it was, and he'd rather be blamed for concealing murder than tell anyone."

Her eyes grew wider and her face more tight and drawn. He knew she had thought the same thing. He was sorry she had had to know this. She would not have had to if he had not brought her here. It was unfair. She was civilian, not police, and certainly not Special Branch. "I'm sorry," he said quietly.

"Wot are yer goin' ter do?" she whispered. "Mr. Tyndale in't never gonna tell yer. An' if it were smashed in a fight or summink, 'e would, ter save yer thinkin' wot yer is now. There weren't no blood on it, though."

"I know that. But if it didn't mean anything, and had nothing to do with Sadie's death, then why is Mr. Tyndale lying about it? And he is lying."

"I know." The misery in her face was naked. " 'E's protectin' 'Is Royal 'Ighness. I reckon as 'e does quite a lot o' that. It's 'is . . . 'is kind o' loyalty. Mr. Pitt . . ." — she frowned, screwing up her face — "d' yer reckon as that's right? Is that wot we're supposed ter do? 'Ave yer gotta do it too? An' me?"

"And let Sorokine spend the rest of his life

in a madhouse for something he didn't do?" he asked.

She shook her head minutely. "Wot are we gonna do, then?"

He sat against the edge of the table. "I'm not sure. That plate wasn't just knocked off something and broken into two or three pieces. It was smashed beyond recognition in an uncontrollable rage. Whether she laughed at him, belittled him, threatened to tell everyone and make a mockery of him, we'll never know. But he flew into an insane fury and cut her throat —"

"Wot with?" she interrupted.

"Maybe the table knife — there was blood on it. Or maybe a different knife altogether, a paper knife or fruit knife he had there. We wouldn't have found it because we haven't looked. The other knife was put into the linen cupboard after we took the body out anyway. The blood could have been from anywhere."

"Then she weren't killed in the linen cupboard, were she?" Gracie said.

"No. She will have been killed in his room. That's why the footmen were up and down with buckets of water, cleaning up."

"You reckon as 'e called 'em?" she said with disbelief.

"No. I think he called Cahoon Dunkeld. I

409

expect the footmen only brought the water. I should think Dunkeld, and possibly even the Prince himself, did the principal cleaning. They wouldn't trust anyone else with a secret like that."

"Wot are we gonna do?" Fear was sharp and bright in Gracie's eyes. "We can't never say as 'e done it! They'll 'ave us 'anged fer treason!"

"I don't know," Pitt admitted. "But if he killed Mrs. Sorokine as well, he has to be stopped. He'll do it again. Dunkeld can't protect him, and I doubt he would want to — not when his own daughter was the victim."

"Then why in't 'e said summink?" she asked. "Why'd 'e let yer blame Mr. Sorokine?"

"He didn't 'let' me, he told me himself that it was Sorokine." He realized as he said it that it made no sense. Did Dunkeld really believe it was Julius who had killed Minnie? Maybe he thought the Prince was innocent, and somehow Julius had done it, or maybe all three of them were involved? "I don't know," he went on. "I don't understand. If the Prince killed her in a drunken rage, then fell into a stupor and woke in the morning and panicked, he could have sent for Dunkeld to help him. Dunkeld moved the body, with the bloodstained sheets, into the linen cupboard, so at least it wouldn't be found in the Royal quarters."

Gracie's eyes never moved from his face.

"The Prince had a bath to clean himself up," he went on. "And maybe sober himself as well. That would explain why the Princess found the bathtub still warm, when she did not expect him to have used it. In the meantime Dunkeld cleaned up the room and had the remains of the broken ornament removed, and everything else tidied up. Then he made a pretense of finding the body himself, to ensure we were called and the evidence kept under some control."

"Only Mrs. Sorokine got too clever, an' worked it out?" she finished. "Did 'e kill 'is own daughter then, to 'ide it? That's 'orrible! 'E don't owe that kind o' loyalty ter the Queen even, nor nobody! An' din't yer say as the way she were cut open were jus' the same as the other poor cow . . . I mean woman?"

"Yes."

"Then stands ter reason it were the Prince as done that too, don't it?"

He felt helpless to deny it, and yet he could not bring himself to say so. "I don't know."

"D'yer still think Mr. Sorokine done it?" she asked.

"I suppose it's possible," Pitt said reluc-

411

tantly. "I can't see Dunkeld killing his own daughter. Killing a wife is different. Tragically, that happens often."

"Ter protect 'Is Royal 'Ighness?" Gracie's expression was one of disbelief mixed with a crowding, terrible fear. "I think ever so much o' the Queen, but I couldn't kill none o' me own ter protect 'er, even if she never done a thing wrong in 'er life. An' I wouldn't put down a dog ter save 'Is Royal 'Ighness, if he done that ter Sadie. I don't care wot 'appens ter the Crown, nor nothin'. I don't want a Crown wot's red wi' blood."

"No, Gracie, neither do I," Pitt admitted. "I don't know what I'm going to do, but I'll do something, I promise you."

Her face brightened.

"Yer'll tell Mr. Narraway, when 'e comes back, won't yer? Mebbe 'e'll know wot ter do?"

"Maybe," he agreed. "He's looking to see if he can find anything in Sorokine's past to show he's done it before."

Gracie gave a little sigh, puzzled and unhappy. "Yer gonna be all right?" she asked anxiously. "Yer in't goin' ter let anyone know wot yer think, are yer?"

He smiled. "No, of course not. And don't you either! As far as we are concerned, the guilty man is Julius Sorokine. We are just

412

tidying up the proof. That's an order, Gracie."

"Yer don't 'ave ter order me." She gave a shudder and pulled her apron straight so sharply that she undid one of the ties. She made a bow of it again, crookedly, then excused herself, closing the door with a snap behind her.

Pitt had not lied, yet he had not told Gracie the exact truth. He felt he had no choice but to speak to the Prince of Wales directly. It was an interview he was not looking forward to. The only thing worse would be to see Julius Sorokine condemned and still be uncertain if he were guilty.

This time he did not ask for Dunkeld's assistance in obtaining an audience, or Mr. Tyndale's either. He had no intention of allowing himself to be denied. He was obliged to wait for nearly forty-five minutes.

"Yes, Inspector?" the Prince said when he was finally shown in. "I have already been informed that Sorokine has been arrested and confined to his room. No doubt Mr. Narraway will bring men to remove him with all discretion. Will that be tonight? I can see that cover of darkness would be better. I thank you for your rapid and . . . and tactful conduct of the matter. I deeply regret that we could not bring it to a conclusion before

Mrs. Sorokine also lost her life."

In one sweeping statement he had thanked Pitt and condemned him for his failure to save Minnie, and concluded their business. It was highly skilled. It forced Pitt into an absurd position if he insisted on remaining.

"Mr. Narraway is looking into Mr. Sorokine's past, sir," he began tentatively. "To see if there is any other incident of a similar nature."

"Quite right," the Prince agreed, nodding his head. "But that is not my concern, nor that of those involved with the railway. We will have to think of replacing Sorokine. That will be our most immediate task. Thank you for your information, Mr. Pitt, but it is not necessary to let us know anything further. Good day to you. I shall naturally thank Narraway for lending you to us in so complete a fashion."

Pitt gritted his teeth and felt his face burn. It was partly a result of being so dismissed that allowed him to stay on the spot.

"I am sure Mr. Narraway will appreciate that, sir, and inform you that we are always at your service. I believe he will arrange to take Mr. Sorokine tomorrow."

"A very sad end. I liked him. But if that is how it has to be done," the Prince said wearily. "It is of little importance now."

"They will also remove Mrs. Sorokine's body," Pitt went on, still standing in the same spot, although the Prince had moved half a step closer, and he felt crowded. There was a battle of wills between them. "I imagine Mr. Dunkeld will wish her to have a Christian burial at some church of his choice, perhaps a family crypt."

The Prince looked taken aback. "Yes . . . yes, I imagine so. It will . . ." He stopped because what he had been going to say sounded callous and he changed his mind and bit back the words. So much was clear in his expression. "I would attend, but it would draw unwelcome attention. Poor man." A flicker of anxiety crossed his face. "I hope you will be discreet with taking Sorokine away. It would displease me deeply if there were to be a fuss now, causing speculation. Perhaps you could have him carried out, as if he were ill? In a way he is." He gave a slight shudder of distaste. "Under proper restraint, of course."

Pitt's temper flared up and he physically ached with the effort of controlling it. He had liked Sorokine too. The Prince would think him very ordinary, very unsophisticated for it, but Julius Sorokine was the only one who had declined to attend the party, even though he was not in love with his wife, and she very clearly had had an affair with his half-brother.

"There are one or two matters I still need to clear up," he said quickly, speaking with his jaw tight, teeth almost clenched, slurring his words. "We must leave the matter beyond any question."

"Surely it is beyond question now?" the Prince said, eyebrows arched. "Sorokine killed the woman, his wife deduced it and confronted him, and he killed her. What else is there to know? He is clearly insane. It is not only discreet, but merciful that we have him committed to private care for the rest of his life. Were he a lesser man he would be hanged."

"He would also be tried first, and given the opportunity to defend himself," Pitt retorted instantly, and just as instantly knew that he had made an unforgivable error as far as the Prince was concerned.

"How?" the Prince said coldly. "By claiming that he is a lunatic? We already know as much."

Pitt was acutely aware that he was in the presence of the man who would one day, perhaps soon, be his sovereign, and to whom he would swear his oath of allegiance. In this man's name all the law of the land would be administered. He felt a traitor even to allow such thoughts into his mind, but they were there.

"Sir, in the course of the killing of the woman, Sadie, a piece of Limoges china was broken into very small pieces indeed. From what is left of it, I can judge its approximate shape and coloring. It appears to have been a pedestal dish, white, with a picture with clear cobalt blue figuring quite prominently and a gold rim. In what room was that dish kept?"

The Prince stared at him, blinking several times. His skin looked curiously sweaty, although the room was cool.

"Sir?" Pitt repeated.

"I don't recall such a dish," the Prince said huskily. "There's a great deal of porcelain . . . ornaments . . . things around. I haven't noticed it." He blinked again.

"Perhaps you might notice its absence?" Pitt suggested. "Since the servants of the guest wing cleared away the pieces, but none of them will admit to it, it has to have been in this wing, and to have been important."

"I can't imagine why." The Prince was annoyed. "A domestic accident, and a servant trying to cover it, are hardly the concern of Special Branch." There was finality in his tone and he seemed about to turn and walk away.

"Was it in your room, sir?" Pitt said abruptly. "That would explain why the servants don't recognize it, except Mr. Tyndale, and he is afraid to tell anyone where it was. I shall have to work it out by a process of elimination."

The Prince froze. "You exceed your duty, Inspector." His voice was icy now, but it lacked the firmness Pitt would have expected. He stared, blinking, the sweat beaded on his forehead. "You know who killed both the prostitute and poor Mrs. Sorokine. Arrest and remove him. That is all that is required of you. I thought that was made clear. If it was not, then allow me to do so now."

"What was explained to me, sir, is that a prostitute had been found hacked to death here in the Palace, and it was my duty toward Her Majesty to find out what had happened, who was responsible, and to deal with it with both speed and discretion. I cannot believe that Her Majesty would not also require that it be dealt with justly. That was not said because I assume it was not considered necessary to say it. And justice is also very practical. Injustice does not lie down quietly."

They stared at each other, the Prince's face mottled with ugly color, and loathing bright in his eyes. "What was this dish like?"

"I think it was probably a pedestal dish, sir, Limoges," Pitt repeated. "There was a lot of white and blue on it, and some gold lattice."

"I had one something like that in my own rooms. Perhaps it did come from there." The Prince hesitated, as Pitt made no response. "I dare say the woman took it. Later, when she quarreled with Sorokine, it got broken."

"Is anything else missing, or broken, sir?"

"No." There was total finality in the single word.

"Obviously you did not see her leave, sir," Pitt pointed out. "She could hardly have taken a pedestal dish and hidden it on her person without your noticing."

The Prince said nothing. He could not argue with such a conclusion without appearing ridiculous.

"Could Mr. Sorokine have come for her?" Pitt went on relentlessly. "How was the arrangement made for them to meet? Why would she take the dish? Surely there are other things of beauty and value in your rooms, sir? Possibly easier to carry or conceal."

"Of course I didn't see her take it!" the Prince snapped. "And I have no idea how she managed to meet Sorokine, or even if she did. I can't see that it matters. It happened. She's dead."

"Where are her clothes, sir?"

"What?"

"She was found in the cupboard completely naked."

The Prince's face was ashen, his eyes blazing. "For God's sake, man! I have no idea! Ask Sorokine. Search his rooms. Although he's had plenty of time to get rid of them by now. Who knows what a madman does?"

"Is it possible, sir, that you were deeply asleep, and he could have fought with her in your room, broken the dish there, and even torn her clothes there?"

"I . . ." He thought about it for a moment or two, and realized that Pitt was using a polite term for asking if he could have been so drunk that he had been insensible. But it was still an escape. "I suppose so," he said grudgingly.

"Then may I look and see if he left any trace, sir, any evidence that would prove it?"

"I can't see why it matters. I've told you, it could have happened," the Prince said crossly.

"It is a matter of justice, sir."

They stood facing each other, staring. Perhaps it was the reference to justice that broke the stalemate.

"Very well, if you insist," the Prince snapped.

"Thank you, sir," Pitt accepted.

But he found nothing of any interest whatever in the Prince of Wales's rooms. There was not even any obvious gap where the Limoges dish might have been. His bedroom and dressing room were gracious, comfortable, but not unlike the rooms of any middle-aged gentleman of his privilege and enormous wealth. Certainly there were no shards of porcelain or crystal embedded in the carpet, and no stains of any sort, blood or wine. Nothing was torn, scraped, or otherwise damaged. If any crime had been committed here, it had been done entirely without leaving a trace.

Pitt left feeling confused and as if somehow he had also been beaten in a game of wits. It felt like a hollow pain inside him. He had escaped a danger, faced a man who had the power to damage him seriously, if not ruin him, and he had found nothing at all. In fact he had made a fool of himself.

He walked slowly along the corridor back toward the guest wing, trying to scramble his thoughts together and make sense out of a miasma of facts that seemed to be without meaning.

He became aware of a calm and very discreet woman standing where the corner turned.

"Mr. Pitt," she said quietly.

He focused his attention. "Yes, ma'am?"

"Her Royal Highness, the Princess of Wales, would like to speak with you, if you can spare a few moments," she said. It was a gracious way of phrasing what amounted to a command.

Pitt found the Princess in her sitting room as before. She was dressed in a high-necked tea gown with a froth of lace at the throat. She sat with her back ramrod straight and her head high. She was a beautiful woman, but more than by her coloring or regularity of feature, he was impressed by her dignity. She was what he expected and wished royalty to be. He stood to attention automatically.

"Good afternoon, Mr. Pitt," she said with a very slight smile. "I hear that poor Mrs. Sorokine has also become a victim of tragedy. I am so sorry. She was an unfortunate young woman." She did not explain the remark, but regarded him as if she assumed he would understand the subtleness of her implication.

"Yes, ma'am," he agreed. "I am afraid so." He inclined his head to make his agreement clearer.

"Is it true that Mr. Sorokine is responsible?" she asked.

He gestured confusion by spreading his hands outward an inch or two. "It appears so."

She understood. "But you are not certain?"

"Not yet, ma'am."

"Do you expect to be?"

"I wish to be. I wish very much to be."

She nodded slowly. Apparently she had understood. There was a flash of what could have been gratitude in her eyes, including a shred of the faintest, self-mocking humor. "I am sure. Is there any way in which I might assist you? I see that you have just been speaking with His Royal Highness."

"Yes, ma'am. There was a piece of Limoges porcelain broken and I was inquiring whether he knew where it was normally kept. None of the servants appears to recognize it."

"And it has to do with the death of one of these poor women?" she asked. "What was it like?"

"It is hard to tell from what is left, ma'am, but it seems to have been a pedestal plate." He outlined it with his hands. "With a lot of gold lattice, I think around the rim, and a picture in the middle with bright cobalt blue." He spoke slowly, but he was still not sure, from the look of total bewilderment in her eyes, if she had understood him at all. "Blue, like the sky." He looked upwards. "And gold around the edge." He made a circle in the air with his finger.

"I hear you, Mr. Pitt," she said softly. "Your diction is excellent. But I am puzzled. There is exactly such a dish in Her Majesty's own bedroom. She is very fond of it, not for itself particularly, but because it was a gift from one of the princesses, when she was quite young."

She must have misunderstood him after all. And yet meeting his steady gaze she appeared to be perfectly certain not only of what she had said, but also the enormity of its meaning. He struggled to think of something to say that was not absurd.

The Princess rose to her feet. "I think, Mr. Pitt, that we had better go and see if Her Majesty's plate has indeed been broken. When she returns, we should have some explanation, and apology for her, if it has. Will you come with me, please?"

"Yes . . . ma'am." He obeyed, walking quickly around her to reach the door before she did and open it for her. He did not know whether he was exultant that she had told him where the dish belonged, or if it terrified him even more. If it was the Queen's dish, how had it come to be smashed? Had the Prince taken it? Why, for heaven's sake? Was he completely mad? If the Princess of Wales realized what it meant, what would she do? Had Pitt, in his blindness, fallen into the middle of a Palace plot? Was the Prince of Wales insane? Did the Princess know it and intend to use Pitt somehow to expose it?

No. That was all delirious thinking. There was a perfectly rational explanation. Probably it was some thieving servant after all. That made infinitely more sense.

He followed a pace behind her along the wide corridors into another wing altogether. She spoke briefly to a servant and then to another. Finally he followed her, with two liveried footmen and a lady-in-waiting, into Queen Victoria's rooms.

They were oddly as Pitt had expected: too much furniture, all large and beautifully carved, pictures, ornaments, and photographs everywhere. The sunlight slanted in through high heavily curtained windows and made colored patterns on the carpets.

"There," the Princess said, pointing to an ornate mantel. On it stood a beautiful Limoges pedestal dish, with gold leaf around the edges, trellises woven of gold, and in the center a painting of a romantic couple on a garden seat. It was not the sky that was deep blue, but his coat, and a robe around her shoulders and down to the ground at the back.

The Princess turned and looked at Pitt, her eyes wide, questioning.

"Was there a matching pair?" he asked, feeling foolish.

"No," the lady-in-waiting answered for the Princess, perhaps fearing she had not heard.

Pitt walked around, making a pretense of looking for a space from which another dish could have been taken, but not expecting to find it. He was puzzled, beaten a second time. He looked at the bed. Did it have the beautifully monogrammed sheets on, like the stained and crumpled ones Gracie had found in the laundry? He dared not look. There was no possible excuse for it, and what did it matter?

He bent and touched the heavy tapestry curtains, feeling the texture of the cloth. It moved very slightly, and he saw a darker patch on the carpet below. It looked like a stain. He bent and put his finger to it. It was dry. He licked his finger and touched it again. His finger came away smeared with brownish-red.

A charge rippled through him like electricity. It was blood. He looked at the skirt to the bed, exploring it with his fingers. He found a seam where there appeared to be no reason for one. He straightened up and moved quickly to the same place on the other side. Here the skirt was even, and there was no seam. A piece had been removed and its absence disguised. More blood? An accident? An illness?

But it was not yet completely caked in. It could not be more than a few days old — in other words, it occurred since the Queen had left and been at Osborne on the Isle of Wight.

He walked back to the Limoges plate again and bent down to the floor below the mantel. It was old, beautiful, weathered by time and years of polishing. But in between the boards there was a fine white dust, as of broken porcelain. Something had been smashed here.

He turned very slowly and stared around the room. They were all watching him, the Princess, the lady-in-waiting, and both footmen. With the horror of certainty, he knew what had happened: For whatever reason, whoever had done it, this was where Sadie had been murdered.

She had been moved from here to the linen cupboard for the most obvious of reasons. But why the extra blood in the port bottles?

To make it look as if she had been killed in the cupboard, so no one would look any further? Was it animal blood from the kitchen? Had someone used the port bottles simply to carry it upstairs?

Three bottles seemed excessive. There had not been that much blood in the cupboard. Had they poured the rest away?

His mind was racing — on fire.

Who had? Certainly not the Prince. He had still been slow-moving with the remnants of a drunken hangover when Pitt had seen him the morning after. The answer was obvious: Cahoon Dunkeld. The Prince had woken to a horror almost beyond belief: Not only was there a dead woman beside him, but he was in his mother's bed. He must have been hysterical. He had sent for Dunkeld, who had come instantly and done all he could to contain the situation, disguise it, and even find someone to blame — his son-in-law, Julius Sorokine, whom he hated anyway: for not loving Minnie, and perhaps for taking Elsa's love, real or imagined.

And of course the Prince's debt to Dunkeld could never be paid. Even all the support he could give for the Cape-to-Cairo railway would be a small thing in comparison with what Dunkeld had done for him. It was the most brilliant piece of opportunism

Pitt had ever seen. He despised Dunkeld's morality, and at the same time admired his nerve and his invention.

Did Minnie Sorokine have any idea how her father had used the crime?

And if the Prince of Wales was guilty, what could be done about it? Even as the question formed in Pitt's mind, he knew the answer. The Prince would be put away quietly. They would claim some illness for him — perhaps typhoid, like his father! There would be no scandal. As with Julius Sorokine, he would simply disappear. There would be a tragic notice of his death. No one would ever know the full truth.

He thanked the Princess and walked out of the room, his mouth dry, his legs trembling, hands slick with sweat and yet cold.

CHAPTER ELEVEN

Simnel Marquand looked exhausted, as if there were nothing of life or passion left inside him. He was in the yellow sitting room with Elsa. They stood side by side, staring through the high windows at the formal gardens in their bright, rigid beauty.

"God knows!" he said bitterly. "Personally I think the man is totally incompetent. If he were worth anything, Minnie would still be alive." The pain in his voice was lacerating.

Elsa avoided looking at him. To do so would be intrusive, like watching someone whose bodily functions were out of control. And yet she was angry with him for blaming Pitt. "What would you have done?" she asked him, her voice almost level in spite of the pitch of her own emotions.

"I wouldn't have spent my time infuriating the Prince of Wales, and the entire staff, about some damn plate!" He almost choked on the words. "The man's a buffoon!"

It was really Julius she was trying to defend, but she spoke as if it were Pitt. "What could he have read from the evidence? There was nothing to prove who killed the woman, or even why anyone should want to."

"Minnie worked it out!" he shouted in accusation. "She deduced it from the evidence."

"What evidence?" Now she swung round to face him, as hurt and desperate as he was. The only difference between them was that Minnie, whom he had loved, was dead, and Julius was still alive, at least for a short while longer.

He did not answer. There were shadows around his eyes and the skin there was puffy, as if he were ill. She knew he had been obsessed with Minnie, beyond his ability to control it. She had seen men be like that over gambling, growing to hate it and yet unable to stop until they had lost everything.

Would she lose everything when they took Julius away and shut him up for the rest of his life? Was he really the man she thought she knew and loved, or a creature that existed only in her own hungers?

It was absurd, she and Simnel standing together in this beautiful room, total strangers at heart, attacking each other, while suffering the same pain.

"If you knew he was going to kill Minnie, why didn't you do something yourself?" she asked. It was a cruel question, but he deserved it for accepting so quickly and so blindly that Julius was guilty. Julius was his brother! He should have had some loyalty, whether they were rivals or not. Minnie had destroyed his judgment, the things in him that were best.

"For God's sake!" he burst out. "Don't you think I would have if I'd known? I loved her! Minnie was . . . she was the most passionately, marvelously alive person I've ever seen. It is as if he had destroyed life itself!"

"Don't you suppose he knew how alive she was?" she asked, hurting herself as she was saying it.

"He didn't love her," Simnel replied very quietly. "He didn't deserve her."

"You say that as if loving and deserving were the same thing," she retaliated. They avoided looking at each other again. "In that case, Olga deserves you. Or hadn't you thought of that?"

"You can't help who you love," he said between his teeth. "You can't love to order. If you had ever really loved anyone, not simply chosen to marry them as the safest and most profitable alliance you could make, then you would know that."

She could not accuse him of cruelty — she had been just as cruel herself. "The marriage where I loved was not offered to me," she answered him. "Any more than it was to you, or perhaps to Minnie. You are totally naïve if you think we can choose to do or undo at will. Or that what you want will turn out the way you believed it would. Olga wanted you. It looks as if she still does, but do you suppose that will go on forever?"

"I loved Minnie," he said again. "I don't think you understand that. You never loved her. She knew you didn't. You were jealous of the affection Cahoon had for her. He admired her in a way he never did you."

Both of these things were true, but strangely it was the charge that she had not loved Minnie that cut deeper. She should at least have tried. She had been so lost in her own loneliness, too consumed in herself to imagine what Minnie felt. She looked at it now, honestly, and found it ugly. No wonder Cahoon had not loved her. She did not love herself very much either.

"I know," she replied aloud. "But did you love Minnie? Or did you love the way she made you feel: passionate and alive yourself? And hate it! She made you behave like a fool. You loved her so much you didn't care if everyone knew — and they did. You betrayed both your wife and your brother. Is that who you wanted to be, what you admired in yourself?" At last she turned to look at him.

His face was white. "You really did hate her, didn't you?" he said very softly. "Why? Over Cahoon, or over Julius?"

She smiled. "At least you haven't the arrogance to assume it was over you! Has it occurred to you that most married women will feel for each other when they are betrayed? Perhaps I hated her for what she did to Olga, as well as to Julius."

His eyes were glittering. "Enough to kill her for it?"

"I thought you believed Julius did it — your own brother?" It was an accusation, all her fear and anger making her voice knife-edged.

"Well, it wasn't me, and she was the one person Cahoon really loved," he pointed out. "If it wasn't Julius, then it must have been Hamilton. And why the hell would he? Face it, Elsa, whoever it is has killed at least three times: Minnie, that poor whore who only came here as part of her job, and the other wretched woman in Africa that we've all been trying to forget. Cahoon wasn't even there, so it couldn't have been him."

"Then it must have been Hamilton," she said simply. "Except that I don't know it wasn't you. Perhaps you were desperate to escape the hold she had over you. You might have been tired of endless lust and betrayal. You couldn't help yourself. Every time she teased you, you responded like a trained dog. Maybe you despised yourself, and that was the only freedom you could achieve."

"You are a passionless, pathetic woman, just as Cahoon says you are." The words were forced out between his teeth, his voice shaking.

"Because I don't go around in a red dress, taunting people?" she retaliated, but the charge stung. She knew Cahoon no longer wanted her. If he wanted anyone at all, it was Amelia Parr. She had seen that in his eyes, but it still hurt that he should say so to another man. It was a complete denial of her as having any value.

"Because you go around in a blue dress, ice cold, and afraid of your own shadow," he replied. "And, God forgive you, you're alive!"

"So are you!" she shot back. "And perhaps if you'd resisted your appetites instead of indulging them, Minnie would be too. Have you ever considered that? If Julius killed her, perhaps you drove him to it?" She had nearly said perhaps Olga did it. The words had almost slipped out.

He was white-faced, blotches of color on his cheeks. "Are you saying that if your wife prefers someone else it is just cause for you to murder her?"

"You had better hope not, or Olga may feel justified in killing you," she answered him. "I would not blame her." That was a lie. Rage against Simnel for accusing Julius, and the disloyalty of it, twisted inside her. And the bitter fear that he could be right was there, tiny, thin as a wire in the gut, but undeniable. She hated herself for it even more, but it was there.

Did she love Julius? Was love an unshakable loyalty, no matter what the evidence? A denial of your own values, your intelligence? Was it something that refuses to believe the ugly and shallow, that sees only the clean in a person, the desire to be brave, kind, funny, and gentle? Or does it also see the fears and the failures, the dreams broken, and still love the person? Is it tender to the bruised hope? Would she still care if Julius were nothing like her vision of him?

Was that love, or obsession, because his face had a beauty that haunted her mind, his smile and his hands, the pitch of his voice? Was it really her own dreams she clung to, and loved? How easy, and how unreal.

The door opened and Liliane came in, followed the moment after by Olga. Elsa made polite remarks. Simnel muttered something meaningless and turned away. No one knew what to say that was honest or anything more than platitudes to break the silence.

Elsa looked at the other women and wondered how many compromises they had made. Were they, in facing reality, in loving men in spite of their weaknesses or failures, more honest than she?

Doesn't all love have a little blindness? How else does it survive? Isn't believing in the possibilities of the good and the beautiful what inspires it into being?

Cahoon came in, and Hamilton Quase. They both looked haggard, skin blotched and hollow, Cahoon especially because he was also scratched by his razor. There was a curious lifelessness about him, as though he were physically smaller. Hamilton had obviously already drunk more than was good for him. An air of miserable belligerence suggested he intended to continue. He deliberately avoided Liliane's anxious gaze.

Dinner was ghastly. The places were set for six, and the absence of Julius and Minnie was glaring. The women did not wear black because they had not brought anything black with them, and the previous night they had dined in their rooms. Instead, they had chosen the darkest shades they had and a complete absence of jewelry. Conversation was halting and desperately artificial until Cahoon shattered the pretense.

"Has anybody seen that fool of a policeman since this morning?" he asked.

No one answered him. Eventually Simnel shook his head, his mouth full.

"It should be over by tomorrow," Cahoon went on. "I don't know why he couldn't have settled it today."

"Will we all leave?" Olga asked, looking from one to another of them.

Hamilton leaned back in his chair and regarded Cahoon overearnestly.

"No," Cahoon was terse. "The course of history does not stop for individual deaths, even of kings and queens, certainly not simply of those we love. I shall complete the negotiations with His Royal Highness, which will take only a little longer. After that we may all leave. Of course we shall have to find a suitable diplomat to take Julius's place."

"In fact, business as usual," Elsa said coldly. "Why should we let mere death or damnation get in the way of a railway?"

"Don't drink any more wine, Elsa. It isn't good for you," Cahoon said, without turning to look at her.

"Did Julius admit to killing Minnie?"

Hamilton asked, suddenly sitting up straight again. "I assume he didn't, and that was why the policeman was still wandering around asking questions. I heard he saw the Prince of Wales again today, and the Princess."

Cahoon sat very still. His knuckles were white where his hand gripped the stem of his wineglass. "I imagine it is true," he said, clearing his throat to try to release the tension half strangling his voice. "He is following the trail of detection that Minnie followed, only, God damn him to hell, he is too late to save her."

"Detection?" Simnel said sharply.

"Don't be so stupid!" Cahoon said savagely. "If Minnie hadn't discovered the truth about that woman's death, Julius wouldn't have killed her too! Even that buffoon Pitt can work that out!"

"What detection?" The words were out of Elsa's mouth before she thought of the consequences, then it was too late.

Cahoon turned in his seat to stare at her. He seemed to be considering an angry or dismissive answer, then changed his mind. "It had to do with monogrammed sheets, broken china, and a great deal of blood."

Everyone around the table froze, food halfway to their mouths, glasses in midair. Liliane let out a little gasp, and choked it off.

Hamilton put down his fork slowly.

Elsa waited. She knew from Cahoon's face that he was going to tell them.

"It seems there was a piece of china broken," Cahoon began. "Limoges porcelain, to be exact. Quite distinctive. The servants swept up the pieces and removed them . . ."

"From where?" Hamilton asked. "Not the linen cupboard!"

Elsa could feel high, hysterical laughter welling up inside her and put her hand over her mouth to stifle it.

Simnel leaned forward. "Are you saying it was from Julius's room, and Minnie knew that? Why would the servants clear it up, anyway?"

A muscle ticked dangerously in Cahoon's jaw. "No, of course not Julius's room. It seems that the wretched woman either was killed in the Queen's bedroom, or else it —"

"What?" Simnel exploded.

Liliane dropped her fork with a clatter.

Olga gave a cry that was instantly swallowed back, and the emotion behind it could have been anything.

"Her Majesty is at Osborne," Cahoon pointed out. "It would be easy enough for Julius to have taken the wretched woman there —"

"But why?" Hamilton insisted. "It makes

no sense!"

"A gentleman guest in Buckingham Palace rapes and guts a whore, and you're looking for sense!" Cahoon shouted at him, his rage and pain at last breaking loose. "The drink has rotted your brain, Quase. I'm talking about what Minnie found out, not trying to explain it!"

Elsa could not bear it. She refused to believe Julius was the man Cahoon was painting him to be. "If Minnie told you all this, why didn't you protect her yourself?" she accused him. "You blame Pitt for not arresting Julius sooner, but you didn't tell him this, did you?"

Cahoon ignored her, but she knew from the tide of blood up his neck that he had heard. "Minnie realized the woman could not have been killed in the cupboard," he said steadily. "And that the broken porcelain was the key."

"Did she tell you?" Hamilton insisted.

"No, of course she didn't!" Cahoon snapped. "I deduced it!"

"Too late to help her," Elsa pointed out.

"Obviously!" he snarled at her. "That is an idiotic remark, and vicious, Elsa, very vicious."

She was too angry, too desperate to care anymore if he humiliated her in front of the others. "But true. You knew Minnie, saw her and spoke to her every day, and you knew Julius," she told him. "If you didn't work it out until it was too late, aren't you a hypocrite to blame the policeman because he didn't either?"

The blood darkened his face. She was perfectly certain that if they had been alone together in that instant he would have struck her. She hated him for Minnie, for Julius, and because of her own guilt over not caring for Minnie. She had not protected her, nor had she been someone in whom Minnie could have confided the terrible things she had discovered. She could not defend herself; she could only attack.

"How does that prove it was Julius?" she asked. "Anyone could have gone along to the Queen's room, if they knew the way. How did Julius know where it was? He had never been here before. How did he even get in?"

They all looked at Cahoon.

"How do you know it was the Queen's room?" Hamilton asked curiously.

"Because that's where the Limoges came from, you fool!" Cahoon snapped.

"How do you know? You saw it there?" Hamilton would not be persuaded without proof.

"The monogrammed sheets," Cahoon was

exaggeratedly patient. "And the fact that it was not the Prince's room. I hope you are not going to suggest it was the Princess's?"

Hamilton shrugged. "That seems logical," he conceded.

"Thank you." Cahoon gave a sarcastic little bow from the neck.

The rest of the meal was completed in near silence. The touch of silver to china and the faint click of glass seemed intrusively loud. When the final course was cleared away, Olga pleaded a headache and retired. The men remained at the table, and Elsa and Liliane withdrew to sit by themselves, both declining anything further and willing to excuse the servants for the evening.

The silence between the two women prickled with suspense and emotion tight and unspoken for years. They were both afraid for men they loved. For Liliane it was her husband, which was obvious and right. For Elsa, her love was so lonely and so burdened by uncertainty that the knot of it was like a stone in her stomach, a hard, heavy, and aching pain all the time. The situation was intolerable.

"Do you think Cahoon is right?" she began, her voice trembling. "I mean that Minnie worked out what had happened, from a few pieces of china and blood on some sheets?"

Liliane kept her back toward Elsa. The light shone on the burnished coils of her hair, tonight without ornament. The skin of her shoulders was blemishless.

"I'm afraid I have no idea," she answered. "Minnie never confided in me."

Elsa refused to be put off. "I had not imagined she would. If she had spoken to anyone at all, it would have been her father. I was thinking of the likelihood of it, even the logic. How did she know about the china when no one else did?"

"I don't know, Elsa." Liliane turned round at last. "I realize that you are naturally distressed about Minnie's death, and that some understanding might ease it for you. It would give all of us the feeling of being rather less helpless than we are now, but I really have no idea what happened. It makes no sense to me, and I'm not sure that I even expect it to anymore. I'm sorry."

She was lying. In that instant Elsa was certain of it. Liliane was afraid. It was there in the fixed stare of her eyes, which were not completely in focus, and the way she stood as if ready to move at any moment, in whatever direction safety lay.

"You don't think it was Julius, do you?" Elsa said suddenly, and then the moment the words were out she knew she had said them too quickly. Her impulsiveness had lost her the advantage.

"I've told you," Liliane repeated patiently, "I have no idea. If I knew anything, I would have told that policeman, whatever his name is."

That too was a lie, but this time a more obvious one. Perhaps Liliane realized it because she looked away.

"What about the woman who was killed in Africa?" Elsa asked. "You were there. Was it just like these?"

Liliane was pale. "As far as I heard, yes, it seems so. That doesn't mean it was for the same reason."

"Oh, Liliane!" Elsa said sharply. "Credit me with a little sense. Hamilton, Julius, and Simnel were all there, and it has to have been one of them here too."

Liliane turned away again, whisking her skirt around with unconscious elegance. "Presumably." She said it with no conviction, in fact almost with indifference.

What was she afraid of? It could only be that it had been Hamilton. Or could it be some secret of her own? Cahoon had said there had once been a question of her marrying Julius, but her father had objected. Then Hamilton had helped so much, and with such gentleness and understanding at the time of her brother's death, that she had fallen in love with him.

Maybe he was a far better man than Julius: more honorable, more compassionate, more loyal — all the qualities Elsa knew she admired. What did it matter if someone's smile tugged at your insides and left your heart pounding and your hands trembling? That was obsession, unworthy to be spoken of in the same breath as love.

Liliane looked back at her, her face softer, almost as if she felt a moment's pity. "Minnie must have spoken to her father," she said quietly. "Who else would have told him that she was asking all these questions? It must have been what she was hinting about at the dinner table the night she was killed. She was taunting him, you must have seen that."

"What for?" Now Elsa's mind raced from one wild, half-formed idea to another. Had Minnie learned it was Julius? Or, fearing that her father's hatred of him would tempt him to blame Julius and even alter the evidence, she had told him that she would defend her husband, whether she loved him or not? She was the only one who was never afraid of Cahoon. Perhaps that was what he loved in her the most.

Had she loved Julius after all? Was the

whole affair with Simnel only a way of trying to stir Julius to some response, a jealousy if not a love? Poor Minnie: too proud and too full of passion to plead, too lonely to confide in anyone, and perhaps wounded too deeply by what might have been the only rejection in her life that mattered to her. Nothing before that had prepared her for it; she might have had no inner dreams to strengthen her.

And Elsa had offered her nothing but rivalry. How miserable, how small and utterly selfish of her. She was ashamed of that now that it was too late.

Liliane was watching her, her beautiful eyes concentrating, seeing beyond the need for answers into the reasons for it.

It was Elsa who looked away. Part of the turmoil inside her was jealousy. She recognized the taste of it with a kind of bitter amusement at herself. Julius had courted Liliane and lost her to Hamilton Quase. Had that always been at the heart of it? He had never fallen out of love with her. Minnie knew it, and it was only Elsa who didn't.

"You can't do anything," Liliane said quite gently. "Nothing can be changed now, except to make it worse."

"I suppose you're right," Elsa conceded, although she was lying even as she said it. She would rather pursue the truth, even if she found that Julius was guilty, than surrender without knowing, and betray her dreams by cowardice. Deliberately she changed the subject to something else, utterly trivial.

Liliane seemed relieved.

They all retired early. There was nothing to say. Even the men no longer had the heart to talk of Africa, and yet conversation about anything else was stilted and eventually absurd. The absence of Julius and Minnie was like a gaping hole that everyone tiptoed around, terrified of falling into, and yet was drawn to by a sort of emotional vertigo.

When Elsa excused herself she was uncomfortably aware that Cahoon followed her immediately, almost treading on the hem of her dress as she went into her bedroom. Bartle was waiting for her and Cahoon ordered her out, closing the door behind her.

Elsa felt a quick flutter of fear. She backed away from him, and was furious with herself for it. She stopped, too close to the bed. He could knock her onto it easily, but if she moved sideways it would of necessity be toward him. She refused to speak first. It was what he was waiting for: the sign of yielding, the impulse to placate him.

"You are making a fool of yourself, Elsa," he said coldly. "If you want to ruin your own reputation, I don't care. But you are still my wife, and I won't have you behave hysterically once we leave here. If you can't control your imagination and have some dignity, then you will have to be looked after, perhaps in some appropriate establishment where you will not damage either of us."

He meant it. It was not just an expression of temper, it was a threat. She saw it hard and real in his eyes. She found her knees were shaking, and it cost her an effort to remain standing straight and looking at him.

"You mean a madhouse, like Julius," she murmured. "That would be convenient for you. Then you can have an affair with Amelia Parr without my getting in the way."

"You are not in the way, Elsa," he replied. It was damning. Nothing else could have obliterated her so completely. "Leave the murders alone, or you will find out a great deal more about Julius than you wish to know." His eyes gleamed, as if somewhere inside himself he were laughing savagely at her absurdity.

In that moment she made up her mind to fight him. If there had been any irresolution in her before, it had vanished. She was ashamed that it had taken her so long. This had nothing to do with Julius; it was for herself, to be the person she wanted to be, not the one too absorbed in her own needs and fears to think of anyone else, or see the possibility that Minnie's bravado hid the fact that she felt pain as well.

She drew in her breath to tell Cahoon, and then realized how foolish that would be. What if Julius was not guilty, but had been made to look it? Wasn't that what she was trying to believe? But by whom if not Cahoon? Was it because he hated Julius for loving Liliane, and not Minnie — because he felt the insult and the pain on her behalf?

No, there was another clearer and much more understandable motive. It was glaring, now that she could see it. Cahoon wanted to put her away so he could marry Amelia Parr. If she were innocent, the good wife she had so far appeared to be, then he had no excuse to set her aside. And he would never damage the reputation he had won with such care. He wanted that peerage desperately. He was like a starving man dreaming of food; only in his case it was respectability, belonging, the acceptance he had longed for and that had eluded him all his life.

He must make Elsa appear so bad in the eyes of society that no one would blame him for putting her aside. They must feel that if they were in his place, they would have felt no choice but to do the same.

If she fought for Julius now, when he seemed undeniably guilty of murder and madness, not once but three times, then it would be simple to convince them she was also having an affair with him. She would have betrayed her husband and his daughter — exactly the sins she had denied herself. But who would believe her?

That meant that she must either not fight, or if she did so, then she must win!

"Really?" she said, keeping her voice level with an effort so intense her fingernails bit into her palms, and she was glad of the folds of her skirt to keep them hidden. "That would surprise me. I don't think we will find out anything at all. I think we are going to keep it all very quiet. You wouldn't want to have taken so much trouble to woo the Prince of Wales and then cause such a scandal that he had to drop you in the end, would you?"

His face darkened and he took two steps toward her. He was so close she could feel the heat of him and smell cigar smoke and the faint odor of his skin. She did not move, although it was hard to keep her balance and not flinch. She had meant what she said as a half-submission, half-evasion. He had taken it as a threat. She was not being clever.

He swung back his hand and slapped her

across the cheek, sending her staggering. The bed caught her behind the knees and she fell onto it on her back, helpless.

He leaned over her, one hand on either side, and bent down so his face was only a foot above hers. "Don't fight me, Elsa," he said between his teeth. "I am not only stronger than you are, I am cleverer, wiser, and braver. I am also your husband, which makes me right according to the law. They won't hang Julius, they will simply lock him away. Don't interfere."

There was nothing she could say, but she did not avert her eyes from his.

He waited for her to answer, still leaning over her.

"Do you intend to remain there all night?" she asked. Her face hurt and she felt it burn hot. Deliberately she relaxed her body. "You will get tired before I do," she added.

He straightened up abruptly and walked out, slamming the door behind him. She got up quickly and locked both the dressing room door, which connected with his room, and the door to the passage. Then she lay down on the bed, shaking so violently she felt as if the whole frame must be juddering with her.

She had no idea how long it was before she finally sat up again, calmer, and began to think. She had left herself no option but to fight. At last she had made a decision. It might be the wrong one, but it was better than losing because she had never found the passion or the courage to try.

Minnie had discussed enough of the truth to be killed in order to silence her. Apparently a broken Limoges dish had been important. Cahoon had described it: white and blue with a little gold. At the time she had imagined it quite clearly; a pedestal dish, with gold lattice around the border and a picture in the center of a man and woman sitting very casually on a garden seat. The blue was in their clothes. She thought of it like that because that was the only Limoges that she could remember seeing. Of course this one could have been any shape or design.

Then she remembered, with a feeling like ice in her stomach, where she had seen it. It was in Cahoon's cases that he had brought with him, here to the Palace. That was how he knew about it! He had not deduced anything at all.

Perhaps it had nothing to do with the woman's murder, but he had seized the opportunity to place the blame on Julius, somehow using that dish.

But how? It made no sense. The dish was

in the Queen's room. Did Pitt know anything about it? Certainly he would not know that Cahoon had brought with him one exactly the same. Tomorrow Elsa would tell him. Of course Cahoon would never forgive her, but she had declared war on him anyway; there was no retreating now. If she did not win, she might be blamed for something unforgivable, put aside as an adulteress — or worse, somehow tied in with the murder of the street woman.

There was no one she could turn to for help. They were all fighting their own battles: Liliane to protect Hamilton from the destruction he seemed determined to find in the bottom of a bottle. Why? Was it because Liliane was still in love with Julius?

Olga wanted to win Simnel back from a dead woman whose fire and laughter she could never equal, and whose selfishness, appetite, and occasional streaks of cruelty she would never sink to.

And Simnel, Julius's brother, who should have been fighting to save him, protect him, was too eaten up by envy to allow himself that loyalty.

If only she could speak to Julius himself. If she could ask him, listen to his answer, surely she would know whether to believe him or not. No one had asked him, they all believed Cahoon's word. For that matter, had Pitt asked him?

He was locked in and only the servants had keys so they could take him food. Tomorrow the police would come; then she would never see him again. There was only one possible decision: She must wait until the household was asleep, then go downstairs and find the keys, even if she searched by candlelight and it took her half the night.

She waited until two o'clock in the morning. She was exhausted but unable to sleep, although she dared not lie down in case she did drift into unconsciousness and waken when it was already light, and so miss her only chance.

She tiptoed down the stairs, feeling ridiculous, as if she were committing some crime. Then she realized that actually she was. It was probably an offense against some law to unlock the door of an imprisoned man. It was certainly a gross abuse of hospitality. If anyone knew, then she would pay dearly for it. She would be disgraced, socially nonexistent from now on. She hesitated only for a moment in her step. What had she to lose? Physical comfort, that was about all.

But what if Julius really were everything Cahoon said of him? Then he might attack her, take the keys and escape. He must know they would never give him a trial, fair or otherwise. It would be his only chance not to spend the rest of his life locked away in an asylum.

Was she tempted to let him go, deliberately? Yes! The thought of him imprisoned forever was hideous. He would be there until he really was mad, and there could never be any escape. The weight of that thought was like a descending darkness, shutting everything out.

But how far would he get? Not even out of the Palace. There could hardly be a better-guarded place in England.

It took her over an hour to find the keys, she had to search almost every cupboard in the kitchens, scullery, still room, and pantries, using separate keys to unlock cupboards where more keys hung in rows. Then she had to put them back in exactly the same place. Even then she was not certain she had the right ones until she tried them. She must be insane herself, breaking into Julius's bedroom in the middle of the night. If Cahoon found her, she would have given him the perfect excuse to have her shut away too.

Still, she did it.

Her hands were quite firm, though a little clammy. Her stomach churned. Then she was inside. She closed the door softly, locked it, and put the key in the tiny pocket in her gown. She listened and could hear nothing, except the pounding of her own heart and her breathing.

Gradually it subsided, and she thought she could hear his breath as well.

"Julius."

Nothing. She could neither see nor hear.

"Julius!"

Movement. A stirring in the bed. Now she felt ridiculous. How on earth could she explain being here? Nothing of love had ever been said by either one of them. Perhaps anything between them was entirely in her own imagination. Probably it was. He would be in his nightshirt, and she had come into his bedroom in the middle of the night, alone. If Cahoon walked in on them, it would ruin them both. It would be exactly what he wished. Had he even planned it? Then she had played into his hands perfectly. How unbelievably stupid! She moved to go back again, her hand feeling for the key.

There was a rustling from the bed, movement in the dark. "Elsa?"

Too late. She couldn't go now. If she opened the door the faint light in the passage would show her face. Have the courage of her beliefs. If she felt anything, grasp for it, fight for it.

"Julius, I have to talk to you."

"How did you get in? If they catch you, you will be ruined." There was fear in his voice. "You can't help me. Please go, before Cahoon finds out."

"They won't try you," she said, standing still because she did not know which way to step in the dark. "They'll just say you are insane, and put you into an asylum, somewhere from which you'll never escape, and no one will ever see you."

He was silent. Had he not realized that?

"I'm sorry." She tried to keep her voice from trembling, and failed. She ached to see his face, and yet perhaps not doing so was the only way she could keep control of herself. "Julius?"

"Yes?" His voice was hoarse, uncertain. The darkness also gave him a degree of privacy. She was grateful for that. She remained standing where she was. She ached to hold him in her arms, give him at least the desperate shred of comfort that touch afforded. But there had never been anything between them to suggest he would welcome it. It would be intrusive, absurd. If his feelings for her were in any way different from hers for him, then it would be offensive, embarrassing, awful in every way.

"You didn't kill Minnie, did you?" she said.

"No," he responded immediately. "I don't know who did. I assume it was whoever killed the prostitute. I can't think of any other reason. Poor Minnie." There was real hurt, and pity in his voice. "She was so sure she was learning the truth. I didn't realize it until she kept saying so at dinner. Obviously someone believed her."

The thought held the kind of coldness that made her feel sick. It was one of the other three men. It could be no one else. She knew them all; in ways liked them, except Cahoon; but she had once thought she loved him. There had been moments that were tender. What was the difference between being in love and thinking you were? Was being in love about what survives after time and temptation, misfortune, change, the need to forget and forgive have all been faced?

"Do you know where Sadie was killed?" she asked him.

"Wasn't it in the cupboard where she was found?" Julius sounded puzzled.

"Apparently not. Cahoon says it was in the Queen's bedroom. That's how the monogrammed sheets got bloodstained."

"What monogrammed sheets?" His voice was a little high. "I don't know what you're talking about."

"The Queen's sheets. They don't belong in the guest linen cupboard."

"Where were they?"

She realized she did not know. "He didn't say. Do you know about a Limoges dish that was broken?"

"No. I haven't seen any Limoges. Mostly it's Crown Derby, Wedgwood, and a few pieces of Meissen. Who broke the Limoges?" His voice was steadier, but he still sounded totally confused.

She was frightened by how little she understood. Even to herself she seemed to be speaking total nonsense.

"I don't know, but Minnie was asking about it. It seemed to matter to her a lot. Cahoon says it was in the Queen's bedroom. That's how they knew the woman was killed there."

"How does Cahoon know it was there?" he asked quickly. She heard the bedsprings as he moved his weight. She could see nothing, but she was certain from the very slight sounds that he had stood up. Was he coming toward her in the dark? She was afraid. Or was it that she wanted him to? "I don't know," she said. "Maybe . . . maybe the Prince of Wales told him."

"If the Prince of Wales could have killed Minnie, I would wonder if he was guilty of the first one too," he said with heavy irony. He was on the edge of laughter, and of grief beyond control.

"Julius!" The moment the word was out, she knew the tone of it would betray her: It was desperate with emotion. He had to hear in it all that she felt for him.

"I know. He couldn't." His voice was tight now, choked with the effort to keep some dignity, some grip on the fear inside him. "It has to be Simnel or Hamilton."

"I wish it could be Cahoon." She meant it, and this was no time to pretend a loyalty they both knew she did not feel. "But he wouldn't kill Minnie. In his own way, he loved her. She was probably the only person he did love. But apart from that, he wasn't in Cape Town when the woman was killed there, and it seems the crimes were exactly the same."

"Elsa . . ." he stopped.

"What?"

"I don't know who did it, and I can't prove I didn't. I know she was sleeping with Simnel a year ago, and if not now, then only from lack of opportunity. I didn't care. I long since realized I didn't love her. I'm guilty of that . . . of not making her happy. If I had, perhaps she wouldn't have turned to anyone else."

"You don't have to make love with someone else because your husband doesn't want you," she said quietly. "That doesn't make it right. Especially if the other person is married also. Even if they aren't, it's a betrayal. How could that other person then trust you?"

The silence pounded like a heartbeat. There were not even any creaks of settling wood to disturb the night.

"They can't," he answered. "But you are speaking of love, and I wasn't. She doesn't love Simnel, nor he her. It's a hunger of a different kind, selfish. It makes you a lesser person, not a greater one."

"And what does a greater one do?" Did she want to know what he thought? Was it not better to keep the dream whole? There would be no tomorrow in which to mend it. This would be all she had, forever.

"It makes you want to be the person they could love," he answered her very softly. "At least honest and generous, and attempt to be brave as well."

The tears filled her eyes and her throat ached almost unbearably.

"I'm trying for honest," he went on. "I didn't kill Minnie, but I am guilty of not wanting to build the Cape-to-Cairo railway. I wish I had had the courage to tell Cahoon outright, and withdraw. We should build railways from inland to the ports, in each region if they want them, but keep the Empire on the sea. That's enough power for any nation. We should leave the heart of Africa alone. It's not ours. The fact that we might be able to take it is irrelevant. But they will be able to build it without me. I can't do any more, but I hope I would have had the integrity to pull out, and tell them why." He hesitated. "Please believe in me, Elsa, that I would have. I can't ever prove it now."

"I believe you," she said immediately. "I . . . I do." She had almost said "I love you," then stopped. He needed trust more than emotion. "Don't give up. I'm going to find Pitt. I have something to tell him."

"Now? What time is it?"

"I don't know. About three, I expect. Something like that."

"You can't wake him up at this hour!"

"Yes, I can."

"Elsa!"

"Yes?"

"Thank you."

"For believing you? That's not necessary. I do."

He had no idea how little she had believed him before this moment, but this was not the time for the self-indulgence of telling him.

Nor was it the time to say she loved him. He knew that. And she did not want to make him feel as if he had to respond. It would betray this gossamer-thin honesty.

She found the key in her pocket and opened the door. She hesitated, almost said something, then changed her mind and went out, locking the door again behind her so no one would know she had been there.

She returned the key to where she had found it, and then went to waken Pitt. Of course it was appalling to disturb him at this hour, but later might be too late. She had no idea when the police would come to take Julius away. Cahoon would have it done as soon as possible.

She was still wearing her dinner gown, which was crumpled now, and her hair was coming loose from its pins. There were probably dried tears on her face. None of this mattered. Another hour or so and it would be light. There was no time to waste in mending her appearance.

It took her a few minutes to find Pitt's room, and then several more to steel her nerve to knock. It was necessary for her to gather her courage again before the door opened. Pitt stood there blinking, the gaslamps turned up behind him. He was wearing a nightshirt and robe, and his thick hair was tousled, but he seemed quite definitely awake.

"Mrs. Dunkeld? Are you all right? Has something happened?" he said with alarm.

"I need to speak to you," she replied as levelly as she could. "Urgently, or I would not have disturbed you this way."

"I'll be out in five minutes." He did not argue but went back into the room. Five minutes later he emerged again, this time fully dressed and his hair in some semblance of order. However, he looked haggard with exhaustion and there was a dark stubble on his cheeks and chin. He led the way to the room where he worked, and opened the door for her.

"What is it, Mrs. Dunkeld?" he asked when they were inside and the lamps lit.

"You found the shards of a Limoges plate in the rubbish, didn't you?" she stated.

"Yes."

"Was it a pedestal dish, mostly white with a gold trellis border around the edges, and in the center a man and woman sitting on a stone garden seat? They both have blue on, a vivid shade of cobalt. I think it is his coat, and a sort of cloak for her."

In spite of his weariness his attention was suddenly total. "Yes. Have you seen it? Where?"

"In a box my husband brought with us."

He looked stunned, as if what she had said were incomprehensible. "Brought with you?" he repeated. "Are you certain?"

"Absolutely. It cannot have been the one which my husband said was broken, in Her Majesty's own bedroom. It must be one exactly like it."

"You are certain, Mrs. Dunkeld?" he insisted.

"Yes." She felt the heat creep up her face. Did he imagine she was inventing it to protect Julius? He knew how she felt, she had seen it in his eyes before, a certain pity. Damn him for understanding! "He couldn't have given it to the Queen," she said aloud. "It would have been in a box, and left for her to open." She was talking too much. She stopped abruptly.

"I know. This one was apparently given to her by one of her daughters, some considerable time ago," he said, and the gentleness was in his eyes again. "But did he bring a gift for the Prince of Wales, do you know?"

She was puzzled. He seemed to have missed the point. "Yes, but it was not particularly personal, just a dozen or so bottles of a very good port. I think they have already been drinking it. Why? How can that matter? It's a fairly usual thing to do."

"Port?" he repeated.

"Yes. Why?"

"Do you know from what vineyard?"

"No, but Cahoon said it was extremely good. But then he would hardly give the Prince inferior wine." She forced herself to ask, whatever he thought of her. "Does the dish not matter?"

"It matters very much, Mrs. Dunkeld. And so does the port — or at least the bottles do. Please don't mention them to him, or to anyone." He was very serious, staring at her intently. "It may put you in danger. Three of them were found with traces of blood in them. Now you understand why you must mention it to no one?"

"Blood?" She was startled, and filled with a sudden hope so erratic and so sweet for a moment she found it difficult to breathe.

"Yes. Now please go back to your room, to sleep if you can. Thank you for coming to me. It must have taken great courage." He stood up, a little stiffly, as if he were so tired that to straighten up was too much effort.

She realized he must be afraid too. He not only had to solve these murders quickly, and discreetly, but he had to find the answer that the Prince of Wales wanted and that his superior at Special Branch could accept. He was a man pressured from all sides. And his own compassion, and his sense of justice, would be compelling him also, probably in a different direction.

There was a sharp bang on the door, and then it flew open and Cahoon strode in. He too was fully dressed, although unshaven, and obviously in a towering rage.

"I assume you have some explanation for interrogating my wife at three in the morning?" he said savagely to Pitt. "Who the devil do you think you are? If my poor daughter hadn't solved the case for you, at the cost of her own life, I would have you removed, and someone competent sent in. However, there is nothing left to do, except have Sorokine taken away and then get out yourself." He turned to Elsa. "Go back to bed," he ordered.

She stood still. "Mr. Pitt did not send for me, I came to see him." She would not have Pitt blamed; it would be both shabby and dishonest. She was fighting for everything that mattered to her, win or lose.

"Do as you are told!" Cahoon said between his teeth.

She did not move.

Pitt also seemed perfectly composed. "Mr. Dunkeld, did you bring a gift of a case of port wine to the Prince of Wales?"

"What?"

"I think you heard me, sir. Did you?"

Cahoon was incredulous. "Three o'clock in the morning, and you want to know if I brought wine for the Prince of Wales?"

"Yes, I do. Did you?"

"Yes. Best port I could find. It's the sort of thing gentlemen do." His tone was acutely condescending.

"And the Limoges dish, was that a gift also?" Pitt asked.

This time Cahoon was definitely taken by surprise. "What . . . Limoges dish?" His hesitation was palpable.

"The one in your case, sir. Is there more than one?" Pitt's voice was polite, but the cutting edge was unmistakable.

For an instant Cahoon obviously debated denial.

"A white and gold pedestal dish," Elsa supplied for him. She was fighting to save Julius, grasping at straws, but all decisions were made and it was too late to go back. "With a garden scene in the middle, a man and woman sitting on a stone seat. Their clothes have a lot of blue in them."

"You have been searching through my cases!" Cahoon accused her.

"I have no interest in your cases," she replied, feigning slight surprise. "Your valet was unpacking and did not know what to do with it. You were with the Prince of Wales, so

469

he asked me. I told him to leave it where it was. If you don't recall it, I'm sure he does."

"Sarcasm is most unbecoming in a woman, Elsa," he said icily. "It makes you seem cold, and mannish." He turned to Pitt. "I am afraid it is a matter I cannot discuss with you, Inspector. It was a favor for His Royal Highness, to whom I gave my word. I am not sure if you can understand that, but if you cannot, and you wish to challenge him on the matter, then you had better do so, at your own risk. I have nothing to say. I have no idea whether you have duties to perform at this hour, but I am returning to bed, and my wife is doing the same. I assume you will be removing Sorokine before I see you again. I suggest that you do so as discreetly as possible."

Elsa's heart tightened and she found it difficult to draw air into her lungs. All her fighting, all the hope, and it was ending like this.

Pitt stared at Cahoon. "If he is taken, it will simply be to a place of safety. There is much yet to learn before the case is over," he answered.

"You don't seem to have grasped the obvious." Cahoon's voice was exaggeratedly weary. "Sorokine is mad. He suffers some form of insanity that drives him to murder a certain type of woman. He killed one in Africa several years ago. We thought then that it was a single aberration and would never happen again. So far as I knew, it hadn't. Then this week he killed the whore. Minnie realized what had happened, and I presume was rash enough to face him and accuse him, so he killed her too. No one else is involved, except possibly my wife in her reluctance to accept the facts. She is not used to the violence and tragedy that can occur in life. She was not with us in Africa, and she tends to be something of an idealist, fonder of dreams than of reality."

Pitt's eyes widened. "Are you saying that Mr. Marquand at least was aware that his brother killed this woman in Africa?"

Cahoon was caught slightly off-balance, but he recovered quickly. "No, but I think he feared it. Watson Forbes was aware. That is why he would not permit his daughter to marry him, even though she wished to. Hamilton Quase was a far better choice. Ask Forbes, if you doubt me. Now I am going to bed. Elsa!"

Elsa looked at Pitt, met his eyes for a moment, then turned and obediently followed Cahoon out into the corridor. She did not know whether she dared to hope, or not.

CHAPTER TWELVE

Pitt went back to his bedroom and lay on the bed, but he did not sleep again. He believed Elsa about the Limoges dish, because Cahoon did not deny it. Certainly she was desperate to save Julius Sorokine because she was in love with him, but even so he did not think she was lying. Were she to do that, she would have done it sooner, and to more effect. She would probably have said that he had been with her at the time of the death of one of the women, or even both.

Would Sorokine have agreed to that, even if it were a lie, in order to save himself? Many men would, regardless of the cost to Elsa's reputation, and possibly her marriage. Pitt did not think Cahoon Dunkeld would be loath to divorce her for adultery, especially one so publicly acknowledged.

If Dunkeld had brought a Limoges dish identical to the one broken, that was surely too extraordinary to be a coincidence.

Was there something in this whole terrible affair that was premeditated? The murder of Sadie? But none of the women had been here before. And surely they couldn't predict which ones would come. Killing her in such a way was the impulse of a madman. Even were it in some way thought of in advance, how would anyone know she would be in the Queen's bedroom, or that that particular dish would be broken? It was not possible. That was why Dunkeld had not taken more care to keep his bringing the dish secret, perhaps unpacked it himself. It was coincidence, something that made sense only afterward. But how?

And the port bottles, at some time filled with blood — there was no proof whether they had come full or been emptied out then refilled, possibly from the kitchen. But if the latter, by whom, and when? How could anyone obtain the blood, and fill the bottles unseen? There was always kitchen staff around. Nevertheless, it must have been the case: a fine example of opportunism.

Bringing them full of blood spoke of detailed and very careful planning for a very precise need.

Was it even imaginable that in some way the murder was foreseen? By whom? Obviously Cahoon Dunkeld. A man does not plan to be insane at a specific time, in a specific way.

But a man might know that someone else is insane and that certain very particular events will fire a breakdown of his usual control. If a man is terrified of spiders, or thrown into a rage by being laughed at, then his behavior is foreseeable.

A man who commits grotesque, uncontrollable murders is triggered into such action by a certain series of events happening in order. The pressure becomes cumulative, and he cannot bear it. Did Cahoon Dunkeld understand such a weakness in someone, and deliberately design the events that would make it explode? Could any man be so evil? Of course. There was no evil imaginable that someone would not commit. But would Dunkeld be so reckless, here in the Palace? The dangers were enormous. But then so was the prize — if it were the African railway that was at stake.

The sunlight came through a crack in the curtains and fell in a bright bar across the floor. Pitt stared at it, bewildered. How could a murder help Cahoon in that project? It looked far more likely to ruin it.

Perhaps it was not the railway that was the prize at all, but something else. Maybe it had to do with Julius Sorokine's love for Elsa.

Did Dunkeld care enough to punish Sorokine for . . . what? Pitt doubted they had ever acted on their feelings. And Dunkeld did not love her, of that he had no doubt at all.

Perhaps it was to free Minnie, and what happened to Julius or to Elsa was immaterial. That was easier to believe.

Then who had killed Minnie? Surely that was never part of Dunkeld's plan. Had Julius Sorokine been a far wilder and more dangerous weapon than he had foreseen? What a vile irony!

And why the Queen's bedroom? That must have been planned, because that was where the Limoges dish was. Had he always intended to move the body and place it in the linen cupboard, or was that improvisation? Why? Pitt's mind was racing. If Sadie had been killed in the Queen's bedroom, by the time she was moved to the cupboard, she would have stopped bleeding profusely. So the extra blood was to fling around so it looked as if she had been butchered there. Then it was meant from the beginning, all of it. But again, why?

And why was she naked? Minnie had been fully clothed. Was the answer that Sadie had been murdered in madness, but Minnie had been killed because in her driving curiosity she had come far too close to the truth?

Again, an obscene irony. Dunkeld had provoked a terrible murder born of madness, in order to destroy his son-in-law and free his daughter from the marriage. Then her intelligence had made her such a danger that in hideous sanity Sorokine had aped his own lunacy and killed her to protect himself. No wonder Dunkeld now looked like a man haunted by far more than grief.

How could Pitt prove that? How much did it matter? If Sorokine were guilty of the murders, then he had to be put into an imprisonment of some sort. That was just. Dunkeld was a man even more evil, in that he had deliberately hired a prostitute with the intention of provoking Sorokine into murdering her, but his plan had exploded in his face, destroying his only daughter for whose freedom the whole tragedy was devised. Surely to live the rest of his life knowing that it was he who had caused her death was a more exquisite punishment than the law could ever devise?

And what would happen to Elsa? She would eventually either sink into madness, clinging to the delusion that Sorokine had been innocent. Or she would eventually realize he was guilty: a divided man, half of him charming, cultured, someone she could love;

the other devoid not only of sanity but of the basic elements of compassion and decency that make one human.

Pitt could not imagine that Dunkeld would afford her any kindness. Her punishment for falling in love with someone else, the man who had also failed to love Minnie, would be continuous cruelty. He would exercise it both privately and publicly.

Pitt needed to prove all of it. Justice required it, whether the Prince of Wales liked it or not and, in turn, punished Pitt.

He must have drifted to sleep because he awoke with a jolt to hear a knock on the door. He sat up slowly, struggling to remember where he was, fully clothed on the big bed. The feeling of claustrophobia was tight in his chest, making it hard to breathe. Before he could answer coherently the door opened and Gracie came in, carrying a tray of tea. He could see the steam rising gently from the spout of the small pot.

"Yer bin up all night?" she said with intense concern.

"No," he assured her, swinging his legs down and standing. He pushed his hair out of his eyes. The stubble was rough on his cheeks and his head ached with a dull, persistent throb. "No," he added. "Elsa Dunkeld woke me at about three, or four.

She said Dunkeld brought a Limoges plate in his luggage, exactly like the one that was broken. I mean identical to it. I presume that was the one I saw in the Queen's room. And also a crate of port as a gift for the Prince of Wales."

Gracie poured the tea and handed him the cup. "It's 'ot," she warned him. "Why'd she tell yer that? 'Ow'd she know the port bottles mattered, if she don't know about the blood?"

"She didn't, I asked her," he explained. "She knew about the Limoges dish because she saw it in Cahoon's cases, and everyone knows we've been looking for one by now. Thank you." He took the tea. She was right, it was very hot. He wished it were a little cooler; he was thirsty for it. The fragrance of it was soothing even as steam. Drinking it would make him feel human again.

"Then Dunkeld done it," she said with satisfaction.

"He didn't do the one in Africa," he answered, wishing it were not so. "I think he provoked Sorokine into it. He knew he was mad, and what it was that made him lose control and kill. He deliberately created the circumstances, then altered the evidence so we . . ." He stopped. He could not think of a reason.

"Wot?" she asked. "Why din't 'e just let us catch Mr. Sorokine?"

"Because he didn't want a scandal in the Palace," Pitt answered. "He still needs the Prince's backing for the railway. He's taking a hell of a chance."

She squinted at him, thinking hard. "If 'e wanted ter get rid o' Mr. Sorokine, why din't 'e 'ave this murder 'appen somewhere else, anytime?"

"I suppose because somewhere else Sorokine might have got away with it." He was thinking as he spoke. "The police would have assumed it was someone extremely violent or degraded. Here we know it could only have been one of three men. There was no possibility of anyone having broken in from the outside."

She nodded. "Wot are we gonna do, then?"

He smiled at her automatic inclusion of herself. Her loyalty was absolute, it always had been.

"Find out what causes Sorokine to lose control," he replied, taking the first sip of tea and swallowing it jerkily because it was still too hot. "And then prove that Dunkeld knew it, and deliberately created a situation in which Sorokine would snap."

"Then you can 'ang 'im?" she said hopefully.

"Sorokine or Dunkeld?"

"Dunkeld, o' course! 'E's the wickeder!" She had no doubt whatever.

"Something like that," he agreed, sipping the tea again, and smiling at her.

Pitt went to see Cahoon Dunkeld after breakfast. He had spent the intervening time shaving and making himself look as fresh and confident as he could. Then he remarshaled his evidence and the conclusions it had taken him to. When eventually he spoke to Dunkeld alone, it was in one of the beautiful galleries lined with pictures.

"What is it now?" Dunkeld said impatiently, facing Pitt squarely, his weight even on both feet.

Pitt put his hands in his pockets and stood casually, as if he intended to remain some time. "I believe you are an excellent judge of character, Mr. Dunkeld. You know a man's strengths and weaknesses."

Dunkeld smiled sourly. "If you have only just come to that conclusion, then you are slower than a man in your job should be. Is it a job, or profession, by the way?"

"It depends upon how well you do it," Pitt replied. "At Mr. Narraway's level, it is a profession."

"I am not so far impressed with Mr. Narraway's judgment of a man's strengths and weaknesses," Dunkeld said pointedly, his eyes looking Pitt up and down with distaste.

Pitt smiled. "How long have you known that Sorokine was insane? Since he killed the woman in Africa, for example?"

"I didn't think he would do it again." Dunkeld was clearly annoyed by the tone of the question.

"No, I assumed that, or you would hardly have allowed him to marry your daughter," Pitt agreed.

"Obviously!" Dunkeld snapped, shifting the balance of his weight slightly. "Have you a purpose to this, Inspector?"

"Yes. I was wondering at exactly what juncture you thought he was mad."

Suddenly Dunkeld was guarded. He sensed danger, although he could not place it. "Does it matter? Sorokine is guilty. The details will probably always be obscure. Your job is to tidy it up in the best, most just, and most discreet way that you can."

"How did you know it was Sorokine?" Pitt pursued. "Given that you are a good judge of character, what did you see that I missed?"

Dunkeld smiled. "Are you trying to flatter me, Inspector? Clumsy, and you have based it upon a wrong assumption. I do not care what you think."

"I am trying to learn," Pitt said as innocently as he could. Dunkeld angered him more than anyone else he could remember. Even understanding his weaknesses, his driving need to belong to a class in which he was not born, his general need for admiration, even the bitter loss of his daughter, Pitt still could not like him. "People who kill compulsively," Pitt went on, "insanely, are triggered into the act by some event, or accumulation of events, which breaks their normal control, so most of the time they appear as sane as anyone else. But I imagine you have realized that."

"I have," Dunkeld agreed. He could hardly deny it. "You seem to be stating the obvious — again."

"What was it that triggered Sorokine?"

Dunkeld blinked.

"Don't you know?" Pitt invested his voice with surprise. "What was the woman like, the one he killed in Africa?"

Dunkeld thought for a moment. "Another whore, I believe," he said casually. "Not young, into her late twenties, not particularly handsome, but with a fine figure. A certain degree of intelligence, I heard, and a quick tongue. A woman who could entertain as well as merely . . ." He did not bother to finish.

"Like Sadie," Pitt concluded.

Dunkeld's contempt was too great for him to conceal. "You seem to have arrived at an understanding at last," he observed sarcastically.

Pitt gave a very slight shrug. "Did you realize this before, or after, you hired Sadie to come here and entertain the gentlemen of the party?"

Dunkeld's temper flared, his eyes bright and hot. "Are you suggesting I knew, and allowed it to happen?"

"Why on earth would you do that?" Pitt inquired, meeting Dunkeld's glare. "Unless it was deliberately to get rid of a son-in-law you dislike, and allow your daughter her freedom."

Dunkeld drew in a deep breath, shifting his weight again. "And you think I would allow a woman to be killed for that?"

Pitt remained motionless. "Do you believe he would have gone on killing, every time the same set of circumstances arose?" he inquired with no edge to his voice.

Dunkeld considered his answer before he gave it. "Do such men usually stop, if no one prevents them?" he countered.

"Not in my experience," Pitt replied.

"Then to ensure he was caught, it is desperate perhaps, but better than allowing him to continue," Dunkeld reasoned. "You did not catch him."

"I was not in Africa."

"Your arrogance is amazing!" Dunkeld almost laughed. "And do you suppose if you had been, that you would have done any better? For God's sake, man, enclosed in the Palace, with only three of us to choose from, you still couldn't do it!"

"Is the Limoges china part of his . . . obsession?" Pitt asked.

"I've already told you, that was a favor to His Royal Highness, and has nothing to do with Sorokine," Dunkeld said huskily. "Now you will have to deduce the rest for yourself, or remain in ignorance. I have a vast amount of arrangements to make. In spite of my daughter's death, the railway will still proceed, and now I must make up for Sorokine's loss, and find someone to take his place. I imagine I shall not see you again. Good day." And without waiting for Pitt to reply, he turned and strode away.

Narraway arrived a little before ten, looking tired and unhappy. His face was deeply lined, accentuating the immaculacy of his clothing. He told Pitt immediately what he had learned, summarizing the murder in Cape Town by likening it to the death of Sadie. There was no more information of significance about Julius Sorokine.

They were alone in Pitt's room. The sun was bright beyond the window, the air enclosed and stale. Narraway sat opposite Pitt, his legs crossed.

Pitt heard nothing that surprised him, but he realized he had been hoping there would be. It was unprofessional to dislike a man deeply enough to wish him guilty of such a crime. Likewise, he felt guilty that he liked Julius — or perhaps it was Elsa he liked, because she was vulnerable, and trying so hard to find her courage. There was something about her that reminded him of Charlotte. It was possibly no more than a way of turning her head, a certain squareness of her shoulders, but it was enough to waken a response in him and make him want to protect her. Disillusionment was one of the deepest of human wounds.

"The similarity is too close to be coincidence," Narraway said finally. "Whoever killed the woman in Cape Town also killed Sadie, and Minnie Sorokine as well. Presumably in her case it was because she knew who he was, and threatened him. He will have mimicked his usual style either from compulsion, or to make it obvious it was the same hand who did it."

"Compulsion," Pitt replied. "It doesn't

matter whether it was the same hand or not; in neither case would it protect him. And although she was a lady, there was apparently a good deal of the whore in her, at least outwardly."

Narraway looked at him sharply. "Are you saying she worked out that the Limoges dish was broken, and that it mattered?"

"And that it was replaced." Pitt told him about Elsa's visit to him, and her story of having seen an exact duplicate in Dunkeld's cases.

"And do you believe her?" Narraway asked with slight skepticism. He uncrossed his legs and leaned forward. "Don't you think, setting personalities and dislikes apart, that the shards were probably something else, and that the dish in the Queen's room was never broken in the first place? Elsa Dunkeld probably has far more grounds for hating her husband than you do."

"If it was irrelevant, then why did the Prince of Wales lie about it?" Pitt retorted. "Tyndale refused to discuss it, and now Dunkeld says he brought one, but as a personal favor to the Prince, and his honor prevents him explaining to us why."

Narraway pulled a very slight face of distaste. "Because it is something foolish and rather grubby, and they find it embarrassing," he said regretfully.

Pitt was unsatisfied. "I want to go through it one more time, step by step."

"If you wish," Narraway conceded. "But only once. Then we must act."

After Gracie had left Pitt with his tea, she returned temporarily to her regular duties. As soon as breakfast was finished, she and Ada began the tidying up and changing the linen. She wanted to investigate the one thing that continued to arouse her curiosity. She had cleaned Cahoon Dunkeld's bedroom and dressing room every morning since she had been here.

Where were the books that were supposed to have come in the box in the middle of the night? There were no more than half a dozen in Mr. Dunkeld's quarters, nor were there many more in the other rooms.

"Where'd they all go, then?" she said to Ada as they were dusting in the sitting room.

" 'Ow do I know?" Ada said indignantly. "Mebbe these is them, for all it matters. Get on wi' yer job."

Gracie looked at the titles. "But these are all poetry an' novels," she said. "An' stories o' the lives o' real people. 'Ere's the Duke o' Wellington, an' there's Prime Minister 'Orace Walpole."

"An' 'ow der yer know that, Miss Clever?"

" 'Cos it says so on the cover, o' course," Gracie replied. "Wot d'yer think, I looked at the pictures?"

"Since when did you learn ter read, then?"

"Since a long time ago. Why? Can't you?" She stared at Ada as if she were looking at a curiosity.

"Yer don't 'alf ta give yerself airs," Ada retorted. "Yer in't gonna last long. Tuppence worth o' nothin', you are."

"So, where's the books, then?" Gracie went back to the original question. "Or is that yer way o' sayin' yer don't know?"

" 'Course I don't know!" Ada spat back. "But I do know me place, an' that's more'n you do! Need someb'dy ter show it ter yer, an' I'll be 'appy ter take the job. I think termorrow yer'd better do all the slops, chamber pots an' all. An' not just your share, you can do Norah's an' Biddie's as well."

Gracie was beginning to wonder if there had been books in the chest at all, but it was obvious Ada was not going to help.

"Yer know so much, Miss Ever So Clever," Ada said, flicking her duster around the ornaments on the mantel. "You should be careful about all them questions yer keep askin'. Yer so sorry for Mrs. Sorokine, 'oo were actually a bit of a cow, if yer ask me.

Lot o' grand ways with 'er nose in the air, but under it no better'n a tart 'erself, jus' less honest about it. Askin' jus' the same questions as she did, you are. Want ter end up wi' yer belly cut open, do yer? Not that yer've got anythin' as'd drive any man wild, 'ceptin' as 'e got cheated, thinkin' as yer was a woman, an' all! Put yer in a matchbox, we could — an' a good idea that'd be, an' all."

Gracie felt the sting of insult. She was very aware that she was small, and too thin. There was nothing feminine or shapely about her. She had no idea why Samuel Tellman wanted her, except that to begin with she would have nothing to do with him. Now the whole idea of their marriage was frightening, in case she disappointed him terribly. But Ada would never know that.

What was important right now was that Ada had told her something she had not known: Minnie was also interested in the box, and what had been in it, or had not been.

"Yer reckon as that was wot got 'er killed?" she asked, forcing the rest out of her mind.

"Yeah! I do, an' all," Ada responded. "Always askin' questions, she was, just like you. If yer don't want nobody ter cut yer throat, then keep yer mouth shut!"

"I'm gonna tidy the bedrooms," Gracie

said, picking her duster up and striding toward the door. Actually she was going to find Mr. Tyndale. She needed his help and there was no time at all to waste. She wished she had realized the possible importance of the box before, but the beginning of an idea had only just entered in her head.

As she crossed the landing she heard Ada shouting behind her. She was tempted for an instant to go back to tell her, extremely patronizingly, to keep her voice down. Good servants never shouted, absolutely never! But she could not afford the luxury of wasting the time it would take.

She found Mr. Tyndale in his pantry and went in without even thinking of leaving the door open.

"Mr. Tyndale, sir," she began. "I know yer got Mr. Sorokine all locked up, but there's still things as we don't know, an' we gotta be right." She drew in her breath and hurried on. "We gotta be able ter explain everythin'. Mr. Dunkeld 'ad a box come on the night Sadie was killed, right about the same time. 'E said as it were books, but there in't no books in 'is rooms, nor in any o' the other rooms neither, nor in the sittin' room."

"The sitting room has at least fifty books, Miss Phipps," he said gravely. "Possibly more."

She kept her patience with great difficulty.

"Yeah, I know that, sir. But they in't books on Africa like Mr. Dunkeld said 'e sent for so urgent they 'ad ter come in the middle o' the night. All the ones 'e got were the same as 'e 'ad before."

Tyndale frowned. "How do you know that, Miss Phipps?"

" 'Cos I looked!" she said as politely as she could manage. Why was he so slow? "I can read, Mr. Tyndale. I think as 'e 'ad somethin' else come in that box, an' somebody's gotter know wot it were."

Tyndale looked uncomfortable. "It may have been something for the party, which could be private," he pointed out.

Gracie felt herself coloring with embarrassment. She had no idea what such a thing would be, and would very much rather not find out. But that was another luxury detection would cost her. "There in't nothin' private when there's murder, Mr. Tyndale. Somebody must 'a seen it, wotever it were. Edwards 'elped carry it in. 'Ow 'eavy were it? Books? Yer can feel if somethin' slides around inside a box yer carryin'. 'Ow 'eavy were it when they took it out again?"

Tyndale still looked just as uncomfortable. "I have no idea what was in it, Miss Phipps. I have no right, and no wish, to inquire into such things. It is better not to know too much of the business of our betters."

She was touched with pity for him, and impatience.

"Mr. Dunkeld in't your better, Mr. Tyndale," she said gently. "An' I don't think anybody 'oo pimps around wi' tarts is either!"

"Miss Phipps!" He was aghast and his voice was probably louder than he had intended it to be.

The pantry door swung open and hit the wall. Mrs. Newsome stood in the opening, her face bright pink, her eyes blazing. "Miss Phipps, I have warned you as much as I intend to about your behavior. Mr. Tyndale may be too kindhearted, or too embarrassed, to discipline you. I am not. You are dismissed. You are not suitable to have a position here at the Palace. Ada has complained about you. Both your work and your attitude are unsatisfactory. And now I find that you have deliberately disobeyed my orders that you were not to come here alone with any gentleman member of staff, and close the doors. You place Mr. Tyndale in an impossible situation. Pack your boxes and you will leave tomorrow morning. I shall give you a character, but it will not be a good one. The best I can say for you is that, as far as I know, you are honest and clean."

Tyndale's face was scarlet. He was mortified with shame, both for what Mrs. Newsome apparently thought and because he had failed to protect Gracie from her wrath. He knew no way to extricate himself now without letting her down. Perhaps also he was disappointed that Mrs. Newsome should think so little of him as to have leaped to such a conclusion.

It was up to Gracie to protect him. He was in this position because of his duty toward her, which he had promised to observe. The case was nearly over. Mrs. Newsome was going to be either a friend or an enemy. Neutrality was no longer an option. Gracie made her decision.

"Mr. Tyndale, I got ter tell 'er," she said earnestly. "It in't that I'm not grateful, I am. But we need 'er 'elp, an' we in't got time ter mess around 'opin'."

He nodded very slowly. "I understand." He looked over Gracie's head. "Mrs. Newsome, would you be so good as to close the door? I find myself in a position where I am obliged to break a trust, or face an even worse situation. I would like to do it as discreetly as possible."

Mrs. Newsome blinked. The color had not ebbed from her face, but she was no longer so certain of herself. She closed the door in obedience, but she still stood as far away from him as possible. The air in the small room was charged with emotion.

"Mrs. Newsome," Tyndale began. He glanced at Gracie, then continued. "Miss Phipps is working here for Special Branch. Mr. Narraway asked me to take her on, and keep her position here completely secret, so she might have as much freedom, and safety, as possible in helping Inspector Pitt to learn the truth of what happened to the two unfortunate women who have been murdered." He was speaking too quickly, gasping for breath. "If she has appeared to take liberties, they have been necessary in order to carry out her primary duty. There was no one she could confide in except me, therefore she was obliged to speak to me alone. Ada is a busybody with a jealous and cruel tongue. If anyone should be dismissed, it is she."

Mrs. Newsome stared at Gracie as if she had crawled out of an apple on the dessert plate. Then she looked past her at Mr. Tyndale again. "I see. I understand why she has behaved so . . . indiscreetly. What I do not understand, Mr. Tyndale, is why you did not feel as if you could have trusted me with the truth. I would have thought after all the years we have worked together, you might have thought better of me, indeed would have known it." She turned round and put her hand on the doorknob to leave.

"I was asked not to, Mrs. Newsome," Tyndale said miserably. "It was not my choice."

She kept her back to him. Her voice trembled. "And did you complain? Did you say that it was necessary to take me into your confidence, and that I am to be trusted as much as you are?"

He did not answer. He had been distracted with anxiety, even fear, and he had not.

Gracie sighed. This was all so terribly painful, and it did not have to be. "Mrs. Newsome, ma'am," she said softly, "if yer 'adn't 'ated me, if yer'd bin nice ter me, like it were all all right, then someone like Ada'd 'ave known there were summink different, an' she'd 'ave worked it out. It weren't until Mrs. Sorokine got killed as we knew 'oo it were as done it. An' ter be honest, even now we in't fer certain sure. Not completely. There's still things we don't know — like wot were in that box wot Edwards 'elped ter carry up the stairs ter Mr. Dunkeld the same night as poor Sadie were gettin' killed. An' wot were in it when 'e took it back down again."

Mrs. Newsome turned and stared at her. The color in her face was ebbing away, leaving only two blotches on her cheeks. She looked at Mr. Tyndale as if Gracie had not even been there. She drew in her breath sharply, then let it out in silence.

"We gotta find out," Gracie urged. "We in't got much longer before they 'ave ter take Mr. Sorokine away!"

Mrs. Newsome reacted at last. "Then I suppose we had better speak to Edwards, and see what he tells us about the box," she replied. "I will send for him, and return."

The moment she was gone, Gracie pushed the door closed again and looked at Tyndale. He was still unhappy. Something had been lost that he had no idea how to replace.

"She's 'urt because she got left out," she observed. "Yer did right ter tell 'er. We in't got no choice."

"Indeed," he replied, but she knew that was not what he was thinking. Mrs. Newsome had not trusted him, and nothing she could say or do now would heal that.

"She don't trust yer," Gracie said aloud.

He did not meet her eyes. "I am aware of that, Miss Phipps." He was angry and hurt that she should make a point of the obvious.

"An' she sees it like yer don't trust 'er," she added.

"That is quite different! I was bound to secrecy by duty. I did not imagine for a moment that Mrs. Newsome had done anything wrong," he protested.

Gracie gave a tiny shrug. "No, Mr. Tyndale, I don't s'pose yer ever done nothing wrong like she thinks neither, but yer works bleedin' 'ard ter protect them as does, an' turn a blind eye ter things wot curls yer stomach. 'Ow's she ter know?"

He looked startled, then deeply embarrassed. He could think of nothing to say, but she could see it in his eyes that quite suddenly he understood, and a wealth of conflict and realization opened up in front of him. Perhaps she had said far too much, but it was too late to take it back.

Mrs. Newsome returned with a very nervous Edwards, who answered Mr. Tyndale's questions without any of his usual insolence.

"Yes, sir, it was heavy."

"Did they rattle around?" Tyndale asked. "Move at all when you changed the balance going upstairs?"

"No, sir, not much moving at all. If it wasn't books, what was it, Mr. Tyndale?"

"I don't know," Tyndale replied. "How heavy was it when you took it down again?"

"Pretty much the same, sir."

Gracie felt her heart pounding. Maybe she was right!

Tyndale looked at her, puzzled, then back at Edwards. "Are you certain of that?"

"Yes, sir. It was still heavy. I reckon as he sent some books back as well."

"Did you look inside it?"

"No, sir! 'Course I didn't."

"Thank you. You can go," Tyndale told him.

As soon as he was gone, Gracie excused herself also and raced up the stairs to find Pitt. It was the last piece of the puzzle.

" 'Ave they took 'im yet?" she said breathlessly.

"If you mean Sorokine, no." He looked up from the paper he was writing for Narraway, a brief and unsatisfying account of the case. There would be no prosecution. Perhaps tonight Pitt would be in his own bed.

Gracie closed the door and came over to the table. "Mrs. Sorokine were askin' about the china pieces, the cleanin' up, an' the Queen's bed linen, weren't she? An' mebbe she saw the dish in Mr. Dunkeld's case too."

"Yes." He seemed too weary, and perhaps disappointed to ask her why she cared.

"An' she knew about the bottles wi' blood in," Gracie went on. "An' mebbe she knew that that case Mr. Dunkeld 'ad on the night o' the murder, wi' urgent books on Africa, didn't 'ave no books on Africa in it."

"How do you know that?" He put the pen down and discarded his writing. The tiredness slipped away from him. "Gracie?"

" 'Cos they in't nowhere," she answered. "Yer know wot I reckon, sir? I reckon as they brought summink else in in that box, ter do wi' the murder, an' it went out wi' summink in it too."

"Something like what?" He frowned, leaning forward now. "What, Gracie?"

It was as mad an idea as anything going on in the mind of whoever was killing people. She hardly dared tell him. He would laugh at her, and never trust her with anything important again.

"Gracie?" His voice was urgent now, a sharp edge of hope in it.

She dreaded being a fool, perhaps making him look stupid in front of Mr. Narraway — and worse than that, in his own eyes. Should she stop now, before she said it?

"Yes, sir," she gulped. "We bin' thinkin' all along that someone went ravin' barmy, off 'is 'ead, an' found poor Sadie, wherever she were, an' took 'er ter the Queen's bedroom and lay with 'er, then killed 'er . . ."

"I know it isn't good." He pursed his lips. "Even lunatics usually have a pattern that makes sense to them. I'm not happy about it, but the evidence shows that's where she was killed, and quite early in the evening. She must only just have left the

Prince of Wales."

"It looks like she were killed there," Gracie agreed, her throat so tight she could hardly breathe. "But it in't all that easy ter get inter that 'e could go there in the middle o' the night an' take a tart there. There'd be servants around. 'E'd take an awful risk. An' why do it?"

"Someone did," Pitt reasoned. "I saw the room, and the blood. And someone broke the dish, even though it was replaced —" He stopped suddenly.

"Wot is it?" she asked.

"By Cahoon Dunkeld," he finished very slowly. "And he hated Sorokine. He wouldn't cover anything for him." His eyes grew bright. "He was covering for someone else, Gracie! Someone whose gratitude would be worth a fortune to him!"

" 'Is 'Ighness?" she barely breathed the words. It was terrible! The worst nightmare she could imagine. What would Pitt do now? He wouldn't cover it up — he couldn't, not and live with himself. And if he said anything, no one would believe him, and they'd all cover it up so he would look like a liar — worse, a traitor to the throne. Perhaps that was what they all did anyway!

Pitt's would be one voice alone, against all of them. He would be ruined. They would see to it. They would have to, to cover for themselves because of all the other things they'd hidden and lied about over the years.

It hurt, all the dreams broken, but there was no time to think of that now. She must look out for Pitt.

"Yes, why not?" Pitt was saying. "He would go along to the Queen's bedroom, and no one would take any notice. In fact he could have arranged to have no servants about. He lies with Sadie, falls into a drunken sleep, and wakes up with her dead beside him, and blood all over the place. He's terrified. He calls Dunkeld to help him. Dunkeld moves the body and . . ." He stopped.

"Wot?" she demanded. She was so frightened every muscle in her was clenched.

He pushed his hair out of his eyes. "No, it makes no sense," he admitted wearily. "I was going to say he put the body in the linen cupboard and used the port bottles full of blood to make it look as if she had been killed there. And replaced the broken Limoges dish. But that would mean it was planned very carefully in advance."

He looked at her, horror deepening in his face. "Gracie, he knew someone was going to be killed, and where! And come to that, how! The only way he could do that would be if he killed her or had someone else do it.

And however sure he was of Sorokine's madness, he couldn't guarantee he would do it in the Queen's bed, beside the Prince of Wales! Or that it would be Sadie, and not one of the other women, or with any of the other men." He bit his lip. "He brought the blood with him, and more important he brought the Limoges dish!"

"So 'e knew wot room it would 'appen in," she followed his reasoning, although it frightened her so she was cold in the depth of her stomach. "Wot if the Prince jus' woke up an' all the blood were over 'im, but not 'er? Then it wouldn't matter where she were killed." She gulped. "Mr. Pitt, I got an idea as she weren't killed 'ere at all. That box wot were brought in 'ad another body in it, not 'er. An' Sadie packed 'erself inter the box again an' were taken out without no one knowin' 'cept Mr. Dunkeld."

Pitt stared at her, a dawning understanding of the entire plan on his face. "Dunkeld was the one who hired the women!" he exclaimed. "They were allies in it. To blackmail the Prince of Wales into helping them with the African railway. Then he couldn't afford not to be entirely on Dunkeld's side, no matter what he actually believed. Dunkeld simply used the opportunity to get rid of Sorokine at the same time!"

Gracie blinked. "Then 'oo killed Mrs. Sorokine? 'Oo did she accuse? It 'ad ter be 'er pa, because 'e were the one wot 'ad the dish."

His face creased in pity. "Poor Minnie. She was far too clever for her own survival. I dare say he didn't mean to kill her, just lost his temper and —"

"Yer don' slit someone's throat 'cos yer lost yer temper," Gracie pointed out. "An' yer certainly don't slice their guts open."

"He had to make it look like the first crime," Pitt reminded her. "And he had to make the first crime look like the one in Cape Town."

" 'Ow'd 'e know wot that one were like?" she asked.

"From someone who saw it, I don't know who. But it fits, Gracie." His voice took on a vibrancy again. "Dunkeld planned it for long before he came. He brought blood, and a replacement dish. He knew it was there. Someone must have shown it to him. He's been the Prince's guest here before."

Gracie shivered.

"He had a dead woman brought in," Pitt went on. "And you're right, Sadie was part of the plot. It could be she who insisted on sleeping in the Queen's bed!" He was speaking more rapidly, his voice eager now. "When the Prince was in a drunken stupor, perhaps aided by a powder of some sort, she slipped out and went to Cahoon.

"Perhaps she even helped Cahoon take the dead woman out of the box, before getting into it herself. After the box was removed, Cahoon carried the dead woman, probably in a blanket or something, and put her beside the Prince, and splashed some of the blood around. He kept the rest to put in the linen cupboard, then went to bed. That's why we could never find Sadie's clothes — she was still wearing them. Cahoon had already arranged for a message to come, and went to waken the Prince himself, and make absolutely certain he was in the spot to see the mess, and offer to help!"

"The bleedin' bastard!" she said with profound feeling. "Wot yer gonna do? Yer can't let Mr. Sorokine be put away for it!"

"Of course not. I'm going to see His Royal Highness." He rose.

"Be careful!" she cried out. "Mr. Pitt, 'e in't goin' ter —"

"When Mr. Narraway comes back, tell him what has happened," he cut across her. "And ask him to wait until I return." He left without even looking back to see if she would obey.

She stood still, hands clenched, her body shaking.

She was terrified for what would happen to him. Suddenly everything that mattered was falling apart. The people she had regarded with admiration were no wiser or braver than she was. The Palace itself was just like anywhere else, full of pettiness, ambition, and shifts of truth. And now Pitt was walking straight into disaster like a child going to feed lions, and she hadn't stopped him, and there was nobody to ask for help.

Hot tears scalded her eyes.

Again Pitt had to wait until the Prince was willing to see him. Time was slipping through his fingers. Any minute Narraway would return with police to take Julius away. Of course he could be released afterward, but it would be far better not to make the error in the first place. People were loath to admit fault; the more important it was, the more reluctant.

He wrote a short letter on a page from his notebook and handed it to the footman. All it said was, "I realize what Dunkeld has done to help. But now more help than that is needed. Pitt."

He was conducted into the Prince's presence five minutes later, and the footman withdrew, leaving them alone. The Prince was white-faced, sweat shining on his brow.

"What do you mean by this, sir?" he demanded, holding up the scrap of paper. "It looks like an attempt at . . . at blackmail!"

"No, sir," Pitt said with as much respect as he could pretend. "It is an attempt to avoid blackmail. I believe Mr. Dunkeld went to considerable trouble, and ingenuity, to make you seem acutely vulnerable, sir, and I intend to see that he does not profit from it."

"I don't know what you mean. You are on dangerous ground, Inspector. Cahoon Dunkeld is a friend of mine, a gentleman of skill and honor, and very great loyalty. Far more than you, I may say, who are paid to be a servant to the Crown!" he accused him.

"Yes, sir." Pitt breathed in slowly, knowing the risk he was taking. If he was wrong, he would be ruined. He would not even walk a beat as a common policeman after this. "You entertained a prostitute of particular intelligence and skill, who insisted she would give her favors only if she could do it in the Queen's own bed."

"How . . . how dare you, sir?" the Prince sputtered.

"You saw no harm in it," Pitt continued. "You took her there, and after she kept her word, you fell asleep, probably assisted by a little laudanum in your drink. When you awoke there was a dead woman beside you, or possibly only a great deal of blood." He stopped, afraid the Prince was going to have a heart attack or apoplexy. He seemed to be choking, grasping at his collar, and he had gone ashen gray. Pitt had no idea how to help. He had not foreseen this.

He turned and strode to the door to call for assistance.

"Wait!" the Prince cried out. "Wait!"

Pitt stopped.

"I didn't kill her!" the Prince said desperately. "I swear on the Crown of England, I never hurt her at all!"

"I know that, sir," Pitt said quietly, turning back to face him. "She was dead before she was ever brought into the Palace."

"She can't . . . what are you saying? I lay with a dead woman? I assure you she was very much alive!"

"Sadie was, yes. But the corpse beside you, and later in the linen cupboard, was not Sadie," Pitt explained. "That is why her clothes had to be removed. The difference would have given it away. And there was probably no time. Dunkeld took care of it all for you, didn't he? Ran a bath, told you to wash away all the blood, and he himself removed the body and the bloody sheets. Later, he had trusted servants clean up the mess, the blood on the floor, and replaced

507

the broken Limoges dish, which you thought you had smashed in your rage with the poor woman."

The Prince simply nodded. He was still gray-faced, his eyes almost glazed. He was mortified with embarrassment at being exposed as such an incompetent libertine in front of Pitt, of all people.

"He told you to say nothing, and it would all be all right. He would get in Special Branch, and they would keep the matter discreet," Pitt continued.

"What about Sorokine?" the Prince floundered. "If he wasn't guilty, why did he kill his wife, poor woman?"

"He didn't," Pitt said simply. "She worked out the truth, and must have faced Dunkeld with it. I don't imagine he intended to kill her, he probably only tried to silence her, and they both lost their tempers. They were very alike. When he realized he had struck her too hard he had to make it look as if it were the same as the other crime, and the one in Africa too, of which he could not have been guilty. It must have been one of the hardest things in his life to have cut her like that, even though she was already dead." He thought of Minnie's body lying with that slit-open abdomen, but her bosom still decently covered. She had not been gutted as the other women were.

The Prince was staring at him in undisguised horror.

"He must have waited all night," Pitt went on. "We can only guess how fearful that was for him, alone with her body. Then in the early morning he went in to accuse Sorokine, and fought with him, his purpose being to mark Sorokine as if from a fight with Mrs. Sorokine, and even more than that, to disguise the marks on himself where she had fought for her life."

"God in Heaven!" the Prince breathed out. "What are you going to do now?"

"Arrest Dunkeld and release Sorokine," Pitt replied. "And hope it is still possible to keep most of this quiet. But we will not be able to shut Dunkeld away and say he is mad. There will have to be a trial, at least for the murder of Mrs. Sorokine. I'm sorry, sir. If another way can be found, it will be."

The Prince swallowed with difficulty. "Please . . . please try . . ."

"Yes, sir. Of course."

Pitt returned to his rooms and found Narraway waiting for him, pacing the floor. Gracie was still present as if she were standing guard.

"Is she right?" Narraway demanded as

soon as Pitt had closed the door. His face was drawn, his eyes haggard.

Pitt did not ask what Gracie had said; he knew she had understood it all perfectly. "Yes," he said to Narraway. "I just confirmed it with the Prince of Wales. Not surprisingly, when he woke and found the corpse of a naked woman, covered in gore, beside him in the Queen's bed, he panicked. He certainly didn't look at her face long enough to see it wasn't the one he went to sleep with — if he looked at her face even then!"

Narraway blasphemed thoroughly and with intense feeling. "What a diabolical shame. A cold nerve, though!" He glanced at Gracie, wondering whether he should apologize to her for his language. In this situation she was not exactly a servant. A certain better nature won. "I'm sorry," he said.

" 'S all right," she told him graciously.

He looked startled, then nodded his appreciation.

Pitt concealed a smile. "We should arrest Dunkeld for the killing of his daughter," he said to Narraway. "Accidental or intentional. And free Sorokine. I'm looking forward to that."

"Just a moment!" Narraway jerked up his hand as if to hold Pitt back. "Can we prove it?"

510

"Minnie knew the whole plot!" Pitt said impatiently.

"Yes, but can we prove that?" Narraway insisted. "And not only that she knew it, but that she would have betrayed him by telling everyone. If we can't do both those things, he could still say it was Sorokine, either because he killed Sadie, or simply out of jealousy over her affair with Marquand."

Pitt took a deep breath, his mind racing. He was certain in his own mind, but was there proof, beyond any reasonable doubt?

"He was the one who arranged for the three women to come. It was his box of books the corpse came in."

"We know it was his box," Narraway agreed. "We have deduced that the corpse came in it, and Sadie went, but there's no proof."

"No books came," Pitt told him. "Edwards carried something up in it, and something of similar weight down again."

"Servant's word against Dunkeld's," Narraway said.

"No books," Pitt argued. "All the African books, of which there are not many, were here already. All the other men will testify to that."

"Moderate," Narraway granted. "Who saw the Limoges dish, apart from Dunkeld's wife, who hates him, and is in love with Sorokine? I think it hangs on that."

"His valet," Pitt replied.

"And he'll testify?" Narraway said with heavy disbelief. "Even if he did, it's his word against Dunkeld's again. From your account the Prince of Wales never saw the dish broken, and he can't be called to testify anyway."

"Tyndale!" Pitt exclaimed. "He knew the dish was broken because he helped clear it away and hid the pieces. He lied to me about it, and to Gracie."

"And you think he'll implicate the Prince in any wrongdoing?" Narraway's eyebrows shot up.

"No, sir, but he'll testify against Dunkeld, who tried to implicate and then blackmail the Prince."

Narraway's face was bleak, his mouth tight. "The newspapers will have a field day with that! It'll never come to trial, Pitt. Dunkeld knows it, and so do I. Perhaps we could prove it, with the dish, the box; we can't prove that he brought the port bottles in full of blood. Certainly someone did a lot of cleaning up in the Queen's room, and Sorokine's never been in the Palace before. But it's all academic. Dunkeld has us. The best we can do is at least not charge Sorokine."

"No, sir," Pitt said in a hard, quiet voice. "Dunkeld was going to blackmail the Prince of Wales, the heir to the throne. If he didn't do it explicitly, it was always implicit, for the rest of his life."

"I didn't think you'd be a royalist after all this, Pitt," Narraway said with irony and confusion in his voice.

"I don't have much respect for the man, but I do for the office," Pitt snapped. "But that isn't the point."

Narraway opened his eyes wide. "Blackmail is a filthy crime."

"Not blackmail," Pitt said tartly. "Treason."

"Treason?" Then in a flash of fire in the mind, Narraway understood. "Of course. We charge him and try him for treason. Secrets of the State — a closed court. Thank you, Pitt. I am profoundly obliged."

Pitt smiled, the blood warming his face again.

Gracie gave a long sigh of relief.

"Who killed the poor woman in the linen cupboard?" Narraway asked almost casually.

"God knows," Pitt admitted. "Maybe He is the only one who ever will. She might be just some murder victim of the night."

"Exactly like the one in Africa?" Narraway

asked sarcastically. "Who the hell brought her?"

"I've no idea."

Narraway raised his eyebrows. "I imagine you would like to find out?"

"Yes, I would. First I would like to go and release Sorokine." Pitt smiled. "I'd take help for Dunkeld, if I were you. He's a big man with a very violent temper."

Narraway looked at him coldly. "I have no intention of going alone, Pitt! Do you take me for an idiot?"

They reached the door together, then Pitt turned to Gracie. "Which one do you want to see?" he asked. "You deserve to take your choice."

"Thanks," she said primly. "I think as I'll come with you and tell Mr. Sorokine 'e's free. 'E were real nice ter me. Let me read in a book by Oscar Wilde, like I were a real sort o' person as could understand it."

"You are," Pitt told her. "How perceptive of him. When we get home, I shall buy you a copy for yourself."

"Thank you," she accepted.

They went downstairs together and found Mr. Tyndale, who gave them the key to Julius's room.

"I'm very glad, sir," he said gravely. "Mr. Sorokine was always very civil." He glanced only briefly at Gracie, confused now as to exactly what her status was.

She avoided his eyes too, so as not to make it even harder for him.

Up the stairs again Pitt knocked on Julius's door, then opened it and went in.

"Your courtesy is very pleasant, if a trifle absurd," Julius said quietly. He was fully dressed but ashen-faced. His hands were clenched by his sides and he stood so stiffly he swayed very little, concentrating on keeping his composure.

Pitt held out the door key in his open hand, offering it.

"I apologize, Mr. Sorokine. I am now perfectly certain that your account of events was a true one. I regret the extreme distress you have been caused."

Julius stared at him, then at the key in his hand. Then slowly he reached for it, took it and held it, smoothing his fingers over it as if to assure himself it was real. Then he looked up at Pitt again.

"Cahoon?" he asked hoarsely. "Why? He's the only one of us who couldn't have killed the poor woman."

Very briefly Pitt explained the main outline of the case to him.

Julius sat down on the bed. "God Almighty!" He breathed out the words so they sounded more like a prayer than a blasphemy.

"If you will excuse me, sir, I need to go and help Mr. Narraway. Arresting Mr. Dunkeld may not be easy. If there is anything you need, Gracie will get it for you."

Gracie moved forward. "Yes, sir," she said with great satisfaction. " 'Ow about a nice fresh cup o' tea, an' a toasted tea cake with currants in it an' butter?"

Julius smiled, but there were tears in his eyes. "Thank you," he said huskily. "I'll admit, luncheon wasn't much. I'd like that . . . before I . . . join the others."

She went to make it herself, choosing the tea cake with the most currants and sultanas, and being generous with the butter. When she took it up to him, he was delighted and ate the tea cake as if it was the first food he had tasted with any pleasure for days.

She glanced over to the bedside table and saw Oscar Wilde's book open on it.

He saw her look. "Would you like it?" he offered.

"I couldn't!" she said intently, blushing that he had caught her looking at it.

"Yes, you could," he replied. "I can get another one. I would like you to have it. I have something to celebrate. Let me make a gift of it to you." He reached out his hand, then saw the butter on his fingers and smiled ruefully. "Just take it. Please?"

She picked it up, holding it tight. "Thank you, sir."

He was still smiling.

Pitt and Narraway found Cahoon Dunkeld with the Prince of Wales. They were obliged to wait until he had finished his discussion and was walking back alone along the corridor toward his own room. They caught up with him at the door and followed him in, to his intense annoyance.

"What the devil's the matter with you?" he demanded, spinning round to face them, his face twisted with fury.

Narraway closed the door behind him. "Naturally, as Special Branch, we do not have the authority to arrest anyone, but in these unusual circumstances, I am obliged to make an exception."

"Good," Cahoon snapped. "You do not need my permission. Get on with it!"

"I know I do not need your permission," Narraway replied tartly. "Cahoon Dunkeld, I am arresting you for the murder of Wilhelmina Sorokine. You will be —"

Cahoon's face turned scarlet. "Her husband killed her," he said between clenched teeth. "If you seek to avoid your duty and blame this on me, I shall speak to the Prince and have you dismissed. And don't doubt he can do it."

"Probably," Narraway conceded with a tight smile. "But he won't, not since he knows that you had a dead prostitute brought in and disemboweled in the Queen's bed, in order to blackmail him for the rest of his life. He will resent that — I can assure you."

"Rubbish! You're hysterical," Cahoon said with disgust, but his voice was slurred and his hands were clenched till the knuckles shone.

"No, Mr. Dunkeld, Minnie was hysterical when she put all the pieces together. She saw the Limoges dish in your luggage; she knew the one in the Queen's room had been broken; but you must have known in advance that it would be, or why bring one identical? She knew the box came in and went out with the same weight in it, and there were very few new books on Africa, if any at all. And she knew you: your nature, your courage, and your arrogance. And you knew that she would want a price for her silence, possibly the clearing of her husband from blame. Profoundly as you loved her, you could not afford to let her ruin you —

and she would have."

Cahoon stared at him. "You can't prove that," he said at last. "None of it."

"Yes," Narraway said, glancing only for a second at Pitt, knowing he could not afford to take his eyes from Cahoon for any longer than that. "I can. A court might not compel your wife to testify, or believe her if she did. They might think your valet merely a distinguished servant, if a frightened one. But they will believe Tyndale, a Palace butler who owes you nothing. He saw the shards of the broken dish, and he saw the new one that replaced it."

"Sorokine brought it!" Cahoon's lips curved in the tiniest smile.

"How did he know about it?" Narraway asked. "He had never been to the Palace before, still less to the Queen's bedroom. You did. He did not arrange the prostitutes to come that evening, nor did he send for the box of books that don't exist. Small pieces of evidence, Cahoon, but many of them, and the Limoges dish was a touch of reality too far. The blood was necessary, but that smashed dish was what caught you."

Cahoon took a deep breath. "Pity," he said, in control of himself again. "But you won't charge me with it. If you think you can ever bring this to the public, then you are an even bigger fool than I supposed, and having seen you and your oaf there," he glanced at Pitt, "even the last few days, believe me, I thought you fool enough!"

Narraway's cheeks paled with anger and his eyes glittered. "Of course we won't!" he said with bitter relish. "I mentioned the murder to disconcert you. I believe in your own way, you loved her. After all, she was a female reflection of yourself, perhaps morally a little better, but then she was younger." His smile widened a fraction. "All of it needs to be proved, of course, but the charge is for attempting to blackmail the heir to the throne."

Cahoon was incredulous. "Blackmail? He'll never bring a charge, you imbecile!"

Narraway stood perfectly still. "I'm bringing the charge, Mr. Dunkeld, of treason. Naturally, to protect the security of the nation, it will not be a public trial."

At last Dunkeld understood. The blood drained from his skin. He swayed very slightly, then, as if catching his balance, he turned and lunged at Pitt, fists flailing.

Pitt raised his foot hard and caught him in the groin. Dunkeld screamed — a high-pitched, tearing sound — and doubled over, pitching violently into the doorpost with a crack that must have knocked him almost senseless.

Narraway gaped at Pitt in amazement.

Pitt shrugged very slightly, a warmth of satisfaction seeping through him. He might be ashamed of it later, but right now it felt good. "No point fighting his fists," he observed. "I'd lose."

Narraway shook his head. "He couldn't have escaped."

"No, of course not. But he would have half killed me, with nothing to lose, and I think that's what he wanted."

Narraway sighed. "Fool," he said sadly. "You'd better tie him up. Can't afford to leave him with his hands free, not that one. Then lock the door."

"Yes, sir," Pitt agreed.

Narraway turned at the door. "Thank you," he added.

The guests met in the sitting room with the Prince of Wales present. He was deeply distressed that the project had collapsed, but with the arrest of Cahoon Dunkeld it no longer had the driving force necessary to succeed. His displeasure was profound, overtaking his earlier embarrassment. But then, as Pitt observed to Narraway in a whisper, anger is always less uncomfortable than shame.

Liliane looked immensely relieved that the ordeal was over. Her eyes shone, her skin glowed, all her old beauty animated her face again. Hamilton seemed sober, the weight of immediate fear lifted from him too.

Simnel was quiet, the death of Minnie wrapping him in a pall of grief. Whether it had been her husband or her father who had killed her made no difference to him. He was still imprisoned by his need, leaving Olga as alone as before.

Julius was subdued. He had been too near a lifelong incarceration with the insane to recover in an hour or two. He had looked into an abyss and he could not dismiss or forget it.

Elsa also sat alone. Her husband had been arrested for killing his daughter. She faced a social nightmare of proportions she could not even guess at, but the man she loved was free, and that joy could not be taken from her. It burned in her eyes with a quiet, beautiful heat.

"Tragic!" the Prince of Wales said fervently. "A great talent, a great driving energy, lost to . . . to . . ."

"The lust for power," Simnel filled in for him.

"Quite." The Prince was irritated by the assistance. He would have found the phrase if he had been given the time. "Now we shall have to struggle to find a man to replace him. Someone who knows the project, understands it, and has the strength of will to guide it through. And the good name and reputation among the people whose investment and support we will need."

Several people murmured their agreement.

The Prince turned to Julius. "You have been through a nightmarish experience, Sorokine. Unjustly suspected. Proved yourself worthy, though. I am sure you could step into your father-in-law's place. Take a little time to grieve for your wife. I'm very sorry. You have my deepest condolences. Inform me when the funeral is, and, with your permission, I shall attend. The Princess of Wales also. Then meet with me privately, and we can make the appropriate arrangements. You will lead the company from now on."

"Thank you, sir," Julius said gravely. "I will, of course, inform you of my wife's funeral, and be most honored if you, and the Princess of Wales, would attend. But I cannot assume my father-in-law's place leading the company."

"After a decent interval, of course," the Prince agreed. "But my dear fellow, whatever private grief may afflict us, the fate of nations does not wait."

"It is nothing to do with grief, sir," Julius said respectfully. "I mean that I am not willing to do it, not that I don't have the skill, although that is certainly also possible. I do not believe it is the right thing to do. I have had time to give it much thought, and I have come to the conclusion that the African Continent should be opened up slowly, according to the will of the many different nations whose land it is. I believe that the British Empire's role lies at sea, as it has in the past. We can ship the great wealth of these people from the ports of the Indian Ocean, the Pacific, and the Atlantic around the rest of the world. It will be more than enough power and profit for us, and leave Africa to its own people."

The Prince stared at him as if he could not believe what he had heard. He looked hard at his face, and saw neither fear nor indecision in it, nor did he see a weakness he could use or ambition he could satisfy. He did not look at Elsa, but Pitt did. Her eyes shone with the radiance of a woman truly in love. She reminded him even more of Charlotte, and the thought was to him a sweetness he could hardly contain.

"You will regret that decision, Sorokine," the Prince said in a hard, tight voice. He did not elaborate on it, but it was a threat, and for a moment the room was quiet and cold.

"No doubt it will have a cost," Julius admitted. "But it is what I believe to be right, sir, and that leaves me no choice."

Liliane moved very slightly in her chair so the rustle of her green-gold silk skirt drew attention to her. "Your Royal Highness, if I may suggest it, my father, Watson Forbes, is an even greater expert in African affairs than Mr. Dunkeld. He has retired from active interest, but in such an extraordinary circumstance as this, he may be persuaded to return, as a service to his country. If you were to ask him, sir, I cannot imagine that he would refuse you."

The Prince's face revealed a sudden leap of hope. "Do you think so? My dear Mrs. Quase, how perfectly excellent! How generous of you. I shall write to him immediately and have the letter delivered within the hour. Thank you so much. You have served the Crown and the Empire most nobly. Please be good enough to give me his address."

"Of course, sir." She rose to her feet and followed him out of the room.

"The King is dead, long live the King," Hamilton Quase said very quietly.

CHAPTER THIRTEEN

"That's not enough," Pitt said. He was standing with his back to the window in the room in the Palace they had given him, and he was still granted the use of it for a few hours longer. It was early afternoon, and time was rapidly running out. Very soon Pitt and Narraway would be thanked and dismissed.

Narraway was standing by the table, facing the light. He looked tired and tense.

"Who was the woman in the box?" Pitt went on. "Who killed her, and where?"

"Well, Dunkeld didn't kill her," Narraway pointed out. "He never left the Palace. So either it was the carter, or whoever paid him to bring her."

"Dunkeld hired Sadie," Pitt continued. "He must have told her a great deal of what was to happen. So where is she now? Keeping out of sight. Which means he paid her well." Other thoughts were swirling in Pitt's mind. "Who would Dunkeld trust sufficiently to have him bring a box to the Palace door, with a murdered woman in it? Would he dare take the risk that the man didn't know what he had?"

Narraway considered for a moment or two. "Hell of a risk," he said finally. "Dunkeld is a gambler, but not a fool. He would eliminate any danger he could. I'd say the carter was the accomplice, possibly even the murderer."

"And Dunkeld disemboweled her when she was here?" Pitt asked. "I think he broke Minnie's neck, almost certainly by accident, and cut her afterward to make it look the same, as if it had been broken on purpose. That's why the injuries on the two women were so similar."

Narraway's mouth tightened into a thin line. "And he made them after he'd knocked Julius senseless in order to mark Julius's face with cuts and bruises, and accounted for the marks on himself. Clever bastard. But who's the accomplice? Thank God we don't have to find him to convict Dunkeld!"

Pitt jerked his head up. "No, but I damn well want him! Are you trying to tell me he came across that girl dead just when he happened to need her? Right height, right build, right coloring, face similar enough, and nothing else wrong with her? No rashes, broken bones, scars or blemishes, no missing teeth, nothing to account for her death except the knife slashes we saw? He may have broken her neck, to make sure there was no blood to seep out of the box, but he killed her to meet his needs. I want him, Narraway, and I don't intend to stop until I get him." That was a warning and he meant it as such.

"Where do you propose to start?" Narraway asked. "By the way, if you have anything at all to ask anyone here, you'd better do it now. You'll never get back in again."

"Not even to trace a murder?"

Narraway gave a short bark of laughter. "Not if your life depended on it, Pitt. You found them the wrong answer."

"I didn't choose who was guilty!" Pitt protested. "The Prince chose the wrong man as his friend."

"A cardinal sin," Narraway agreed. "In fact completely unforgivable. Don't fool yourself he will ever excuse you for pointing that out! Now he has to admit to Watson Forbes that he made a mistake, and he will not like that either."

"Will Forbes accept? You said he'd retired, didn't you?"

Narraway bit his lip. "He seemed adamant to me that he didn't believe in the idea. He thought it would be bad for Africa, and in time destroy what was beautiful and unique. He said such a railway would cut through the heart of the country and vandalize the soul of it."

"He said that?"

"Not in those words." Narraway looked vaguely uncomfortable at the vividness of his own imagination. He was acutely conscious of the fact that he had never been to Africa. "But that was the essence of it. He might well turn the Prince down."

"Two women murdered, and for nothing," Pitt observed. "We don't even know who the first one was."

"The African one? We never will."

"No, I'm not sure she had anything to do with it, except as a tragedy to make us think Dunkeld had to be innocent, and Sorokine guilty. I meant the woman in the linen cupboard, whom we thought was Sadie. Who was she? Did the carter who brought her here kill her simply for Dunkeld to use? Did he do it knowing what it was for? Or does he simply kill for money?"

"Too dangerous," Narraway said immediately. "Dunkeld would be a fool to put himself in the hands of a man like that."

"Then he was a conspirator. And he had to know Sadie in order to find a woman sufficiently like her," Pitt added. "So he's intelligent, resourceful, devious, and has a hell of a cool nerve. He's not just an assassin for hire."

"You've made your point, Pitt," Narraway agreed with the ghost of a smile. "We have to find him, and Dunkeld isn't going to help us. It is almost certainly the carter, but there is no reason to suppose he actually looks anything like the man the servants glimpsed on the night he brought the box. His clothes were nondescript and dirty, he wore a hat, and fingerless mittens to protect his hands. Usual enough if you're driving a horse, or lifting boxes. We'd better start with looking for Sadie."

"She'll have disappeared," Pitt told him. "Dunkeld will have paid her to do that."

"I know!" Narraway snapped, his temper closer to the surface than he wished to betray. "I mean where she used to be. Dunkeld found her in some brothel, or through a pimp. London can be a small city at times. He met her somewhere. Other women will know her. They might have seen the carter."

Pitt nodded. "I'll find him if he's in London."

Narraway swore. "We may not have long. Since the scheme has failed, as soon as he knows Dunkeld's caught, he may make himself scarce. He could go anywhere: Glasgow, Liverpool, Dublin, even the Continent. I'll call every contact I have in the police. Thank God for inventions like the telephone. I don't think we have anything more to do here."

Less than half an hour later, when Pitt was in the sitting room and Narraway had returned to his office, the Prince came in, closely followed by Watson Forbes. It was instantly apparent that Forbes had accepted the Prince's offer. How it had been phrased, or what additional incentive had been offered, was not mentioned. Everyone was introduced, although only Olga Marquand had not previously known him. Pitt was merely mentioned. Forbes's eyes lingered on him in a moment's interest, but he did not speak.

"Mr. Forbes has accepted the responsibility of Dunkeld's position to lead the building of a Cape-to-Cairo railway," the Prince announced with a smile. "He is by far the best man in England for the task; in fact, very possibly the only man who could succeed. We are very fortunate that he has agreed to pick up this burden, immediate from today. I have promised him that he will have the total co-operation of everyone involved, and the freedom to make any decision in the furtherance of our cause that he considers wise and just."

Complete control. Was that the power Dunkeld had had? Or was it Forbes's price? The very slight emphasis the Prince placed on the words suggested that it was the latter.

"Her Majesty will return from Osborne in two days," the Prince continued. "I am very pleased at that time to present to her such a magnificent project for the Empire she loves so dearly." He turned to Forbes and made a small gesture of invitation.

Watson Forbes stepped forward, smiling. "Thank you, sir. It will be my privilege to serve my country, and future generations in that great Continent of Africa. Gentlemen, we have a momentous opportunity before us. It will call for every resource of mind and body that we possess. Let us not underestimate it. We shall require all the honorable assistance that we may be offered, or lay claim to. And we must be of a single mind. This is not for the glory of any one man, but of our Queen and country."

Pitt slipped away without excusing himself, and no one except Julius Sorokine noticed.

Pitt left the Palace and took a hansom cab to Narraway's office. It had been only a matter of days that he'd been on the case, and yet his sudden sense of freedom was immense, as if he had escaped from enclosing walls, opulent as they were and hung with some of the greatest works of art in Western civilization. Now he was surrounded by the noise of traffic, hoofs, wheels, voices shouting, and occasionally the barking of dogs. It was midafternoon, hot and dusty, but the sense of space, even crowded as it was, and the urgency that drove him, was exhilarating. He found himself sitting forward as if it would somehow add to his speed.

Dunkeld was to blame for much. He was an arrogant and callous man, but he had not killed the prostitute, whoever she was. Whether the man who had was a willing colleague, Pitt did not yet know, but he was guilty of a brutal murder, purely for the convenience of having a body with which to blackmail the Prince of Wales. He, at least, would be someone they could charge, try, and, in the end, hang. There would be no secret incarceration in an asylum for him. Not that death, even on the end of a rope, might not be better than the rest of one's life in a place like Bedlam.

Pitt alighted a street away from Narraway's office — a precaution of habit — and ten minutes later was upstairs in his usual chair at the far side of Narraway's desk.

"Forbes accepted," Pitt said briefly. "Complete control."

Narraway nodded. "I think the carter was a colleague, not an employee. Dunkeld would never be fool enough to trust anyone with that sort of power over him."

"I'm not sure what I think," Pitt said thoughtfully. "I'm not certain if the plan originally was Dunkeld's or the other man's, or even if it changed halfway through, when Minnie died. Perhaps each of them thought the plan was theirs, and in fact there were two?" He saw the wry look in Narraway's face. "But I am absolutely certain that I want to find the man who killed that girl, whoever she was. If we don't care about justice for her as much as for Minnie, or Julius Sorokine, or the Prince of Wales, then we are the wrong people for this job."

Narraway's face was wry, and for a minute uncharacteristically gentle. "There are plenty of wrong people in jobs, Pitt, but I admire the sentiment, even if we may not be able to live up to it. I've sent orders to every police station in the city within an hour's travel of the Palace to see if they know of a prostitute missing from her usual patch, if any brothel's lost a girl, or any street woman known as missing, whatever the reason."

"We can't sit here and wait!" Pitt protested. "How long is it going to take before someone reports her, or any police station cares? It could be —"

"Hours," Narraway cut across him. "Or less."

"Days," Pitt contradicted him. "Or not at all."

"I don't think you understand the importance, Pitt," Narraway observed drily. "One has only to mention bombers or anarchists and even the busiest and least sympathetic policeman will take notice. If there is any report at all, we will have it before dark."

Pitt had to be content. Narraway forbade him to leave, and it was as dusk was beginning to close in that the report came. It was still barely dark when they alighted at the police station on the Vauxhall Bridge Road, less than three miles from the Palace.

Narraway did not waste time or energy on niceties. He introduced himself and came immediately to the point. "You reported a prostitute missing, possibly dead," he said to the constable on duty. "I need to see your superintendent."

"He's busy with —"

"Now," Narraway said grimly.

"But —"

"Don't argue with me, Constable, unless

you wish to be charged with treason," Narraway snapped.

In less than five minutes a local dignitary had been hurried out, and they were in Superintendent Bayliss's office where he stood uncomfortably, a pile of papers on his desk, and a mug of gently steaming tea.

"Who is missing?" Narraway asked quietly. "When, and from where? Describe her."

"I don't know what she looks like," Bayliss began, then changed his mind. "Charming enough, I'm told. Brown hair, nicely built."

"When was she last seen, and where?"

"About a week ago, Bessborough Street, just short of the Vauxhall Bridge, sir. There's a house there that looks perfectly respectable, but it's a rather good brothel. Caters to the carriage trade."

"Who brought in the report?"

"Constable Upfield."

"Get him. I need him to take us there, in an hour. They'll be open for business, and I want a local man who knows them to be with us."

"Can you tell me what it's about, sir?" Bayliss asked reasonably.

"No, I can't, and you would prefer not to know."

"If it's on my watch, sir, I need to know, whether I like it or not."

"It's not on your watch. This is Special Branch business. Get me Constable Up-field."

"He's off duty . . . sir."

"Then get him back on," Narraway snapped.

"Yes, sir."

It was a long night of questioning, arguing, threatening. It was after midnight by the time they elicited the information that Kate, the missing girl, had gone out to see a client in the mews. He had wanted to look at what he was buying and she was willing to oblige. This particular man had had very precise tastes. Apparently he had already tried one or two other houses, and found nothing to his liking. However, Kate suited him, ac-cording to the boot boy, and she had gone with him.

"Gone?" Pitt said quickly. "Not into the house?"

"No, poor stupid cow." The boot boy shook his head. " 'E spoke nice, but that don't mean nothin'. Don't even mean 'e got money, let alone sense. Some o' them up-market toffs is the worst."

"When did she go?"

"Gawd knows."

"Didn't you go after her?" Narraway snapped. "Later, if not then."

The boot boy gave him a dirty look. "I'm 'ere ter 'elp business, not drive it away!"

Pitt knew that whether the boot boy had followed her or not — and he probably had — he was not about to admit it. He would have known roughly what had happened, and been very willing to keep it secret rather than help the police investigate the establishment. The quality trade they aspired to would take their patronage somewhere else rather than risk visiting a house that was the subject of any kind of police interest. In the service of survival he would have concealed the crime, had there been one. If they could find who had killed her themselves — and they would try — then they would execute their own justice. Pitt realized he should have told Narraway that before they came.

"Of course," Pitt agreed aloud. "No one wants a Peeping Tom when they've taken a girl along the street a little. Who found her? You? Or should we ask someone else?"

"I . . . er . . . I dunno."

Narraway glanced at Pitt, and was silent.

"It would be better," Pitt began judiciously, "if we didn't have to discuss this with anyone else. Let us just suppose you were unlucky enough to have been the one who found her. The wisest thing would be to move her somewhere else, wouldn't it." He said it as an observation of fact, not a question. "It all comes down to the same thing in the end. She'll be found by police, if it makes any difference, which it doesn't really. If it was a toff, they're never going to find him. She'll get a decent burial, and your business is safe. Isn't that right?"

Narraway's eyes widened very slightly in the lamplight. In the distance a cart rumbled by them, the horses' hoofs louder on the cobbles in the comparative stillness of the night.

"Yeah," the boot boy agreed reluctantly.

"So who did you find to take her away for you? I don't suppose you have any idea what they did with her?"

"I don't wanter know!" The boot boy's voice rose indignantly.

"Of course you don't. Well, she will get a decent burial, I can promise you that."

The boot boy looked relieved, his sallow face easing a little.

"In return I would like to know exactly what the man looked like who took her away, and how he took her, cart, carriage, wagon, dray?"

"Cart," the boot boy said immediately.

"What color horse?"

"What?"

"You heard me! What color was the horse?"

The boot boy swore under his breath. "Gawd! I dunno! There was Kate lyin' in the street wif 'er neck broke. An' yer think I'm carin' wot color the bleedin' carter's 'orse is? Light color — gray, summink like that. 'Oo cares?"

"And the carter?" Pitt persisted.

"Scruffy old devil. I gave 'im a guinea ter put 'er somewhere else, at least a mile away. Best the other side o' the river."

"Can you remember his face?"

"No, I bleedin' can't!" He swore again under his breath.

"Try. It's worth your guinea back."

"Sharp face, wi' eyes like coals," the boy said instantly. "An' 'e 'ad mittens on 'is 'ands, I remember that."

"Thank you." Pitt turned to Narraway. "Have you got a guinea?"

Narraway also swore, rather more fluently, but he produced the guinea.

They returned to the police station and mustered all the men they could, from that station and the two on either side. They spent all night asking, probing, questioning to trace the passage of the cart from Bessborough Street to Buckingham Palace. By dawn they were certain of it.

Pitt and Narraway stood by the magnificent wrought-iron railings, the first light tipping the gold on them, the wind rustling in the leaves across the park. Pitt was so tired his limbs ached, and his eyes felt full of hot grit.

A troop of Horse Guards came out of the Palace yard, uniforms magnificent, harness and spurs gleaming in the broadening light, horses' hoofs crisp on the road. They looked like a cavalry from some heroic dream.

Was that what the Cape-to-Cairo railway was: a heroic dream? Or just single-minded, oppressive empire-building at the expense of a more primitive people? Who was right, Cahoon Dunkeld or Julius Sorokine?

"Where did the carter go from here?" he said aloud.

Narraway dragged his attention back to the present. He was so tired his face was seamed with lines, dragging down his features and hollowing his eyes. It was clear it cost him an intense effort to control his mind and focus it. "It must have been about this time of day, possibly a little earlier," he replied. "But some of the same people will be about. I suppose we'd better begin asking."

Pitt nodded and led the way across the street toward the nearest sentry. He asked the man if he had been on duty a week ago.

The man ignored him. Only then did Pitt remember that they were not allowed to speak. They were trained to ignore all comments or actions unless they constituted a threat. He turned and saw Narraway smiling behind him. It gave his face life again.

"All right," Pitt said, shaking his head. "You ask him."

Narraway produced his identification as the head of Special Branch. After a moment's doubt, the sentry replied that he had been on duty.

Narraway asked him about the carter, and if he had seen him, which way he had gone.

"To the right, up the Buckingham Palace Road, sir," was the unhesitating reply.

Narraway thanked him, and he and Pitt set out, footsore and hungry. A sandwich from a peddler, a cup of hot tea from a group of cabbies around a brazier, and sixpence worth of bootlaces from a one-armed soldier on the corner of Buckingham Palace Road traced the carter at least that far.

They asked around Wilton Place, Chester Street, and Belgrave Square, then into Lowndes Street and beyond. No one had seen him.

"Probably all still in bed," Narraway said miserably, shivering with exhaustion. "He could have gone anywhere."

"Servants wouldn't be in bed at this hour," Pitt replied, moving his weight from one foot to the other to ease the ache. "There was somebody putting out rubbish, beating a carpet, or carrying coals. Look around you."

Narraway turned obediently. There were sounds of movement everywhere. A sleepy scullery maid fetched a scuttle of coal, her hands dirty, apron crumpled. A message boy strode along the pavement, whistling cheerfully. Somebody opened an upstairs window.

They tried again, knocking on areaway doors, kitchens, stopping the few people in the street. No one had seen the carter they described.

"He must live here!" Narraway said in disgust an hour and a half later. "We haven't got time for this, Pitt. We'll never find him this way."

"I need breakfast," Pitt replied. "I'm so thirsty I feel as if my tongue is as trodden on as the soles of my boots."

"There's nowhere around here to get anything." Narraway looked miserably at the elegant façade of Eaton Place. "I know people in this damn street! But I can't go and ask them for breakfast."

"Who do you know?" Pitt inquired. "Which houses?"

"No!" Narraway was aghast. "Absolutely not!"

"To avoid them," Pitt explained patiently.

"What are you going to do?" Narraway was too tired to hide his apprehension.

"Go and question someone's servants inside," Pitt replied with a faint smile. "Preferably in the kitchen. I'm not above asking the cook for a cup of tea and a piece of toast. I'll even ask for one for you, if you like?"

"I like," Narraway said grudgingly.

"Then I can think," Pitt added. "We're going about this the wrong way."

"Couldn't you have told me this ten miles ago?" Narraway asked sarcastically.

Fifteen minutes later, sitting at the table in a large and very well appreciated kitchen, they were sipping tea and inquiring about strangers in the neighborhood, possible break-ins, theft of harness or other stable supplies. They gained no information of any value whatsoever, but at least they had done it sitting down with tea, toast, and rather good marmalade.

The scullery maid returned to her chores and the cook resumed the preparation of breakfast for the household. They had both answered the brief police questions and satisfied their charitable consciences.

"I didn't see it until now," Pitt replied to

Narraway's original question.

"What? You are trying my patience, Pitt." Narraway took another slice of toast from the rack and buttered it.

Pitt passed him the marmalade. "We lost the carter because he changed appearance. Which says he was in some form of disguise, even if only different clothes, attitude, and manner, and a good deal of dirt on his face."

"Because he was not a carter by occupation," Narraway agreed. "We know that too. It doesn't tell us who he was, or more importantly, where he is now."

"It tells us he might be known without the disguise."

"Ah . . ." Narraway took the point this time.

"What do we know about him?" Pitt went on. "Dunkeld must trust him, not only not to betray him, but his competence, his nerve, his ability to find the right sort of woman who would be taken for Sadie at a very rough glance . . ."

"Very rough?" Narraway questioned. "She was identified as Sadie."

"By Dunkeld himself," Pitt reminded him. "She only had to answer a verbal description: brown hair, blue eyes, average height, handsome build."

"But he had to be there at the Palace doors

with her in a box, not long after midnight," Narraway agreed. "So he was someone Dunkeld trusted. We've no idea who that is. Could be dozens of people."

Pitt leaned further forward over the table. "But who told Dunkeld how the woman in Cape Town was slashed? He wasn't there. He made a point of saying that, and you confirmed it. The murder wasn't common knowledge; in fact the whole episode was pretty well covered up."

Narraway frowned. "Are you saying he was there?"

"No! I'm saying that someone who was there told him about it. And he trusted them enough in this for them to conspire together. He put his career, even his life, in their hands. Why did they do this for him?"

"Someone equally interested in the project," Narraway answered. "Which comes back to Sorokine, Marquand, or Quase. But none of them left the Palace! They could have told him about the woman, if one of them killed her, but why in God's name would they trust him with information like that? It could get them hanged! And if they'd trust Dunkeld never to use it against them, either they truly are insane, or else they had a hold on him so great he wouldn't dare betray them? Is that what you are saying? It doesn't tell me who the carter is. A three-way conspiracy?"

"No, just two," Pitt shook his head. "Dunkeld wanted to get rid of Sorokine."

"Sorokine could still be the madman from Cape Town," Narraway cut across him. "Perhaps he's done it again, since then, and Dunkeld knew, and that's how he found out the method."

"Too complicated, and still doesn't tell us who the carter is," Pitt told him, at last taking another bite of his toast and drinking half his tea before it was cold. He filled the cup again from the pot.

"Then what does?" Narraway ignored his own tea.

"We are assuming the plan is not working." Pitt's mind was racing from one improbability to another. "What if it is?"

"Dunkeld will hang for treason," Narraway replied. "His daughter is dead and his wife despises him and is in love with Sorokine, whom he hates. I would say that is about as much failure as it's possible to have."

"Not Dunkeld's plan, his co-conspirator's," Pitt corrected. "The carter, whoever he is." At last it was beginning to clear in his mind, threads were emerging. "Who has won?"

"No one, unless getting rid of Dunkeld was what they wanted," Narraway replied.

"But Sorokine turned down the leadership, and neither Marquand nor Quase were offered it. They have even less autonomy under Forbes than they had before."

"But Forbes had no part before, and now he has complete control, and the Prince's profound gratitude," Pitt said.

Narraway stiffened. "Forbes? But he doesn't even approve of the damn railroad! His financial interest is in shipping!" A sudden spark lit in his eyes and slowly they widened.

"Exactly," Pitt breathed out. "And what better position than leader of the project from which to make certain it never succeeds?"

"God Almighty!" Narraway breathed out. "He was the carter! He knows about the murder in Cape Town because he was there too! You're not saying he killed her. Are you?"

Pitt thought for a moment. "What is Quase so afraid of? And he is, he's terrified. Liliane too, but she doesn't know of what."

"He killed the woman, and Forbes knows it?" Narraway shook his head. "You're wrong, Pitt. He would never allow the man to marry his daughter."

"It's not something Quase did." Pitt was still making his way through the myriad of facts in his mind. "It's something he knows."

"Forbes killed them himself?" Narraway struggled with it.

"I don't know."

"We can't prove it . . ." There was an anger and deep frustration in Narraway's eyes and in the tight line of his lips. "There's nothing we can do."

"I don't know what he did," Pitt went on as if Narraway had not spoken. "But he did something, before he killed Kate. And Hamilton Quase knows about it, but Liliane doesn't." An idea was forming in his mind, one that Narraway would hate. "At least I think she doesn't, although like Minnie, she may be working her way toward it. I wonder whom she loves more, her father or her husband."

"Pitt!"

"Yes?"

"Don't look at me with that air of innocence, damn it! We can't prove anything against Forbes. All we have are guesses, and we could be wrong."

"But we aren't," Pitt said it with growing assurance. "I don't know if it was just to get rid of Dunkeld and take over the project, so he could see it fail, or there were other reasons as well . . ."

"Such as what?"

"I don't know." He didn't, but he was beginning to guess, though it was not yet a thought he was prepared to share with Narraway. If his plan failed, and it well might, Narraway needed to be able to deny any knowledge of it. Pitt believed that to be fair. It was also the only chance he had of putting it into action. If he knew, Narraway would stop him. He would have to.

Pitt finished his tea. "We had better go back to the Palace. See if there is time to wash and shave before the Prince of Wales makes any formal appointment of Watson Forbes. I've got a clean shirt there. Perhaps Tyndale can get something for you."

Narraway gave him a filthy look, but he did not argue.

At the Palace, Pitt changed hastily into a cleaner and less crumpled shirt, then went straight to the anteroom where they were all waiting to be ushered in for the Prince's announcement. They looked somber and more than a little nervous. Neither the Prince of Wales nor Watson Forbes was there, but Gracie was. She looked unfamiliarly formal in a black stiff dress. Her white, lace-trimmed cap and apron were crisp and cool as snow. Her face showed intense relief when she saw Pitt, but since everyone else turned to look as he came in, she did not dare approach him.

Narraway was not there yet.

Pitt hesitated a moment, aware of what he was risking: Narraway's anger; perhaps even the loss of his support, which might mean Pitt's job. If he were right, the Prince of Wales would not forgive him. Even when he was king, his enmity would last. Above all, Pitt's disgrace would cost Charlotte any hope she might have of once again being part of Society. All doors would be closed to him, and his children.

And if he did not try, he would deliberately have let go a man who would kill again and again in order to gain what he wanted.

He walked forward to Liliane Quase, who was standing a couple of yards from her husband, who was talking to Simnel with his back to her. But as always she was close, as if guarding him.

"Good afternoon, Mrs. Quase," Pitt said quietly. "This must be a desperate decision for you."

Her marvelous eyes widened, dark with sudden terror. She started to speak, but the words died in her throat. She moved away from him, a step closer to her husband, her hand out, as if she would touch him.

Pitt made a guess, not certain what he meant. "He was willing to pay any price to earn your love, wasn't he? Are you willing to let him? Even his life?" He was still guessing. "He was originally the one meant to take the blame for that woman's death. Only his hatred of Julius made Dunkeld change the plan."

"You can't know . . ." she began, shaking her head from side to side.

"Your father won't let the project succeed, you know. All his own money is in shipping," Pitt went on.

She shook her head harder. "No . . . you're wrong!" Her voice was no more than a whisper.

"Why does your father want your husband dead? What does he know that is so dangerous?"

She turned away from him and for an instant he thought he had lost.

Sensing her panic, Quase swung round toward her. Simnel Marquand moved away.

Liliane stared at her husband.

"What did you do for him?" she asked, her voice trembling now. "It was Eden's death, wasn't it? Everything was different after that."

He looked at her with such pain and such gentleness that it met her worst fears. Pitt saw her body stiffen.

"It was Eden who killed that woman in

Cape Town, wasn't it?" There was no doubt or hesitation now. "Did he really fall into the river with the crocodiles?"

Hamilton did not answer.

"By accident?" she said hoarsely.

"Don't ask, Liliane. It was best that way, cleaner than a trial and . . ." He could not say it.

"Hanging," she finished for him. "And family disgrace. My father killed him, and you covered for them both, why? For my sake?"

"Of course. Why else would I do anything?"

"Even though he would have had you hanged for killing that poor woman in the linen cupboard?"

"I didn't know that."

Her eyes did not leave his. "You know it now."

Two liveried footmen came and opened the doors, announcing that His Royal Highness would receive them.

Liliane glanced at Pitt, and the ghost of a smile touched her lips. Then she took her husband's arm and walked into the throne room beside him.

Olga and Simnel Marquand followed, then Elsa on Julius's arm, as was proper for the survivors of Dunkeld's family.

Pitt offered his arm to Gracie, who hesitated, uncertain what to do. Then with a tight little grip, she took it.

Narraway followed last, a little breathless and in a borrowed shirt.

The throne room was magnificent, pale-walled, gleaming with gold, high windows letting in the shimmering sunlight. There was hardly any furniture to fill the space. The Prince and Princess of Wales stood at the far end ready to receive them. On either side were other members of the royal household, the Prime Minister and several members of his cabinet.

Gracie gasped and would have tripped on her skirt were she not hanging on to Pitt's arm with a grip of iron.

Even Pitt was impressed more than he had ever intended to be. His courage wavered. He was absurd even to think of doing such a thing. He would be betraying Narraway's trust in him.

Watson Forbes was in front of the Prince, a little to one side. The Princess stood apart, isolated by her deafness.

The Prince gestured for them to come forward.

Gracie's hand tightened on Pitt's arm so hard her fingers hurt his flesh. They stopped just behind Elsa and Julius. Pitt was pleased that they were so close to each other. They had moved in step, instinctively. He thought of Charlotte and wished she were here, and yet Gracie deserved to be present. And perhaps it was better Charlotte was not with him; thinking of her might destroy his courage.

Simnel was presented, with Olga beside him, and the Prince thanked him for his loyalty and skill.

Hamilton Quase was presented, and Liliane. Hamilton's engineering brilliance was praised.

Julius was presented next, and the Prince sensibly excused his withdrawing from his diplomatic role because of the very recent death of his wife, for whom he was still in mourning. Elsa was presented as his mother-in-law, also very naturally mourning. Nothing was said of her being a second wife to Dunkeld, who was not mentioned at all.

Narraway was presented in his capacity as head of Special Branch, here to make certain every safety precaution was in place. The Prince thanked him also.

This was the moment of decision. Pitt stood face-to-face with his future king. It would never happen again. Either he condemned Forbes now, or his silence made Forbes safe forever.

"Your Royal Highness," Pitt said, trying to keep his voice from trembling. He must be fair to Gracie. "May I recommend to you, ma'am, your most loyal and brave servant, Miss Gracie Phipps, who has assisted Special Branch in the service of the Crown."

Gracie stood frozen in awe. She looked about thirteen.

"Indeed," the Prince said with some surprise. "I am obliged to you, Miss Phipps."

Suddenly Gracie's legs gave way and she dropped a far deeper curtsy than she had intended. She managed to rise again only by hauling herself up on Pitt's arm.

Pitt remained where he was.

The Prince of Wales stared at him with slight irritation. Pitt took a deep breath. This was the moment. "I regret, sir, that the railway will not be built by Mr. Forbes," he said.

"Nonsense," the Prince said savagely. "Please step back, sir! Do not compel me to call for assistance. It would be most embarrassing for you."

"Mr. Forbes has misled you, sir," Pitt said relentlessly. His voice was trembling, but he made it loud enough for the whole room to hear him. Was he ruining himself and his family? "He has expressed his belief that such a railway would be injurious to Africa and its peoples, and his own personal fortune is invested in shipping. He wishes to lead the project only in order to sabotage its success. Also, regrettably, he was responsible for a murder in Africa, and for the murder that His Royal Highness sent for Special Branch to solve. I am deeply sorry, sir. Could a resolution have been found earlier, you would not have been troubled at this late date."

The Prince's face was gray but for two spots of hectic color in his cheeks. "What the devil are you talking about?" he hissed. "He wasn't even in the Palace when the woman died, you nincompoop! What murder in Africa? Have you taken leave of your wits entirely?"

"His own son, sir," Pitt said as levelly as he could. "Eden Forbes. Tragically, he was mentally unbalanced, and murdered a half-caste prostitute in Cape Town. Rather than have him publicly tried and hanged for it, and knowing that it was a compulsion he would continue to follow, Mr. Forbes took him to a lonely place and executed him himself."

The Prince stood paralyzed.

Watson Forbes swung round and took a step toward Pitt. Liliane interposed herself between them, facing her father. He looked at her eyes, and saw grief, and rage, and loyalty to her husband.

There was utter silence in the vast, glorious room. Every man and woman in it stood like figures in a painted tableau, gorgeous, lifeless.

Gracie's nails dug into Pitt's arm.

Pitt felt the sweat break out on his body and the instant after he was cold again.

Narraway was the first to move. He stepped up beside Pitt and bowed deeply to the Prince. "The matter is entirely closed, Your Royal Highness. The innocent have been vindicated and the guilty discovered and will now be arrested. I regret profoundly that it had to be done in your presence. We would all much rather you had not had to be distressed by it."

The Princess of Wales stepped forward at last, linking her arm in that of her husband, and then she turned to Pitt, her eyebrows raised.

"I am deeply sorry, ma'am," Pitt apologized humbly. "But I could not stand here and lie to His Royal Highness, and thus cause him to approve someone, in ignorance of their nature, and then be embarrassed later."

"Your timing is unfortunate, sir," the Princess said drily. "But I suppose your information is better late than not at all. You may go and finish your business. His Royal Highness is obliged to you."

Pitt bowed again. "Ma'am." Then he turned and withdrew as commanded, knowing that the Prince of Wales's eyes followed him all the way to the great doors. He would neither forgive nor forget this wound, dealt in the throne room, in front of his court and his future ministers.

"'E in't gonna get over that," Gracie said in a hoarse whisper when they were back in the anteroom. "But yer done right." She took a deep breath and smiled up at him. "I knew yer would."

"Thank you, Gracie," he said shakily. He thought of putting his other hand over to loosen the fierce grip of her fingers on his arm, but then decided not to. Perhaps it was enough.

ABOUT THE AUTHOR

Anne Perry is the bestselling author of two acclaimed series set in Victorian England: the Charlotte and Thomas Pitt novels, including *Seven Dials* and *Long Spoon Lane,* and the William Monk novels, most recently *The Shifting Tide* and *Dark Assassin.* She is also the author of the World War I novels *No Graves As Yet, Shoulder the Sky, Angels in the Gloom, At Some Disputed Barricade,* and *We Shall Not Sleep,* as well as the holiday novels *A Christmas Journey, A Christmas Visitor, A Christmas Guest, A Christmas Secret* and *A Christmas Beginning.* Anne Perry lives in Scotland. Visit her website at www.anneperry.net.